A Friendly
Killing

by

Michael Davies

A Friendly Killing

First Printing 2008

ISBN: 978-0-9818087-5-8

First Printed in Australia

Published by The Mickie Dalton Foundation
Kempsey, NSW
Australia

To Forbes Hunter

The very finest of men, badly missed

Other Books by Michael Davies

The Nightmares of God
The Janus Conspiracy
Accounts of a Killing
Dreamkill
Ready, Steady, KILL!
Helix Dreams

For the Young Adults (12-18)
The Many Worlds of Mickie Dalton
The Many Galaxies of Mickie Dalton
The Many Universes of Mickie Dalton
The Strange World of Mark and Anna

For the 8-12 age group
The Quest for the Locket
The Julie Malloy Gang and the Smugglers
The Secret of Yuri Kirilenko
The United Nations and the Extra-Terrestrial
The Secret of Charlotte's Cello
The Star of the Yshan Kings
The War of the Yshan Empire
The Red Fog of Time
The Mysterious Recorder and The Door to Elsewhere
Prisoners of the Picture

For the Little Ones (3-5)
Mary's World

And in non-fiction
The Business School Approach to Writing Your Novel

Prologue

"He'll die," said the unidentifiable voice in the phone message that the BBC had received. "And lots of other people with him. His death is for Scotland."

The voice had promised bloody mayhem. The accent was neutral, unidentifiable. The section's analysts played the tape time and time again, analysed it, dissected every vowel and consonant, every inflection, every pause. They ran the tape through electronic gizmos that drew exotic graphs on video screens, and they matched them against known speech patterns from the files. They enhanced minute background sounds to detect where the call came from, but, after all their wizardry had been expended, the experts were unhelpful.

"Scottish," they said. "Probably. Could be Aberdeen, but spent some years in the south of England. Or it could be a Sussex man who lived in Aberdeen for some years. Could even be just somebody with high mimicry skills. We're almost certain he was calling from Euston Street Station, judging by the public address system we could hear, but that's all we could determine. Difficult. Certainly not anyone we know."

So Scott went north to Edinburgh and baby-sat a large, overweight politician who had openly scoffed at Scottish nationalism and who had to attend a conference on hefty

1

economic matters. The politician's bluster faded after the first hour, and his pale face and big, worried eyes reflected the raw fear he had so vehemently denied when the trip began.

But nothing happened.

The bomb-squads tore the conference room apart and rebuilt it, and the guards examined everyone who came in through the metal-detector bars. The dogs sniffed them, too, causing a few embarrassed giggles, but nothing caused the sharp cry of havoc to sound. Scott's Browning nine-millimetre automatic remained in its shoulder holster, while his eyes tried to rip away the layers of anonymity from the faces around and see the blood-lust and killing rage, but he saw nothing. The mayhem didn't materialize. No blood was spilled over the carpets of the Edinburgh hotel. Nobody screamed in horror. Nobody died.

The absence of violence didn't alleviate Scott's nerves one bit.

"Nothing?" Jamieson's voice echoed down the line from Birmingham.

"Nothing, sir."

"And our man's gone home?"

"I've just put him safely back in his pad in Knightsbridge," Scott said. Post-mission letdown had hit him, and he was having difficulty keeping his eyes open.

"Okay. Come back, McIntyre."

"Yes, sir," Scott replied and replaced the phone.

Nothing had happened.

Chapter 1 - Whispers Through the Night

The radio had just switched itself on when the phone rang, and the BBC's morning traffic report into the city was murmuring gently into his ear. Birmingham was having a heat wave this Monday morning and a number of cars had broken down with boiling radiators. The situation was the polite chaos that only the British could organize.

Scott picked up the phone, and listened to the brief sentences from the emotionless voice at the other end. When the voice had finished, he replaced the phone. The woman by his side stirred slightly.

"So where to, this time?" she murmured into the general region of his neck.

"Chicago," he said to the ceiling. On the far wall, the brown curtains with the orange and white patterns of Australian Aboriginal bark painting moved softly in the light breeze from the open window. The curtains had grabbed his attention one day while killing time in a department store in Sydney. He had bought them on the spot and had them shipped home.

He was very comfortable and felt most unwilling to move. She had snuggled up when the radio first came on, as was her habit when she stayed over at his apartment, and this was a sufficiently rare event that the delight had not faded. In the cool of the morning breeze, not yet corrupted by the city's heat wave, her smooth skin felt delicious to him.

3

"Who is it? Do we know?" Her long red fingernail was tracing the line of his jaw and it tickled faintly.

"No idea. All we've got is a possible event."

In fact, he did have some idea, but Janette was not cleared for the details yet. As the senior decoder and analyst in the department, she got most of the stuff that came in through the wires, but this one had come in by diplomatic bag, according to the voice on the phone. Her curiosity would have to remain unsatisfied until Jamieson told her. The voice had said that the people in Karachi had sniffed some possibility that it would be al-Yaffi again, but they couldn't be certain. Somebody, mumbled the jungle drums of international undercover intelligence, *somebody* was going to kill a top Defence Official of the German government. It would happen in Chicago during a visit to a couple of defence contractors said the drums, and it had to be stopped.

On such whispers through the night was Scott's life scheduled.

"I hate it when you go away." Her voice was muffled, probably because she knew that such a comment was unprofessional. Going away to interfere with assassins was his job. But he hated having to be away from her too, which made him just as unprofessional.

"Your turn to make breakfast," he said, turning the conversation from the unpleasant realities of the next few days.

"Oh God, is it really?" She dug her face deeper into his shoulder. "After last night, I really don't want to move for a few more minutes."

Yesterday, they had driven down to Sonning-on-Thames in Berkshire, wined and dined at The French Horn while the Thames gurgled happily past the floodlit weeping willows. They had returned to Birmingham in rosy happiness at one-thirty in the morning.

4

"Tough!" Scott said. "Extra Special Super Extraordinary Secret Intelligence Agents always need their breakfast, you know that! Can you imagine James Bond leaving on a mission without his Scots Oats, green figs and coffee? To the kitchen, woman!"

"James Bond you are not, Scott McIntyre," she said, unmoved by his authoritative command. "And anyway, seeing as you're going to be away for a few days, I thought perhaps you might like to take it out in trade."

"You did, huh?"

"Uh-huh."

"Oh."

They were twenty minutes late leaving for the office.

* * *

The traffic was fierce all the way into the city and the relief when he finally drove the Honda down the ramp and parked was like reaching shore after swimming against the tide. Janette was with him, because everybody knew about them anyway, and nobody cared a damn. After all, trying to hide any part of one's private life from Jamieson's spooks was a useless task, and both of them were well up on security clearances.

The elevator stopped at the third floor.

"British Council of International Economic Analysis" said the sign on the door. Scott had always been amused to think that anyone visiting the place would most certainly see the computer terminals and printers gushing out reams of statistics, the newsletters on the wall racks, the official publications which the Council put out every month. Scott knew that many of the people in this room flew around the world to talk in esoteric terms to economists and business leaders. He had learned that if any visitor to this office addressed the pretty girl behind the reception desk and asked her where to find any official statistics on the world's trade health, Julia would smile in her best British manner and direct the visitor to the appropriate stack of books. And if the

visitor asked ninety percent of the people in the place what was the function of their office, he or she would receive a perfectly sincere answer about economic analyses and trade news, because the people who worked for the Council genuinely and correctly believed that such was their function.

But Scott knew that just like his Australian curtains, the whole decorative extravaganza was there simply to hide from outside watchers what really went on in the place.

He followed Janette down the long central aisle, past the battery of computer terminals and the jabbering printers, past the three rows of study desks with their high screens, past the racks of journals and newspapers and computer printouts, and reached the far wall. The atmosphere was alive with study as thirty or more intelligent people beavered away to produce useful trade data that would be read with interest by an amazingly large number of people around the world.

Several of the beavers greeted them as they passed down the rows of desks. Most of them believed Scott and Janette to be systems people in the computer section. Only Julia and two others in the room knew that the real reason for the existence of the entire office was the set of rooms on the other side of the door at the back. The sign on this door said simply *"Computer Room - Authorised Access Only."* This was only a partial lie, since access was certainly for authorised people only.

Scott took a plastic card from his wallet, pushed it into the slot and a small chime rang out, audible for only a few feet. He entered four digits on the security lock pad and the door opened. The numbers were changed every few days, and Jamieson advised each of them personally when that happened. Not by memo, not through his secretary, not in company with anyone else. He did it face to face. Across his desk. In private. Nobody ever wrote the numbers down. Breaking that rule would have brought down the wrath of God, or Jamieson, which might have been worse.

Scott gently nudged Janette ahead of him, gave one more admiring look at her long brown hair and slender form, dressed in neat secretarial garb of dark blue skirt and crisp white blouse and wondered again whether this was a good idea. He was dangerously close to being serious about her.

She gave him a small smile and turned off to her own area, the decoding room.

"Drop in and see me before you go," she whispered. *Thank God for women who understood the job,* he thought. No need to lie, to pretend, to hide one's fear. She knew what he did and what it cost him. He smiled back and watched her walk along the corridor and enter her office.

Scott raised an eyebrow at the neatly dressed woman sitting at a computer screen outside the plain wooden door to her left. She replied with an infinitesimal movement of her head towards to the door and Scott walked in to see the Old Man.

Jamieson's office was not luxurious. During his training, Scott had learned that the British intelligence community didn't work the same way their foreign cousins did. Britain had no equivalent of huge office complexes in the Virginia countryside, massive brick monuments in Washington, or fearsome prison blocks in a bleak city square in Moscow. In Britain there were no signs, no pointers, no big organisation. Most British intelligence operations were just small groups like this one, hidden behind some inoffensive cover, Spartan accommodation, cheap decor and very short lines of command. The British had always understood the attractions of power, Scott had learned, the ease with which security organizations could acquire it and the corruption that could follow. Small, independent operational units were the norm, therefore, controlled by somebody like the man sitting at the desk in front of Scott.

Air Marshal (Retired) Sir Martin Beresford Jamieson reported directly to the Prime Minister. The red phone used for that purpose was kept in a drawer, hidden from the gaze of the common herd. It hardly ever rang, and for every time Jamieson opened the drawer to make a call, there was a story of pain and tragedy that probably never made the news.

The Air Marshal was writing in a small notebook as Scott walked in. He looked up briefly and pointed to the coffee pot. A box of donuts provided the only colourful break in the grey and green monotony of British Service-issue decor. Scott had heard that Jamieson had picked up the taste for these cholesterol fiestas while serving as Air Attaché in Washington some twenty years ago. The habit was probably the chief reason why Jamieson was heavy-chested and broad, no longer the muscular young Pilot Officer Jamieson leaning against the nose wheel of a Vulcan bomber in the photograph above the coffee pot.

"Good morning, Scott, I'll be with you in a moment," he said, his deep voice slightly muffled because of his head-down attitude. "Help yourself to coffee."

Scott did so gratefully, taking a long chocolate mass of calories from the box as well. As much as he had appreciated Janette's reasons for keeping him in bed, he was still hungry, and the gathering tension in him needed something to distract him. Mission nerves started earlier, each and every time.

He watched Jamieson as the Air Marshal worked with his back to the vast panorama of a gold-framed painting of a Lancaster Bomber flying through storm clouds. The brutally functional war machine would have dominated the room, except for the presence of Jamieson. The Air Marshal was in his late fifties, his full head of hair turning, like his moustache, gently grey. His deep brown eyes could be disconcertingly secretive, but sometimes the harsh face would crack into a genuine smile of amusement or affection. He had been the dominant force in Scott's recent life.

Four years ago, Scott was in the middle of interviews with MI5, after finally checking out of the Royal Air Force. He was sitting alone in a scruffy office in Whitehall, filling out an extensive and intrusive form, when the door opened behind him and he heard metal-tipped heels walking across the hard linoleum-covered floor. He finished the answer with which he had been having so much difficulty, and turned round.

"Squadron Leader McIntyre?"

The thick-set individual exuded authority the way only senior military commanders can. It was in the way he stood, evidence of hours on a parade square, the way he looked at Scott with complete understanding of what he did, what he thought and what would push his buttons. Even in his well-cut, grey suit and black waistcoat, he looked as if he were dressed in full ceremonial uniform. Scott could almost see the white belt and gleaming brass, the rows of medals and the sword.

"Yes, sir," he responded, automatically standing up, not quite at attention, but almost. He knew he had seen this man before, but could not identify him.

"Martin Jamieson," the older man said and put out his hand. He was two or three inches shorter than Scott, considerably wider, and he filled the room with his presence.

Ah yes, now I know, Scott thought and took the proffered hand. "Air Marshal Jamieson, I believe?" he said, remembering the photographs on the walls at the Royal Air Force College at Cranwell. "Number Eighty-Three Entry, C Squadron, if I remember correctly?"

"The very same!" Jamieson's moustache wiggled gently. "I'd like to discuss an idea I've had for a while."

Their voices echoed slightly in the bare room. Through the dirty glass of the sealed windows, the honks, whistles and roars of London were a dull backdrop to the sudden tension that rose in Scott.

Jamieson took a seat on a battered wooden chair on the other side of the small table Scott had been using as a desk, leaned one elbow on the table and crossed his legs. His shoes reflected the subdued daylight from the window.

"You're really sure you want to do this stuff?" Jamieson asked, lightly touching the form on which Scott had been expending so much sweat and frustration. The Air Marshal's voice was the well-mannered, educated voice one would expect, but Scott could just hear the tiny note of Yorkshire. Legend had it that Jamieson's father had been a coal miner.

"To be honest sir, no." It seemed natural to call him "Sir" even though Scott knew that Jamieson was retired. "It's just that the idea of becoming a desk-bound business type scares me. Not even sure I know what else I could do."

Jamieson nodded briefly, with obvious understanding. "Searching for smugglers, watching ports and air terminals, checking out applicants for political jobs, all that sort of stuff, it appeals to you?" His eyes watched Scott closely.

"More than building warehouse shelves or tractor engines, yes, sir." Scott's intrigue was growing. The Air Marshal was moving toward something, and Scott felt like a butterfly spread out on a board under the other man's inspection.

"Hmm." Jamieson shifted in his seat, recrossed his legs and looked out through the grimy window. "Know what a mongoose is?"

The subject change threw Scott off balance for a second, but he managed to hide it, he hoped. He had read Rudyard Kipling as a boy, and the adventures of Rickki-Tikki-Tavi were familiar to him.

"Something like a weasel or ferret, common in India," he answered. "It kills snakes."

Jamieson looked back and smiled, ever so briefly. "That's what we do," he said. "How would you like to kill snakes?"

This was not small talk. Men like Jamieson didn't indulge themselves that way. Scott didn't smile back at him.

"Any particular type of snake, sir?"

"Mustapha al-Yaffi type snakes."

For an undefinable length of time, they stared at each other. Jamieson had not walked in here on impulse. The Air Marshal knew about Scott and Mustapha al-Yaffi.

Nightmare memories erupted in Scott's head. Shattered building, metal girders sticking out like broken bones, pulverized white stone of a Spanish hotel, a complete wing of the two-storey building reduced to waist-high rubble. And three pathetic bodies, broken like the building, laid out on cold white tables, no longer his mother, his father and his sixteen-year-old sister, Leanne, but husks of what they had been. One year ago.

Al-Yaffi, they said. Probably. That's what all the information indicated. Really after three French diplomats staying in the same hotel. The other wing. Not like him, they said. Usually kills at close quarters with a pistol. Doesn't make mistakes. Not like him at all. Terribly sorry, Mister McIntyre. The bodies will be flown to England for burial.

"Yes sir," Scott said clearly, so that there should be no misunderstanding, working hard to keep his voice level. "I'd like that very much."

Jamieson stood up and smiled. "Good," he said and gently touched the form on the table with a well-manicured hand. "Tear that thing up, will you?"

Jamieson coughed, bringing Scott sharply back to the present. The Air Marshal put down his pen, folded the notebook and leaned back, sighing slightly. "Got a meeting with the minister this afternoon," he said. "Needed some notes."

Scott took a sip of coffee and wiped his hands on a napkin.

"You got the message from Communications okay?" Jamieson folded his hands in front of his chin.

"Yes sir, I did. You think it's al-Yaffi again?"

Jamieson shook his head. "Not certain. Our Karachi people said they thought it might be, but it's only a sniff. The only solid thing appears to be that somebody has been contracted to take out a senior German official while he's in the USA. He's visiting Boeing in St. Louis, then going to Chicago to see APV about an order for their armoured personnel carriers."

The trace of Yorkshire was in his accent was a little stronger than usual. Jamieson was probably under some stress, Scott decided. He stood up to refill his coffee cup. "What's the target's name?" he asked. Jamieson waved at his own empty mug, a huge blue one with the RAF crest on it, and Scott poured fresh coffee over the dregs still in the bottom, replacing the mug on a coaster on the desk. He gestured at the doughnut box, and Jamieson shook his head. Scott selected something cream-filled and returned to his seat.

Jamieson looked severely at him. "I pay you to keep fit, McIntyre, not gorge yourself like some schoolboy in a cake shop."

"Yes, sir, that's right." Scott was unaffected. This game was a common one and he know that Jamieson was fully aware of just how fit he was, having devised the brutal training program and regular work-out torture sessions that his Mongoose agents undertook.

"Wilhelm Scheidinger's one of the biggest officials in Germany's military procurement group," Jamieson said, picking up on Scott's question. "Having him killed would be one hell of an embarrassment to the Americans. The Prime Minister offered your help because you probably know more about al-Yaffi than anyone else. They're not happy about having some Limey help them out, but they'll take anything they can get."

"Do we have any leads at all?" The information seemed very thin, but Scott had gone chasing around the world before on far less substantial twitches of the grapevine than this.

"Very little," Jamieson said, breathing in the fumes of the coffee. "Perkins in Karachi says he heard that some neo-Nazi group has taken out the contract because Scheidinger was in the East German government before unification, and they want to make a stink with Bonn about trusting ex-communists. But he's a bit small for an al-Yaffi contract." He took a small sip of the brew and replaced the mug on the coaster. "On the other hand, a political assassination in Chicago could cause a real commotion with the Yanks, so it's possible."

"Do our contacts in the States have anything?"

"I don't know, as yet." Jamieson opened a drawer to his desk and extracted a package of documents. He slid the package across to Scott. "The word only came through a couple of hours ago. Your instructions are in here. Contact the FBI chap in Chicago and he'll fit you up with a gun and give you any recent gen they've picked up."

Sometimes the old boy dated himself with his vernacular, Scott thought in amusement. He put the coffee mug back on the cabinet by the doughnut box and picked up the package from the desk top.

"Leaving today or tomorrow, sir?" he asked.

Jamieson looked pointedly at his watch. It was a massive aircrew watch that was standard issue at Cranwell many years ago. "You do have your bag and passport with you?" he asked, staring up at Scott.

Oh-oh, thought Scott, *I'd better check the package rapidly. I've probably got five minutes to get the shuttle to Heathrow.* He closed the door gently, with just enough delay to see the older man rising from his desk to go to the doughnut box.

As it turned out, Scott had nearly two hours before leaving. He did have his bag and passport with him, because he always had his bag and passport with him. That was Standard Operating Procedure. Working for Jamieson was not a nine-to-five, come to the office, hour for lunch and go home business, ever.

He took Jamieson's package to his own desk in the office he shared with three others whom he saw perhaps once every couple of months. The area consisted of one room, with four desks, no windows, dull cream walls and a few screens to give an appearance of territorial claims. Desk lights partially alleviated the gloom of the inadequate ceiling lamps.

Mongoose Four was still in training. His desk was bare, the walls around it unadorned. Scott didn't even know his name, let alone his origins. Mongoose Two had a poster of every ship which had ever borne the name "HMS Ark Royal" taped to the wall, and a colour painting of the latest of the line, the light aircraft carrier, next to it. The picture showed a Harrier fighter taking off from the "ski-jump" over the bows of the ship. A wall map of the world was the sole touch of decoration in Mongoose One's cubicle. Scott's desk bore a photo of young Pilot Office McIntyre in his flying suit, holding his silver bonedome with its dark plastic sun-visor, and leaning with affected nonchalance against the nose wheel of a Nimrod of 18 Group, Coastal Command. On the portable fabric screen in front of him, was a color poster, blown up from a photograph he had taken at an air show at Lyneham. It showed a Hercules under rocket-assisted take-off, climbing at an impossible angle into a pure blue sky.

The same cheap carpet that lined the corridor covered the floor, the elderly desks had been obtained from an army navy surplus store, leather chairs bought at a used office supplies shop in Sutton Coldfield. Decor was not a strong point of the British secret services, Scott had discovered.

He separated the airline ticket and other travel documents from the package that Jamieson had given him, and settled down to work. There was a separate envelope together with the tickets. 'Mongoose Three - FYI' said the label on the seal. He broke it, and spread out the few sheets of paper from within.

Mustapha al-Yaffi was believed to be behind the killing of an Egyptian politician recently and the murder of a Canadian businessman in London two months earlier. Before that, he had a whole string of professional assassinations around the world to his 'credit.' He killed for hire said the conventional wisdom, but many of his assignments indicated that killing for Allah was a preferred option. Scott knew the details of al-Yaffi's life, as far as any of them were true. Not that the details were plentiful. Al-Yaffi was a Palestinian, born in one of those merciless camps that the world pretended to abhor but did nothing to help. He fled when he was thirteen, joined the PLO and trained as a killer. Mongoose Section believed he had transferred to Colonel Ghaddafi's personal bodyguard then went solo when he was about twenty-five. After that, it was all conjecture.

Even in a job where uncertainty was the rule, the facts before Scott were meager at best. The Karachi office *thought* that a plot existed to hit Scheidinger, *possibly* a contract by Knights of Aryan Dawn, a neo-Nazi group which had been stirring up the old ugliness for a couple of years. They *thought* it would be in Chicago. They *believed* that al-Yaffi was behind it. They *hoped* that the FBI in Chicago would have more information *(more gen, Scott, more gen,* he mused, smiling in the empty office) by the time Scott got there. There were contact numbers, an address, a name: William Patrick Webster. FBI Special Agent Bill Webster. Scott hoped somebody would be there to pick him up when he got to Chicago.

He looked at the airline tickets. British Airways Flight 297 leaving Heathrow at five minutes to one, window seat in business class, his standard request with the travel agency who booked them all for the economic conferences and meetings for which they were supposedly travelling. The agency never questioned the suddenness of some of the departures.

One could hardly plan ahead to stop a killing.

Scott examined the package again. He found another photograph of a man believed to be al-Yaffi, but could just as well have been an unfocused, wavy shot taken in a hurry on a gloomy, wet evening, of any dark-featured man running through a crowd, shielding his head from the rain. As an aid to finding his man, it was as useful as wet toilet paper, he decided. A single sheet contained some more notes, but nothing he didn't already know. He wrapped it all up again and went to see Janette.

Her office was two doors down from his. He opened the door quietly and looked inside. He saw four desks, each with its burden of a microcomputer and laser printer. The mass of wires extending from the computers were all neatly gathered together by heavy duty rubber bands, and the strands vanished like a rabbit down a circular hole in the floor. From this room, he knew they could contact almost any place on earth and access the computers of organizations and governments that ruled the universe.

Two of the laser printers at unoccupied desks were wheezing away, ejecting a sheet of paper every few seconds with a smug click of the feed mechanism. The computer screens next to them were an uninformative blank stare of light blue. A high-speed printer stood against the far wall, within a cabinet of acoustic screens to prevent the crashing noise the thing could make from damaging the eardrums of anyone sentenced to be near it. Right now, it was silent.

Scott leaned against the wall next to the door while Janette stared in intense concentration at the computer screen on her desk, unscrambling recently received signals. He watched her gentle, serene face, currently screwed into a fearsome frown, and again thought how dangerous their affair was. Agents weren't supposed to have entanglements that could distract them. Some day it would probably end, and then they would have the usual unpleasantness of two people who were no longer an item still working in the same place. *It's dangerous,* he thought, *because I love her and I don't know what I would do if I lost her.*

Oh shit! he thought. That was the first time he had actually admitted how much he loved her. Now what the hell was he going to do?

She suddenly looked up and caught him watching her. A slight flush began in the small 'V' of her blouse and reached her face. She smiled, putting her hand to her throat. "Why, Mister McIntyre!" she said. "How nice of you to drop by!"

"I'm catching the shuttle down to Heathrow. I'm leaving in a few minutes." Mission nerves had racked up another notch, and he was tense, harsh, without the gentle touch that she deserved. But she had seen him leave like this, before. He knew that she understood.

"Yes, I know," she said, standing up and walking over to him. "We just got a signal in saying that the contact in Chicago would meet you at O'Hare. I faxed him a picture of you."

"Oh."

"Please take care, Scott."

"I will. See you in a few days."

He touched her hand and for a second she clasped his fingers firmly. *When you're an Extra Special Super Extraordinary Secret Intelligence Agent, he thought, that's about all you can do when saying goodbye to your best girl in a public office. Revealing the fear and the pain, clasping her in your arms, telling her you love her and need her was not on. It simply wasn't British.*

* * *

He checked his watch. Unlike Jamieson, he had returned his aircrew-issue chronometer together with the flying suit, bonedome, oxygen mask and all the other flying gear, uniforms and paraphernalia when he had finally cleared through the exhaustive, complex routines of returning to civilian life four years ago. Scott had to make do with a simple Seiko digital watch that he had picked up at the duty-free store in Sydney, the same trip on which he had bought his curtains.

He had twenty minutes before he needed to leave for Birmingham's airport to catch the shuttle down to Heathrow. He decided to give Nick a call and set up an evening out with him and Janette when he got back. *Assuming you do get back Scott,* said a little voice in his head. *Shut up,* he said to the little voice.

Making such post-mission arrangements before leaving was encouraged by Jamieson, which made it a law engraved in granite.

"Creates a mind-set that you're returning, removes any internal doubts," he told Scott before his first mission, a minor and totally inactive jaunt to Belfast to protect a member of the British Cabinet. The Dublin accent on the phone to a London newspaper had warned of an attack by some previously unknown Irish Nationalist faction, but, like the trip to Edinburgh, nothing had happened. "It also confirms your general cover. If everybody sees you planning to attend the Queen's Garden Party or an evening at the Symphony, they won't think you're on some exercise requiring guns and stuff."

Scott picked up the phone and dialed Nick's office.

"Europharm, good morning," said the German-accented voice at the other end. Scott knew that Kirstie was actually Swiss, but she spoke the High German of the north. She looked Spanish, spoke French, Greek and Italian as well, and Nick said that she was simply invaluable to him.

"Let me speak to Nick please, Kirstie."

"I'm sorry, Mister McIntyre. Mister Wallace is in Europe this week."

"Oh!" Scott was surprised. Nick had said nothing about another trip. But as a senior marketing executive for a small pharmaceutical firm based in Switzerland, he travelled often. "When did he leave?"

"Last Wednesday."

"And when do you expect him back?"

"We're hoping he'll return by the end of this week."

"Okay, leave him a message that I called. I'll call him again in a few days."

"Of course, Mister McIntyre, I'll make sure he gets the message."

"Thank you," said Scott, and hung up.

He packed his briefcase, took another look around the office and walked out, deliberately not looking into the coding room where Janette would be fighting her own demons as he left. This was by far the worst part, walking away, not knowing when or even if he would return, frightened but unable to show it, wishing that perhaps he had taken a job building tractor engines or warehouse shelving.

"Mongoose Three leaving on assignment," he reported formally to Marjorie, a grey-haired woman in her fifties, who had served as Sir Martin's personal assistant ever since he had replaced his uniform with a clerical-grey three-piece suit. She nodded, logged the details in her book and carefully didn't look at him. He knew from Janette that seeing an agent off on a mission still tore holes in Marjorie's psyche.

He took the elevator down to the car park, climbed into the Honda and headed toward the airport.

Chapter 2 – Chicago

"Your reason for entering the USA, Mister McIntyre?" The immigration officer, a young, black woman, studied Scott's passport and face with disconcerting intensity.

"I'm researching trade developments in US-European tariff agreements," he responded.

"Your occupation?"

"I'm a public servant with a British Government economics research group."

She carefully examined the visa stamped into his passport. Then she smiled, a most glorious, sincere smile which seemed to warm up the sterile immigration area at Chicago's O'Hare Field.

"Welcome to the USA, Mister McIntyre," she said, added a stamp to the passport and handed it back to him.

"Thank you!" he said, slightly dazed by the brilliance of the smile, and walked on through to Customs, who ignored him totally. Outside the gate, he stood looking around like a tourist. Crowds of people passed him, chattering, exhausted, squealing pleasure as they met friends, lovers and relatives. Somebody would meet him, Janette had said. He stood quietly, trying to look like somebody who should be met.

"Scott McIntyre?" asked a voice behind him. It sounded like "Scart." Somewhere in the crossing of the Mayflower, Scott thought, the Americans had lost control of their vowels. Maybe it had been a rough trip. He turned to see a tall young man with a long face and exhausted eyes. He was about thirty, blond hair already growing thin on the top. He wore a dark suit and white shirt, both rumpled.

"I'm Scott McIntyre," said Scott, and held out his hand. The American took it with a small smile.

"Special Agent Bill Webster, sir."

Scott looked round hurriedly, but nobody was near enough to hear them. "Glad to meet you, Bill," he said. "Maybe we can forget titles in public?"

The young man looked confused for a moment. "Sorry, you're right. You'll have to forgive me, I've been up all night."

Scott grinned at him. "You look like it. Was that because of me?"

Webster's expression seemed to loosen up, as if he had been worried about meeting Scott. *Maybe he had*, thought Scott. He had found that many Americans got a little shy in the face of the English. Finally, some humor shone from the young man's tired eyes. "Only partly," he said. "We're all a bit worried about this mad dog that may be here."

He began to lead Scott toward the stairs heading down. "No other bags?" he asked with an approving glance at Scott's leather overnight case. "Good, my car's in the terminal parking lot."

They walked and rode elevators, and eventually they reached the fourth floor of the huge parking building. Webster led Scott toward a massive, tank-like, white vehicle that Scott recognized as a Lincoln Town Car. It seemed the size of a whale to his eyes, more accustomed to cars built for fuel prices at which filling the tank almost needed a second mortgage. He mentally christened the car "Moby Dick," and sank deeply into the leather luxury of the right hand seat as Bill closed the door behind him with an expensive clunk. They drove out of the building and onto the freeway toward Chicago's Loop. The Lincoln flowed in elegant silence.

"Scheidinger came into town last night, sir," said Bill, breaking the silence.

"Bill, for Christ's sake, you make me feel old!" said Scott, raising his head from the leather seat back and looking at him. "It's Scott, okay?"

Webster grinned. "Okay!" he said with a brief sideways look at Scott. "He's in the Regency tonight. We have a couple of rooms on either side of him. At all times, we plan to have two people with him so one can get some sleep. My partner is with him right now with orders not to move out of the room until we get there."

Scott nodded. "Sounds like Standard Operating Procedure. What are Scheidinger's plans after tonight?"

Bill paused while he slowed down to allow an unbelievably shabby old car with neither a signal nor tail lights to pull in front of the immaculate radiator of the Lincoln. The jackhammer clatter of a broken muffler defeated the soundproofing of the Lincoln. Bill muttered something under his breath and shook his head.

"He goes on to St. Louis tomorrow morning," he continued. "He'll be on a government Gulfstream with some of his group and two of us. A second Gulfstream goes along too, with the rest of his team and the other one of us. We land and taxi straight into the Boeing hangar and close the doors before we let anyone out."

"Excellent."

"Reverse procedure that evening for coming home. We'll take him alone from the airport in this car with you, me and Allison."

"Allison?"

"My partner."

"Oh."

Webster looked sideways at him. "Don't worry," he said. "She's good."

"I hope so."

"*Very* good."

Allison had to be pretty special, decided Scott. He looked forward to meeting her.

The towers of Chicago loomed ahead. The solid black pile of the John Hancock building was clearly visible, but the silvery spire of the Sears Tower was almost lost in the haze. The summer afternoon was hot and humid, and the car's powerful air-conditioning was a blessing.

"Been here before, Scott?" Bill asked, breaking the silence that had taken over for the last ten minutes.

"A few times. Visited once with the Air Force when we showed the Nimrod at the Lakeside air show."

"You were a pilot?" Scott sensed his glance.

"Ten years. Nimrods, choppers, academy instructor."

"No shit?" The younger man sounded impressed, and Scott smiled at him.

"No shit," he assured him solemnly.

They turned off the freeway and drove along city streets, finally turning up the ramp of the hotel. Bill left the car at the front, and they entered. They took an escalator up the main floor, found the elevator bank and ascended to the twelfth floor. Bill led them to a room at the end of a corridor and knocked gently. A female voice asked, "Who's there?"

"Scott McIntyre and Bill," he replied, looking directly at the spyhole lens. He held his right hand up, touching his left shoulder. It looked silly, but Scott knew that if Bill hadn't done that, it would have signalled to the watcher through the spyhole that he was not acting under his own free will and a hostile player had entered the game.

The door opened.

Allison was about thirty, ebony-skinned and stunning. She stood a couple of inches above Scott's five-foot-ten, dressed like any businesswoman in a dark suit with a light blue shirt, open at

23

the neck. Scott felt his jaw drop and he stared at her, speechless. Her long black hair was tied in a simple ponytail, revealing a slender neck and jawline. Her amused expression said she had seen similar male reactions before.

"Come on in, gentlemen." The voice was like a church organ playing softly, the power on call, but unused. The two men moved inside and she closed the door behind them. The room was not at all like Scott's offices in Birmingham. There were three comfortable lounge chairs and a three-seat sofa, all decorated in subdued burgundy. Drapes of a neutral cream color hung at the windows. A round table sat in the middle of the room with four chairs, papers on the table and a tiny cellular telephone. One door led off to the left, one to the right. A refrigerator sat in the corner with a table holding a coffee pot and packets of instant coffee, tea bags, sugar and powdered cream.

"I'm Allison Monroe," she said with a smile and shook hands with Scott. He was still feeling off-balance at the magnetism of the woman. Bill was smiling slightly, also amused at Scott's reaction.

"Scott McIntyre," said Scott, and coughed to clear the slight obstruction in his throat.

"Mister Scheidinger is asleep in the next room, jet-lagged to death," said Allison. "Why don't we get the logistics sorted out?"

She led them to the small round conference table and pulled a small bag out from under one seat. Scott sat down on her left, Bill across from him. She opened up the bag.

"First essentials," she said. "Hardware!"

She extracted a Browning nine-millimeter automatic pistol and pushed it across to Scott, followed by a box of bullets and a silencer. He pulled out the magazine, and began to load bullets into it. A shoulder holster was next, and he stood up to take off his jacket and strap the leather case around his shoulders.

"We reckon we'll be indoors almost the whole time. So you've got low-velocity shells," Allison added as an afterthought.

Scott nodded his approval. A silencer was not much use if the bullets were supersonic. He put the jacket back on and practised a couple of quick draws. It was smooth enough, and he felt more properly dressed for the occasion with the comforting weight under his left arm. The other two watched him with professional intensity until he sat down again.

"So, about al-Yaffi?" said Bill, leaning forward on his elbows. "They say you're the expert."

"Expert?" said Scott, shaking his head. "Hell, nobody's an expert! It's just that I've been trailing the bastard for four years and I know something of his style."

"Any idea of what he looks like?" Allison's tones were so beautiful, thought Scott, he wished he could persuade her to keep talking. He'd be very happy just to listen.

He took the few alleged photos of al-Yaffi from his bag and laid them on the table. "We think, and I stress the think part, that these are pictures of him," he said. "They're not much use."

The other two fanned out the photographs and leaned over the table. Their disappointment was obvious.

"I'm afraid that's all there is," Scott responded to their unspoken question. "Looks like he's about five-foot-nine or so, Arabic or Semitic features, small beard, moustache, long hair, light build. Maybe early thirties. Not a lot to go on."

"What about methods?" Allison was obviously perturbed by the poor photos but seemed determined to press on. She collected up the pictures and returned them to the envelope.

"Fairly predictable," answered Scott. "He will occasionally use a bomb if he wants to get more than one person at a time, and we think he's done that twice." He didn't amplify that statement. His private history had no bearing on this mission. "But otherwise he's a face-to-face killer. Some element of a sense of honour, or warrior mentality. He's never used a long rifle, always a pistol at close quarters. So far as we know, that is. Very secretive character, our Mustapha."

25

The door to the bedroom opened and they all turned to face it. Wilhelm Scheidinger stood before them, a short, stocky man dressed in a beautifully cut grey suit. His crisp white shirt displayed gold cufflinks and a dull red tie knotted in a perfect Double Windsor. His hair was full, still glossy brown, though he looked in his sixties. *Not the archetypal East German Communist politician,* thought Scott. *Obviously he's been able to get some decent suits since reunification.*

Scott stood up and walked over to meet him. "*Guten Abend,* Herr Scheidinger," he said with a smile and offered his hand. The German shook it briefly but firmly.

"I think we can manage in English, Mister McIntyre," he said with no discernible accent whatever.

"Yes, sir," said Scott, feeling silly. Scheidinger sat down across from Allison. Scott returned to his own seat.

"You were discussing the possible attempt on my life?" said Scheidinger. The question was universally addressed, as he looked at each of them in turn. Allison chose to reply.

"Yes, sir, we were. I would rather you played no part in this, Mister Scheidinger. We have many things to work out."

"Nevertheless, Miss Monroe, it concerns my life, and I would like to listen in on whatever arrangements you will be making."

He could be a British diplomat, so perfect is his diction, so immaculate his appearance, thought Scott, trying to keep a straight face. *The old Communist bloc traditions had died goddammed quick with this man.* Both Bill and Allison were obviously impressed by the flawless English accent.

Bill sneaked a look across the table to Scott with a slightly helpless look, and Scott nodded briefly. It could hardly hurt to have Scheidinger aware of what they would be planning.

"Okay, sir," said Bill, moving to the cabinet by the wall and pulling some papers from a drawer. He brought them back and laid them on the table. "The first sheet is a diagram of the secure hangar at St. Louis. We will taxi directly there after landing, both jets will enter the hangar, and the doors will close before we open the aircraft door."

"Who will be allowed in the hangar?" asked Scott.

"Only the Boeing executives scheduled for the meeting," replied Webster. "You and Allison will be on the first aircraft with Scott, and up to six of your party. I will be on the second craft with the remaining four of your party." He pointed at the diagram with a pencil and traced a line to the doorway. "We will all leave the aircraft at the same time and move in a close group around you, through that door and into the offices. A special room has been prepared alongside the hangar with washrooms and dining facilities, so that we don't have to leave the area before returning home."

"What happens while the meeting is going on?" asked Scott.

Bill looked at him briefly and pointed again at the chart. "Two of us will at all times be in the meeting room. One of us will always accompany Mister Scheidinger any time he moves away from the table. The third will be outside, checking everything, including the twenty men of the National Guard who have been loaned to us for the day by the Governor of Missouri."

Scott sat back and smiled. "Nice," he said. "Very nice. What about the aircraft themselves?"

"Both craft will be fully fuelled on leaving O'Hare," replied Allison, with a satisfied expression. "And we depart from the Air National Guard depot where a guard has been placed on them since we got the word about this mission. We don't need to refuel in St. Louis. All four pilots are security-cleared Bureau men."

Scott nodded, also satisfied.

"Mister McIntyre?" The clipped, British-sounding tones of the German pulled Scott's attention away.

"Yes, sir?"

"Do we know who wants me dead?"

"Uncertain, sir," said Scott, looking up at the German's clear gaze. "One possibility is a new neo-Nazi group we've not met before, Knights of Aryan Dawn, but we have nothing definite."

"I see," the German replied, looking thoughtfully at his hands on the tabletop. "I have heard of these people. And who is the intended executioner?"

So very British, thought Scott again. *I could be talking with a senior member of the Diplomatic Corps, Eton and Oxford, and all that Establishment stuff.* "Again, uncertain," he answered. "It's possible that it's Mustapha al-Yaffi, however."

"Al-Yaffi?" Scheidinger looked pensive and raised his eyes to Scott. "I should be honoured, I suppose, to be attracting such exotic attentions. You are aware, are you not, that some people think that the celebrated al-Yaffi is actually a German national?"

"German?" Scott was surprised. He had never heard any theory of al-Yaffi's origins other than the Palestinian one. "No sir, I was not aware of that. Do you have evidence for that?"

Scheidinger shook his head. "Not personally. But contact our security people in Bonn. They will give you what we have."

"Thank you, I will." Scott felt confused, a little angry. *How the hell could such a wildly different theory of al-Yaffi's origins and history be in circulation without the ears of the Mongoose Section picking it up? What was going on?* Under his confusion, he sensed a tiny tremor of awareness that something horribly wrong was stinking up the works.

They resumed the briefing and Bill ran them through the tiny details of position, timing, coordination and support that should keep their charge alive until he left. Bill wrapped up the final arrangements.

"When we return here tomorrow night, there'll be a small dinner in this suite for you and three executives of APV and their spouses. As we agreed, dining in public areas is thought to be dangerous."

Scheidinger nodded. "You three will be here still?"

"Yes, sir," they replied in chorus.

For the first time, he smiled. "Splendid!" he said. "I hope, Miss Monroe, you will act as my hostess for the event? So tiresome, being a bachelor for these formal dinner affairs."

"It will be my pleasure, sir," she replied, the organ tones of her voice providing a musical close to the business of the evening.

Scheidinger moved to the sitting room of the hotel suite.

"Mister Webster, could you summon Miss Hollesteller and Mister Lederer from their rooms?" he asked. "We have considerable work to do."

Bill nodded and went to the phone. A few minutes later, Scott heard a knock on the door. The three of them looked at each other. Bill went to the door and waited until Allison was on the side that would leave her covered when it opened. Scott stood by the far corner so he could see through the first crack. They moved as if they had been partners for years. Three guns were drawn smoothly and held ready.

Bill studied the outside corridor through the spyhole, nodded to them and opened the door. Despite the assurance, Scott felt his tension rise. Two people came in. Bill closed the door, and the others put their guns away. A middle-aged man in a pinstriped suit carried a briefcase, a heavy-set woman in her forties held a green leather handbag that did not match the severe blue suit she was wearing.

"Sorry," said Bill. He took the briefcase from the man, who merely stood in a resigned manner. Allison took the woman's handbag. Both bags were examined thoroughly and returned to their owners. The woman sneered slightly, as she and the man walked into the other room.

The three agents smiled at each other.

"Bill, you need to get some sleep," said Allison. "Why don't you head for your room and sack out? Scott and I will hold the fort."

"Yeah, fine." Bill looked on the verge of collapsing. "I'll do that."

Scott checked his watch. Seven-thirty in the evening, it said, one-thirty in the morning by his internal clock.

Allison saw the movement. "We'll get Bill back in here at one, then we can get our rest," she said with a smile of sympathy. "We'll start again at seven."

Bill nodded at them and left. Scott checked the door latch, looked around the room again as dusk began to fall, and checked that all the curtains were closed before switching on the lights. Allison went to a small cabinet by the refrigerator and extracted a pair of glasses.

"One drink is permissible, I think," she announced. "We have scotch, brandy, bourbon, vodka and gin, and all the fixings a man could want."

"Scotch, teaspoonful of cold water, no ice."

She looked sideways at him with a half smile. "Very specific. I always like a man who knows what he wants!"

Scott laughed. "My very Highland granddaddy in Dundee taught me to drink scotch when I was ten," he said. "Never could abide these newfangled ways of mixing horrible things like soda water or ginger ale in God's drink. As for ice...." He switched to the old man's deep brogue. "... Only those godless heathens in the south and those damned rebels in the colonies would do that!" He rolled the "r" ferociously.

She chuckled happily and brought a bottle of Glen Grant to the table with the glasses. "In that case, I'd better do as Grandaddy would have it," she said, her melodious voice providing a background to the chinks of glass. "I'd hate to be either a godless heathen or a damned colonial rebel!"

Scott filled a glass with water from the bathroom, joined her at the table and poured two healthy slugs of the Glen Grant. With exaggerated care, he dribbled a few drops of water into each and handed her one.

"Sláinte Mháth!" he said and raised his glass to her.

"Who?"

"Sláinte Mháth. It means good health!"

"Oh. In that case, *Sláinte Mháth!"*

"Well said!"

She chuckled again, a deep-throated, beautiful sound, and they drank each other's health.

For about two hours they talked softly, learning about each other's past, present and hoped for futures. They compared notes about their jobs, talked shop and kept an ear tuned to the muted conversation they could hear in the sitting room. Hard to recall a more pleasant, relaxed time spent with anyone, thought Scott. Except Janette.

At ten, the door from the next room opened and all three Germans came out. Speaking quietly, they worked their way to the door that led to the corridor. Allison and Scott rose and went to join them. Scott checked the spyhole, saw an empty corridor, opened the door and checked again. Still empty. He nodded at Allison. She stood aside and let Scheidinger's colleagues leave. Scott closed and locked the door again.

All SOP, Standard Operating Procedure.

The lines of fatigue on Scheidinger's face were deep. Shadows under his eyes spoke eloquently of overlong hours, excess tension and huge responsibilities.

"I think I shall return to my bed," he said with a deep sigh and left them without waiting for an answer.

Lucky you, thought Scott. *My eyes are getting gritty. I have three hours before I can do the same.*

Those three hours passed in occasional comments between Allison and Scott, intermittent jokes, no more scotch, and Scott knew that he dozed off a few times. Allison was polite enough not to mention it. At one-thirty, Bill returned, looking much more alive than when he had left. He showed Scott to the room next door, a smaller version of the suite they had been occupying, and the next thing for which Scott was fully awake was breakfast at seven.

* * *

The next day was a bore. Everything went exactly as Bill had laid it out. Allison, Bill and Scott drove to the airport in Moby Dick with Scheidinger, the ten members of the German entourage travelled in a minibus. They flew down to St. Louis in two Gulfstream executive jets then sat around for six hours. The three agents took turns sitting in the conference room, strolling around the hangar checking on the locations and alertness of the National Guard contingent, found nothing to bitch about, and everyone flew home again.

Nothing else happened. It was all good old SOP, the Standard Operating Procedure that was the bible of military life.

The bright spot for Scott was to take the jump seat in the Gulfstream behind the flight deck for the take-offs and landings and swap flying anecdotes with the two frighteningly youthful pilots. He got a great view of The Arch on the approach into St. Louis. He thought a little sadly of owning the left hand seat of a Nimrod years ago, tried to wipe his mind clear of nostalgia, and returned to the question of keeping Wilhelm Scheidinger on the operational side of The Veil.

The landing at O'Hare was uneventful, and the two vehicles were waiting for them as the Gulfstream jets stopped at the terminal. Bill piloted Moby Dick back through the freeway with Allison in the front seat, Scheidinger and Scott in the back. The evening traffic heading toward the Loop was heavy with more than the usual number of cars pouring in. It caused the single break in the silence during the ride.

"Heavy traffic tonight. What's up?" asked Scott.

"Night game at Wrigley Field." Bill was distracted with the driving problems.

"Baseball?" sighed Scott. "God, I haven't seen a baseball game since I was here for the Lakeside Airshow."

"Can you take a day off when this is over?"

"Not a chance."

"Pity."

Silence resumed its grasp on the interior luxury of the Lincoln. They got back to the hotel suite and Scott began to think of leaving for home the next evening. Just a dinner tonight for the executives, spouses and their host to get through, and tomorrow, they would take Herr Scheidinger of the immaculate suits back to O'Hare for Lufthansa's afternoon departure.

In carefully choreographed shifts, they showered, changed and tried to ease jangled nerves. Scott checked the free movement of the Browning with the silencer screwed on to the barrel, felt the tension growing and tried to ignore it. At seven, they went through Standard Operating Procedures again as the visitors arrived: two heavy-set men, high-level executives, with willowy, elegant, interchangeable wives and a petite, strong-faced young woman in her thirties, Vice President of Something, accompanied by her husband who looked a mite uneasy in the rarefied company. Allison worked deliberately on him and soon had him chatting cheerfully, to the relief of the Vice President of Something who was secure enough not to feel threatened.

Allison was wearing a deep blue Cheongsam with a split up the thigh that caused a spark in Scheidinger's eye, disapproving glances from the interchangeable wives, and sneaky side looks from the heavies when they could. The scene provided Bill and Scott with a constant side-show of small-group sexual dynamics.

The two agents kept a low profile. They stood by the walls, occasionally checked the curtains if anyone passed near enough to disturb them, listened to snippets of conversation. Scott wished he could have a drink.

"...took Sheila to Lake Placid for a week's skiing at Christmas...."

"...could shave a millimeter of plating at the rear, sure...."

"...next time you come, we'll...."

A knock on the door signalled dinner and the hair on Scott's neck rose. *Scott, for God's sake, you're getting paranoid. Check the spyhole, it's the waiter with the food cart just as expected, and Miss Hollesteller with a file of papers. Must be okay, so why the ghost fingers on your spine?*

He opened the door. He watched the cart pushed in, watched Miss Hollesteller advance on her boss with the papers. He heard a sharp cry from Allison and everything went into slow motion.

The waiter reached under the cart. He stood up with an Uzi. Miss Hollesteller pulled a Walther PPK from under her left breast. Training and instinct took over. Scott threw a high kick at the waiter's arm and heard a gasp of pain. Scott's gun was in his hand. *(How the hell did the gun get into my hand?)* There was a gusty sneeze of a silenced nine-millimeter and the waiter went down with a small bloody spot mathematically in the center between the eyes. *(Nice shooting Scott, your first kill... it's not al-Yaffi... he always works alone... a pistol, never a sub-machine gun... who the hell is it, then?).* Scott twisted his head, frantically searching for the other woman. He heard a flat crack of a thirty-two. *(Where in the name of heaven did she hide a gun under that Cheongsam?)* There was a snap of a cleanly broken arm as Allison's shot hit Miss Hollesteller, a scream of pain and the thump of a pistol falling to the expensive carpet...

Time returned to normal.

The only sound at first was heavy breathing, with a tiny whimpering from Miss Hollesteller who sat in a silk-covered chair, clutching her arm. Allison was standing over her, motionless, the muzzle of the Colt pistol resting against the woman's bowed head. The wives were white, clutching their identical gold handbags, eyes staring at the red ruin of the waiter's forehead. The smell of burnt explosive mixed with expensive cigar smoke and perfume. The Vice President of Something was standing with her husband, both looking with calm interest at Allison and Scott.

"Jesus CHRIST!" One of the heavies took a deep draught of his bourbon and water and ground his cigar into an ashtray. The wives broke into tears simultaneously. *(What is it with these two?* thought Scott. *Are they twins or something?)* Bill had already pulled a tiny cellular phone from his breast pocket and was talking calmly into it. His eyes met Scott's and he smiled. *A very cool customer, young Bill,* thought Scott. As for Allison... as Bill had said, she was *very* good.

"Outstanding, Scott!" she said, her voice only a shade higher than her regular contralto. Scott bowed slightly in her direction.

"Miss Monroe, gentlemen," said Scheidinger. He was totally calm, not breathing hard, no sweat on his face, no sign of nerves at all. "That was very well done indeed. I believe we all owe you our lives."

Scott looked at him briefly then went to the body on the floor, his automatic still pointing at the corpse's head. He gently kicked the Uzi away from the dead hand toward Bill, who picked it up and removed the magazine with a metallic snap. Scott bent over the man. The body had light brown hair, a muscular build, well over six feet tall. He was very dead.

"That's not al-Yaffi," said Bill Webster.

"No, it's not," agreed Scott, still bending over the body. "But who the hell is it, then?"

"Knights of Aryan Dawn, Mister McIntyre."

Scott stood up and turned to face Scheidinger who was standing next to him. "How do you know, sir?"

With the toe of his beautifully polished dress shoe, the diplomat delicately pushed at the body's right wrist. He turned it over so that the back of his hand faced upward, and forced back the sleeve. Scott saw a small tattoo, twin red lightning flashes on a black square background.

Scheidinger walked away, all interest lost, and stood over the woman crouching in the silk chair, clutching her arm, silent now. For a long moment he stared down at her.

"Really, Miss Hollesteller!" he said. The edge to his tone would have sliced through armour plating. "How pathetic."

He walked to the table and poured himself a glass of white wine from the bottle that stood in the silver ice bucket. He sipped calmly at his glass, checking the label on the bottle with interest.

"Herr Scheidinger?" said Scott.

The German looked up. "Yes, Mister McIntyre?"

"If you ever want a job in our section, you will call, won't you?"

For the first and last time that Scott knew him, Scheidinger grinned cheerfully. "Thank you, Mister McIntyre," he said. "I shall always remember that!"

Bill opened the door. Scott hadn't heard the knock, nor seen Bill check the spyhole, but in came three men in working overalls, wheeling a large laundry basket. They hauled the body off the floor, dropped it unceremoniously into the basket, covered it with a sheet, and wheeled it out. Not a word had been said.

All SOP, it seemed.

As midnight struck, two more young men arrived. They greeted Allison and Bill with a happy grin and an incongruous "How about them Cubs, then?" and walked out again, leading the white-faced Miss Hollesteller.

The heavies and the cloned, willowy wives left after a few words with Scheidinger, who seemed happy to see them go. The Vice President of Something had stayed a little longer, and exchanged a quiet sentence or two with Allison and Bill, which brought smiles to all three faces. Then she took her husband's hand and led him out with a stage whisper of, "Okay, Jim, one more look at her legs and then we really must go!" Both of them chuckled to themselves as they walked out. *Tough cookies, the pair of them,* thought Scott.

Tougher than he was, perhaps. As the door closed behind them, the trembles began. *I have killed a man, swiftly, professionally, without thought,* he said to himself. He knew he would have nightmares about this. *Maybe this was the character flaw they had seen at the Central Flying School fourteen years ago.* They had taken him off the track for fast jets and assigned him to coastal surveillance in the massive Nimrods, and later converted him to helicopters for air-sea rescue. Perhaps they had seen that killing would never come naturally to him. Jamieson's training school instructors might disagree with that conclusion if they had watched him this evening, but Scott knew the nightmares would strike him later.

Allison went to the cabinet, brought out the Glen Grant and four glasses. Bill closed and locked the door. They sat round the small table. Scheidinger took off his jacket, hung it carefully away in the closet. He smiled briefly and sat down with them, looking expectantly at the bottle of Glen Grant. Allison laughed, a deep, wonderful laugh, took off the cap and poured four generous helpings into the glasses.

Then she threw the bottle cap into the wastebasket in the far corner.

* * *

With the danger removed, security procedures were relaxed. Bill went to sleep in one suite, Allison in the other. Scott stretched out on the couch in Scheidinger's lounge and slept a woozy, disturbed sleep until breakfast. At that point, Bill came in, carrying an envelope.

"Came for you overnight," he said, placing it by Scott's coffee cup. Scott looked up with a question.

"One of the guys brought it in from the office," said Bill in answer to the unspoken question. Scott opened the envelope and found a print-out of an email from Jamieson.

"German Minister of Finance shot dead at close quarters in Milan last night. Believed that the killer was al-Yaffi."

Carefully controlling his emotions, he read the words to the others. Jamieson's man in Karachi had got the victim's nationality right, and the killer's identity. It was just that he had got the wrong event and the wrong continent. They had saved a man's life, but they hadn't got al-Yaffi. In this game, batting 500 was not enough.

Chapter 3 - A Friendly Meeting

Scott flew home on the British Airways Wednesday evening flight, slept not at all, and got to the office by mid-morning feeling scummy and fogged. He shaved in the washroom and took a clean shirt from his office drawer, a trick Mongoose One had taught him when he joined.

"Always keep a change of basics in the office," Mongoose One had said. "Our schedules are a mite untidy." British understatement at its best, Scott had realized. Jamieson gave Scott little time to relax, and called him into his office within minutes of Scott's rapid clean-up. The doughnut box had been half-emptied by that time, but the coffee was fresh.

"What's this about al-Yaffi being a Kraut?" he snapped as Scott sat down, cradling his coffee mug. Jamieson had refused Scott's offer of filling his own mug, which was a sign of tension.

"Scheidinger merely raised the possibility," said Scott, trying to play down the possibilities of the German's remark. "He suggested we talk to his people in Bonn."

"Then why are you still sitting here, Mongoose Three?"

Scott hurriedly replaced his coffee mug on the desk and stood up. He had managed one small sip. "Me sir? Sitting? Never, sir!"

He heard a slight "Humph" as he closed the door behind him on the way out.

Janette was disappointed that he was off again immediately, but she knew the rules. The smile of delight when Scott walked into her coding section would keep him going another twenty-fours hours, he thought.

"I'm glad you're back," she said softly. More British understatement it seemed, if the embrace he got was any real indication. She lifted his spirits wonderfully.

"Just nipping across to Bonn," he whispered into her ear. "I'll be back tomorrow night."

"I'll meet you at the airport. Then we can have the whole glorious weekend!"

"What a great idea! I'll call you when I reach Heathrow and know what shuttle I'm getting."

Regretfully, he moved away and headed home to repack his bag and take a shower before returning to Birmingham's Elmdon airport.

* * *

"We have very little factual information, Mister McIntyre," the young security man said. His name was Henning Staude and he looked about sixteen. His unlined face looked anxiously at Scott, as if worried that his paucity of data was somehow a black mark against him. The order to cooperate with Scott had reached him from somewhere rarefied, and he was impressed and formal.

He took Scott to a small, bare room on the ground floor of the lovely old brick building in the center of Bonn when Scott arrived by cab from the airport. Excellent coffee was served on a silver tray with an antique cream jug and sugar bowl. A small plate of sweet biscuits was ignored by both of them.

"What you've got is obviously more than we've got, so you're ahead of us right away," said Scott with a smile, trying to put the young German agent more at ease. Data would flow more freely if they both relaxed. It seemed to work, because Staude returned Scott's smile and looked even younger. His blond hair and bright blue eyes would have made him a recruitment poster for the Hitler Youth sixty years ago, thought Scott, and smothered the unkind idea immediately. That was the trouble with talking about the Nazi movement in Germany, he thought. It kept bringing back long-gone memories.

"I must emphasize, it is all guesswork," said Staude. *His English was excellent*, thought Scott. There was just the merest hint of an accent, and the formal phrasing of one being careful with his words. Scott had come prepared to speak his competent German, but it had been unnecessary.

"So, let's have it," said Scott, looking at the small pile of papers and binders in front of him.

Staude opened up a black ring binder with a magnificent crest of the German eagle on the cover and scanned his notes. "The first thing we noticed," he said, slowly turning over a couple of typed pages, "was that, while the man known as al-Yaffi certainly had killed people who might be unpopular with Moslem fanatical groups, every single one of his targets was also what might be termed to the left of the political spectrum."

Scott nodded. He had spotted this fact, also. He refilled his coffee cup from the white china pot on the tray while Staude continued.

"So we ran some deeper analyses of his targets," said the German, "and found that, apart from the obvious PLO, Iranian, Libyan and Syrian choices, all the others had at some point in their lives been highly critical of German reunification aims, or of neo-Nazi groups here, or of suspected old Nazis still in power. Some, in addition, had strong communist connections."

Scott looked at him with respect. He had not caught on to this common feature. Staude saw the look.

"We have been working on this for six years, Mister McIntyre," he said with a deprecating shrug. "Ever since al-Yaffi emerged. And we had a few hints from the Israeli Mossad at the beginning that obviously never got to you."

Scott was grateful for the efforts to ease his wounded ego. "Have you any leads as to possible identity?" he asked.

Staude shrugged again. "That is much harder," he said, turning more pages until he reached a section with photographs in small sleeves. "But we did get one picture from the Israelis that helped. It gives us little idea of his facial details, but at least we get a clearer indication of body shape and age."

He drew a snapshot from one of the sleeves in the binder and passed it over the table. Scott took it eagerly. This was by far the most concrete picture he had ever been given of his quarry. The photograph showed a man ducking into the middle of a group of bystanders. The face was hidden behind the muscular arm of a large, matronly woman in a ridiculous flowered hat and silk dress. She seemed to be screaming and waving her arms. Next to the other people in the photo, Scott could see that the man was taller than previously thought, and slender of build.

"Mossad believes that is our man," continued Staude. "It was taken by their operative just after the Henderson shooting in Stockholm four years ago."

"Can I get a copy of this?"

Staude nodded. "Keep that one. The negatives are on file."

Scott put the photo back on the table. "But why German?" he asked, feeling frustrated. "How did I manage to have the Palestinian identification and story?"

"I cannot give you concrete facts, Mister McIntyre," the German replied, turning more pages. "I have only a combination of possibilities and rumours. The first possibility came when we captured a Libyan gunman in 1993 during a failed terrorist attack in Cologne. He claimed to have been close to Ghaddafi during the years al-Yaffi was supposed to have been on the Colonel's staff."

"Was he credible?"

"Perfectly!" Staude slid the binder toward Scott and pointed at another photograph. "This is the man. You can see he is standing next to Ghaddafi. We have other pictures of him with

Ghaddafi, spanning a couple of years. That's how we recognized him in Cologne."

Scott stared at the black and white picture of the thin man in a burnoose standing by the familiar image of the Libyan strongman. "Oh dear," he said, inadequately. He began to feel depressed at the possible ramifications of what Staude was telling him. He sipped his coffee and studied the photograph.

"He said he knew of nobody fitting al-Yaffi's history as we knew it," continued the German security agent. "Then a year later, the French seized an Algerian terrorist during a gun fight in Rouen. Under questioning, it seems, and I stress the "*seems*" part, he told them al-Yaffi was German. The French didn't believe him, thought he was laying false trails or bargaining for something. He died before he said any more."

"Good for the French," Scott said ironically. Staude shrugged with a cynical twist of his lips.

"Who knows with the French?" he said. "Anyway, just for the exercise, we ran a computer analysis. We looked for any German male between fourteen and twenty-five who disappeared between 1984 and 1995, fitting the general physical descriptions. We picked those years because al-Yaffi is thought to have started operations in 1998, and he would have needed at least two years to get to the proficiency level he has. The general view also is that he's probably in his mid-thirties."

It was broad, and the information was weak, thought Scott. But it was as good an idea as anyone else had suggested. Staude finally relented in the face of temptation, picked out a biscuit and chewed it thoughtfully.

"We came up with twenty-three possibilities," he mumbled. "With most, we were able to get pictures, but of course, they are all several years old, dating from when the man was still a child or perhaps a youth."

"You have them?" Scott felt a small surge of excitement. Something concrete, at last!

43

Staude grinned. "Of course, Mister McIntyre!" he said, pulling a flat package from the pile in front of him. "German thoroughness. It's our greatest pride!"

He seemed to be thawing out at last. Scott reached for the packet of photos, spread them out, arranged them in groups of four and examined them. There were only sixteen. The selection of young faces looked back at him. Some smiled. Some frowned. Some were cut out of group pictures and then blown up, a little fuzzy. All were young, unformed features giving little hint of the men they might become.

Scott picked one of them up. Something about the face intrigued him, but he couldn't say what it was. "Who's this?" he asked, holding out the small, square piece of card.

Henning wiped sugar grains from his fingers, took the picture from Scott and turned it over. Scott could see a typed paragraph on a piece of card taped to the back.

"Dieter Konig," Staude read. "Born 1970. Vanished from his home in Hanover in 1985 when he was fifteen. His family was working class, not educated. The boy had a history of violence at school. Nothing was ever heard of him again."

He's my age, thought Scott. He took the photo back and studied it again, wondering briefly what tragedy had taken place with this young boy of which the world would never hear. He placed the picture back on the table with the others and their associated stories, looked again at the selection, but none of them gave him any reason for further study.

"Yes, we have copies for you," said Henning before Scott could ask. Scott grinned with appreciation.

"Herr Staude, I am very impressed!"

"In that case, you can buy me a beer," the young man smiled. Scott laughed at his expression.

"Are you sure they'll let you in the bar?" he asked

"If there's a problem, I show them my police card," replied the youthful agent with a small grin. "I have to do it very often."

In good spirits, they drove to Scott's hotel, and Scott bought them both several beers.

* * *

That weekend, Scott and Janette finally got to have their long-promised dinner with Nick. They met at a lovely old country pub in Solihull, on the south side of town. Scott drove into the car park, recognized Nick's Jaguar and parked his Honda next to it. He was not in Nick's financial league at all, he thought. He walked into the restaurant hand in hand with Janette, who looked beautiful in a dark blue dress with a white silk scarf round her neck. The dress emphasized her immaculate complexion and light hair, and Scott enjoyed the glances they received from other patrons as they walked through the lounge to the bar.

Nick's dark, lean face was easy to spot in the crowd standing by the bar. He was talking to a rangy blonde in an astonishingly short black dress, who seemed to be trying to drape herself all over his slender frame. Not an uncommon sight with Nick. They were also attracting some attention from drinkers nearby. Nick saw Scott and Janette coming in and waved cheerfully, unwrapping the blonde as he did so. He looked in excellent spirits.

"Nick, how lovely, it's been a while!" Janette gave him a hug that he returned enthusiastically. When Scott had first introduced him to Janette a year ago, he had been quite nervous and insecure about the whole thing, knowing Nick's capabilities with women, but he had not had cause to worry. The two had got on well, but Janette had confessed later to Scott that while Nick certainly was devastating, the lean, piratical sort had never been her type.

Once untangled from Janette's embrace, Nick put his arm back round the waist of the blonde and introduced her as Kathleen. She was, he said, something in Production at Granada Television in Birmingham.

"Hello," she said, in a slightly affected husky whisper. Ah well, one can't always like one's friends' choice of lovers, Scott thought. Still, the evening started well, the warmth and the comfortable atmosphere smoothing away the rough edges that might exist between strangers. They ordered the house speciality from the harried barman, dry sherry off the wood, and gathered closer around the two bar stools. Nick slid off his and offered it to Janette who took it. The two women could have posed for an advertising photo, sitting with considerable expanses of thigh displayed. Scott exchanged a glance with Janette to share their amusement at the picture then he took a glass as the barman deposited the four capacious tumblers of sherry on the bar by her elbow.

"So how was the week in Europe, you old bastard?" Scott finally got round to asking Nick. "You didn't tell me you were off again."

Nick grinned happily. "Didn't have time, kid! It was marvellous! Cut a great deal with one major distributor, put in a bid with another I should get next week. Made a packet!"

His excitement was infectious, and all of them responded. He had always had that effect on people.

"Any more travels in the offing?" asked Janette. Kathleen looked interested in the reply. Nick took a sip of the sherry, and put the glass down, leaning a little against Kathleen. She seemed pleased by the contact and put a hand on the back of his neck.

"Looks like another visit to Berlin this coming week," he said. "One of the big drug stores is starting up a new chain there now that the city's open, and I have a whole range of stuff to sell them. Might be there a week or more."

The blonde pouted. "Can't I come with you on one of these lovely trips? I hardly ever get to travel in my job."

"Sorry, love," he said, hugging her round the shoulders. "These things tend to be total pandemonium from go to whoa. I don't get a moment to myself the whole time."

She looked unhappy at the idea and got a sympathetic smile from Janette.

"I have the same problem," she said. "This jet-setting executive won't take me along, either!"

She gave Scott's hand a quick squeeze to share the private joke. The two men exchanged glances, which on the face of it, were understanding looks of sympathy. *In our own ways, Nick and I are lying to each other,* thought Scott. *I imagine Nick's got a whole line-up of women in just about every major city in Europe, and he's not going to admit it in this group. Still, it's a better lie than mine.*

"That's the trouble with these orphan boys," said Scott with a smile at Kathleen. "No ties at home, off they go, trotting off around the world at the drop of a hat!"

"I didn't know you were an orphan!" the girl said with a burning look at Nick. He grimaced.

"Both parents were killed in a road accident when I was a kid," he said shortly, as if unwilling to talk about it. "I was brought up in an orphanage till I was ten, then got fostered out."

"Oh you poor darling!" The blonde looked ready to strip him naked at the bar. *Nick looks like he'll have an exhausting night when he gets home,* said Scott to himself. Maybe before.

"You were off somewhere yourself, weren't you, Scott?" said Nick. "Kirstie said you phoned." The change of topic was obviously a relief to him, and a temporary block to the blonde's ambitions. It didn't surprise Scott; Nick had never talked about his childhood to him.

Scott nodded. "Just a quick flip to Chicago to sit in on a conference on trading developments," he said. "Nothing too exciting."

"Chicago?" Nick looked interested.

"Yeah, just a couple of days. Hardly saw anything of the city at all."

Nick leaned back against Kathleen again, raised his glass, drained the last mouthful of sherry and looked around for the waiter. He had that much-envied ability to catch waiters' eyes, and it didn't fail him this time, either. His wide, white-toothed grin lit up the bar.

"Looks like grub's up!" he said, and pulled his lady off her barstool to lead her to their table.

Janette drove them home. Somehow, with Nick, there always seemed to be a lot of booze, and Scott was well over any legal limit. Nick's enormous cheerfulness and excitement over his completed contract and possible pending one were too much to resist, and the wine had flowed freely. It didn't seem to have affected Nick, but the blonde Kathleen was almost asleep by the time they left, and Scott was definitely unsteady. Janette rarely drank anyway, so her sherry and one glass of white wine automatically designated her as the driver.

Scott relaxed in the passenger seat, confident of her excellent driving skills, and let the wine have its effect on him. He felt detached, happy, yet pensive. He kept seeing the photos of the young men and boys he had been shown in Bonn the day before, and wondering what horrors had happened to them. He had no idea why one of them had caught his special attention.

Dieter Konig. About my own age. Tall, slim, thin-faced. Vanished when he was fifteen. Hell, at that age I was a kid at school in Reading, playing rugby for the school's second team, and rowing in the junior crew. I worried about pimples before the school dance and the girls I might meet at the Saturday night hops at Palmer Park Hall. Dreamed of flying fast jets for the RAF, owning a sports car, wondering whether I could get a driver's licence when I was sixteen. Simple things, teenage things, emotions awash in testosterone and battles with baffled parents. Not running away from home and fighting to stay

48

alive in a hostile universe. Poor little Dieter Konig. I wonder what the hell happened to you.

She stopped the car outside Scott's apartment in Acock's Green and chuckled. "Drunk, asleep, or miles away?"

He shook himself awake. "A bit of all three, I think!"

She smiled at him as they stood by the front door while he reached for his key. They had a lot of making up to do this weekend and thoughts of Dieter Konig vanished from his mind after Scott closed the door behind them.

Chapter 4 – Toronto

Jamieson was at his desk, writing a note to somebody in his immaculate copperplate. He was the only person Scott had ever known who used this old-fashioned, beautiful script. He never used his secretary for letters, always writing his own.

"Modern kids, forgotten how to write!" he had complained, soon after Scott had joined the Mongoose Section. Scott had said nothing, well aware that his own penmanship, awful since he was a child, had suffered even worse degradation by his constant use of the computer keyboard.

Jamieson was finishing off the letter, and Scott could read the "I have the honour to be, Sir, your obedient servant" lines which they both had once used in official letters as air force officers. *So it was a formal letter*, thought Scott. *Probably to Air Ministry to one of his ex-Cranwell buddies, or somebody in close proximity to the Prime Minister.*

Two jelly-stained paper napkins lay on Jamieson's desk. *The old reprobate had been at the doughnuts again,* smiled Scott inside himself, but nobody ever saw the Old Man actually eat one. Marjorie, his assistant, said that six were delivered every morning, and she regularly got one or two of them. This morning, Scott had eaten one with his coffee, but Jamieson had refused Scott's offer to pass him one. So they played the game, and everyone pretended he never touched them.

Silly old bugger! thought Scott with affection. *Probably thinks it's not appropriate Air Marshal behaviour to be seen eating the damn things!*

"Do you think the Germans might be right about al-Yaffi?" Jamieson spoke without lifting his eyes from the completed letter, which he was reading over. The question caught Scott off base for a second.

"Insufficient evidence, sir."

"How so?" Jamieson recapped his pen and put it down on his desk.

"All they have is the word of a Libyan terrorist, the dying words of an Algerian ditto, reported to them unwillingly by the Frogs, and a few hints from Mossad. I might be willing to take the Israelis' words seriously, but they're unconfirmed. As to the others...." Scott shrugged. "Who knows?"

"What about those pictures and the German computer analysis?" Jamieson finally looked up from his letter.

"SWAG, sir."

"SWAG, McIntyre?"

"A scientific wild-ass guess, based on conjecture and unreliable witnesses."

The moustache twitched. "Not enough to bet the crown jewels on, is that what you're saying?"

"Exactly, sir. But there was enough in those files to give me a double problem."

"Yes?"

"We've been geared up to look for a fairly short, slightly-built, Arabic sort of gent, and I have to keep looking for him that way. But, just in case Staude was right, I also have to look for a six foot or so, slim, European type."

"Hmm." Jamieson folded the letter up carefully and placed it in an envelope. He reached for the fountain pen again, uncapped it thoughtfully, and began writing the address. The gold pen nib squeaked on the heavy bond paper. "What about the analysis of al-Yaffi's targets?" Jamieson lifted his head and stared at Scott. The old bomber pilot's eyes were deep in shadow and unreadable.

"That was certainly spot on, sir. I've reviewed every one of al-Yaffi's hits, and young Staude was right on the button."

"Does all this leave you with any questions, McIntyre?"

Scott knew he was being tested. "A number of them, sir."

Jamieson waited, dark eyes fixed on his agent's.

"The first one," began Scott, "is how can Karachi have received such specific indications that the event was an al-Yaffi strike in Chicago, when in fact it was for Milan?"

"And...?"

"So, was my trip to Chicago a deliberate red herring? If it was, then not only was al-Yaffi given a clear look at his real target, but it means he's got a contact in our system."

"Any more?"

"The second one is how can we have had such misleading information on al-Yaffi all these years, when more current and quite possibly better stuff was on file in Bonn?"

"Yes...?"

"Who supplied those photos of the obviously wrong man?"

Jamieson looked down at his desk and tapped his pen gently on the blotter for a few moments.

"Sir?"

Jamieson looked up at Scott blindly, his thoughts far away.

"Did any other information originate with the Karachi office?" asked Scott.

Jamieson turned his head and looked hard at the photo of himself as a young Pilot Officer leaning on the Vulcan nose wheel. It was a sign of heavy thinking and a decision to come. Scott had seen it before.

"I'll look into that," Jamieson muttered. "As soon as Mongoose Two gets clear, I'll ask him to go and talk to Perkins in Karachi."

If Perkins is going to be questioned by Mongoose Two, then my sympathies are with Perkins, decided Scott.

Mongoose Two was Allan Hopkins, two years younger than Scott, a one-time Naval Lieutenant who had joined Jamieson after serving on destroyers and then the aircraft carrier Ark Royal. He was quiet, thoughtful and totally lethal if the situation called for it. Scott and Allan had got happily drunk one night in Scott's apartment, and after reaching that quiet, introspective stage which commonly occurs, Hopkins had told Scott about the three men he had killed during an ugly incident off the coast of Libya, which the Royal Navy had kept well hidden. Two drinks later, he added the story of the two terrorists he had encountered in Athens on service for Jamieson. Silence had been essential, and he had broken both the terrorists' necks. Every one of the deaths clearly was branded on his soul.

Scott's sympathies were decidedly with Perkins.

"You'd better go with Richardson," said Jamieson, breaking the heavy silence that had fallen on the small office.

"Richardson, sir?"

"Arnold Richardson. Labour Member of Parliament for somewhere in Yorkshire. Very bright boy, very outspoken. Still hostile to German reunification, tends to make a lot of noise about the numbers of old Nazis left alive and kicking in the German political machine. Very pro-Israel. Wanted us to drop nukes on Baghdad during the last little unpleasantness."

"All of which makes him a perfect target for our boy, certainly," said Scott. "Where's he going?"

"Toronto. Three day meeting of the Socialist Brotherhood of something or other. We've had calls from both Mossad and our Egyptian contacts that someone is planning a hit on him, and he'd make a high-profile target, especially at a conference of that sort. Go and look after him."

"Yes, sir. When?"

53

The Air Marshal looked at his watch. Scott sighed. Just time to catch the shuttle to Heathrow again.

* * *

Toronto was cool and pleasant when Air Canada touched down almost exactly on time. The Immigration Officer distinctly spoiled the atmosphere by grilling Scott in a hostile fashion for fifteen minutes about his reasons for visiting Canada, and then sent him to cool his heels in another office for over an hour before the grilling continued. Keeping his temper, and suspecting that this torment was a result of Richardson's avowed politics rather than a personal attack on himself, Scott was eventually allowed out to collect his bags and depart.

Two hours after landing, Scott finally got out of customs and into the public areas. Nobody to meet him this time. The rest of Richardson's party of four had apparently gone on ahead. He waited for a cab in the cramped area outside the terminal entrance, reaching the Royal York Hotel a little after six. The room was reasonable but not luxurious. He had a view of the immense CN Tower and thought that a great deal of effort would be required to get him up that thing. The idea of being so high up with nothing but a building to support him made his hands sweat.

The telephone rang while he was in the shower. "Murphy's Law is alive and well and living in Toronto," growled Scott as he padded damply to the phone.

"Carstairs, S.I.S.," said an abrupt voice in his ear, while Scott stood depositing a large part of Toronto's water supply on the Royal York's carpet.

"Hello, Mister Carstairs, would you like to come up?"

Carstairs hung up without answering. *Was there something in a new diet they had begun feeding to Canadian officials?* Scott wondered. He had been here many times, on both personal and business trips, with the RAF and as a Mongoose. He had never met a Canadian before who was not friendly, cheerful and prepared to go out of his or her way to help. He decided he had obviously hit a bad batch on this occasion.

He hurriedly dried himself and flung on clean underclothes, a shirt and his suit. He was knotting his tie when the rap on the door came with the power and rage of a police squad making a drug bust. Pulling a face, Scott opened the door to find a forty-something individual with a briefcase, wearing a loud checkered jacket, grey pants and a scowl.

"McIntyre?" he snapped, before Scott had a chance to speak.

"No," said Scott. "I am Elizabeth Windsor, Queen of England, Canada and Australia, Empress of the Colonies and purveyor of fine wines to the gentry."

"What?"

"Please come in," Scott sighed. Lack of a sense of humor was about the one thing he could not tolerate in people. *Apart from noisy sniffing, bad table manners and lousy flying discipline, that is,* he thought. *God, I'm feeling crabby.*

The man in the loud jacket followed Scott into the room and closed the door with a slam. He too, seemed to be in something less than a mellow mood.

"Let me see some ID," demanded the Canadian.

Conviviality doesn't appear to be part of Canadian Security Intelligence Service training programs, thought Scott. *No, that couldn't be right, I've met these guys before. Maybe Carstairs was sick during those classes.* "You're the one who demanded to see me and claimed to be CSIS," Scott pointed out reasonably. "Let me see some of yours first."

Carstairs seemed about to argue, but saw the point. There was hope for him yet, decided Scott. The Canadian fished out a wallet from his appalling loud jacket and opened it for Scott's inspection. Scott checked the badge and the card next to it and nodded.

"Good," he said and showed Carstairs the plastic Mongoose Section card with his hologram image. It was really a British Military Intelligence card. The hologram and the serial number would identify Scott as a member of the Mongoose Section only to the initiated. Carstairs studied it hard, checked with Scott's face at least three times, and finally seemed satisfied. He slapped the briefcase on the tabletop and opened it, still scowling.

"You don't approve of this, do you Mister Carstairs?" asked Scott gently. The Canadian didn't look at him but pulled a leather holster with another nine-millimeter pistol in it from the case. *A Browning again,* thought Scott. *Janette would have advised him of my preferences.*

"No," rasped Carstairs. "I don't. Firstly I don't approve of that commie bastard Richardson coming here, and I don't like having to give a gun to some Britisher to protect him. We can do the job as well as anyone."

"I have no doubt whatsoever about that," said Scott, as reasonably as he could in the face of the man's hostility. "I've worked with you guys before. But we both report to other masters and neither of us has any choice. Richardson's political opinions have nothing at all to do with it. Our job is simply to keep the peace while he's in Canada. So please don't take it out on me. I'd rather be watching the Blue Jays, anyway."

At long last, the stiff shoulders relaxed and the resentment eased. "Yeah, well, it's been a shit of a day," said Carstairs. "And I don't like having my boss suddenly tell me I've got to let some unknown Britisher on to my turf with a gun."

"I'd hate that too," Scott agreed with a laugh. "I'm Scott McIntyre. What can I get you to drink?"

A smile broke through the storm clouds. "Jack Carstairs. Bourbon and Coke."

Scott poured two of the same drinks from the small collection of miniature bottles in the fridge. Truce was finally declared over glasses of Kentucky's finest product.

"Okay, Jack," said Scott, breathing a little harder after a quick gulp. "Let's go and look after our baby, shall we?"

He put on the gun under the careful inspection of the Canadian agent, checked the magazine and received a nod of approval. Together, they went to see their baby.

As agreed by Richardson, following a short note from the Prime Minister, nobody had been allowed into his suite other than his own immediate party of four who had come with them over the Atlantic. Because of Scott's hold up at Lester Pearson Airport, Richardson was not in the best of moods when the two agents finally knocked on his door.

"I'm sorry, sir," said Scott, soothingly. "Immigration decided to delay me for a couple of hours."

Arnold Richardson was a slightly built man with a pale complexion and heavy spectacles. In his tweed jacket with leather patches on the elbows, he looked more like an academic than a member of Her Majesty's Loyal Opposition. From his briefing, Scott knew that Richardson had been a lecturer in political science at Durham University before entering the political fray three years ago.

"Bloody swine," muttered Richardson with a look of irritation. "Probably deliberate obstruction because of my politics."

Scott agreed, but declined to say it aloud. The look he got from Jack confirmed the view.

"Sir, this is Jack Carstairs of Canadian Security," said Scott. The two men didn't shake hands, merely nodded at each other. *Oh well,* thought Scott. *They don't have to like each other. We only have to keep the man alive for three days.* "Now, as I understand your schedule," he continued, "your conference lasts all day tomorrow, Wednesday and Thursday, and you have a reception here in the hotel tomorrow night."

"That's right," replied Richardson. "And I don't care what you spooks say, I'm not cancelling it."

"You have that right, of course, but I wish you would reconsider."

"No. That's final."

"Very well," said Scott. "Then the conference will continue for two more days, and you return to England on Thursday evening?"

"That's right."

"And tonight you are not doing anything?"

"Planning an early night," said the politician with a grin. "Never did like flying long distances and the jet lag really hits me."

"I agree," said Scott with feeling. "I take it you'll dine in your room and not go to the bar or restaurant?"

"I suppose so. The PM was rather forceful on the subject."

"Okay." Jack took over the briefing, which Scott felt was appropriate. "In that case, here's the procedure," said Carstairs. "Tonight, I'll leave it in Scott's hands. Keep your door locked, and when you've ordered dinner, call Scott. He'll come here before the meal arrives and will stay until the waiter has left with the meal trolley after you've finished. Then lock your door again. Okay so far, Mister Richardson?"

His hostility to Richardson was not well disguised, but the English politician had probably got used to being unpopular, and it seemed not to worry him. He simply nodded at Jack, who continued. "Good," he said. "Same arrangements for breakfast tomorrow and the next two days."

"Okay." Again Richardson nodded, and Scott did the same.

"During the conference, Scott and I will be next to you at all times." Jack was well in control now, delivering instructions in the manner of someone accustomed to command. "The room will have only one entrance. All the other doors will be bolted and guarded. Everybody coming in, and that means *everybody*, will pass through metal detectors, and if necessary, they'll be searched personally. Three female RCMP officers will be present to take care of lady guests."

More nods from Scott and Richardson.

"For tomorrow night's reception, the same arrangements."

Richardson looked irritated at that. "Is all this really necessary? It will certainly put a damper on the evening."

"Yes, sir," Scott said carefully. "But being shot dead is not the greatest party trick in the world, either."

Richardson looked suddenly shaken, as if the idea had not occurred to him before.

"In addition," continued Jack. "Scott and I will be wearing radio units with which we can both speak and listen to any of the other agents in the room. They will be similarly equipped."

"And just how many of those will there be?" Richardson was irritated again. *Maybe he's concerned about all the extra food and drink that will be consumed,* thought Scott.

"I'd prefer you didn't know sir," Jack said stolidly. Scott smiled to himself. SOP again.

"If Scott sees anyone remotely fitting the description we have of al-Yaffi..." *Or Dieter Konig,* Scott suddenly thought, for no obvious reason. *Dammit, why should that name, of all the others come to mind? Do I really think the Germans could be right?* "Then he will point out the suspect and someone will check him out at once. If no identity can be fixed immediately, we'll remove him and make a more thorough check."

"Damn!" snapped Richardson. "Having people suddenly rushed out and searched is hardly what I had in mind! McIntyre, this will kill the conference as well as the party!"

"I'm sorry, Mister Richardson," said Carstairs. "Rather the party than you."

Richardson didn't have an answer to that.

At seven o'clock, Jack left with a brief handshake, a warmer parting than their meeting. Ten minutes later, Richardson called Scott's room to say he had ordered dinner, and it would be delivered within half an hour. Scott walked along the corridor to his room, knocked and made the pre-arranged signal again, this time his left hand over his left ear, to show to Richardson that he was acting freely. The door opened, and Richardson was looking irritated again.

"Bloody hell, Scott, this flaming spook act is giving me the shits!" His Geordie accent from England's north-east was even more pronounced than usual. Scott tried to smile reassuringly.

"That's the state of the world, sir," he said. "Live with it, if you can." Richardson seemed unconvinced.

At ten minutes before eight, the door was tapped firmly, and Richardson let in the waiter with a trolley of food. Scott went through the standard operating procedures with considerable care. He checked every container on the trolley, checked the waiter, who looked extremely alarmed at the process, and looked under the trolley. Then he let the waiter take the rare rib of roast beef, vegetables, apple pie and a bottle of California Burgundy to the small table and watched carefully until he had left. He went to the door. "Lock it after me, please, Mister Richardson," he said, "and call me when you've finished."

"Tell you what," said Richardson. He was looking very sleepy by this time, which was one in the morning by his internal clock. "Go to bed. I'll leave this lot inside and not bother having it removed. I'll probably drop off before it's finished, anyway."

Scott nodded approval. He returned to his room, had another bourbon, watched part of a baseball game for half an hour and tried to fall asleep. But he couldn't overcome the jet-lag this time, and managed only a few fitful periods of dozing before he had to get up again.

Day One passed without incident.

* * *

Day Two began the same way Day One ended, with the ritual of having breakfast delivered on a cart. At nine, Jack Carstairs arrived. Scott checked him through the spyhole, let him in and they escorted Richardson down the corridor to the elevator, to the lower level and the conference room. Richardson looked like a schoolboy between the two agents.

Jack's team had been busy. The room had been painstakingly checked for metal, for bugs, for guns, anything. The microphones had been tested for electrical supply to ensure no lethal jolt could be released and the waiters who would bring in water, coffee and eventually lunch had been searched and checked against Scott's description of the two versions of al-Yaffi which he still maintained, although Scott simply could not yet believe in the German theory.

Grumbling to himself about the boring and totally unglamorous life that this job gave him, he walked Richardson to the podium, and sat down in a chair behind him, studying the crowd. Not even a ride through Toronto to see the place, he muttered internally. Just three days within the walls of the Royal York Hotel.

At the entrance to the conference room, more of Jack's people checked every one of the arrivals. By nine-thirty, the place was full, and Scott spent an unbelievably stultifying day listening to speeches full of clichés, delivered with fire and passion, or didactic, bone-numbing monotony. *Definitely one of the worst days I can ever remember,* he decided to himself. The idea of two more such days was like the expectation of immediate and painful dental surgery. At five, the misery mercifully ended, and they prepared for the evening session.

Eight o'clock in the evening and the security team all had radios strapped to their belts, ear pieces firmly in place, and throat microphones placed under their collars. "Testing, testing, one, two, three...." said Scott for yet another time and sighed inwardly.

"This is Six, reading five by five," said the male voice in Scott's ear piece.

"Thank Christ for that," muttered Scott, forgetting his microphone was live.

"I think Northern Telecom might deserve our thanks rather more than any Divinity," said a woman's amused voice in his ear.

Scott grinned. "Gather round, people," he said. "It's get-to-know-you time."

The communications worked. All but one door was bolted and Toronto's police were handling the guard duties. Metal detectors were installed at the door, the room had been swept for bugs and other metal in case someone had come in earlier and hidden a gun. All the waiters had been checked with management and yes, everybody had been in the hotel's employ for at least three months.

The six agents of Jack's team, four men and two women gathered round Scott. "Who's One?" he asked, looking at the two women, having already allocated the first two numbers to them, but unsure which was which.

"I'm One," said one of them.

"I've no doubt you are, ducky," quipped one of the men, and a round of chuckles swept the group. Scott waved for silence and studied the woman.

Number One was tall, elegant, almost a model, with high cheekbones and much poise. She was dressed in a calf-length, slinky red number and carried a purse holding little else but her Smith & Wesson thirty-two. Hers was the voice that had admonished Scott for his wrongly addressed prayer.

"And, of course, you're Two," Scott said. The second woman was more homely in her appearance, an ordinary face alleviated by beautiful violet eyes that seemed to let nothing slip by her.

She wore a dark green trouser suit with a loose jacket that covered her pistol in its holster on her belt.

"That's me," she said and smiled. "Obviously."

"Obviously," agreed Scott.

The four men were almost interchangeable in their dark lounge suits, and Scott had more trouble fixing their numbers to their faces, but eventually he had it. Aware of his slipshod work in Chicago the previous month, he was firm in his instructions to the agents.

"Check every cart and trolley which comes into the room," he said. "Inside the bowls, under the shelves, everywhere."

Just in case they had a repeat of Chicago and it was somebody other than al-Yaffi, they closed all the curtains and sealed them so that no sudden gap could occur to let a rifleman get a sight of Richardson. *And what if it wasn't al-Yaffi, and the killer used a knife? thought Scott. Or poison? Oh hell, trying to think of every possibility was what Jamieson said I was paid for, but it makes my head spin. Sufficient unto the day is the evil...*

By nine-thirty, all the guests were in and Jack agreed with Scott that it was safe to let Richardson leave his room and join the party. The two agents came up to Richardson's room where he had been waiting with ill-disguised impatience accompanied by two of Jack's men. Jack knocked on the door and they were carefully scanned from within. Jack made the pre-arranged gesture to his agent, which indicated nobody was forcing them to stand there. Richardson came out, gave a bad tempered growl and allowed them to walk him down to the elevator, along the corridor and to the reception room.

A burst of applause erupted as the group entered the ballroom, and both Jack and Scott flinched with raw nerves at the sudden noise. *Christ, I'm getting soft for this game, thought* Scott. He stood next to Richardson with twitchy fingers half reaching for the gun, carefully examining the people who approached and said the things people say at these occasions...

"Arnold, what a pleasure...,"

"...socialists of the world appreciate your efforts for the fight...,"

"...the people of Canada express their support...,"

The room was spacious, carpeted in dark red with heavy, cream-colored drapes. Tables lined one wall, loaded with the snack foods that were always laid out at these affairs. Bowls of chips, dips and salads, crackers with things of indeterminate nature on top of them covered almost every inch of the tables' surfaces. At the bar, two solid-looking waiters in white jackets dispensed various mixtures with considerable speed and dexterity. People gathered in clumps and chatted, while eyeing up the passing throng for anyone more interesting or useful. Occasional lone observers drank quietly, waiting for someone to show up to kill their isolation.

A tall, slender man, blond hair and light moustache stood in the crowd by the punch bowl, smiling at an elderly woman. A suspect in the German image, Scott decided. He spoke into his hand to disguise the words.

"Number Three, check out the tall, fair-haired man at your five o'clock, moustache, tuxedo, red cummerbund." He watched as the agent moved to the target and gently took his arm, saw the expression of astonishment as the man was led firmly away. He listened to the words coming from Three's microphone.

"It's okay Scott, his picture checks with the master list, he's Peter Cunningham, a reporter with the Globe & Mail." Scott relaxed again, kept his eyes turning.

The throng mixed, swirled, changed the distribution of its mass from the food tables to the middle of the floor as Arnold Richardson and the other celebrities mingled. Nervously, Scott moved with him, trying with his icy gaze to dissuade people from standing too close to him. He was not too successful.

* * *

Ten-twenty. Scott saw slightly built man in a grey suit, chatting up a vacant-looking redhead in a green dress that had a lot more fabric below the waist than above. The man had a dark complexion and black hair. Scott searched for the nearest agent. "Number Six, dark individual drooling over tatty redhead in the dress at your two o'clock, yes, *that* dress... ignore *her,* check *him* out..." He felt sweat in his palms, this could be it. He watched the young man of Jack's team gently touch the dark possibility on the shoulder. The quarry gave a smile and took a wallet from his inside pocket. Scott saw Jack's man give a reflex twitch for his shoulder holster, then control it. He listened to the conversation from Six's throat mike.

"Jack, do you know this guy? Say's he's on the Premier's staff, named Colin Hawkins. Okay, Jack. Scott, did you get that, Jack confirms this guy's true blue."

Eleven o'clock. The atmosphere was a little foggy, but nowhere as bad as it would have been twenty years ago when everybody smoked. Bursts of laughter erupted from a group of tuxedo-clad young men in one corner, all drinking their beers straight from the bottle in macho style. People swung round to look and the room's color lightened as all the faces were turned in one direction for a time.

A tall woman caught Scott's eye. She had strong features and long black hair. She wore a full-length gown with a high neckline. *Christ,* thought Scott, *who said he couldn't disguise himself as a woman?*

"One and Six, tall, dark woman, black evening gown, your nine o'clock. Be careful, don't want to upset Toronto royalty if she's genuine. Give her the gentle touch, Six."

He watched the agents approach the woman, heard the preliminary enquiry from one of them, then jerked his head as his earpiece crackled.

"Oh SHIT!" said Six. "She's furious! Jack, help!"

"Two, get over there and lend a hand," snapped Jack from somewhere in the room. "This needs diplomacy of the highest order, but check her out! She's who?... Wife of *who*?... Well, fuck a duck! Stop laughing Three, this is serious!" Scott located Jack near the bar and could see that Jack was having difficulties keeping a straight face, his shoulders were shaking.

Oh God, begged Scott, *I want to go home...*

Eleven-thirty and people were beginning to show signs of leaving. There were handshakes for Richardson.

"That's three more gone," muttered Jack to Scott. "Maybe this will work out okay."

Scott vaguely noted that Richardson was rubbing his hand, looking with irritation at his right palm and scratching it with the forefinger of his left. A face caught Scott's attention. It diverted him from Richardson for a second then Scott returned his gaze to his charge. Another five people were leaving. One of the men gave a slap on the back to Richardson who was now back to the high-powered pressing of the flesh. Another group of six or seven walked from the ballroom. Very few left now, thought Scott, feeling the tension start to ease. But a memory slammed into his mind like a car crash. *That face! What the hell, I know that face! Where the hell have I seen that face?*

Richardson screamed, a high, terrifying scream of such pain as Scott had never heard before. He arched his back, his face contorted. People were shouting and gathering round him. Sudden image of the scenes when Robert Kennedy was shot rushed into Scott's mind.

Oh God, Scott groaned inside, *where have I seen that goddammed face?*

Richardson was dead.

Before he even got to the body, Scott knew it. Richardson had collapsed, rigid on the floor, still arched backward at a terrible angle, eyes staring in impossible pain.

For an hour or so, the world was insane.

* * *

"Looks like a puncture of the right palm, administered by a hand-held device during a handshake. Simple enough, just a tiny reservoir of something I haven't yet been able to identify, a needle, a handshake and bingo. One dead politician."

The doctor had a lugubrious sense of humor. He stood at the head of the body stretched out under a sheet, holding out the pallid hand of what had been Arnold Richardson. The sheet went only to the corpse's neck, and the white face of Richardson still showed an expression of pain.

"Whatever it was that killed him, it took a few minutes to go from the hand to the heart," continued the pathologist. "Clever pharmacology. Your killer had plenty of time to get away before the noise started and the exits were sealed."

Jack looked unemotional. Scott stood staring, the almost sleepless twenty-eight hours since he had got up from his bed in Birmingham making him feel as if he had been thumped on the head continuously with a sandbag. *What the hell was the boss going to say?* he thought. *Go and look after Richardson, Jamieson had said. Yeah, right! That's one profoundly dead Richardson looking accusingly at me. Great job, Scott. A gorgeous woman in a blue Cheongsam saves your neck on one mission, and you screw up the second one all on your bloody own. A proud record, Scott.*

Jack finally turned away from his study of the lifeless shape under the sheet on the morgue table. "Sorry, Scott," he said softly. "Looks like we blew this one."

They began to walk away from the miserable sight.

"Thanks, doc," Scott said over his shoulder as they left the room. The pathologist nodded with a small smile and replaced the corpse's hand under the sheet. The two agents walked out of the morgue and the door swung closed on the depressing scene.

"You think it was al-Yaffi?" asked Jack.

"Yes, I do," said Scott. "I know he's never used this method before, but the whole close quarters bit, that's al-Yaffi all the way."

They reached the elevator bank of the hospital building, and Jack pressed the button to go up from the basement. The elevator door slid open immediately.

"I think he's laughing at us." The idea had suddenly hit Scott. "It's a joke to him. See the silly plod run and jump and shout. He's got some sort of pipeline into British Intelligence, and he's having himself a ball!"

"Come off it, Scott! You're getting paranoid!"

"I don't think so. He led us off his track in Milan and pointed us to another killing in Chicago where the killer was just some dumb schmuck all set up to shout 'Knights of Aryan Dawn' at us and get killed himself."

Jack sniffed. "Bit far-fetched, I'd say. Why would he want to play that sort of game?"

The door opened onto the lobby of the hospital, and they walked round to the rear entrance and the car park where Jack had his car. They walked out into the dawn. Rain had started during the night, and a fine mist hung over everything. Scott didn't have an umbrella. They got into Jack's white Chevy Nova. Droplets hung on Scott's eyebrows and dripped down his face.

"I think he's the type to try and get some spice back into his work, by adding some extra danger," Scott said, taking his handkerchief and wiping his face. Jack started the car and drove out into the pale, shining streets. The tires hissed as they drove, and the wipers held Scott's sleep-deprived eyes in deep thrall.

Jack grunted, but said nothing.

"Look at the way he does his stuff, normally," continued Scott. "Nearly always at close quarters, except for two bombings when he was going for multiple killings in Barcelona and Munich." He stopped for a second, images of his parents and his sister still too fresh in his mind. "All the other times," he continued. "A pistol, face to face, *mano-a-mano* and all that quixotic crap. We've never come close to him, it's all been too easy. Maybe he wants the added tingle of a larger risk element. Give the cops some warning, tweak their tails, that sort of thing."

"Maybe." Jack was concentrating on the slippery roads.

"There were... what? A hundred and thirty people at the reception, Jack?"

"That's what it says on the list."

"Your people are going to have to check out every single one of them."

"Yup."

"Oh hell, Jack, I need some sleep."

"That's where you're heading, my son."

"Thanks, pop."

Jack grunted again.

Scott's mind had nearly stopped working by this point, but the memories of a face that he both knew and didn't know still haunted him through the thick, dense insulation of fatigue.

* * *

Mid-day when Scott awoke, and Jack was waiting for him in the hotel lounge, cradling a mug of Upper Canada dark beer. Scott asked the hovering waiter for a coffee and a hamburger. He'd missed breakfast. *We British hate to miss breakfast*, grumbled Scott, internally. The day didn't start properly in the RAF without bangers and mash, fried bread, gallons of coffee, toast and marmalade and a suitably respectful silence once the dawn chorus of "good mornings" had been played through. The

British Empire had been *built* on breakfast. Anything else was simply not cricket. It was *foreign*.

"Crabby hour is it then?" asked Jack with a gentle grin. He seemed to know the rules of British social conduct. Scott felt his black mood lifting.

"It would have been at seven, but I was asleep at that point," he muttered. "Don't spoil a good crabby hour, please."

Jack hid his laugh in the Upper Canada beer. The early business drinkers were beginning to fill up the lounge. There were circles of earnest young men and women in snappy suits, elderly, affluent business leaders, and the occasional group of secretaries.

"My men have been checking every one of the revellers of last night," Jack murmured, his voice not carrying far in the growing noise of the bar. He put his beer mug down on the table.

"And?"

"All but three of those on the list check out as the real McCoy. Two didn't turn up at all. One did, but didn't."

"You *will* get round to explaining that to me?" Scott was irritated. Word games and crabby hour didn't mix.

Jack smiled briefly, took out a notebook from his breast pocket and consulted a page. "Miss Angeline Carter, aged twenty-three, stayed at her home in Weston with a touch of flu. The list is marked to show that she did not arrive. An unlikely candidate."

"Bit hard to disguise himself as her, I suppose."

"I agree. She's five-foot-one." Jack's tiny smile was rigidly suppressed. Scott took a bite of the hamburger and spilled gravy on the tabletop. The food tasted good but needed salt. He reached for the steak sauce as well, and poured some of the rich, brown fluid over the meat. *To hell with my cholesterol level,* thought Scott, *I need breakfast.*

"Doctor Adrian Westover of Forest Hill was also on the invitee list," continued Jack. "He's stinking rich, seventy-two, an unlikely socialist but renowned as such. But the good doctor was unable to get away from the hospital before midnight."

"Could be, I suppose. Easy to disguise yourself as an old man. Was he checked in to the party?" Scott sipped the coffee. It was excellent. A waiter appeared from nowhere and topped up the cup. Scott waved a casual finger in thanks.

"He's six-foot-six. And black." Jack looked up at Scott with a straight face. He seemed to be enjoying himself, despite the grim circumstances.

"Christ!" Scott buried his dismay in the coffee.

"Exactly. Almost as difficult as Angeline."

"Almost," muttered Scott, feeling the hot brew doing great things for his battered and abused brain cells.

Jack nodded. "Anyway, Doctor Westover didn't turn up, either," he said.

Scott shrugged. Clearly, Jack's emphasis was on the third candidate.

"The last one however, is interesting," Jack said. All signs of humour had vanished. "The record shows that Peter Callahan, a sales manager with some pottery firm in Scarborough, did set out to come to the event. He was apparently hit by a dark Chevy Impala a few minutes after leaving home, forced off the road and injured. He went to the hospital with a broken wrist, reported the incident to the police, but he didn't see the license plates. Said he'd tried to see them, but they were obscured with mud or something. He left the hospital at midnight and went home."

"And?" This was clearly the crux of Jack's report.

"But the list says that Peter Callahan *was* at the party," said Jack with some urgency in his voice. "He was clocked in at nine twenty-five, an hour after the accident happened, when Callahan was still having his wrist reset. The guard says he matched the description of Peter Callahan on the check sheet."

"And is Peter Callahan tall, slender and European, or slight, dark and Arabic-looking?" The answer was terribly important.

Scott moved the coffee cup and hamburger away. Jack looked at the English agent, his face weary. He too had seen all the previous information on al-Yaffi that Scott had seen before he went to Bonn.

"Tall, slender and European," he said quietly.

"The Germans were right, then."

"Seems so."

"It's a new ball game, Jack."

"Thus crumbles the cookie, Scott."

"Shit!"

"Absolutely."

That evening, Scott flew home to face Sir Martin.

Chapter 5 - Lovers, Friends and Children

Everything had changed. All the old stuff about al-Yaffi being a Palestinian went out the window. For lack of anything more concrete, he was now a German national, approximately six foot one inch, or one hundred and eighty-five centimetres, slim build, probably weighing eighty kilos or about one hundred and seventy-five pounds.

With the changes, some nasty questions had to be asked. They ran through Scott's mind like cockroaches frantically escaping insecticide spray.

Where had all the garbage about the Palestinian history come from? Who had supplied it? Who had verified it? How had they been misled about Chicago? Had they been deliberately pointed at the Knights of Aryan Dawn? Did the poor bastard Scott had killed know he was being set up?

Did the one-time al-Yaffi have a contact within British Intelligence? If so, where? Who? Could it be within the Mongoose Section?

Who the bloody hell was this man?

Scott spent days sitting at the table in the small conference room next to Jamieson's office with the sixteen photos given to him by Henning Staude laid out in random patterns, staring at each in turn. He could do nothing about the other seven of the twenty-three missing youths for whom no picture had ever been located. Supposing there had been others? All this could be a total waste of time, much like his visit to Toronto. A waste of a life, too.

Jamieson had been remarkably gentle about the whole thing. "We've been chasing the wrong dog for eight years, that's all there is to it," he said. "Somehow we were given duff gen..." *(Duff gen? Jesus, boss!)*. "And the new MO with the poison handshake? Well, hell, impossible to anticipate. Forget it, McIntyre. Let's just start again."

Yeah, sure.

Janette tried much the same, in her own unique style.

"Let's go to bed," she said. It certainly helped Scott to forget his depression while they engaged in those wonderful, cathartic activities in his apartment. But the whole dreadful mess in Toronto kept coming back to him; Richardson's scream, his arched back, his wide, pain-filled eyes. *Go and look after him, the boss had said. Well done, Scott.*

He stopped sleeping well, and he began to buy antacid tablets.

Where the hell had he seen that face?

Scott caught himself almost nodding off with the dreadful sense of falling that sometimes wakes a person from the edge of sleep. He had sixteen pictures on a conference table. Maybe the answer was there. Maybe not.

Time and time and time again he kept returning to Dieter Konig. The missing youth was fourteen when that photo had been taken. The eyes still had the luminescent innocence of a child, the skin was fresh, unmarked by razor blades, though a faint trace of hair on the top lip indicated little time before that changed. It was a thin face, a sad face, the face of a depressed boy, a lonely boy. Violent at school, Henning Staude had said.

What had happened to Dieter Konig? thought Scott. *Where was he now? Could he be al-Yaffi? Why do I keep returning to his picture? Who was screwing us around? Where had I seen that face in Toronto?*

Round and round and round and round...

* * *

On the Saturday night, Scott and Janette went out to dinner again with Nick and a replacement for the rangy Blonde. This time, Nick brought along a tall brunette with hair down to her waist, model's emaciated cheekbones, and legs that went to the stratosphere. *Where the hell did Nick find these women?* Scott wondered to himself. She was called Cheryl. She didn't speak a lot, but the fire in her eyes when she stared at Nick, which was most of the time, could have broiled their steaks. She was almost an interchangeable version of the previous Barbie Doll, dressed differently, but of the same generic mould.

Janette was unconcerned about Scott's occasional study of the Brunette's physique. The day he stopped admiring such natural wonders of the universe, she had once said, she'd have cause for concerns about him. Scott hoped she had meant it.

They met at an ancient restaurant in Henley-in-Arden, a little country town famous for its ice-cream made from goat's milk, though Scott preferred its lovely old buildings to its dairy products. The restaurant had low ceilings with blackened beams, brass wall-lights and a huge fireplace, unlit on this mild summer's night. The barman served sherry and port from massive oak barrels. It was ye olde English pubbe, and all that.

Nick was in ebullient mood again. "Got that second deal!" he said, ordering the house's best champagne at sixty pounds the bottle. "Dinner's on me!"

He nodded to the applause they gave him round the table.

"It's been a hell of a year for you, kid!" Scott grinned when the waiter had taken their order for the champagne and retreated with a happy smile.

"Has it ever!" replied Nick with his glowing grin. "And lots of splendid possibilities for the rest of the year."

"Good, profitable business?" asked Scott.

"For sure! But last week I was able to clear up an organizational problem too. A bloke in one of our overseas offices was going to cause me real problems, and I managed to get him removed before he did."

"So you're set for an astronomical year, it seems!"

Nick smiled with that glittering, overwhelming smile which was probably the heart of his sales success. "Positively galactic! See the new car when you came in?"

"Not again, Nickie!" Janette was the only one who could call him that. "You've only had the Jag a year!"

"Hey, a man can get tired of the same set of wheels!"

"So no doubt you've really splurged this time?" Scott was intrigued. The playboy role was sitting well on Nick's shoulders, but something was bothering him a little. Perhaps plain old-fashioned jealousy he considered, and squashed the slightly unpleasant emotion.

"And how!" Nick was clearly enjoying the moment, and Cheryl was providing a splendid supporting role. She was leaning against him, stroking the back of his neck.

Scott remembered the car park when he drove in. In a country where fuel prices made small cars the norm, luxury cars stood out, and one of them had done it with distinction.

"The blue Mercedes? That's yours?"

"You bet!" said Nick, and punched the air with his fist.

Holy jumping nuns, thought Scott. *He must have really made a packet this year! The Mercedes is worth nearly twice my annual salary. That's an awful lot of pharmaceuticals sold.*

"It's been a life-long dream of mine," said Nick with a grin at Cheryl. "Ever since I was a kid, I've promised myself that one day I'd be rich enough to get a Mercedes. And tonight's the night!"

"Well, that's worth drinking to!" said Janette with a brilliant smile. The champagne arrived at that moment, and they watched with the usual fascination as the waiter went through the rituals of showing the label and removing the cork with enough of a pop to cause a small cheer around the table. They raised their full glasses and clinked them over the middle of the table.

"To Nick! More of the same!" said Scott, and took a mouthful of shooting stars. They sat back in their seats again.

"Your parents would have been proud of you, Nickie," smiled Janette. *Trust my lady to think of nice, gentle things,* thought Scott. But a slight shadow passed over Nick's eyes before he smiled back.

"Thanks, gorgeous. I hope so."

"How about ordering?" Scott suggested quickly, hoping to avoid the evening descending into sadness. It seemed to work, because all of them opened up the lavish menus and began to study them.

The gentle nibble at the back of Scott's mind was still there, and he had no idea what was causing it. But something was worrying him. Was it something somebody had said? An expression on somebody's face? Try as he might, he couldn't pin it down.

Oh, hell, he swore internally. It was probably still the shock of the failure in Toronto and his own sense of inadequacy, despite the different assurances from both Janette and Jamieson. Maybe his distress was exacerbated by Nick's sudden, extraordinary affluence.

"Something wrong, old son?"

Scott looked up from his blind stare at the menu. Nick was watching him. Just for a second, Scott thought his eyes gleamed with sardonic amusement, but he quickly rejected the idea as being a trick of the glow from the candles on the table and his own slightly sour mood. Janette touched his left hand with a private look of worry. She understood his depression, but couldn't tell anyone at the table about it.

"No! No, just got side-tracked into some private thoughts there," said Scott. "Actually," he leaned forward over the table with a conspiratorial sideways look at Janette and took her hand in his. "I was trying to work out how to seduce this gorgeous woman on my left here. I was hoping you could advise me."

All of them laughed happily and the brunette called Cheryl ignited the table with another burning look at Nick. He pulled the champagne bottle from the ice bucket and refilled all the glasses.

"Get more of this down her, that'll do it every time!"

Janette feigned modesty but accepted a refill. The brunette drained her glass and held it out with a sultry expression.

"In that case, another one for me, too!"

In the laughter, Nick called for another bottle, they returned to inspecting the menu, and they got down to the serious matter of the evening. Scott tried to put the black shadow behind him and almost succeeded.

* * *

Two in the morning. Occasional traffic noises rumbled from the Solihull Road a hundred yards away and once, a police siren dopplered its way toward the city. They had thrown off the blanket, and only a sheet partially covered them. Scott lay on his back and Janette cuddled comfortably against him in the confines of his left arm while he stroked her shoulder. She was weary but sensed his distress and couldn't sleep any more than he could. Orange glows of street lighting crept through the gaps in the curtains and tentatively explored the bedroom walls. Occasional summer breezes moved the curtains, and the orange light filled the room, bathing their bodies with a friendly aura and sending shadows to play around them.

"Jamieson is really not blaming you for Richardson," Janette murmured into his neck. "I've seen all the signals he sent to Downing Street, and there's nothing but confidence in you."

"Clever bastard!" muttered Scott. "He'd know you'd tell me that! If he was going to crucify me, you can bet the signals would have been sent by Marjorie."

"That's right."

"You know, I don't think that's what's bothering me. I'm missing something, and it's giving me the running squitters!"

A muted chuckle fanned warm air to his neck and he tightened his grip on her shoulders.

"Okay, try telling it to me, thought by thought," she said. "Are you sure it's not jealousy about Nick? You said earlier that you felt a bit inadequate in the face of all that money."

"No, I'm not really sure, but I don't think so. I'll never have that sort of money, but I'm pretty comfortable. I came out of the RAF with a nice nest-egg, my parents left me a solid little lump, so even on Jamieson's miserable pay, I'm fine for life."

"All right, so is it something about the event in Toronto?"

"Probably. I'm furious with myself about that, and I still keep seeing Richardson's body on that ghastly morgue table. I'm personally embarrassed as hell about the Chicago thing, too."

He had told her how Allison had saved the day with her rapid warning, and the astounding way her gun had appeared from nowhere. *But I should have checked under the waiter's food cart,* he snarled at himself. *No way I could escape blame for that, it was so damn amateurish.*

"Maybe you're stuck on Allison. You said how she looked in that Chinese thing." Janette's tone was a little anxious, and Scott turned his head to kiss her gently.

"Not a chance, lady. I seem to have got myself totally entangled with my gorgeous colleague in the Mongoose Section."

"Who? Marjorie?"

He laughed out loud. "Of course! You've guessed my secret!"

She pounded his chest gently with a clenched fist. "Rotten male pig!"

Suddenly, he grabbed her hand. "No! Dammit, I know what it is! It's the face!"

"What face?" She freed her hand and raised herself to lean on her right elbow and look at him.

"I saw a face. Somehow it meant something to me. It was a man, and he looked at me just for a split second. I'm absolutely certain that I know that damned face, but for the life of me, I can't place it."

She said nothing, letting him think. Then he realized that some loose ends could be tied, and that he had to do the tying if he was ever to get any peace.

"Honey, I'm going back to Germany."

"Dieter Konig's parents." It was a simple statement, not a question. Scott knew he was cuddling one very bright woman.

"Dieter Konig's parents," he agreed, and a load of worry came off his mind as a course of some action at last gave him a light in the middle of a jungle of confusion.

"Well, now that we've got settled, perhaps we can go back to sleep?" She relaxed back against him.

"Sleep, woman? When we've just arrived at a momentous conclusion like that? And when I may have to be away a few days again?"

"Well, if you put it like that...."

"Put what like what?" he asked innocently. She giggled, and it was quite some time before they finally did get back to sleep.

* * *

"Yes, I agree you should. Just don't go yet." Jamieson had seen Scott in the corridor, standing with Marjorie, asking her to arrange his travel to Hanover that Monday afternoon.

"Why's that, sir?"

"Come into my office." Jamieson turned and walked toward

his door with that total assurance which came from a lifetime of command that Scott was following at his heels. He was, of course, dead right. Scott trailed along two feet behind as if a string connected them.

Inside, the scene was as eternal as Michelangelo's paintings in the Sistine Chapel. The Lancaster with its four Merlin engines almost bellowed on the wall behind the Air Marshal's desk, and the forty-year-old photograph of Pilot Officer Jamieson leaning against the Vulcan with his arms folded and a bright "Look at me, what a steely-eyed jet ace I am" grin on his face looked at them from over the coffee pot on the adjacent wall. The coffee pot was half full and the box of doughnuts which magically diminished each day provided the only garish colours in the room.

Jamieson walked round his desk, looking at the Lancaster for a second as he always did. He waved Scott to a seat and sat down.

"Can I pour you a coffee?" asked Scott. It was standard ritual if the Air Marshal's big blue RAF mug looked unused.

"Ah yes, yes, why not?" said Jamieson, as if the idea were startlingly new and original. "And have one yourself."

"Thank you, sir." It was almost Japanese Kabuki theatre, stylised, detailed, graceful and followed with faith and enjoyment. Everybody in Mongoose Section laughed about it and would cheerfully have followed the Old Man to the far side of the River Styx.

Scott poured two mugs, delivered the big one to Jamieson and sat down.

"I certainly think you should go and see Konig's parents, and as soon as possible," said Jamieson, moving the blue mug closer. "You've checked with that young chap in Bonn?"

"Henning Staude? Yes, sir."

"Good. Mongoose Two should be getting in from Karachi at any moment. I believe we should hear what he has to tell us first."

"He went to see Perkins? Has he reported to you at all?"

"Patience, McIntyre. I just got the bare bones of it over a bad line yesterday. I'd rather you heard it straight from the ... er... Mongoose's mouth, as it were."

My God, the old boy has made a joke! thought Scott. He refused to play along and laugh at it, but looked seriously back at the Air Marshal. "That does sound appropriate, sir."

Jamieson searched Scott's face, looking intently to see if he had got the joke. Scott stared back at him. Jamieson seemed disappointed. It was a game they played regularly. It seemed to provide an easing of the tension that lived permanently in the offices of Mongoose Section.

The buzz of the intercom broke the small silence, and Jamieson pressed the button.

"Yes?"

"Mongoose Two reporting in, sir." Marjorie's voice was as cool as ever, but Scott knew that she looked on Allan Hopkins with a special regard.

"Send him in."

Silent tension floated in the air until the door opened and Allan came in. Scott stood up to greet him, but naturally, Hopkins spoke his first words to Sir Martin.

"Good morning, sir." Very formal, very British.

"Good morning, Allan, take a seat."

"How are you, you old bastard?" Scott grinned at the other agent and took his hand. Hopkins gripped it firmly and clapped his other hand on Scott's shoulder. Hopkins' astonishingly brilliant hazel-green eyes made a face which otherwise was quite ordinary, into one of authority and strength. His grip was another misleading indicator of the man, for the power in it was not advertised by Allan's long, bony shape.

"Still better looking than you, you ugly sod!" Hopkins said with a smile. "You've aged horribly!"

"It's all the clean living," replied Scott, and they sat down. After Nick, Allan Hopkins was Scott's closest friend, and certainly they understood each other better than Nick and Scott did, if only because Scott had to keep half his life hidden from Nick.

"If you two love birds have stopped slobbering sweet nothings in each others' ears, can we get to work?" said Jamieson dryly.

Allan looked at Scott. "He's in fine form today, is he?"

"Oh, excellent!" replied Scott, deadpan. "He almost made a joke before you came in."

"Good heavens!" Allan looked at his watch. "It's only August!"

The Air Marshal's moustache twitched quite violently. Score another one for the good guys, decided Scott.

"If you two clowns will cease and desist," grated Jamieson. "I'd like to hear what happened in Karachi."

The game over, Allan became stone-cold serious. "I flew to Karachi from Johannesburg as you asked, as soon as I had cleared up the Porterson matter. I got there on Wednesday. I called Perkins as soon as I had cleared immigration, but the receptionist said he was in New Delhi until the next day."

"New Delhi?" Jamieson stared at him.

"Yes, sir. For the previous three days, she said."

"What in the name of Gunga Din was he doing in New Delhi?"

"Beats me, sir. I asked the girl, but she said she didn't have the information."

"You identified yourself?"

"Absolutely. Correct code word for the day, correct code names, everything. I asked her for his arrival time, she said he'd be in the office by late afternoon. So I got into the hotel and caught up on some sleep."

A small grunt from Jamieson signified approval. One thing the Mongoose agents always learned early in the game was to get sleep when you could. As Scott had discovered on both his last two missions, sometimes it could be a precious commodity. He resolved to ask Allan what the Porterson caper had been, but probably he wouldn't find out. The rule of "Need to know" would deny him the information. If he didn't need to know the facts for his own work, he didn't get them.

"Next morning, I checked all the possible flights arriving from New Delhi that day," continued Hopkins. "I called each airline in turn and asked them if a Mister Kenneth Perkins was a passenger in any of them. He wasn't."

Whoops! Scott saw Jamieson's face tighten up. Something was clearly not according to Hoyle. He looked sideways at Allan. Hopkins was perfectly calm.

"I went to the airport in the afternoon," continued Allan, "thinking I'd check and see if he was unlisted for any reason, and I watched each of the flights arrive. Finally, I used my identification card with the airport security police to see the passenger lists directly on the computer, and he simply wasn't there."

The room felt as if a lightning bolt had streaked through. The air almost crackled with the contrast between Allan's calm manner and the words he was using. Heads of station simply did not move away from their desks without several key people being informed of where they were and how to contact them. And if Jamieson knew of no valid reason why Perkins should be in New Delhi, the thing smelled like an open sewer.

"So, I called the office again," continued Allan. "Same girl, same code words, everything. She said he hadn't come in. It was after five by that time. So I called Records Section here and got his address and went to see if he was at home."

Jamieson nodded.

"I had to break in." Hopkins' face was perfectly calm as he delivered the blow to departmental security. "He was in his lounge, sitting upright, but somewhat dead. Bullet hole smack between the eyes. Very clean. Very professional. Been dead one or two days, I thought. I called the clean-up crew and that was that."

Oh bugger it! thought Scott. *No certain answers, but the crown jewels to a barrel of squirrel-shit it means that Perkins had been in the pay of someone. And that someone wanted to make sure he kept quiet.*

"Sir?"

"Yes, Scott?"

"Who else knew that Allan was going to see Perkins?"

"Nobody," said Jamieson. He was sitting forward, leaning on his elbows, his hands clenched in front of his mouth. "I called Allan on the secure line to our Embassy in South Africa while you were in Toronto. The first anyone other than Perkins would have known Allan was arriving was when he phoned the Karachi office."

"That's what I thought," said Scott. "Allan, did you see any signs that Perkins had actually been away?"

"Oh, he'd been travelling okay," Allan replied with an energetic nod. "His bag was still packed in his bedroom. But there were no airline tags on the bag, no tickets I could see. I went through the stuff inside, but all I found was dirty laundry. He wanted his destination kept under wraps."

"Did he have any alternative passports for secret travels?" asked Scott.

"Not that I knew of," replied Allan. "Did he, sir?"

Jamieson shook his head. "Simply an administrator. No field work."

"So if he did travel," said Scott, "it was under his own name."

"Unless he had other sources of false documents that we don't know about." Allan was calm, but he was indicating the possibility of a double agent.

"Then, it's time we put Janette's special talents to work," said Scott.

"Really?" Allan gave him a leer.

"Wash your mind out, Hopkins," said Scott calmly. "Janette can tie into any major communications network from her terminal. Let's do a search of the airline registers and see where the hell Perkins did go."

"As the man says," said Jamieson, rising to his feet, "let's do it."

In line astern, as Allan would have put it, they walked out of Jamieson's office, down the short corridor and into the coding room. Two of the analysts were at work at their computer terminals, with Janette at her own desk. The high-speed printer was chattering away under the acoustic screens, the dreadful racket muffled to a dull rumble. Janette's expression was worth seeing, thought Scott. When she saw Jamieson, her jaw dropped, her eyes went wide and she froze at the keyboard of her computer terminal. The Boss' visits were rare enough, but together with two senior agents, it was almost an historic occasion. The other two girls in the room also stopped work and watched the three men advance on Janette.

Jamieson smiled sweetly at the other girls. "May I suggest a short coffee break, ladies?" he said. Like any suggestion by Jamieson, it had the force of an imperial decree. Two chairs scraped as they were pushed back, and the girls left, leaving the three men surrounding Janette. She stayed sitting down, almost rigid, as Jamieson took a seat next to her. Allan turned a chair round and sat astride it, his elbows on the back rest. Scott sat on the desk behind her, and finally she turned round to query them with her eyes.

Scott gave her a reassuring smile. "Janette," he said. "Sometime between the ninth and fifteenth of this month, Kenneth Perkins of the Karachi office flew out of Karachi to somewhere and returned. Assuming he was travelling with his legitimate papers, can you find him?"

She looked briefly at Jamieson, who nodded approval at the request. She glanced at Hopkins, and turned back to Scott.

"Of course," she said simply. Scott smiled at her, and she stood up, walking toward a small safe against the wall. She pulled a key on a thin chain from under her blouse and opened the safe, extracted a black notebook and returned to her seat.

"I have legitimate access to the main airline computer systems," she said, tapping a few characters on her keyboard. "That's by agreement, as you know."

Jamieson grunted. Janette opened the notebook, scanned a page and began entering a series of complex codes into the computer, each entry receiving a response of a line of data on the screen. Occasionally, the screen beeped at her. She had to pause frequently between entries as the computer deliberated whether to accept the input and took its own sweet time thinking about what to say to her. Several times, she referred intently to the notebook. Finally, a column of airline names appeared on the screen. From his seat, Scott couldn't read the data.

"Those are the airlines which flew into or out of Karachi between the dates you mention," said Janette, looking over her shoulder at Jamieson. "All I do now is enter Perkins' full name into the system and let it do the search."

She keyed in the name, pressed the 'Enter' key and sat back. "It could take a few moments," she said apologetically. "Our programs get lower priority than the regular booking transactions."

"That's fine, Janette," murmured Jamieson. Janette had been with him for five years, and Scott knew that the Old Man had complete faith in her abilities. Scott took the signal from his boss and tried to relax, ignoring the anxiety within him. What the hell were they going to find on that computer screen?

All four of them were silent for over five minutes as they stared at the screen. Just for a few seconds, Scott was distracted by the smooth line of Janette's back, her waist and legs under her dark blue skirt, and how the cloisonné earrings he had given her for Christmas gleamed under her hair.

Scott swallowed as the computer screen beeped gently, went blank for a second, then filled with lines of data. Both Allan and Jamieson lost their relaxed postures and leaned toward the screen. Scott knew that they were about to uncover a traitor in the organization. Jamieson would have a great deal of trouble with this one.

"Mister Perkins flew on Emirates Flight 605 from Karachi to Geneva on Sunday the eleventh," Janette read aloud. "Arriving in Frankfurt at seven-twenty in the evening after a change of flight in Dubai, then catching Lufthansa 3668 to Geneva, getting in at five to six. He left again on the thirteenth, in the afternoon on Lufthansa, changed in Frankfurt again to an Emirates flight, and arrived back in Karachi at four-thirty-five the next morning."

"Geneva?" Jamieson looked puzzled.

"I can examine his credit card transactions too, if you like, sir," Janette said quietly. Clearly she understood how damaging it was to the department that Jamieson and two senior agents had been unaware of the location of a head of station for a few days. Jamieson nodded and folded his arms. *As a defence against further shocks, it won't help,* thought Scott.

Janette returned to the keyboard, turned to a fresh page in the black notebook, and spent a further few minutes in entering data. Against the wall, the high-speed printer fell silent, as if recognizing the gravity of the events taking place in the room.

"Nothing on his Visa card," she said at one point, and began another series of transactions.

"Nor Mastercard." More tapping. Half an hour had passed since they had come in, and Scott found that the desk top was getting uncomfortable. But Jamieson had not moved, nor had Allan shifted from his relaxed stance on the chair. Scott stood up and remained leaning against the edge of the table while his muscles relaxed.

"American Express," Janette announced suddenly, and a series of lines appeared on the screen. She read the details aloud again. "Avis Rental Cars at Geneva Airport on the eleventh... *Le Bon Ami*,' a motel in Versoix, that's about ten kilometres east and north of Geneva, along the lake toward Lausanne. He checked out on the thirteenth, had dinner the first night at a restaurant in Versoix. He had lunch the next day in Geneva. Must have paid cash for dinner on Monday, or somebody else paid. The car was returned at the airport. That's all, sir. I'll print the data for you."

"Well done, Janette!" Jamieson stood up and stretched. Allan did the same and they waited another few moments while the computer data wheezed its way out of the laser printer. Scott took the sheet, then followed Allan and Jamieson from the room. Scott put his hand on Janette's shoulder as he passed her. She put her own hand over his and gave him a smile. It lifted his spirits for the day.

* * *

Back in Jamieson's office, they resumed their seats, ignored coffee and the doughnuts and gnawed at the problem instead.

"Can I suggest a possible sequence of events?" Scott asked the room at large. When they got to a stage of analysis like this, Jamieson was clever at diminishing his stature, rank and presence so as not to interfere with anybody else's comfort and thinking process.

Scott took the Air Marshal's silence as approval. "Let's assume for now that al-Yaffi is truly a German, or at least a European and not a Palestinian. Let's also assume it was al-Yaffi who conducted the Toronto event, and that Perkins has been his conduit for misinformation into us. Okay with you so far?"

"We're going to have to give al-Yaffi another name if these assumptions are correct," Allan said softly. Jamieson was wearing an expression of distaste, as if he had just got a whiff of a long-dead animal.

89

"Eventually," agreed Scott. "Maybe when I get back from Germany later this week."

Nods flickered around the room.

"I flew with Richardson to Toronto on Monday the fifth," Scott continued. "Al-Yaffi must have been there a few days already, preparing for the hit."

"Casing the joint," nodded Allan.

"*Casing* the joint?" snapped Jamieson. "You've been reading too many gangster books, Mongoose Two!"

Allan grinned at Jamieson. Let him have one win, he seemed to be saying. It was a bad day for the Air Marshal.

"Our man takes a few days casing the joint, as my young naval colleague said, and looking for somebody to replace at the party," continued Scott. "He must have made some connection inside the caterers or the organizers, because he obviously had a list of attendees and probably their pictures as well. Or perhaps he just had the list and went looking until he found some bloke he could pass for with a little assistance. He selects this Peter Callahan and arranges to sideswipe him in some car he probably stole for the occasion."

More small nods ran around the room.

"The hit takes place on Tuesday night. Al-Yaffi flies back to Europe the next evening, reaching wherever he was going on Thursday morning." Scott was reeling off a desk calendar in his mind as he was speaking.

"The eighth," murmured Jamieson, making notes on a pad.

Scott nodded. "I flew the evening of that day, and got back to England on the ninth. Now, sir, you said you and Allan talked while I was in Toronto and asked him to get to Karachi when he had finished an operation in South Africa?"

"That's right," said Jamieson, finishing a line of notes and putting his gold pen on the desk top. He opened up a small desk calendar. "On the seventh, early afternoon, one hour earlier in Johannesburg."

"Right," cut in Allan. "The consular people patched it through to me in Port Elizabeth. I managed to make contact with Perkins the same day."

"Port Elizabeth?" Jamieson looked astounded.

"Yes sir, Porterson had flown down there to meet his contact."

"Good lord!"

Scott coughed delicately and snapped them out of a debate on an operation of which Scott knew nothing. They looked a little shamefaced and returned their attention to him.

"Now we get into some wilder guessing."

"SWAG, McIntyre?" Jamieson raised a single eyebrow.

I don't care how bad a day he's had, thought Scott. *I'm not going to let him score one.* "Not that wild, sir."

Allan stifled a snort and looked hard at the photo of the Vulcan. Scott ignored him and continued.

"I suggest that Perkins got his knickers into a tight knot when Allan called him, and he immediately tried to call al-Yaffi in Europe. Because al-Yaffi didn't get back till the eighth, that's... er... Thursday, the conversation probably took place sometime in the afternoon of the eighth, or the next day. Perkins asks for a meeting, flies off to Geneva on the Sunday, meets with al-Yaffi who drove, took a train or flew down, depending on the location of his base."

"Could we check all the airlines and locate a possible candidate?" asked Jamieson.

"Unlikely, sir." Allan shook his head. "Travel within Europe for European citizens is so unregulated there'd be no record. The chances of his having flown are maybe fifty-fifty at best. If he drove or took the train, there's no chance at all, and we have no idea what name or names he could have used. If his organization is well set up, and you'd have to believe that it is, he could have any number of complete identities nicely documented with passports and stuff."

"Hmm." Jamieson sat back. "Then what, Scott?"

"Al-Yaffi decides Perkins' value is questionable. He's panicked, probably broken security procedures. But if he kills Perkins in Geneva, it might give some indication of his base, so he decides to follow Perkins back to Karachi and kill him in his home. He comes back to Europe and he's in the clear."

"Except that he's lost his conduit into Mongoose Section and his misinformation capabilities," said Allan calmly.

Scott shrugged. "Probably no real loss," he said. "He'll know by now that we suspected Perkins, so he's probably sure that the whole Palestinian cover is blown. And anyway, I'd say that suits him. He's clearly looking for a bit of excitement. The whole thing was getting too easy."

Silence fell as Jamieson and Hopkins looked for holes in Scott's line of thinking. Holes there were, too, Scott knew. The entire thing was simply conjecture, but unfortunately, like a lot of simple theories, it fitted the picture all too horribly well.

"There's something else, too," said Scott, the idea sliding into his mind like a hunting python. Two faces turned to him.

"Yes?" said Jamieson.

"It's rare that we get such specific leads to events as we got in Chicago and Toronto, or with such accuracy. We all know how often we've missed hearing about events until afterwards, or gone scooting off to exotic locations where nothing happened."

Allan was looking intently at Scott. His mind seemed to be working overtime behind those brilliant green eyes.

"But here," continued Scott, "in the space of a few weeks, we get direct, accurate leads to two events which happened on time, just as forecast. Even though the Chicago killing was not an al-Yaffi event, we still got information we didn't have before and which may turn out to be vital."

"Interesting," said Jamieson calmly. *More British understatement,* decided Scott with an internal grin. Allan gave

Scott another sharp look, then put his chin in his hands and stared at the carpet.

Jamieson turned his swivel chair around and stared at the huge painting of the Lancaster. Allan sat back, stretched his legs, folded his arms and studied the ceiling with intensity. Scott leaned forward, his elbows on his knees and examined the depressing broadloom of service-issue floor covering. The office was sound-proofed, so no noise invaded the room from the working areas outside. Scott was aware of the tiny hissing and popping of the coffee maker and the faint scent of doughnut that occasionally drifted in his direction. Lunchtime was getting close, said a random thought.

A squeak of the swivel chair broke the frozen scene. Jamieson had ceased his meditations and he turned back to the other two men. "Scott, time for you to head off to Germany," he said.

Scott nodded.

"And Allan," continued Jamieson. "Start digging into Perkins' past. You know the drill. Look at everything. Find out if he or anybody, including his grandmother's cousin's nephew's cat had pro-Moslem leanings."

Both agents laughed. The old boy definitely deserved a couple of wins today, considering the sort of day he'd had. Jamieson smiled with satisfaction.

"Well, don't just sit there!" he said. "Piss off, both of you!"

"Look for pro-Nazi leanings, too," Scott muttered to Allan as they stood up. They had reached the door when Jamieson called out.

"Scott?"

"Yes, sir?" Scott returned and eased the door almost closed. Allan had continued walking and was well down the corridor.

"When you've finished with the Konigs, go and have a look at that motel in Geneva," said Jamieson. "The trail could still have a sniff or two left in it. You might be able to find out who he met."

"Yes, sir," said Scott again. Then he pissed off, too.

* * *

There was no direct route from Birmingham to Hanover, so Scott had to put up with the tedium of the shuttle down to Heathrow and then to Germany. Scott caught the afternoon flight and spent the time in deep thought.

A call to Henning Staude in Bonn had given Scott the last known address of the Konig parents and a telephone number in Hanover to call if he needed help or got on the wrong side of the local police. *He's proven to be a complete godsend, that young man,* thought Scott. *Without his input, I would still be chasing a mythical PLO gunman, running round in silly circles while the real killer laughed his insides out.*

But then, he thought, *if I hadn't been sent on a wrong path to prevent the killing of Wilhelm Scheidinger in Chicago, I wouldn't have discovered this lead either. And Scheidinger would probably be dead. And I'd be chasing Arabs....*

How would he approach Dieter Konig's parents? Should he tell them who he was? Would that cause them great distress? Could he possibly avoid any grief? How? What if they had moved away? What if the search proved a failure? What could he do next? Would he find anything in Versoix?

Round and round and round and round went his mind.

Hanover was cool and pleasant. Scott hadn't been there for over six years since he took a leave with a few friends from the squadron, and came to check out the German night life. Three days later, he had returned to active duty with one hell of a headache, a deep respect for local beer, general affection for the people and very specific affection for one Madeleine Kruger. Scott grinned at the memory as he walked along the airport corridor.

He rented a Merkur from Avis, and tentatively worked his way into the late afternoon south-bound traffic. He drove gingerly to the city centre and, after a few false turns, halts in side streets and bus stops to check his map, and a couple of queries at gas stations, he located the main station and then the Thuringer Hof on Osterstrasse. The hotel looked most unprepossessing from the outside, all white brick and undecorated windows, and he wondered why Marjorie had recommended it. But when he had parked the car and entered the lobby, he realized why. The magnificent, red, oriental rug reflected in warm gleams off the polished wooden panelling of the walls, and in the welcome he received from the middle-aged woman at the check-in counter. The room was delightfully airy and would be sunny during the day. The welcoming room was a surprise, given the institutional white walls of the exterior. He unpacked his small overnight bag, took a quick shower, and collected his thoughts.

Activating his German language skills, he had his first try at telephoning the Konig household at the number which Henning Staude had supplied. But, as might have been expected, the Konigs had moved away and the woman at the number he reached seemed hostile to his obviously non-German accent. He put the phone down with a grimace, having severely extended his capacity to stay polite.

It was too late to find the local post office and trust to German orderliness and record-keeping to find the Konig's new address. Too tired to look for a restaurant, he decided on an early night. The next day promised to be hard. He turned down the bed covers and was asleep within minutes.

The following morning, he got an early start and was out of the hotel by seven. He had a difficult task in locating the old Konig residence, even with the street map he had bought the previous evening at the airport, but by eight, he had parked outside the elderly, two-storied brick house south-west of the city. The house looked blindly onto the street. Lace curtains provided a shield against the outside world's snoopers. The whole area had an air of genteel, working class dignity. Good people lived here, thought Scott, working long hours, worrying about the kids, what the neighbours thought of them, being seen on time each Sunday at church. Suburbs like this existed near every prosperous town in the western world.

Scott left the car and stretched to ease the tension caused by the drive through morning traffic. He advanced on the door of the white painted house with its perfectly-manicured, tiny lawn in the front. His gentle tap on the door was met with a rattle of heels on wood, and the door opened to reveal a tall, bony woman in her sixties. *Time for my German to be exercised properly,* thought Scott with a touch of nervousness.

"Good morning," he said. "I was looking for the Konig family. I believe they used to live here."

He received a look of intense suspicion. Beady black eyes looked hard into his. "You are police?"

"No, I am from England," said Scott. He launched into a prepared story about doing a magazine article on children who had lived during the world war and wanting to talk to Herr Konig about his experiences. It was pretty weak, but Scott had found that most people loved talking to reporters, especially about somebody else. But this sweet old dear wasn't biting.

"Nobody of that name here," she snapped, cutting into his rambles, and shut the door firmly.

He spent a fruitless two hours trying the same story on a number of neighbours and got exactly nowhere. Finally, he did what he knew he should have done at the start, and went to find the local post office.

* * *

Yes, they would have kept all the records, Herr McIntyre, and yes, Herr McIntyre, the records would be stored locally, but no,

Herr McIntyre, we cannot show them to you without suitable authority.

Ah yes, thought Scott. *Balance out all that wonderful orderliness and record keeping discipline with the need for authority.* He sighed, suppressed his unreasonable irritation, decided that a post office in Birmingham would have probably done the same thing, and pulled his mobile phone from his pocket. Henning Staude was putting him in his debt again.

The call was short, business-like, cool. The woman on the other end of the line sounded young and she was fully aware of Scott's mission, his status and his needs.

"Wait fifteen minutes, Herr McIntyre," she said. She spoke the softer German of the south, rather than the local dialect. Scott did as he was told. Sixteen minutes later, the clerk from the post office walked over to him.

"This way, Herr McIntyre," he said smiling, and pointed to the swing door by the postal counter. He displayed no evidence of hostility about being over-ruled. He had received legitimate orders from legitimate authority. *Alles in ordnung.* Everything in order.

Half an hour later, Scott had a new address for the Konigs. Six years ago, they had moved to Osnabruck, about a hundred and twenty kilometres west. Scott checked his watch. It was just after eleven. He could be in Osnabruck by soon after lunch.

* * *

The two elderly people regarded him with a mixture of sadness and wariness from the settee in the immaculately neat sitting room. They sat straight, with dignity. They seemed very close.

"You had no other children?" Scott asked gently.

They shook their heads in unison.

Conducting the interview, Scott felt like an archaeologist unwrapping the Dead Sea Scrolls. He spoke softly, worried that if he raised his voice, the old couple might bolt or simply fall apart. It had taken him half an hour to explain who he was, but he had not raised the question of what he thought might have happened to their son. Behind him, the windows opened onto a postage-stamp garden that had run to seed. The lawn was scrubby, full of weeds and showed several bare patches of earth. There were no flowers. The small table in front of the window was perfectly polished and a tiny lace cloth covered the surface. On it rested a white earthenware vase containing what looked like artificial pink tulips. The room smelt of wax polish and little use. Scott felt that they were probably the first people to occupy it in months.

"Dieter was fourteen when he disappeared?"

"Just fifteen." Her voice was like old muslin cloth, no substance, no timbre. Ancient grief sat in her face. She took her husband's hand and looked down in her lap. He smiled gently at her and stroked her fingers with his other hand.

"I read in his file that he had been rather violent at school," said Scott, praying that the question would not cause a problem.

"We couldn't understand it." The man's voice was much like his wife's. They probably spoke little to each other, thought Scott, communicating with almost telepathic skill acquired over forty years of marriage. Their voices were like the room, used only for special occasions.

"He had been a very quiet boy, always reading," continued the old man. "Then when he was twelve, the bullying started. His teachers came to us, but we couldn't help them. He was not a big boy, but he was tall for his age, and very strong."

"Did he have any friends?"

"A few. We didn't like any of them, and he never brought them to the house."

"Did he play any sports or games?"

"He loved to go camping in the woods," said the woman. "They would build a fire, and sing songs." A tiny smile appeared on her face at the memory of a time when her child was like any other German child. *Interesting cultural difference,* Scott reflected. British families head for the sea when they can. Germans make for the forests. His specific questions were getting him nowhere.

"Frau Konig, what can you tell me about Dieter that might tell us why he left? What were his dreams, his aims?"

She shook her head doubtfully. "There was very little," she whispered. "He didn't talk to us much once he had turned twelve or thirteen. He read a great deal in his room. Everything he had is still up there. We brought all his possessions with us when we moved here. Would you like to see it?"

Oh my! thought Scott. *Who would have thought it?* After twenty years, they still hung on to the memory of their vanished son, perhaps had dreams of his return, still fifteen, still the sad-faced, lonely boy they lost so long ago.

"Yes please, I would."

They rose, and the husband opened the door for Scott. Scott waited for them at the foot of the stairs and the couple slowly preceded him to the top and halted outside a closed door.

"Please, Herr McIntyre, go in. We will stay outside. It is a small room."

"Thank you." Scott walked in and met the smell of dust. Books, lots of books, lined on shelves, piled on the floor, cardboard boxes, their lids folded over each other like cloverleaves. A vanished boy's room.

He started with the book shelves and studied each row in turn, looking at every title. Adventure stories, war stories, a complete set of a Children's Encyclopaedia dated 1967, *Mein Kampf,* a stack of comic books from the sixties....

Mein Kampf? Hitler's infamous creed which once had been mandatory book-shelf and coffee-table items in all German homes? What the hell was a pre-teenager doing with that dirt? Scott extracted it from the shelf. It was well-read, well-thumbed, many scrawled notes in margins in a child's hand, not the fully formed script of an adult.

"... *the Jew systematically endeavours to lower the racial quality of a people,"* said the paragraph in front of him, *"by permanently adulterating the blood of the individuals who make up that people."* Scott closed the book with a snap, raising a small puff of dust. He put it back in its place, feeling soiled, wanting to wash his hands.

A single photograph in a cheap metal frame stood at the end of the bookshelf. Scott picked it up. It showed a group of six boys. One of them was the face that Scott had seen in the office of the German security agent in Bonn, and had obviously been copied from this group. This picture was a little clearer than the copy he had seen. Scott studied the face and felt the same echo of familiarity as before. Was this the face of the man seen as he killed the English politician in Toronto?

There was a shelf of histories of World Wars One and Two and more German histories of the Twentieth Century. Again, he opened one of the World War Two books. Beautifully hand-drawn swastikas adorned the fly-leaf. More scrawls ran up the margin, in the same childish, unformed hand as before. In the section that dealt with the inter-war years, there were numerous large flourishes of "Rubbish!" and "Crap!" He read one of the paragraphs that had been disfigured this way. The section described the violent methods of Hitler's early supporters, and referred to sections of *Mein Kampf* as being reflective of a damaged, corrupted mind. The reader and creator of the angry comments had clearly objected to the conclusion.

Interesting, thought Scott.

A lot of books on cars filled three shelves. A thick, well-illustrated manual of Porsche racing cars was followed by lots of smaller books on the general history of the automobile. A complete shelf was devoted to Mercedes Benz. *The boy had been a car freak,* thought Scott with a smile. He turned to the cardboard boxes and knelt alongside them.

The first contained a large model of the classic Mercedes gull-wing sports-car, built in plastic from a commercial kit. It was beautiful, painstakingly finished, carefully wrapped in cloth, and extra rags had been used to pad the box. Scott closed the box again and opened the second. He found a similar model of a Mercedes limousine, perfectly painted, carefully wrapped.

"Ah yes," said the muslin voice from the doorway. "Dieter loved Mercedes cars. He told me one day, *'Mutti,'* he said, 'when I grow up, I'll be very rich and I'll buy a Mercedes.' That was his biggest dream."

The old couple were standing together, watching Scott. The sparkle of tears lay on the woman's cheek, and her hands were clenched at her bosom. The man's left arm rested across her shoulders.

For a few minutes, Scott remained on his knees with the cardboard boxes, running his finger-tips along the lines of the two Mercedes models, trying to think why they bothered him so much. He opened up a third box to find a model of the old 'D' Type Jaguar racing car of the mid-fifties. An old hero of Scott's, Stirling Moss had made the name of Jaguar synonymous with racing victory in that car. For a time as a child, then, Scott had shared Dieter Konig's dreams, before his heroes became the great pilots like Roland Beamont and Chuck Yeager, who flew him beyond the clouds to show him the face of infinity. The small glow of pleasure from that thought rapidly dispersed before the sour worry that something was horribly wrong.

He drove back to Hanover in a contemplative mood. Almost without knowing his whereabouts, he drove through Harpenfeld and Lubbekke. Through Nenndorf, he got the occasional whiff of sulphur of the spa region, and he finally hit the B65 into

Hanover, took the airport signs and returned the Merkur with some regrets. It had been fun to drive.

He was lucky and was able to get a Swissair flight to Geneva, though had to put up a wait of over two hours in Zurich on the way. On the short second leg he sat in the window seat of the small commuter jet, watching Europe slide away beneath him, idly tuning in to the voices around.

He looked down on the night gathering over Europe and sensed his own darkening mood. Just as the picture of Deiter Konig had disturbed something in him, the discoveries of that day had also plucked some jarring chord. Maybe it was the dignified, controlled grief of the parents as they watched him resurrect old pain while he worked through the remnants of their long-ago life. It could be simply his own distaste at the obvious passion for Nazi philosophies which he had uncovered, which went a long way to proving his theories about Dieter Konig. Or perhaps he was distressed at finally having to abandon a long-held view about the nature of Mustapha al-Yaffi. That identity was obviously a myth, a smokescreen. But there was something else under the doubts, something which skittered and jumped around in his head like a nervous bird. He couldn't identify it.

And what of Perkins? It was clear now that Perkins had been the source of the misinformation on al-Yaffi, had been a double agent within Mongoose section. But if that were so, and if his function was to draw Scott away from the assassin, why had he pointed him so closely to the killing in Chicago that had led to the Knights of Aryan Dawn? Why not just point him to some place where nothing was to happen and nobody was to get killed? All the Mongoose agents had experienced such non-events often enough. They had gone chasing around the world, tense and nervous with expectations of bloody mayhem, only to meet with perfect peace and tranquillity.

The lead to the Toronto killing had been accurate, a genuine al-Yaffi strike. Was that a Perkins leak, too? Jamieson had said that the word had come from the Egyptians, but could Perkins have initiated it? If so, why the hell did he? What was he trying to achieve by exposing his masters to the threat of a Mongoose? Why had he flown so urgently to Geneva, presumably to meet with one of his other masters? Had Perkins met with al-Yaffi who had once been Dieter Konig? What could Scott possibly find in Geneva?

The aircraft landed on time at eleven o'clock, and again Scott rented a car, this time a tiny Ford that almost gave him cramps as he tried to ease into the driver's seat. But the little car was sprightly enough, and he had no trouble finding the city centre. Marjorie had said the Lido Hotel on Chantepoulet was the place for budget accommodation, and again she was right. Muttering a little about the undoubtedly more luxurious travelling style that Nick would experience on his sojourns in Europe, Scott checked in.

This was definitely not the life of a James Bond, he groused to himself. No luxury hotels, first class travel and Aston Martin DB6 automobiles. There was not even a bosomy Russian agent to attempt to divert him from his mission. At midnight, he had little time to do anything but take a short walk, find an all-night coffee shop, add a slice of *apfeltorte* to the basic snack that Swissair had served, and turn into his tiny room by soon after one.

He drove the few kilometres from Geneva, first taking a slight spin around the lake front to make sure he saw Geneva's trade mark, the enormous fountain bursting out of the surface of the water, then carried on to Versoix. The motel was easy to find. It was small, neat, painted white and red, picture-postcard perfect, like the whole of Switzerland.

"Yes, Mister McIntyre. Mister Perkins stayed here for two nights on the eleventh and twelfth of August."

The young man at the reception desk of *'Le Bon Ami'* pointed at the signature in the register lying open on his desk. The rich, blue sheen of Lake Geneva was just visible through the door on Scott's right.

"And this is the man?" Scott slid the photograph of Perkins under the clerk's gaze. He had obtained a copy before leaving Birmingham.

The young man studied the picture carefully. "Yes," he said. "I believe that is the man who checked in."

Very careful with his commitments was this man, said Scott to himself with an internal smile.

"Did he see anyone or have any visitors while he was here?"

"I have no idea," said the man, shaking his head. "Our guests have keys to their chalets. They do not pass through this lobby once they are registered. His bill does not indicate any telephone calls made from his room, however."

As Scott had expected, beyond confirming that it really was Perkins who had stayed here, this visit was providing nothing new.

"Thank you," he said, and put the photo away into his wallet.

Lots of good restaurants in Geneva, said the guidebooks. They were dead right. By midday, Scott had been into twenty-two of them, each time flourishing Perkins' picture and asking if anyone had any memories of seeing him for lunch or dinner over ten days ago. A fool's chase, by any criterion. Not unnaturally, he received a slightly contemptuous curl of the top lip from the majority of waiters to whom he talked. This was high season in Geneva. None of them had time to scratch, never mind remember one face out of thousands.

He had a beef sandwich and a cup of coffee at an outdoor cafe, watching the world go by for twenty minutes, glad of the cooler-than-average, late-August day. The sunlight was clean and organized, like the city. The fountain performed for the tourists, and the roar of cameras was a constant background drone, like a flight of restless insects. He paid his bill and returned to the hunt.

Restaurant thirty-four provided the break. The head waiter was cool to Scott's request as they stood talking in the dark alcove next to the dining area. However, he agreed to let Scott question the team of waiters and waitresses who had been working on the two days Perkins had been in Geneva. It was four in the afternoon by this time, and business had slowed a little. Scott followed the tall, balding young man along an ugly, narrow corridor lined with wooden cartons and cardboard boxes waiting to be thrown out. Smells of old grease, food remnants and off-cuts of vegetables assaulted his sinus passages. They walked to a small room next to the kitchens, where three waitresses and one waiter were sitting in various attitudes of exhaustion. The man was sitting at the table, his head on his arms, two of the women were curled up in a pair of well-worn armchairs, and the third was sitting on a hard chair by the window, reading a magazine.

"Two of the waiters will not be in until this evening," the head waiter said calmly. He was not really interested.

"No matter," said Scott. "May I ask those who are here?"

The man nodded and explained the situation, speaking in English, and the three young women carefully inspected Scott. The man at the table lifted his head for a second, peered at him and laid his head down again.

The head waiter passed the picture around and the women gave it serious attention. The sleepy waiter raised his head again with an expression of irritation, looked briefly at the photo and shook his head. Then one of the waitresses stood up, came back to the table, studied the picture in silence for a few moments and suddenly squeaked.

"Oh, yes!" she said with a brilliant smile. She was fair-haired and very slender. "He was sitting in the corner by the fish tank. He came in quite early, about seven o'clock."

"How is it that you remember him so clearly after ten days?" asked Scott, smiling at her. She flushed delicately, and looked sheepishly at her feet.

"It was the man who came in later to join him," she said, looking up at him with her eyes glowing. *He must have had one hell of an impact,* thought Scott with a tinge of envy.

"Tell me about him," he nudged gently. She put her hands over her mouth to stifle a giggle, and the other two waitresses laughed at her. She had obviously spent much time telling them about this man.

She turned lovely green eyes to Scott, her mouth still smiling at the memory. "He was very handsome," she said. "Tall, dark, beautiful smile. And rich!"

"How do you know he was rich?"

"He gave me a very large tip!"

"The handsome one paid for dinner? Did he pay by credit card?" A sudden hope flashed into Scott's mind. Maybe a clue had been left. But his hopes were short-lived.

"Oh no! By cash!"

Of course, Scott. The guy was a professional, not like Perkins, who had left a paper trail of every move between Karachi and Geneva.

"How old do you think he was?" he asked.

She considered the question for a few seconds, one finger against her chin. "Perhaps your age, I think," she said.

"And how tall?"

"As he walked out, he passed me. I think I would have reached to about...." She moved her hand from the top of her head across to Scott and touched him at the base of his neck. The gesture was obviously sexually provocative, and Scott hid his amusement.

"Perhaps a couple of centimetres taller than I am?"

She smiled. "Yes, I think so. Maybe a little more."

He talked to the girl for another few minutes reviewing the information she had given, hoping to prod some more details from her. But she remembered nothing beyond how handsome the man was, how he smiled at her, and how much money he seemed to have. She remembered nothing of their conversation other than that the two men had spoken in English.

But Scott now had a general description of a man who might stand out in a crowd, not just to women. He was dark, slender, a little taller than Scott, about Scott's own age.

"Christ!" he said aloud, as he drove toward the border. "The bastard could almost look like Nick!" He shook his head at the stupidity of the idea. Nick had been his best friend, almost his brother for half his life. Mustapha al-Yaffi was an international assassin. "Get real, McIntyre," he muttered. "Let's keep this thing rational, shall we?"

He began the search for travel clues with the entry by road from France. The drive up the mountain to the entry point was spectacular, and the tiny Ford was panting hard by the time he got there. He went to the Swiss guard post first and showed his Mongoose Section identification card. He talked to the group of officers for half an hour, but none of them could remember seeing a man of the description Scott gave them. The senior officer promised to pass the request to his other off-duty guards.

Scott walked the few yards to the French post where he performed the identical procedures and received identical results. Nobody had seen Scott's man cross this border in either direction.

When he got back, Scott decided, he would get Jamieson to make the necessary motions to have similar inquiries made at all other road entry points from Italy, Germany and Austria.

He drove back to the airport, returned the car and began similar inquiries with Customs and Immigration. Scott was lucky in his timing, reaching the airport just half an hour before a change of shift, and the customs supervising officer made the officers' lounge available for his inquiries. Scott had no expectation of learning anything valuable, as any European passport holder would be passed through immigration with minimum fuss. He talked to the group of men and women who would go on duty in a few minutes, and after describing as well as he could, the man he was hunting, a silence had fallen on the room.

"He appears to be very attractive to women," said Scott, rather apologetically. But he had to try because nothing else seemed to be working.

"Ah! Yes! I saw this man!" It was a customs officer who suddenly clicked his fingers and spoke up. Scott smiled at him.

"How so?" he asked.

"A man like you described walked through about the day you mentioned," said the officer. "I cannot be certain, but I think it was one of those days, in the early afternoon. I remember him, because he had two young women walking with him. The two girls, they were extremely pretty, so I saw them first, and thought how lucky the man was." He grinned, and a murmur of amusement ran around the room.

"Hey, Jean-Paul," called one of the other men. "Are you sure it was the girls you noticed and not the guy?"

His grin was unembarrassed. "Definitely the girls! And they were obviously competing for him, so I think he had just met them."

"When were you on duty that day?" asked Scott through the laughter which rang round the room.

"Between three and ten that evening, though I was not always in the customs area. Ah! I have just remembered! I saw them in the general lounge area, not going through customs."

"What flights arrived from outside of Switzerland that evening?"

A small stir shuffled round the room as everybody chuckled. A small, dark-haired young woman chose to enlighten him, keeping her smile to a minimum. "Sir, this a major European hub. Flights arrive from all over the world every few minutes!"

Scott felt rather silly and wrapped up the proceedings quickly. "Thank you all so very much, ladies and gentlemen," he said with feeling. "You have helped me enormously."

He picked up his bag and left the lounge. The hunt was still dreadfully wide in scope, but at least they were further along than they had been the day before. Al-Yaffi had flown into Geneva, so he lived a fair distance away. But it meant that they could tighten the search and find out who had flown on those dates. It might be a total of several thousand people, this being Switzerland in tourist season, but the number was at least finite.

He boarded a British Airways flight to London in the evening. When he got home a little before midnight, he realized that he'd had an icy feeling of something dreadful about to happen ever since leaving Osnabruck. Despite the progress made these last couple of days, the horrors stayed with him. They were unaffected by a short call to Janette and untouched by the stiff belt of good scotch he took. He unpacked his small bag and immediately repacked it so that he would be able to travel at a moment's notice again.

Mustapha al-Yaffi didn't exist, Scott was certain of that. The Palestinian identity had been created to divert attention from Dieter Konig. Scott tried to recreate the moment of humour he had felt when he realized that Dieter Konig probably looked something like Nick. It didn't work.

"Christ," he muttered aloud, "I wish I could tell Nick about this. He'd wet his pants!" He realized that the surface similarity was what had made the picture of Dieter Konig stand out from the rest. "Nick, you'll never know how you helped me track down the bastard," he said to his reflection in the bathroom. He tried to laugh, but felt only a streak of anxiety. The worry was untouched by the hot shower, and despite his exhaustion, kept him awake till after two in the morning. He had no idea why.

Chapter 6 - Electronic Hunting

Thursday morning, and Scott was early into the office. At five, he had realized he would get no more sleep. He got up and took a long, long shower to try and clear the fuzz from his brain. He still had the horrors. He picked up a Jamieson-style breakfast of coffee and doughnuts on the way into the city, taking a small pleasure from the relatively empty streets at that hour. He put his plastic access card into the slot of the restricted door at ten minutes after six.

That early hour was not totally unfamiliar to him. He had met it from both sides, coming in early or working through the night. After ten years of active service with the RAF and four years as a Mongoose, weird hours were nothing new. He was not alone in the office. The night shift of signals staff were still there, and would be until Janette came in from her own apartment in Edgbaston at eight-thirty. The two young girls seemed fresh and bright, despite their overnight session. What this job did for their social life was anybody's guess, thought Scott. He sat at his desk and wrote up his notes for Jamieson.

At seven, the security door chimed and opened and another of the decoding team came in carrying a fresh box of doughnuts. Scott assumed Jamieson had them delivered at the front desk of the outside office, and whoever saw them brought them in. He was tempted to steal one but he felt that such an act would constitute dangerous and life-threatening behaviour, and he had

111

already eaten the two he had bought earlier. Instead, he put a short note on Marjorie's desk that he needed to see the Boss and went back to complete his report.

* * *

"Run me through it then, Scott." Jamieson looked tense and drawn. He had been summoned down to the prime minister's offices at Number Ten Downing Street, and the meeting could not have been easy on him. A traitor had been discovered in the Mongoose organization and a high-profile politician had been murdered in Toronto, despite the presence of one of the supposedly crack Mongoose agents. Unpopular as Richardson had been, his murder was a blow to British security.

And worst of all, thought Scott, *Mongoose intelligence on al-Yaffi had been exposed as a deliberate construction of falsehoods.* The department had been made to look silly. Rather, the Prime Minister had been made to look silly. The value of the British system of intelligence organization was proven again, Scott decided. Practically nobody had heard of the Mongoose Section and few people knew who Jamieson was. If necessary, the whole section could be wrapped up and dismembered without fuss. The CIA, FBI, KGB or BOSS could not have ridden such a wave with such ease. Jamieson had survived dismemberment but he was hurting and it showed.

"I believe it's Dieter Konig, sir," Scott said firmly.

"Why?"

"The kid was obviously a rabid Nazi believer. His library of German history was heavily read, and his comments scrawled all over any comments critical of *Der Fuehrer* show a keen support of the Nazis. Lots of swastikas drawn with loving care in the flyleaves of the books. He had thoroughly read his copy of *Mein Kampf.* The whole thing is totally beyond the standard interests of a normal twelve- or thirteen-year-old kid."

"That's it?"

"No. He'd been a quiet, withdrawn kid up till that age, then suddenly he becomes a bully at school. Classic pattern. I'd say he'd been got at by that time, by some form of Neo-Nazi recruiter."

"And this is enough to confirm your case?"

"No, it's not. The rest is pure hunch. Very strong hunch. I'm certain of it but I can't give you any more than I have."

Jamieson leaned on his elbows, studying his clenched hands. His strong face was immobile.

"What about the man in Geneva?" he asked.

"Definitely a meet with Perkins," said Scott. "I think he flew into Geneva on the afternoon of the twelfth the day after Perkins got there. He met with Perkins at the Golden Hind restaurant in Geneva at about seven-thirty. He's in his mid-thirties, in fact my age less a couple of months, if it really is Dieter Konig. He's tall, about six-one, dark, but definitely European, slim, good looking, seems to have a lot of money. Appears to have a hell of a way with women."

"Can we locate him?"

"I want to put Janette on to it. Depending how many identities he used for his travels, we might be able to identify somebody who flew in and out of Geneva on the same day and then flew to Karachi and back."

Jamieson fell back into his pose of deep thought, leaning backwards in his chair. His interlinked fingers rested against his mouth as he studied the desk top. He stayed like that for over a minute before sitting up again.

"We've established some better links with other agencies as a result of this almighty balls-up of the last few weeks," Jamieson said, breaking the silence. "It wasn't just us who got screwed over al-Yaffi. The Americans are hopping mad, the French are embarrassed as hell, the Germans are being politely smug, and Mossad has realized that the information they were supposed to give me got diverted. Probably by Perkins."

"Has Mongoose Two got back with anything more on Perkins?"

Jamieson shook his head. "Not yet. Allan's with Mossad in Tel Aviv right now. Nonetheless, because of all this sudden wave of embarrassed cooperation, we got some sniffs in the wind of an event in Singapore. An Australian industrialist is going there in a few days to discuss a joint venture in a high-technology plant. This chap, Benny Moskowitch was originally English. He migrated there about ten years ago and made a fortune."

"Moskowitch? British?"

"Aha. His parents fled Poland in the mid-thirties, when the kid was six. He grew up in Cheetham Hill, a strongly Jewish part of Manchester. He was active in Jewish affairs and a popular man. Made millions in textiles, then electronics."

"Then did the same in Oz?"

"You've got it. He lives in Brisbane, which is a bit unusual because most of the financial heavies live in either Sydney or Melbourne. Maybe he likes the warm climate. Anyway, Moskowitch is going to Singapore in a couple of days to arrange a new electronics plant. Mossad sent us a note saying they've picked up rumours of a possible hit. Go and look after him."

Ah, those gentle words again, thought Scott. The last time Jamieson had said that to him, a man had died in a particularly painful manner. The doubts must have shown in his face.

"Scott?"

"Yes, sir?"

"Every one of my people has a few events they'd rather forget," Jamieson said gently. "So have I. You and Mongoose Two are the best I've ever had. Mongoose One told me he thought that even at his best, he was less than you are now, and you have some development ahead of you."

"Thank you!" Scott was so astonished he sat in his seat staring at the Air Marshal. Those were the first words of praise

Scott had ever received from him beyond a snappy "Well done!" on a couple of occasions.

"You still sitting there, McIntyre?"

"Er.. no sir, I just left!" Scott rose quickly, almost gave him a full, long-way-up, short-way-down RAF salute, remembered where he was then moved to the door. He was just closing it behind himself when Jamieson called out.

"Scott?"

Scott leaned his head back into the office. Jamieson was still sitting, leaning on his elbows and staring at his hands, but he looked up as Scott came in.

"Good luck, son," he said.

"Thank you, sir," replied Scott uncertainly. That was a first also. The meeting with the PM must have shaken the old man to his boots, he decided. This time, he closed the door fully and went to see Janette.

There was nobody in the decoding room when he got in, apart from the lady herself scowling ferociously at the computer screen. He went up behind her, put his arms round her and kissed the side of her neck. Her hands left the keyboard and covered his.

"Good morning!" she said, the smile audible in her voice. He nuzzled her left ear and she squealed softly.

"Sexual harassment in the office!" she said. It didn't sound complaining.

"Good!" agreed Scott, kissed her again and let her go. He pulled a chair from a vacant desk to a location next to her and copied Allan's position of a few days ago. He reversed the chair and sat astride it, leaning against the back.

"Busy?" he asked.

"Just for a while. Got one more signal from Jerusalem to decode. Need something?"

He grinned with an evil leer.

"Apart from that!" she smiled. "Though if you're free tonight we could discuss that, too."

"Not sure, yet," he said, returning the smile. "Jamieson has me flying off to Singapore, I hope not till tomorrow. I'll know when Marjorie gives me the details. If it's tomorrow, let's have dinner at my place tonight?"

He received a beautiful smile in return as agreement.

"Let me finish this last signal," she said, turning back to the computer screen.

He was happy to spend ten minutes watching her. She had perfect skin and a clear complexion. Her hazel-green eyes could sparkle with intelligence, flame with anger, or be soft and languid in candle light. Her features still showed traces of the child she had been, but in her late twenties, were firming into the beautiful woman she was becoming. She was a delight.

You're very lucky, McIntyre, he said to himself. *Don't screw it up.*

Her smile was so glowing he almost thought he had spoken aloud. "Finished!" she said. "They're printing out at Marjorie's desk now. So, what do you need?"

All business now. They were both professionals.

"Same sort of thing you did the other day when we found Perkins' travel agenda," said Scott. "But a bit more complex."

"Okay, give me the details."

He thought in silence for a few seconds while she went to the safe and extracted the black notebook that held the computer codes. "Run a search of all flights arriving in Geneva on the twelfth of August," he said, finally. "Look for a male flying in and leaving again on the same day."

"That'll be a long list, Scott."

"I know. But the second phase should shorten it. Can you retain the list for a subsequent comparison run?"

"Oh yes! No problem. But this will take time. It's a complex extraction with a lot of source data to search."

"No worries. Just get it going."

Again he had the pleasure of watching her work. She concentrated, referring to the notebook before each entry of a code into the system, and sometimes half a minute or longer elapsed before the computer responded to her probes.

"As I said," she murmured at one point, about ten minutes into the exercise, more to herself than to Scott. "We get lower priority than the booking transactions and it's pretty busy right now." Her voice tailed off as the frequency of response increased. Scott had no real idea what she was doing but assumed she was logging into the network of airline computers and entering her authority codes.

Five minutes passed in silence.

"Good!" she said, suddenly. "That's got us hooked into the main network." She looked sideways at him. "Into and out of Geneva on the twelfth, you said?"

"Yes."

"Okay." Silence descended for another few minutes, while only the background noise of her keyboard tapping accompanied his study of her profile, soft hair and graceful hands.

Suddenly she sat back. "This will take some time," she said, giving him the full force of her smile again. Even as an Extra Special Super Extraordinary Secret Intelligence Agent at the grand old age of thirty-four, thought Scott, that smile did amazing things to his insides.

"Let's go and get a cup of tea, then," he suggested.

"Brilliant thinking, McIntyre," she said and stood up.

The department had a small lounge in one corner of the area. They walked into the pleasantly-decorated little room, the only spot in the whole place which was not decorated in basic institutional style. No windows looked out onto Birmingham's streets. The only way in or out of the entire office was through the door between the Mongoose Section and the facade of the British Council of International Economic Analysis. The lounge contained three soft, red, leather armchairs, a small modern table with six chairs around it, a coffee pot that brewed real coffee and a kettle for the tea drinkers.

They stood close together while brewing the kettle for the mint herbal tea that they both liked so much. There was no undue show of affection, however. Even though the whole office knew about them, good manners were still required. So they simply stood while Scott let the scent of her hair mingle with the mint from the tea packets.

Tea made, they sat in the leather armchairs.

"Singapore?" she said, breathing in the steam of her cup.

"Possible event with an Aussie businessman. Actually he's originally from your part of the world."

"Manchester?"

"Cheetham Hill. Emigrated down under about ten years ago. Stinking rich. Classic poor Polish immigrant family running from Adolf before the war, worked like hell and made it big on sheer guts and persistence."

"An al-Yaffi target, it seems," she said with a nod.

"Ah! Let me update you on al-Yaffi!"

She gave him an inquiring look. "You're convinced it's Dieter Konig?"

He hadn't seen her since getting back from Germany, and although he had called her on the telephone, such topics were not for unsecured lines.

"I am, though I've nothing concrete to stand on," he replied. "Just the gut feeling."

"Have I ever told you, Scott, what a lovely man you are?"

Scott laughed at the suddenness of the change of topic. "No, never, Miss Colley. And I feel very deprived as a result!"

Her tiny smile was astonishingly sensual. "Then let us hope you don't leave till tomorrow and I can un-deprive you."

"Crossed fingers."

"And toes," she nodded.

He looked at her intently. He was extremely lucky, he decided for the ten thousandth time.

"Maybe we'd better go and check the computer?" she said, her breathing a little ragged.

"Either that or a cold shower!" he agreed.

With a laugh, she led him back to her hi-tech domain.

They were a little early returning but that was probably good for their nerves. Sitting with her in the lounge was damaging Scott's resistance and threatening the policy of no overt shows of affection. Five minutes longer, and Scott felt they might have added an unexpected chapter in the annals of Mongoose Section.

A couple of minutes after resuming their seats before the screen, the screen beeped at them.

"Good," she said. "That's the list of male day-trippers to Geneva on international flights. There were...." She leaned forward to study the screen, "eighteen hundred and sixty-three of them."

"Eighteen hundred...? Ye gods!"

"It is high season still."

"Yes, I know, but over eighteen hundred! Oh well, so be it! Let's move on to phase two."

"Which is?" She moved her hands to the keyboard in preparation.

"Identify all male travellers arriving into Karachi and leaving again between the twelfth and thirteenth."

Her light brown hair floated around face for a second or two as she nodded vigorously. "And then see if anyone from the first list is also on the second?" she asked.

"Presactly! What a bright young decoder analyst you are, Miss Colley! You'll go far, I'm certain."

She blew him a small raspberry from a lipsticked mouth and concentrated on the screen.

119

"Go back to your desk," she said, her voice already fading as her concentration focused on the task. "I'll bring it in when it's done."

"I'm being thrown out!" wailed Scott in mock grief.

"Absolutely!"

He left, unwilling to distract her further. But forty minutes later, his excitement was cooled drastically.

"No match!" she said, swinging the door open into his office and walking up to him with her free-swinging stride that he found so attractive.

"Oh shit!"

"Very likely," she agreed. "But still no match."

Scott sat back in his chair. He had been so certain he would hook Konig this way, even though it was an absolute certainty that Konig had travelled under another name. Scott had to rethink his logic.

"Honey, I'm going back to the lounge," he said. "I need to sit and contemplate the mysteries of life, and this damn chair is giving me piles. And your perfume is distracting, too!"

"Okay. I'll save these data files for further use."

"Sure," he said, more confidently than he felt. He stood up and they walked back to the door of her office where Scott opened the door for her and let her in, then he walked on to the lounge. He took the same leather armchair he had occupied before and began to review the whole thing.

Perkins had arrived in Geneva on Sunday, the eleventh of August, that was a known fact. Konig, assuming that it was Konig he had met for dinner at the Golden Hind, had flown in the next day, arriving in the afternoon. Assuming, that is, that the customs officer at Geneva airport had correctly identified Konig and not merely seen some other handsome young stud on vacation.

Two pretty loose assumptions, he said to himself. But he had no alternative but to follow through with this.

Perkins flew back to Karachi on the thirteenth, the Tuesday. Now, did Konig go home first then decide to follow Perkins to Karachi and kill him, or did he make the decision immediately? Probably the latter, decided Scott.

So amend my initial logic right away, he thought. No wonder Janette's search had resulted in no match. He had asked her to identify any male flying into Geneva, then returning to his original point of departure. More likely, Konig flew into Geneva on the twelfth and then flew to Karachi, probably on the thirteenth, on a different flight from Perkins. He went to Perkins' house, shot him and flew back on the fourteenth, either to Geneva or directly home.

Scott was about to get up and take the new logic to Janette when...

"... have just remembered! I saw them in the general lounge area, not going through customs."

Jean-Pierre, the customs officer! Maybe Konig had not arrived by an international flight after all! Perhaps he had come in via Zurich or Berne, then taken a domestic puddle-jumper into Geneva. That would certainly muddy the waters of any search such as Scott was conducting.

This time, he did stand up and returned to see his lady of the keyboards.

"Revise the whole thing?" she said with a grin.

"Yup! Sorry! I didn't think it out clearly enough the first time."

"No matter," she said gently. "We just start again."

"Janette, you're a darling!"

"Yes, I know! And I have news for you!"

"Good or bad?"

"Depends on your values. You don't leave for Singapore until Sunday morning."

Scott pretended to consider it. "Well, I suppose..."

"Yes?"

"Taking every factor into consideration..."

"Ah?"

"With all things being equal..."

"McIntyre, I'm going to beat your brains out!"

"I would say that it was good news."

"I'm relieved to hear that," she said with a grave look. "Otherwise you have undergone sudden and enforced surgery."

"In that case, I'm relieved, also."

"Good. Let's do some work. We need the evening off. And then we have nearly the whole glorious weekend!"

"Agreed. Mind on the job, woman! Try this approach..."

She turned to the keyboard.

"First," he said, "extract all males flying into Geneva on the twelfth as you did before. But this time, do it for both domestic and international flights and make it for say, after midday and before five o'clock. That'll be one hell of a list, I know. Then find all males flying into Karachi on the thirteenth and out again on either the thirteenth or the fourteenth. That'll also be a hell of a long list. Then analyse for a match. That should be a short list."

She nodded, fingers already flying on the keyboard.

"When you print out the final list, will you show both destination and arrival airports of all trips?"

"Natch!" she said, not looking away from the screen. After a couple of minutes, she paused and looked up at him.

"Scott, go and do some work," she said, a tiny vein of irritation showing. "This will take a long time and you're distracting me."

"My aftershave lotion?"

"Something like that. Now run away and play, there's a good little boy!"

Stifling a laugh, he left her to it.

She was right. Three hours passed before she came into his office with a computer printout. He raised an eyebrow at her.

"Oh yes!" she replied to his silent question. "Longer list than I might have imagined."

She put the printout on his desk and came round to his side, leaning her left hip lightly on his right shoulder.

"Twenty-seven of them," she said.

"The world is full of jet-setters, it seems."

"You're certainly not the only one, Scott!"

"Hmm." He studied the list. There seemed to be more data on the two sheets of sprocket-punched, eye-lined computer paper than he had asked for. "What have you given me here?"

She leaned over the paper and pointed out the individual details with the eraser end of her yellow pencil. "That's the passenger name, that's the departure airport in the three letter international code. I've brought in the code book for you. GVA is Geneva, KHI is Karachi. The rest you'll have to look up."

"Good thinking, young lady! What else?"

She pointed again. "That's the airport they arrived at after leaving Karachi."

"Okay. What are these numbers?"

"Date and time of arrival and departure. That's the airline. And the last one is courtesy of my brilliance. I extracted the passenger's contact telephone number."

He looked up at her and put his arm round her waist. Just for a second, she put her hand on his shoulder and he leaned his head against her hip.

"Janette, what would I do without you?"

"I'm really not sure I want to answer that," she said with a light laugh and extracted herself from his arm.

"See you tonight!" she waved and left. The room seemed horribly dull and lifeless without her.

Twenty-seven names! *Do I really have the infamous Mustapha al-Yaffi or Dieter Konig on the two sheets of characterless computer stationery on my desk?* he asked himself. If he did, how would he know? He began to study what he had. He opened the airline code book left for him by Janette to check the airport codes.

His first read through the list left his head swimming. People seemed to flying all over the world into and out of Karachi. This was getting to be more complex than ever, he thought. He might have to track down the complete itineraries of every one of these people.

Six had arrived from Paris then gone onto Karachi, all on the fourteenth. Two had arrived on the same Swissair flight from London, gone on the same Lufthansa flight to Frankfurt and then Emirates to Karachi and left together to go onto Bangkok. He stopped examining the list. He would get nowhere that way. Janette's idea of extracting the contact telephone numbers might turn out to be the brainstorm that broke the camel's back. Or something.

He'd have to give this list to Jamieson, he decided. It was probably the best chance the Mongoose Section had ever had of identifying their man. Even then, the chances of that being so were pretty small. Perhaps the customs man in Geneva had simply seen a handsome young man on vacation who had struck lucky with two girls at the airport. Even if it was Konig, maybe he had driven down or up to Geneva from somewhere else, gone to the airport for another reason and therefore wouldn't be on any of these lists.

Scott knew he was missing something, some other connection, some other test to isolate his quarry. It was simple, but he couldn't pin it down.

Perhaps, what if, maybe, on the other hand, how about...

Round and round and round and round...

He wrote a short note to Jamieson asking for the domestic police in each of the indicated countries to start a check on every one of the men on the list, stapled it to the computer printout and took it to Marjorie.

124

"This should exercise his little grey cells," he said. She gave him a small smile, looked at the sheet and raised her eyebrows.

"Very likely," she said.

We British are not famed for excessive demonstrations of excitement, thought Scott with amusement.

"Here's your packet," Marjorie said and passed him a bundle of envelopes. He had more instructions, travel documents, contact names and numbers. He took them back to his desk to read until Janette was able to leave at five.

She left her car in the basement and went home with him. They spent a wonderful evening of absolute normality. They went shopping at the supermarket in Acock's Green, came home, changed into casual clothes and cooked dinner. These evenings were all too rare, decided Scott. The idea of experiencing them a lot more was gaining in his mind.

By nine, they were lounging in the blue Queen Anne sofa that had come to Scott from his parents' home in Reading after the bombing in Barcelona. His compact disk player was softly emoting the wondrous songs of the Mamas and the Papas from the sixties. Mama Cass was in great voice and Janette was lying back across his chest, his arm round her waist. He felt good.

The apartment was warm and homely. Scott had rented it for the whole time he had been living in Birmingham and it was the first sense of permanent home since leaving school in Reading, seventeen years ago. His books were in shelves instead of boxes, his records were in racks, the stereo system had been assembled without change for four years and some pictures hung on the walls.

As a student at Nottingham he had lived in a series of scruffy pads. In the RAF, home was merely a series of rooms in the Officers' Mess of whatever station to which he had been posted. The gypsy life had been fun, but tonight, with a feeling of calm well-being, and his best girl in his arms, he was in contemplative mood.

"Janette?"

"Yes, love?"

"Do you realize I'll be thirty-five next month?"

"I do. I've already ordered the solid gold elephant with diamond-covered ears for your birthday present."

"Gold? How very tacky! All the best elephants these days are platinum."

"Yes dear, but my budget was a shade limited this year."

"Oh, I see." He nuzzled her neck and she squealed gently. "Has it really been three years since we first went out?"

"Two years and nine months," she replied. "Presactly."

"You know, that's the longest relationship I've ever had with anyone."

She turned her head and looked up at him. "Getting you worried, Scott?"

"Quite the opposite. I feel very happy about it."

She seemed to relax a little and leaned back against his chest. "Good. Me too." He could hear the smile in her voice.

"Do you think you could consider a formal agreement to extend it a while longer?"

"How much longer?" She chuckled, a pretty, feminine laugh.

"Say about forty or fifty years?"

He felt breathless waiting for her answer through the melodious harmonies of 'California Dreaming.' She turned her head again and looked directly at him.

"I'd like that very much," she whispered.

"I think we just got engaged!" he said, touching her cheek.

"I think we did!"

It was a while before any more meaningful conversation took place. Breakfast, in fact.

Chapter 7 – Singapore

Singapore Airlines, his favourite way to travel. Scott had his regular window seat in business class. He tried to settle his jangling nerves by accepting a king-size Manhattan cocktail from the tiny, exquisite Chinese flight attendant soon after take-off from Heathrow, just before noon. The wonderful, private cocoon of modern business class left him isolated from the rest of the passengers and he blessed the fact, knowing he had a lot of thinking to do.

He leaned back and idly watched Europe pass below, just as he had done on the recent trip from Hanover to Geneva. He still had a ragged sense of having missed something in his analysis of the airline passenger lists which Janette had generated.

That was not the only sense of inadequacy he carried with him. The big questions jumped around in his mind. Had he picked on Dieter Konig as being al-Yaffi just because he had no other indications? Clutching at straws? How long could he last with Mongoose Section if he performed as tackily as he had in the last two events? Despite Jamieson's astonishing farewell statements to him, he was all too aware that he had screwed up in Chicago and Toronto. It was not a good feeling.

Night fell as they headed east over northern Europe before curving south, crossing southern Russia and over the troubled Afghan provinces. The flight attendant was called Kim Ling Soo she said, when she brought dinner to him and served it with a small bottle of Australian Cabernet Sauvignon. She had the soft, immaculately-spoken English which well-educated Chinese so often possessed. Scott had no trouble finishing the excellent meal of beef and vegetables, washed down with the superb sample of the vineyards of the Hunter Valley. Ling Soo took the tray away with a glowing smile and left the rest of the bottle with him. He sipped at his glass and tried to think about realities.

Was Dieter Konig really al-Yaffi? he pondered. *Whose was the face I had seen in Toronto? Why had Konig's photo disturbed me from the start? What was bugging me about the description of the man in Geneva? Was I just jealous about someone who so clearly did what I had never been able to do, attract women with a wave of his hand?*

The cabin lights faded. Scott didn't bother unwrapping the headphones or checking out the movies on the tiny screen built into his seat. He finished the wine and waved at Ling Soo for another Manhattan. This was way above his normal ration for booze and he normally did not drink alcohol on long airline flights because it dehydrated him so badly. But tonight, he needed something to still the nerves.

"...always wanted to be rich enough to have a Mercedes...."

What?

The voice had echoed through his head like a warm wind appearing from nowhere. Dieter Konig's mother had said that to him, surely? But somehow, that wasn't the voice he had heard. Why did it come to his head just then? Scott's mind was becoming fuzzy under the effect of the alcohol.

Konig as a boy had been tall and slender, a sad faced urchin with violence implanted in his mind by some neo-Nazi recruiter. The thin, sad face had filled out into a lean, muscular, smiling killer.... killer.... lady-killer.... Nick.... Now there was a *real* lady-killer....

"...ever since I was a kid, I've promised myself that one day I'd be rich enough to have a Mercedes...." Hah! Some coincidence. That was Nick at dinner with the leggy Cheryl

stroking his hair. He'd had an expression of pain when his dead parents were mentioned. Pain? Somehow, as Scott recalled it, there was a lot of tension in his face, too.

Damn! Scott stirred restlessly in his seat. *I've been through this already. Nick? He's my best friend. Why is my heart slamming into my ribs like a frightened animal in a cage? Why is my breathing suddenly irregular, as if I was having an asthma attack?*

Ling Soo placed the huge cocktail on the tray of the seat next to him. He grabbed it and took a heavy gulp. Already he was feeling the effects of too much alcohol, too quickly. Soon he'd be asking her to bring him long drinks of iced water.

Scott lost his focus. Nick's face swam in front of him, grinning cheerfully.

"...always wanted a Mercedes...."

"...both parents killed in a road accident when I was a kid...."

Scott saw a pretty fair-haired young waitress with enchanted eyes as she remembered the man of her dreams. Scott had already let his mind acknowledge the similarity between Nick and her description of the man talking to Perkins. But he'd firmly rejected the idea of anything more significant. It was insane. But now he remembered the love of Mercedes cars shared by Dieter Konig and Nick.

How can I be thinking this way? Oh God! I hate this.

Scott fell asleep somewhere over Saudi Arabia...

..and woke up over India, with gummy eyes, dry throat, and aching limbs from sitting sideways and resting his head against the window. All the seat lights were out, leaving the cabin in almost total darkness. The Boeing droned through the night, occasionally twitching like a restless dog as it hit small disturbances in the atmosphere. He stood up, stretched and walked to the rear of the business class compartment. Ling Soo was sitting in the seat nearest to the kitchen area, talking quietly to one of the pilots. The pilot was Chinese also and looked like a teenager with unlined cheeks and dark eyes in a boy's face. Both of them smiled at Scott as he stood over them.

"Can I have a very long drink of iced water?"

"Of course!" Ling Soo jumped up and moved into the kitchen area and began breaking out ice from the fridge.

"Dehydrated?" The pilot had an understanding smile on his face. Scott nodded, his mind chasing evil tracks through his head. Ling Soo handed him a large glass filled with iced water, and Scott returned to his seat and his dark thoughts.

Nick. My best friend. Seventeen years of friendship. What nonsense was this, just because he had a similar appearance perhaps, to the international killer Dieter Konig? Just because he had bought a Mercedes and had a gift with women? Ridiculous.

Nick had been away in Europe when I was in Chicago. In Milan, shooting the German diplomat? Don't be stupid, Scott. He had been away in Berlin, he said, when I was in Toronto. He was away this week, Kirstie had said, when I called his office on Friday afternoon. Where? I had asked. Naples, she said. When did he leave? Four days ago. When was he due back? Uncertain, but probably the week after next, she said. Benny Moskowitch was thought to be the target of a hit in that time.

The image came to his mind of a doctor with a weird sense of humour, holding the pale hand of the corpse of Arnold Richardson in the morgue in Toronto. Clever pharmacology, the doctor had said of the poison which had been injected into Richardson's hand and took long enough to work its way to his heart to give the killer time to get out. Then bingo! One dead politician, he had said.

Nick. A pharmacist with a small, rich, drug company in Switzerland. A very bright pharmacist, apparently. With resources immediately to hand.

Alright, Scott, he said to himself, looking out into the clear night. *This is just business. You have to think about it because the possibility has suggested itself. Yeah, right. Think that your best friend is the most sought-after killer in the world. Think that your best friend might have murdered your parents and sister. Think that your best friend watched you trying to protect a politician in Toronto, and laughed at you while he killed the man you were guarding.*

Good God! That would mean he was fully aware of my identity while we wined and dined in close friendship last Saturday night. This is horrible!

In the darkened cabin, his thoughts flew around in his head like agitated sparrows watching a hawk patrol nearby. Six or seven people were asleep, while two oases of light showed that others were like himself, reading or thinking. Scott doubted that their thoughts were as dark as his.

"...last week I was able to clear up an organizational problem too. Bloke in one of our overseas offices was going to cause me real problems, and I managed to get him removed before he did."

Nick at dinner in Henley-in-Arden telling them about his triumph in Europe. Or was the organizational problem the leakage of data from Jenkins in Karachi? By 'getting him removed,' did Nick mean he had killed him? *Oh God!* groaned Scott. *This is getting unreal.*

What really did he know of Nick? They had met in their freshman year at Nottingham during a lengthy drinking session at the famous pub carved into the rock of the equally famous castle. "A Trip to Jerusalem" was the finest pub in town, the loudest, the most fun, the place to meet the girls. Nick had stumbled over Scott's knees and spilled his beer while leading

131

some amazingly curved redhead to the bar. He had immediately brought Scott another beer back from the bar, sat down at his table with the redhead on his knee and introduced himself. He became Scott's closest friend.

He was an orphan with no relatives he said. So Scott met no family. But neither did he meet any friends of Nick's earlier years from school, either. After six years at a large school in Newcastle-on-Tyne, Nick should have had some friends who visited. He stayed in Nottingham during the vacations because he had nowhere else to go, he said. The women of Nottingham were the best looking in England, he told Scott with a leer, so it was no hardship. And that was certainly the city's reputation, well supported by their own empirical research.

Occasionally, Scott invited him home to Reading to stay with the family, and Nick always accepted, always enjoyed the time with them, as they seemed to enjoy him. He got on well with Scott's father but had a special fascination with his mother. He spent hours talking to her and taking photographs of her alone, as well as with the rest of the family. Scott teased him about being sweet on his mum, and Nick laughed it off.

"She has oomph and pizzazz!" he grinned, and Scott had to agree. His mother was something special.

In the long summer vacation of their second year, Nick went to Europe. He bought a motorbike and roared off down the motorway into the summer night to catch the morning ferry from Dover. Scott got a postcard from Munich a month later.

Nick was never short of money but he never worked at the traditional student jobs in the vacations. He never delivered Christmas mail, never tended bar at a pub or took casual labour at the cigarette factory. Scott didn't think about it then. He was only a kid himself, with his own worries of passing exams, pursuing girls and planning his wondrous future flying Jaguars, Tornadoes or Harriers with the RAF.

But now he did think about it. And it didn't compute.

Dawn slipped cunningly into view, sneaking behind some low clouds until it could pounce on the unaware watcher. Interior lights flickered into being and sleepy travellers stirred in seats around the cabin, making the first forays into the washroom. Ling Soo, looking as if she had just dressed in a new gown after stepping out of the shower following a solid night's sleep, appeared with a tray of fresh fruits, coffee and scrambled eggs, and slipped it onto Scott's table with a smile which competed with the sun, now lighting up the walls.

He had got nowhere with his thinking except round and round in circles, horrified at the possibilities he was raising and beginning to wish he had taken the job in Peterborough making tractor engines. He washed and shaved in the bathroom, changed his shirt and returned to his seat, feeling a little more human.

The Boeing glided down the coast of Thailand and Malaysia, and Scott detected the minute change of pitch as the four Rolls Royce engines reduced power for the descent path. With a professional ear and sense of balance, he followed the changes of engine noise, the variations in angles of descent and the occasional vector changes as the two men in the front cockpit delicately rode the enormous bird down into Changhi Airport in Singapore. Wheels touched the tarmac with a sister's kiss, reverse thrust pushed him into his straps for a few seconds, and he was there.

* * *

Scott had always loved Raffles Hotel. He stayed there the first time as a teenager with his parents and fell in love with the entire British Empire feel of the place. They had rooms over the Writers' Courtyard and they had revelled in sitting on the balcony over the garden and swimming pool while they breakfasted on egg *foo yong* and fresh tropical fruits. Some nights, they dined in the garden while the band, dressed in military uniforms and white solar helmets, played excerpts from Gilbert and Sullivan, or Strauss waltzes. The whole history of Raffles fascinated him, the stories of Hemmingway's visits, the silver tea trolley buried in the garden to hide it from the Japanese in the Second World War, the legend of the tiger shot in the tea room. His father and mother drank Singapore Slings in the Long Bar, occasionally letting him have a sip as a change from the endless cokes of a teenage diet.

He loved it. They went shopping along Orchard Road, explored old Chinatown, ate amazing meals in tiny restaurants, the food selected by pointing, to the delight of the locals who cackled with each other and discussed the evidently English family in Mandarin without any offence being caused. Apart from breakfast and the occasional dinner in the garden, they never ate in the hotel, preferring to explore this extraordinary city and dine out in the manner of its inhabitants. Scott's parents even let him go with them to Bugis Street where the transexuals and transvestites paraded in head-shattering clothing, stretching the imagination to believe that these sensually beautiful woman, many of whom would shame the models in Vogue or Cosmopolitan, were actually men. His father lost dollars to the ten-year-old kid who played tic-tac-toe with the tourists, they bought drinks, ate the cuisine and loved every minute of it, knowing that the New Zealand armed forces men sitting around in relaxed attitudes were the informal guardians of peace and tranquillity in this crazy, wonderful, magic place.

Scott checked in and got his pre-arranged Writers' Courtyard room. He walked up the wooden stairs to the balcony, fatigued from the flight but emotional with memories of previous trips here. Since the first visit with his parents, Leanne a toddler left with nannies in Reading, he had come several more times, mourned the destruction of old Chinatown, but never lost his love for the city or the hotel. He scorned the modern luxury palaces and never stayed at any of them. The Old Man carefully ignored the steep costs of a Raffles room, apparently happy to let his agents be comfortable.

By the time he had unpacked his few belongings and changed into a light safari suit, the only additional item of clothing he had brought with him, noon was rapidly approaching. He was not at all hungry, so he left the room and walked round the wooden balcony, looking down at the sunbathers lying by the pool of the Writers' Courtyard, the palm trees and flowers making the view wildly exotic after England. Down the wide stairway he continued into the main building and out to the front door where the uniformed doorman in his solar helmet called for a taxi. He ignored the rickshaw drivers lining up for tourist traffic. He couldn't take the time.

Seventy miles or so north of the equator, the heat was to be expected, but it was still a shock. It slammed into his body, brought out the sweat in his armpits and down his back and almost drove him indoors again. The cab was not air conditioned, but with the windows open a breeze of sorts blew into him and within a few minutes he had adjusted enough to start enjoying the sights, sounds and smells of the city again. The cab took him past the beautiful white government buildings, to the stone merlion on the river side and over the Connaught Bridge to the water-front commercial stretch.

The bank building lobby was wonderfully cool. He stood still for a few moments, revelling in the cold, dry air which wafted around the cathedral-like expanse of marble pillars. Around the walls, bank-teller cubicles stood with customers talking in low, deferential tones to the people behind the wrought iron grilles. He had not been brought up in any religion, but the scene reminded him of the confessional line-ups in a church. The reverential atmosphere was similar.

Cooled off, he found the elevator banks, waited for a few seconds while a phalanx of people evacuated from the opening door, then entered and pressed the button for the thirty-third floor. The elevator sighed gently and accelerated rapidly, taking only a few seconds to get him there. He walked out, looked left and right then saw the board on the far wall listing the tenants.

Champlain Literary Services was shown as being in room 3306. Scott walked along the silent corridor and located the office, a single blank door with only a number but no name. He walked in.

No receptionist, but a bell sat on an empty desk. Behind the desk there was a sliding window of frosted glass behind which he could see the shadow of a smallish person wearing something red. He pressed the bell, the window slid back and the vague shadow became a petite, solemn-faced Chinese girl, black hair cut short, and red lipstick matching a bright red silk blouse, buttoned high at the neck in Chinese fashion.

"Hello!" she said, the solemnity shattered by the most welcoming, eye-sparkling smile anyone could desire. He couldn't help but smile back.

"Scott McIntyre to see Mister Ong Liang Sien," he said.

"Ah yes, Mister Scott! Mister Ong will be right out!"

She seemed so happy, his spirits rose dramatically. She slid back the window again and almost immediately, the door next to it swung open to reveal a large Chinese man displaying a wide grin.

"Scott! What a delight to see you again!" The accent was pure Oxford University.

"Liang Sien, you drunken old rogue! Great to see you!"

"Of course it is! Why else does anyone come to Singapore?" He seized Scott's hand and ground it dangerously.

"I can't think!" Scott chuckled. "Perhaps merely to listen to your extraordinary modesty and wisdom?"

Ong laughed out loud, and led Scott through the door. "This is Jessica," he said, pointing to the receptionist and Scott rapidly revised his view of the young woman. He had read the file on her a week earlier, but had not connected the pretty, solemn-faced receptionist with Ong's impressively-qualified assistant in Mongoose Section. She was the daughter of a senior public servant whose lifetime friendship with Lee Kwan Yew, a former Prime Minister had given him access to many of the affairs of the island state and provided Jessica with training in politics second to none. She spoke Mandarin, Cantonese, Hokkien and two other Chinese dialects, plus Malay, English, and French. She looked barely into her teens but was a thirty-year-old with degrees from Cambridge and Stanford.

"Good morning again, Jessica," Scott said and they shook hands. Then he followed the retreating frame of his colleague.

Ong Liang Sien's tall, heavy physique was unusual in a Chinese. His grandparents had trekked to Shanghai from the mountains of the northern provinces where such a build was not uncommon, he had once told Scott. The two agents had met a year ago when Ong had come to England on a meeting of Station Heads to discuss new policies and strategies. They had got on famously, checking out restaurants and bars, and Scott had taken him to some of his favourite country pubs in which Ong demonstrated the capacity for beer which had made him famous as an undergraduate at Balliol College fifteen years earlier. Six months later, they had met again on a training program, and the friendship had firmed.

Behind the door by which Scott had just entered was a short corridor with several office doors and small open-plan area with four desks. At each of these a young person was reading a manuscript, and each had a pile of large envelopes, presumably containing more manuscripts in front of them. They were busily making red marks on the pages and not one of them looked up at the two men as they passed. Just as the British International Economic Analysis Council provided a perfect, functioning and valid cover to Mongoose Section in Birmingham, this small literary agency provided a genuine front for the one-man, one-assistant operation of Ong Liang Sien, Mongoose's man in Singapore.

"This way, my little *fahn gwai-loh*," Ong murmured, and led Scott to the end of the corridor past the open area, where the last of the four offices provided a private area. The "foreign devil" comment managed to lift a couple of heads from the study of manuscripts, but only briefly as the Chinese work ethic took over again. Ong opened the office door, let Scott walk in ahead of him and closed the door.

The office was pleasantly cool. Paintings of mountains and forests in traditional Chinese style covered two of the walls and the window looked out onto the docks. Ong's desk was bare of papers, but two telephones, one grey, one green took up a corner of it. The green one had a red button on the side. Ong opened a small refrigerator and extracted two bottles of fruit juice, placed one in front of Scott and opened his own, putting a straw in it. His humorous face had turned serious.

"Jamieson believes al-Yaffi will strike the Australian here?" he said, lifting his face from a study of the juice.

"That's the rumour." Scott took a long gulp of cold grapefruit juice and washed some of the travel dust from his throat.

"Not good, my friend," Ong said. "That would do a great deal of harm to us all."

"Not least to Benny Moskowitch."

"That is true. But all you occidentals look the same to us!"

Scott laughed at the other man's dead-pan expression. Then he brought the conversation back on track.

"Let me give you an update on the inestimable Mustapha al-Yaffi."

Ong sucked noisily on his drink, threw the straw in the waste paper bin by his desk and placed the empty bottle on the bookcase together with four others, remnants of his morning's thirst. "I read the summary that came in by coded signal," he said. "He's a German?"

"I think so. Looks increasingly like a neo-Nazi operative, maybe with links to the PLO and other Moslem terrorist groups, but that could just be for money."

"Any leads to the man?"

"Don't know. I've got some ideas but they're very tenuous. Nothing I'd bet the house on. I need to call Birmingham later on. Is that line secure?"

Ong nodded and looked at his watch. "With summer time, England is six hours behind us. So it's not quite seven in the morning there. Call in an hour or so."

"Right. What are the plans for Moskowitch's visit?"

Ong opened a drawer in his desk, extracted a manila folder and opened it. "This isn't going to be easy. Our security forces will not give you the same sort of support as you got in Canada and the States. They're pretty jealous of their own turf."

"So no gun?" Scott had expected that.

The Chinese agent nodded. "No gun. And don't chance it, they'll put you away for a squillion years if they find you with one."

"What's a squillion?"

Ong looked seriously at Scott. "It's a one followed by a lot of zeroes and commas and stuff," he said without expression.

"Not nice."

"No," Ong agreed. "However, they will let you join them to meet him at Changhi Airport tomorrow afternoon, and you can ride into the city with him. He's in the Westin Plaza, and the meetings with the various people he's seeing will be either in a conference room there, or at a government office nearby."

"And can I sit in those meetings?"

"No problem."

"Fine. Do you carry a gun?"

Ong nodded. "Took a year of negotiations with the local chaps about five years ago. Went right up to the Prime Minister and he finally agreed."

"Good," Scott said. "At least one of us is properly dressed. Has there been an alert for al-Yaffi at entrance points to the Island?"

"Of course, but without any success. We've had a watch for anyone of that description...."

"Which description? The Palestinian version or the European?"

"That's the problem," the Chinese agent said, looking uncomfortable. "We got the revised description of the man only yesterday and he's probably been in the country for at least a week. So we've been looking carefully for him at the airport and at the Johore Baharu causeway from Malaysia, but you can bet your life we missed him."

"Yes," Scott said firmly. "We've missed him. He's in the country already."

"Indubitably. Scott, what do you know about this man?"

"Nothing certain. But I have some thoughts. It's all vague, can't prove a thing yet. But you can have what I've got."

"Please." Ong settled back in his chair, looked once at his watch. "We'll call Birmingham in an hour."

Scott nodded. "I think he's a German called Dieter Konig. He's about my age, thirty-four. Ran away from home when he was fifteen after showing a lot of pro-Nazi inclinations as a kid. I suspect he was recruited by a mob calling themselves Knights of Aryan Dawn. He's living somewhere in Europe with another identity. It looks like Ken Perkins in Karachi was his man."

"Ken? Good God!" Ong Liang Sien sat up with a jerk. "I had dinner with him in Bangkok last month! But, Holy Christ, Scott, it means he must know you!"

"Not a nice thought, is it?" Scott tried to look casual, but the fact was an unpleasant one. And undeniable.

"Bloody horrible! Any leads to the identity?"

This was the worst part of it all. Scott couldn't tell anyone yet of the ghastly suspicions which were forming in his mind. He shook his head. "Nothing worth making public yet."

Ong looked once more at his watch. "We have some time before calling Birmingham. Let's go and get you some decent food."

Scott stood up. Hunger was at last getting to him. "Good idea," he said. "Somewhere close and quick."

"Of course. My favourite restaurant."

Ong led them out to the elevators, down to the bank lobby and out into the thunderous heat. His favourite restaurant turned out to be a tiny ground-floor location, open to the air, with just a tarpaulin cover as a protection against the regular rainfalls. The owner evidently knew Ong well, for they were received with many bows and rapid chattering in Mandarin and were led to a table in the corner where a large bowl of seafood soup and two glasses of fruit juice were placed on the table before they had sat down. Ong ladled out the soup, which was as delicious as Scott had learned to expect.

"We will be having pork and braised prawns," Ong said. "Alright with you?"

Scott grinned at him. "You know very well it is!"

"Good," he smiled and proceeded to slurp the soup rapidly.

While they were outdoors they kept the conversation innocent of business. Within minutes, a bowl of rice and two plates of steaming delicacies were added to the pile on the table. With these, came the tiny bowl of fresh-chopped, red chilli peppers which Scott was never able to get at any Chinese restaurant in the west. They busied themselves pouring some soy sauce into miniature, patterned bowls and dropping peppers into them to soak. Added to the rice, pork and prawns, the peppers made a piquant, spicy enhancement to the already delicious flavours.

Ong was eating at twice Scott's rate, with that rapid shovelling movement of food with his chopsticks from the bowl placed by his lips which the Englishman had never been able to copy. Scott filled up at a more leisurely speed but got his fair share, regardless. 'Defensive eating' Ong called it, that custom of grabbing what one could from the central plates.

"You are improving your technique, little *gwai-loh*," Ong smiled while spooning more rice into his bowl. "Soon you will reach Level Three of competence."

"Level Three?" Scott was amused.

"Ah yes. Level One is to be able to get food generally into your mouth. Level Two is to be able to pick up those little button mushrooms. You are good at that."

"And Level Three?"

"To be able to catch a fly on the wing with your chopsticks." He lifted a pile of vegetables on his chopsticks and deftly pushed it into his mouth.

"Uh-huh. Is there a Level Four?"

"Of course," he said, swallowing delicately. "To catch the fly without hurting it."

"I know I shouldn't ask this but you know I could never resist sticking my head in the dragon's mouth. Four is not the top level, is it?" Scott had always enjoyed his colleague's sense of humour.

"No way! Level Five is the top." Ong studied the table and pincered two pieces of pork from the plate.

"And Level Five is..?"

"To castrate the fly on the wing with your chopsticks."

Scott nearly choked on a braised prawn. "Time to get back to the office," he gasped, trying to keep a straight face.

Behind his desk again, Ong opened two more bottles of fruit juice. Scott took one gratefully, conscious of the sweat drying on his back in the cool office air and resumed the topic of Benny Moskowitch.

"Let's assume we can keep him alive while he's in the hotel," he said. "Mind you, after Chicago and Toronto, that's a pretty loose assumption." Ong smiled sympathetically, while Scott continued. "Does he have to go out at all?"

"He does," Ong replied. "Wants to see a number of sites for the new factory he plans to set up."

Scott took a deep swallow of the apple juice. "That'll be tricky," he said.

"It will," Ong agreed. "But there'll be an armed guard with him at all times. We can go too."

It all sounded highly risky, thought Scott. He looked at his watch. "Can I call Birmingham?" he asked.

"Of course." Ong picked up the green telephone and dialled a series of numbers, waited for a few seconds with the earpiece pressed close to his head and then pushed the small red button on the base of the phone.

"It's scrambled. Want me to leave you alone?" he asked, his eyebrows raised.

Scott shook his head. "You might as well hear what's on my mind," he said.

Ong passed him the phone and settled back in his chair. Scott took the handset just in time to hear Marjorie's voice at the other end. The line was so clear she could have been next door. But it was well scrambled so no outsiders would be able to listen in. If they tried, they would hear nothing but a random warbling, like a bunch of drunken starlings.

"Mongoose Three for Analysis Section." Social amenities were not required on these calls. A faint click sounded on the line, then he heard Janette's lovely soft voice.

"Hi!" she said brightly. *Well, perhaps some amenities could be allowed,* he decided with a small grin.

"Janette, I need some research doing, rapidly."

"Not alone, huh?" He heard her smile down the wire.

143

"Right. Janette, this is going to be unpleasant. I won't give you the reasons for it, I'll explain later."

"Go ahead." She was all business, now.

"Run a check on Nicholas Wallace." He heard her gasp, but she said nothing. "Graduated from Nottingham University with a Bachelor of Science in Biology, 1992. Check his references, his High School records, everything you can. Find an address for him while at school. Find out which orphanage he was in, who his foster parents were, and where they are now."

"Yes, Scott." He could hear the shock in her voice.

"Has Jamieson come up with any results of the checks on the people we identified in your airline analysis?"

"Nothing yet of interest. So far, six of them have checked out clean, according to the local police forces."

"OK. Signal me here if anything comes out."

"Will do. Anything else?"

"No, love."

"Okay. Take care, McIntyre."

He hung up. Jamieson would not object to the tiny deviations from strict operational procedures. Despite being one of the most ruthless men in the service if the situation demanded it, Scott thought the Old Man was also a real pussycat at heart.

Ong was looking hard at him.

"Nick Wallace?" He had met Nick one night in London. Scott had introduced Ong as the Council's South East Asian Consultant, and the three men had got on famously. They had left the pub near London Tower as the last light was being switched off by the patient publican. "Our man?" Ong looked disconcerted. The old saw about inscrutable orientals did not apply at the moment. Liang Sien was clearly shaken.

"Liang Sien, I have nothing to prove it, and I know it's crazy," Scott said, almost pleading for understanding. "Just some tiny coincidences which could mean nothing and some gaps in my knowledge of the man that I should never have had. He's my best friend, dammit!"

He ran Ong through a shortened version of his discoveries to date on Dieter Konig and his horrors at the realization that a minuscule case existed for some possible suspicion of Nick.

"Bloody light, isn't it?" he said quietly, when he had finished.

"Certainly would be laughed out of any court of law in the civilized world," Ong agreed. "But we're neither a court of law nor civilized in what we do. You have to check it out."

Even that little confirmation that he was not totally crazy was enormously comforting to Scott. But it did little for the crawling hatred of himself which he felt for even thinking this about Nick, nor the sick sensation that he might be right.

"But man, it's crazy!" Scott exploded in a sudden burst of fury at himself. "There must be a million men out there with Nick's general appearance. What are the odds that the man we've been looking for turns out to be my friend? For God's sake, I've known him since I was an eighteen-year-old kid at college! He sure as hell wasn't al-Yaffi then!"

Ong was looking sympathetic and not the least inscrutable. "It makes no sense at all," he agreed. "But you've opened the can of worms. If it turns out to be empty then you know your friend is clear. The quicker we get to that point, the better."

"Yeah, I suppose so." Scott felt the weariness of many hours in the air.

"How about going for a nap at the hotel?" Ong suggested. "I'll pick you up this evening and take you out to eat something. Maybe even a beer or three. Moskowitch gets in tomorrow evening, we'll meet him. Till then, relax."

"Sounds like a good idea," Scott agreed. "I'll have a Gin Sling in the Long Bar, look at the tourists, maybe sleep an hour or two."

Ong walked him out to the elevators and waved gently as he disappeared from sight behind the closing elevator door. Scott found a cab and returned to Raffles to follow what seemed an excellent action plan until dinner that evening. The Gin Sling helped the depression a little, pushed it behind the nostalgic wave which came over him as he remembered sitting here with his parents twenty-five years ago.

His father had been a lawyer running a small practice with three other partners in Reading, his own home town once Scott's Dundee-born grandfather had moved south to live among the hated "Sassenachs" for reasons he had never made clear. McIntyre Senior was a strong-willed man who built a lucrative practice by being afraid of nothing and good at most things. He had been such a loving parent to Scott, then later to Leanne as well, so obviously adoring them both that Leanne and Scott waited by the front room window each evening to see him drive his big Rover car into the driveway of the old house in the pleasant suburb of Earley. Then they would rush out to meet him and the big, muscular man would swing them both up and around. Even at fourteen, when most boys would scorn such childishness, Scott looked forward to each evening's homecoming.

His mother was tall, slender, dark-haired. She taught music at a girls' school in Wokingham, a small town a few miles east of Reading and she sang in the Reading Festival Choir. Each Christmas, Father, Leanne and Scott would go to Reading Town Hall and hear the choir perform Handel's Messiah. Their greatest triumph was the year his mother sang the soprano solo part and the audience gave a standing ovation. She was the forceful initiator also, of the combined performances in opera and dramatics her school did with Scott's school. Each year, the two schools got together and did one musical work, usually a Gilbert and Sullivan production, and one dramatic work. These ranged from comic tragedies like *"Maria Martin, or Murder in the Red Barn"* to Chekhov's *"The Cherry Orchard."* These were wonderful times for Scott, the few occasions when two single-sex

146

schools got together, and the fact she was his mother did Scott's reputation the world of good with the girls.

He always remembered the excitement of those days, the rehearsals, the dress-rehearsals, eventually the performances and the teenage love affairs which inevitably started up. After every one of those productions he had to travel to Wokingham a lot to see the latest girlfriend. His mother stayed quiet about the whole business but she gave him a grin occasionally when talking about her day and happened to drop the girl's name into the conversation.

She travelled a lot during the school vacations, doing research in Europe or taking groups of girls on cultural visits. Scott, his father and Leanne missed her badly when she was away. Father seemed to go quiet during those weeks and the anxiety and loneliness in his face used to haunt the young Scott.

Carrick McIntyre, his father, a large, bulky man on whom suits hung shapelessly however expertly cut, only really comfortable in baggy pants and sweater. Short on words but not on love, he was everything a boy's father should be. Elizabeth Manning, his wife, Scott's mother. They had met at a Hogmanay party in Edinburgh, that New Year's Eve riot that for most Scots far exceeds the importance of Christmas. Their love affair had begun immediately and never stopped growing deeper and more beautiful to them. A month after that party, she had left her position as a music teacher at an elite school for young ladies and moved to Reading. Six months later, they were married.

Once each summer, until Scott left home to go to University, the family went on vacations together. Not always so exotic a locale as Singapore, but more reasonably to the Lake District, Cornwall and, of course, Scotland. The trip to Barcelona was his parents' first visit to Spain and Scott had taken a weekend's leave from St. Mawgan in Cornwall where he was stationed with his Nimrod Squadron to see them off at Gatwick Airport.

A week later, he was granted compassionate leave and he flew the same flight they had taken, to collect the three shattered bodies from the morgue.

Dangerously close to feeling tears near the surface, Scott left the Long Bar and walked through the Writers' Courtyard which was full of sunbathers lounging by the pool. He climbed the wide wooden staircase to the upper level and slept an hour under the gently rotating 'punkah-wallah' fans in his spacious room.

* * *

The following morning, he was up late. Dinner with Liang Sien had turned out to be a marathon banquet at a tiny restaurant off the Orchard Road. Like many Chinese, Ong's favoured drink with dinner was brandy, and the two men had polished off a complete bottle of five-star Courvoisier by the time they had reached the ninth and final course. Even though Ong had consumed most of the bottle, Scott had still drunk too much. Once the delicate slices of red bean paste tart had been demolished, Scott was hauled to a night club in the Mandarin Hotel where a traditional jazz band threatened the foundations. Trying not to feel too discombobulated by the sight of six Chinese men playing *"South Side Stomp"* and *"Tiger Rag"* with all the pounding enthusiasm and genuine feeling of any band in Chicago or New Orleans, Scott was finally able to get back to Raffles at three in the morning.

At eight, he was sitting on the balcony outside his room, enjoying the morning cool with just a hint of the furnace to come, admiring the palm trees and colourful flowers in the courtyard below. The scrambled egg and crab meat was exactly what his insides needed to settle down and a plate of fresh tropical fruits was restoring his tongue to something almost human again. The bellow of the telephone was most unwelcome, but he carried the fruit plate into the room and picked it up.

"Scott, you'd better get down here. Message for you from Birmingham." Ong sounded perfectly healthy.

"Urgent?"

"Can't tell. You'd better see it."

"I'll be there in thirty minutes."

"Move your Scottish bum, little *gwai-loh!*"

Scott made a rude noise, put back the telephone and hurriedly polished off the fruit plate. Then he left.

Jessica wore a bright yellow dress this morning, and the colour scheme with her red lipstick and black hair reminded Scott irresistibly of a set of coloured wooden bricks with which he had played as a little boy and still kept in his storage trunk, maybe to give to his own child one day. Her solemn face broke out into an even more welcoming smile and sparkling eyes than yesterday.

"Hello, Mister Scott!" she beamed, almost like a toddler welcoming Santa Claus, and opened the door for him. Inside, the four book readers did not appear to have moved since yesterday and they did not lift a single head to see the foreign devil walk past them.

Ong was into his second bottle of the morning, judging by the empty one on the book case. For a change, he was into soy milk, a taste Scott had never been able to acquire, but might be the only sign that Ong had drunk more than he should have last night. He had pulled out an orange juice for Scott already and had it standing by the sheet of paper on the front edge of his desk. His straight face as he looked at Scott's slightly haggard sense of hang-over was clearly a struggle for him to maintain.

"You primitive barbarians never could hold your booze!" he said. "I was in here at seven, decoding this!"

"How terribly sweet of you," Scott muttered. He slumped in the seat across from his partner and took a long drink of the orange juice. Ignoring Ong's tiny chuckle, Scott picked up the sheet of paper. It was from Janette and she had sent it at midnight, local time. She tended to work long hours when Scott was away. Better than sitting in her apartment in Edgbaston worrying about him, she had said.

Part 1 - Airline Passenger Analysis, the first heading line said. *All passengers identified in Geneva-Karachi list check out clean. No sign with any of them of possible involvement.*

Part 2 - Subsequent Airline Analysis, the second heading line said. *An analysis of passengers leaving Canada and the USA following the Richardson event was conducted. One name showed up that had appeared on the Geneva one-day list.*

Scott's heart kicked, and he swallowed. Janette had caught on to the one thing he had missed. So that was what had been bothering him while on the flight from London, he realized. *Dammit, I knew I had missed something,* he thought. *Bless you, Janette, you've pulled me out of the poo, possibly.*

He went back to the sheet of paper.

A Mister Paul Unsworth appeared on the list of passengers visiting Geneva for one day on August 12th, Janette's message continued. *Unsworth also flew by British Airlines flight 0177 from Heathrow to New York Kennedy Airport on July 31st, returning to London on August 8th. He flew from New York's La Guardia to Toronto on 31st, and back to New York on 8th. Checks are being conducted of his name on flights into or out of London prior to or after the United flights. His airline contact telephone number in England was false. Search will continue. Research on your request of yesterday also continues.*

British based! Dammit, he's based in Britain! At first, the hunter's excitement ripped through Scott's veins like champagne. It was the first genuine, concrete lead. Any way you want to look at it, he decided, they were ahead of where they had been a few weeks ago. *Al-Yaffi or Dieter Konig,* thought Scott, *you live in Britain, you bastard! Janette, you little darling, I owe you lots!*

Then the cold reality hit him. It was another pointer, tiny as it might be, but still a pointer to the horrible possibility that Nick, his best friend, almost his brother, was the most sought-after, brutal killer in the world today and the man who had slaughtered Scott's parents and sister. Distractedly, Scott took another draught of the cold orange juice. His throat was dry, not entirely due to the dehydration of alcohol excess.

"Useful?"

Ong's soft tones broke into his thoughts. Scott looked up. Ong was examining him calmly, his deep black eyes wide open under the Chinese eyelids.

Scott nodded. "Al-Yaffi," he said. "Or Dieter Konig, whichever he is. Looks like he's based in Britain. Adds another factor into the Nick Wallace possibility. Indicates that our belief that he did the Toronto event is correct, also."

"And would confirm that he certainly knows you, in that case." Ong spoke softly, as if to cause minimal disturbance to his colleague.

"Yes," Scott agreed. "He knows me. Whoever he is, he knows me now."

"Not so good, Scott."

"No, it's not... Shit! I've just thought of something else!"

"Yes?" Ong leaned over to put his empty soy milk bottle on the book case.

"There's no indication here that he flew to Karachi," Scott said. "Unless he used yet another identity for that trip, and that's always possible, I suppose. But if he didn't kill Perkins, who the hell did?"

Ong leaned forward on his elbows, his black stare still fixed firmly on Scott. "My little *gwai-loh*," he said gently. "This affair is getting dirty."

"Listen here, slant-eyes! Understatement is for us British, okay? Keep off my turf!"

Ong cackled with delight. Insulting one's friends was a uniquely British characteristic which he had adopted with enthusiasm while picking up his degree at Oxford. His laugh helped break the bleakness seeping through Scott's body at the prospect of just what sorry mess would eventually be uncovered.

Ong stood up abruptly. "Our man gets in this evening," he said. "We'll go to his hotel now and have a look around, check his room, all that good secret agent stuff, okay?"

"Okay. Do the local people know?"

"Sure. I told them yesterday we'd do that. No problem. Let's go."

They went.

* * *

Qantas Flight Fifty-One direct from Brisbane was three minutes early and they waited outside the exit from the plane until all the passengers had left. The attending group with them was quite extensive. Four uniformed cops who spoke Mandarin to Liang Sien and ignored Scott completely, plus the two Mongoose operatives, the six of them stood quietly while the noisy crowd of what sounded predominantly like Australian travellers poured out of the gateway.

Finally, the two Mongoose agents walked down the tunnel and into the massively spacious body of the Boeing 747. Benny Moskowitch sat calmly in a seat in the first class section, reading a copy of *"The Australian,"* the national newspaper. As the two men entered, he looked over his reading glasses at them, put the paper down and stood up. He gave them a problem immediately. The man must have measured a good six-foot-five, thought Scott, with a huge spread of shoulders. No surplus poundage round the waist, he stood straight with his head back. His hair was thick and plentiful, giving an image of a man many years younger than his recorded sixty-three. Energy exuded from him. He stood at least a foot taller than any of the uniformed cops and a full head above either Ong or Scott.

"G'day!" he smiled, folding his spectacles into an inside pocket of the blue denim jacket he was wearing. His words were standard Aussie greeting protocol, appropriate for a first meeting between strangers or after a twenty year gap between relatives or close friends. The voice was strong and confident and his smile looked more a regular fixture than would a scowl.

"Good evening, sir," Ong said in his best British accent, extending his hand. Moskowitch took it and shook it firmly, peering closely into Ong's face. "I am Ong Liang Sien," continued Ong. He released the Australian's massive hand and gestured at Scott.

"And I am Scott McIntyre," Scott said. "A pleasure to meet you, Mister Moskowitch."

The huge Australian mangled his hand in the same enthusiastic way he had treated Ong's and with the same intent stare into Scott's face.

"You're the two security blokes supposed to keep me alive, eh?" Moskowitch asked.

"Correct, sir."

"Well, bloody start by calling me Benny! Can't be formal with blokes looking after my skin!"

Both agents laughed. Benny had clearly adopted the Australian style of informality in his decade of living there, as well as the accent.

"Got any bags, Benny?" Scott asked.

"Sure do," Benny replied, opening the overhead compartment and pulling out a plush leather briefcase. "Got a couple of ports I checked in."

"Suitcases," Scott said with a grin at Ong before his puzzled expression got too extreme. Port was purely a Queensland term, short for portmanteau.

"We'll have them collected for you, Benny," Ong said. "Customs have already cleared you through."

"Fair enough. Not likely I'd be bringing in ten kilos of dope on a trip like this, now, is it?"

The uniforms did not look amused at that.

"Benny, we'll take you straight to the limousine." Scott was beginning to feel tension in his throat. "We're going to walk you out of here straight to the car parked at the door." They began to move out of the aircraft's cabin to the obvious relief of the flight attendant shuffling his feet by the doorway. "I think the best thing will be for Ong and myself to walk on either side of you, and the police to walk two in front, two behind," Scott continued. "They're armed. If either of us yells to you to get down or just assaults you, do it, get flat, stay there. Leave the crude stuff to us."

The smile had faded and Moskowitch stopped still, staring at the Englishman.

"You blokes are for real, ain't you?" he said.

"Fair dinkum, mate!" Scott replied in his best Aussie.

Benny grinned again. "Alright, last one in the bar buys the beers!" He resumed the progress out of the aircraft.

"There's a case of beer in your room," Scott said to the massive retreating back. "No bars, I'm afraid."

"No worries," Benny said over his shoulder.

The sliding door into the concourse slipped open and Scott's tension rose sharply. Crowding as close as they could to the mountainous crag of Benny Moskowitch, they shepherded him like tiny sheepdogs to the last door to the outside world. Scott's head was swinging rapidly around, as was Ong's, both of them looking for a face which might be frighteningly familiar. Benny was horribly exposed and Scott made a mental note to get Ong to request larger scale bodyguards for the rest of this assignment. His fingers itched for the comforting feel of the handle of his

Browning pistol, but it was an itch that could not be satisfied while in Singapore.

They made it to the car. Ong opened the door hurriedly, they almost crammed Benny's enormous mass inside, then scrambled in after him while the uniforms formed a second barrier behind them. The police piled into a marked police car behind the limousine and they slid away from the hotel heading for the city. Ong extracted his pistol and laid it casually on his knee.

"Jeez, I feel like a bloody convict under guard," the huge man complained.

"Sorry, Benny," Scott murmured, looking quickly at him. "Paranoia is a useful job characteristic in this business!"

"Bloody oath!" The Australian looked with dismay at Ong's pistol. "I didn't reckon on all this lot, just because I want to build a factory up here. And you really think it's all because some Nazi shit-head wants to get me?"

Scott nodded, looking left, right, behind and through the glass partition, in a constant circular inspection, the way he had when flying helicopters and jet trainers. Just like the sky, the surroundings were attractive but could be lethal to the unwary.

Benny's face was sad. Scott took a rapid glance as he swung his head from the right hand window to the front, and the expression was mournful.

"My parents left Poland because of thugs who hated anyone who wasn't one of their Master race," Benny said. "And sixty years later, I have to have half a dozen blokes with guns keeping me in my room because those same thugs are still running loose. This is progress?"

Scott didn't look at him but he shook his head. "Not to us, no. But there are people who would think so, it seems." He sensed rather than saw Benny's shrug.

"The world's going to hell," the large man muttered.

They made it safely to the Westin Plaza Hotel.

"Just this short walk through the lobby," Scott said softly. "Benny, let's get at those beers in your room!"

"Best offer I've had all day!" he laughed, and the three of them shuffled out of the limousine, protected by the ring of four uniforms. The group moved like a squadron of frigates round an aircraft carrier, through the doors of the hotel into the lobby.

The fear wouldn't leave Scott. Benny was still dreadfully exposed with his huge size and Scott's head revolved like a weathercock in a whirlwind as they made their way to the elevators. Check-in procedures had all been completed before they arrived and a cop was waiting at the door to Benny's suite. He opened it as the group arrived.

The layout was just like the suite in Chicago, thought Scott. A large room with a small conference table, comfortable lounges and armchairs, a refrigerator in one corner next to the television, tea and coffee facilities. A door led off each of the two opposite walls, presumably to a bedroom and a study. Benny walked straight through, dropped his briefcase on the table and immediately flung off his jacket, advancing on the refrigerator.

Ong stayed by the door and a rattle of Mandarin followed with the cops who immediately left. Ong closed the door.

"Aha!" Benny emitted a cry of delight as he opened the fridge door to reveal a stack of yellow beer cans. He pulled out three, closed the door and stood up, walking back to the middle of the room.

"Cummanavadrink!" he said to the room at large, and they needed no further words. The click and hiss of three cans being opened, followed by glugging sounds as they were upturned and emptied were the only sounds in the room for a few moments.

Benny emitted an explosive sigh, putting down what sounded like an empty can. Scott had managed less than a third of the can but was enjoying every mouthful. Ong was still drinking. Benny moved back to the fridge, opened the door and looked back at the other two with an enquiring eye. Scott shook his head, as did

Ong, and Benny took a single can, opening it as he came back to them.

"So now what?" he asked, sitting down at the small round table. The other two joined him.

"It's not a tourist trip, Benny," Scott said. "Keeping you alive is the priority and that means no sight-seeing."

"I have to look at a couple of possible locations for the building," the Australian protested.

"Sure," Scott agreed. "But that means moving around with the same sort of bodyguard as we had coming in. Which reminds me," he said, turning to Ong. "Taller cops!"

"All taken care of! Told them that as they left."

"Good!" Scott turned back to Benny who was well into his second can of beer, looking depressed.

"So no tours of the best local restaurants tonight?" Benny said, looking at Scott.

"Not tonight, nor any other night on this trip. Sorry."

"When does it end, Scott?"

"When we get the bastard!"

"And who the hell is the bastard, anyway? They didn't tell me much before I left Brisbane."

"There's a lot we don't know yet for certain," Scott replied. "But we think he's a German called Dieter Konig. He's either a member of, or supports a neo-Nazi group called Knights of Aryan Dawn. What we don't know is whether he does this for kicks or for money. Or both."

"Any idea of what he looks like?"

"Tallish, a bit over six foot, slim, dark, mid-thirties. I may have a better idea of his face than I know, but I can't be sure."

"I don't understand that."

Scott sighed. "It's a bit tricky, Benny. I've had some loose, very loose pointers to a specific man. I could be pissing in the wind or I may be right. I'll be on the lookout for him."

Benny sat back, then finished his beer with a loud gurgle, placing the empty can on the table next to the other three. "So what now?" he asked.

"Dinner in here," Ong said. "Then Scott can go back to his hotel. I'm armed, so I'll stay here tonight in the second bedroom. There's a cop outside at all times. Tomorrow, we'll take you to the government building for your conference."

Benny shrugged. "Well, alright. If you say so."

The telephone rang with a shrill shout. Benny looked at the other two with a raised eyebrow. Liang Sien nodded at him.

"Could be for me, but answer it anyway," Ong said.

Benny stood up and went to the phone, picked it up and listened for a few moments.

"For you," he said, indicating Ong who stood up and took the phone from him. He stood still, listening to the voice at the other end, then switched his eyes to Scott.

"Coded signal for you at the office," Ong said. "I'll have to go and decode it and bring it back here."

"Okay," Scott said. "Want us to hold dinner for you?"

Ong shook his head, said something short into the phone and replaced it. "Could take a while."

"Right," Scott said. "Benny, what's your choice?"

"Well, we have time to kill," he answered with a wide grin. "A good Chinese banquet will hit the spot, and a couple of bottles of good white plonk!"

"I'll order it on the way out," Ong said. "That'll make sure you get the real stuff!"

"In that case, I need another beer!" Benny seemed resigned to his fate. Ong left and Scott locked the door after him, catching a quick look at the guard outside the door. Benny collected another beer can from the fridge and snapped it open with a small hiss.

"One for you, Scott?" he asked.

Scott shook his head. "One's my ration for the night, Benny," he answered.

"Help yourself if you change your mind," Benny said and sprawled out on the lounge. For a multi-millionaire and chairman of a massive organization, he was a most egalitarian man, thought Scott.

Three hours passed easily. They chatted lengthily about Benny's history and his life in Australia, and why he lived in the sub-tropical town of Brisbane rather than the more conventional Sydney or Melbourne.

"Climate!" Benny said shortly. "I lived in Melbourne the first year, but my wife has arthritis and the cold really gets to her. So we moved up north. It's just perfect for most of the time though you can get some hellish storms."

"Doesn't the political system bug you?"

Benny laughed. "Biggest outdoor lunatic asylum in the world, that place! But still nowhere near as crazy as it was back in the sixties and seventies!"

Dinner came, three full cartloads of plates, bowls, basins and spices. After standard checking procedures, Scott let the waiter in, and the two men attacked the magnificent spread with enthusiasm. The wine was a superb Barossa Valley Reisling from South Australia, and by eleven in the evening, the quantities of both food and drink were sharply reduced, mainly by Benny Moskowitch. A few minutes later, Ong called from the lobby to say he was on his way up.

Scott opened the door for him after checking through the spyhole and getting the secure signal. Ong came in carrying an envelope which he passed to McIntyre. Scott ripped it open with the nagging sensation that the news was going to hurt. He read it out loud to an attentive audience of two.

"The Nottingham University records of Nicholas Francis Wallace show that he had attended Matherson Grammar School in Newcastle-on-Tyne from 1981 to 1988, leaving with General Certificate of Education, Ordinary Level in seven subjects and Advanced Level in Mathematics, Biology and Chemistry. He paid his own University fees, rather than have them paid in the conventional manner by the County. No record exists of any student grants made to him by any local authority in the North East of England.

No record of his attendance exists at Matherson Grammar School. The GCE certificates are not recorded with the issuing authorities. His references, signed by teachers at the school appear to be forged.

No record can be found with any regional orphanage organization that anyone of that name was ever under their care.

The home address shown in his university file was a genuine location, but the owners of the house denied any knowledge of anyone of that name ever living there."

The room was silent. Scott felt numb.

"This Wallace bloke, is he the one you think might be it?" Benny's voice was low. Scott nodded, not looking up from the sheet of paper.

"That would seem to settle the matter," Ong said gently.

"He was my friend!" Scott snapped. "How the hell could my best friend turn out to be al-Yaffi? It makes no bloody sense at all! You just don't get coincidences like that! It's crazy!"

His world was splintering around him. It was insane. Out of millions of men of his age, how could the maniac he had been hunting for four years suddenly turn out to be the friend he had loved like a brother since he was eighteen?

"I agree." Ong's voice broke into the private bedlam inside Scott's head. "As a coincidence it's totally off the wall. Way outside any odds. So remember what Sherlock Holmes said."

"When you have eliminated all the possibilities...." Scott muttered. They'd had this conversation before, in a brainstorming session on a case study during a training program together.

"Whatever remains, however improbable...." Ong continued.

"Must be the answer," they said together, looking at each other.

"Not a coincidence?" Scott asked. A black hole was opening up before his feet and he felt the pull of helpless fury.

Ong shook his head. "Not a chance, little *gwai-loh.* You need to talk to Jamieson."

"Bloody right! As soon as I..." Scott stopped, blasted into silence by the sudden picture which blanked out the room and replaced it with another scene.

...People milled around, saying their goodbyes, shaking hands... '...Great party, Arnold....,' '...May see you at the Copenhagen Conference next September...,' '...Look forward to the seminar tomorrow morning, Arnold....' The tall figure with shoulder-length, blond hair, narrow face, strong eyes, bright smile, light moustache and neat beard clinging to the jaw line....

Nick.

Scott had not recognized the face because it appeared totally out of any expected environment, blond and bearded when Scott knew dark and clean-shaven. But the eyes, the smile, they were the triggers in his dulled memory. Scott had known the face for seventeen years.

My best friend, Nick Wallace, supposedly in Europe but actually in a Royal York Hotel conference room in Toronto. I saw him grinning at me as he killed Arnold Richardson before my eyes.

"Scott?" Ong's voice was hesitant.

Scott snapped his mind from Toronto back to Singapore and looked at Ong steadily. "It's Nick Wallace," he said.

"Definite?"

"Definite."

He should have seen it before, Scott knew that. All the pointers had been there. Nick's surprise at Scott's visit to Chicago. Nick's absences for every al-Yaffi strike. The love of Mercedes cars, the ability to be the man of almost every woman's dreams. Scott should have seen it. But how could he have thought Nick was al-Yaffi? His subconscious had seen it, hence his distress over recent weeks, but Scott had only caught on when alcohol had removed the inhibition to thought.

Nick Wallace, his best friend for half his life was the international assassin, Mustapha al-Yaffi, once called Dieter Konig.

Scott slept badly that night.

* * *

At seven the following morning, he strolled across the road from Raffles, and was back in Benny's hotel suite. Getting in was not easy. He was stopped by a uniformed guard holding a pistol as soon as he walked out of the elevator. He was frisked professionally and identification was demanded. The guard was not the same one as had been outside Benny's door last night, so the action was appropriate. The new cop was also Scott's height. Ong's request had been heard and activated.

"Please check with Ong Liang Sien for my identification," said Scott calmly. Black eyes stayed staring into Scott's as the guard pulled a compact radio unit to his lips from the leather strap up his right side and spoke briefly into it. He stood motionless, his right hand holding his gun pointing at Scott, still staring into his eyes, awareness in his whole body like a cobra ready to pounce. Scott froze every muscle.

The door to Benny's suite opened and the guard still didn't move. A real professional, this one, decided Scott. Ong leaned out and spoke shortly. Only then did the guard move away.

"Excellent!" Scott said softly to him. The guard nodded briefly. Scott walked into the room.

Benny was polishing off a plate of fruit, and waved a fork at him. "G'day! Had breakfast?"

Scott nodded. "Same as yours. Could use another orange juice, though."

Benny cackled. He seemed in a good mood and pointed at the jug on the table. "Grapefruit juice, better for you. Help yourself."

Ong closed and locked the door again. He was dressed formally for the day, in a white shirt and blue tie, with tiny stainless steel cufflinks and no jacket. It was the standard alternative to the safari suit for business.

"I called Jamieson last night," Ong said. "Had to use the telephone in here, so I was careful. I told him your thoughts had been verified."

"Did he say anything?" Scott carefully filled a large glass from the jug, checking that his hands did not seem to be trembling from the rotten tensions of last night.

"Highly verbose he was, for Jamieson."

"Oh?" Scott gulped down the juice and the tartness almost convulsed his tongue and cheeks and went rampaging round his body, shaking out the smelly little lumps of a poor night's sleep.

"Yes. He said 'Thank you, Ong. Carry on.'"

"Sounds like Jamieson, alright."

"Who the hell is this Jamieson bloke?" Benny had been listening intently, not hiding his amusement.

"The boss," Scott replied. Further identification was inappropriate.

"Obviously," guffawed Benny. "And a real comedian."

Scott thought about the Old Man's twitching moustache, the occasional weak attempts to make a joke, and the way Jamieson let his subordinates speak with total freedom, sometimes pushing out the envelope of what was an appropriate way to address a much-decorated hero of the Middle East and Malayan conflicts.

"Yes," Scott said in affection. "He really is!"

Ong refilled his glass from the jug of grapefruit juice. "Change of venue for today's conference," he said. "The Prime Minister has offered a conference room at his lodge. It's close, it's the best-guarded place on the island."

"Perfect!" said Scott. "Who organized that?"

"I imagine the boss was a little more talkative after speaking with me," said Ong. "He probably pulled out the red phone in his desk and called Downing Street."

A beep from Ong's pocket interrupted further discussion. He pulled a radio unit out and listened, spoke a few words in Mandarin and replaced it. "Our escort is outside," he said.

"Good!" Benny stood up, pulled on a lightweight safari jacket of similar pattern to Scott's over his thin cotton shirt and picked up his brief case.

"Same routine as yesterday, Benny," said Scott. "Any sudden action, hit the floor and stay there."

"Sure thing. You're the boss."

Scott opened the door and moved into the corridor to find himself surrounded by six uniformed police, all armed, all around the six foot mark. They were probably the tallest men in the entire force. Scott felt a little more comfortable and nodded back at the suite door.

Benny and Ong came out together. They took up similar stations to yesterday's phalanx and walked to the elevator. When it came, it was luckily empty, so no poor civilian had to be evicted. One of the cops took out a key and inserted it into the control slot of the elevator to ensure no stops would be made at any other floor. They crowded in and waited the few moments to race down to the ground floor. Scott felt tension growing sharply, some paranormal feeling of wrongness.

The door opened and they eased their way into the lobby, which was swarming at this hour. Scott began his neck-twirling act, Ong was doing the same, so were the armed guards, and they were attracting a great deal of attention. People stopped in their tracks and traffic backups began to build up. *This is bloody dangerous,* thought Scott.

One clump of Europeans, twenty or thirty of them in colourful Batik shirts flowed in their direction from the front and right of the group. Ong rattled a sharp warning at the leading cop. Another bunch of tourists materialized to their left, talking loudly to each other in German. Scott frantically twisted his head to try and see what was happening. A shout came from one of the cops, his gun was raised. Screams from the crowd filled the air and all the dogs of war broke loose.

The first bunch of tourists flooded all over, breaking into panicky droplets of colour. People were running in every direction, some to avoid the suddenly dangerous atmosphere of the lobby, others running in from the restaurants and coffee shops to see what was happening. Scott saw a tendril of humanity float out from the middle of the bunch on his left like the arm of an amoeba in his direction. Scott grabbed Benny's shoulders.

"Down!" he bellowed, and the huge Australian collapsed to the floor.

One person suddenly left the moving tendril and with frightening speed was almost within touching distance of the nearest cop. A shot thundered into the cavern of the lobby and more screams erupted, much louder than before. Scott was kneeling by the side of Benny, desperately craving the feel of his Browning in his hand. Two more cops joined him round Benny, guns drawn, looking frantically in all directions.

"That one!" Scott yelled, pointing at the figure moving so terrifyingly toward them. The attacker was tall, thin, looked Chinese. Scott couldn't see a gun in the man's hand but the marauder reached behind his back and suddenly there was a gun. *A Beretta automatic pistol, probably a nine-millimetre,* said Scott's coolly observing mind, somehow not caring about the physical danger in the area. More shots erupted, one of the cops next to Scott aimed carefully. His shot didn't seem to make a noise, but the approaching man swerved. He raced through the crowds milling around in massive confusion. *He seems to be holding his side,* thought Scott, watching helplessly from next to Benny's massive shape. The cop next to him aimed then snarled in frustration, unable to shoot in that direction with so many people around.

The noise subsided gradually. Scott thought calmly about what a weird tableau this was. One huge man was lying on the ground, three men were kneeling around him, two of them in uniform with guns drawn, one looking into the crowd for a glimpse of the running assailant. Six more uniforms stood in a circle, guns aimed outwards. Another man, dressed in a natty white shirt, colourful tie and stainless steel cufflinks stood in the same stance.

The silence was total then sounds began to roll in from the edges of the lobby like a slow tide encroaching on a vast, empty beach. People began breathing, talking to each other, comparing notes, telling latecomers what they thought they saw. Memories were being carved out for telling and retelling for years to come, a base for arguments about what really happened and why. Scott's calm was replaced by the feel of his heart pumping furiously and the coldness of damp sweat on his back.

Scott placed a hand on Benny's shoulder. Muscles which could pull a railroad car moved under the expensive smooth fabric of the tailored shirt, a neck which could have graced a lineman in the American National Football League twisted round.

Benny's huge face turned from the carpeted floor and looked up at him.

"Well, shit, eh?" said the Australian.

"Very likely, Benny. No damage?"

"Hell, no! You blokes were too quick for that."

He pulled himself to his feet and brushed down his suit. The ring of police contracted around him, professional eyes studying their charge. Ong walked into the circle.

"You saw him?" he asked.

Scott nodded. "The right shape and size, but looked oriental. Probably a wig and decent make-up. Wouldn't need any more."

"Tell you what," swore Benny. "That bloke was fair bloody dinkum going for my arse, alright!"

Benny was not as cool as he liked to pretend, decided Scott, but he was doing one hell of a job of keeping his composure. Scott nodded then tapped the shoulder of the young cop who had fired at what he knew to be Nick as he charged them.

"That was well done, officer," he said. "I think you winged him, or hit his side."

The officer nodded, but said nothing.

"Scott, let's get to the car, quickly," broke in Ong.

The uniforms picked up on that and rapidly moved them through the front door to a black Mercedes Pullman standing between two police cars. The two agents hustled Benny into the luxurious interior and jumped in after him. Within seconds, the three machines were moving in the direction of the Prime Minister's Lodge.

The tremors subsided in Scott, and he could see all three of them gradually recovering.

"Who provided this tip, Mossad?" asked Ong, sitting in the front seat of the limousine's passenger compartment, facing Benny and Scott in the rear. Scott nodded.

Benny grinned smugly. "Top people, those guys!" he said.

"You were pretty good yourself," Scott smiled at him, and Benny's grin widened.

"Not bad for a senior citizen, I suppose!"

"It may happen again," said Scott. The grin faded.

"You think so?"

"I'm certain. It's the first time to my knowledge that this guy has tried a hit and failed. I think it's the first time he's been hurt. Not only his body but his reputation, and that's far more important to him."

"You think he'll try it the same way again?" Ong looked dubious and Scott shook his head.

"No, I don't. He'd never get through the sort of cordon we've got round Benny, especially not now that we're expecting it. He's probably hurt remember, so his mobility may be reduced. And if he's got a contract riding on this hit the results are more important than his macho man-against-man stuff. I think we have to be prepared for anything, rifle, bomb, anything."

"Seems logical." Ong looked unhappy. "On the way back we'll have the car drive into the hotel basement and have the place cleared out first."

"That'll take care of a rifleman," agreed Scott. "Can you get a tight search of the room too, before we get back. Get shutters placed on the windows then seal it off?"

Ong nodded, smiled and plucked out his mobile phone. "The wonders of modern technology!" he said, and spoke rapidly and at length into the unit.

As his words were flying through the ether, the limo was turning into the ornate, wrought iron gates of the Prime Minister's Lodge. A smart, British Guard's style salute came from the military uniforms, the gates opened in front of the leading police car and all three vehicles cruised slowly along the driveway to the beautiful house set in lovely manicured lawns and garden.

Benny got no time to admire the view. The agents hustled him into the doorway and the spacious lobby then followed the police down a corridor to a conference room. The door opened and Ong and Scott were left to take Benny inside, closing it after themselves.

Seated at the long oak table were eight men. All but two were oriental, the exceptions being Indians. They all stood as the group entered, and for a moment, Ong, Benny and Scott stood confused as the eight bowed at them. Benny recovered his composure first. He was at last in an environment familiar to him.

"Good morning, gentlemen," he said, his rich, strong voice filling the room. "I am Benny Moskowitch."

As the other eight performed their introductions, all of them in perfectly intoned English, Ong and Scott moved to the back of the room where two chairs were placed. Scott studied the room and saw oak panelling, leaded windows with stained glass patterns and plush carpet. *This could be the cabinet room at Chequers, the British Prime Minister's country retreat,* Scott thought. He looked carefully around the gardens outside, and was unable to see any other building. That was perfect, he decided. Nick could never get into the grounds and he had no place from where he could fire a rifle.

The day proceeded in total dullness and safety.

The meeting split up at a little after six in the early evening. *How Benny does it fails me,* thought Scott. The conversation had been heavy on rates of return, leveraged loans at various international interest rates, labour utilization factors and a number of legal issues which had reduced Scott's brain to a stultified porridge by midday. But Benny had obviously been alert the whole time, eyes flashing from speaker to speaker, noting everything, evaluating, measuring, missing nothing. Several times he had referred back to minor comments or figures from an hour or more earlier, to show the logical error in some argument, and it was clear to Scott that by the end of the meeting, Benny Moskowitch had the whole table eating out of his hand.

"So we will examine the two potential sites tomorrow, gentlemen," Benny said, standing up for the first time since lunch at twelve. Only then did he show some signs of his age as he stretched with difficulty and, apparently, a little pain.

Murmurs of agreement ran around the room and a fairly confused round-robin of handshakes began which took up over ten minutes before everybody was certain that all the essential hands had been gripped, heads bowed at each other, and political smiles of varying degrees of sincerity. While this went on, Scott exchanged a few words with Ong.

"Everything arranged with the hotel?" he muttered.

"Management is not too happy about this morning's episode, but they've made all the arrangements," replied Ong. "They practically wept over the phone, begging me not to permit a repeat of the gunfight at the OK coral. I said you'd guarantee it with your life."

"Gee, thanks! What a pal!"

"Thought you'd like it." Ong smiled modestly.

The group began to ooze out into the black and white tiled corridor outside the conference room. The six uniformed cops were waiting by the front door, outside of which were congregating a number of chauffeurs of the Mercedes limousines parked in a sedate row in the driveway.

A quick discussion took place between Ong and the police lieutenant in charge of the escort, and they shepherded Benny into the car, moving away tucked in neatly behind the similar vehicle in front. By the time the lead car had reached the gateway onto the main road, twelve cars were in the convoy and gradually they filtered off, leaving just the two police vehicles to accompany Benny back to the Westin.

The rest of the evening was much like the previous day. Dinner was served in Benny's suite, the fridge, now restocked with fresh cans of Queensland beer, was emptied by Benny, and the conversation flowed. Benny seemed unaffected by the day's events. He had the two agents in hysterics with anecdotes of what life was like for a large, successful Jewish businessman in Brisbane. Under the humour, the pain was often evident, however. Benny had met the appalling impasse of being rich in a place where wealth was worshipped but where parochialism and bigotry were still common.

"That's why we call it The Deep North in Australia," he said, walking back from the fridge, carrying three more cans of beer. "It's the same culture as the Deep South of the States. One American mate of mine says it's a bit like Alabama in 1950."

"Surely not!" commented Ong. "In this day and age?"

"Well, it certainly used to be, though things have improved a lot in the last couple of decades. But hey, you've got to remember, they were the bunch that wanted to cede the northern half of Australia to the Japanese in the second world war." Benny snapped open his beer, and took a healthy swallow. "One of their Federal Members of Parliament wanted to censure some other bloke for being unpleasant about that valiant man, Adolf Hitler! In 1943, yet! They're also the same people that rejected daylight saving time on the grounds that God would object to any interference with His time, and also that the cows would get upset! As you might imagine, trying to join a golf club was like hitting a brick wall. I could have bought the damn place out of the week's petty cash, but join? Forget it!"

Ong and Scott nearly choked with laughter, and Benny spent the next hour telling them amazing tales of life in the tropical north of Australia.

At ten, he faded and retired to his room. Scott set off to return to Raffles and Ong retreated to the second bedroom. Scott gave a cheery goodnight to the cop at the door, received a blank stare in return, and walked across Bras Basah road back to Raffles.

Sleep was still not good, despite the exhaustion. Had that really been Nick this morning? he pondered, sitting under the cool breeze of the *punkah-wallah* fans. Had he been hit? How badly was he hurt? Had he seen Scott again? What would he try next? Would he give up? What was the source of his support? Who had supplied the gun? How had he got into Singapore? How would he get out, now that the manhunt was stepped up?

Round and round and round and round...

* * *

At seven the next morning, safely steering his way through the intensive search by the guard on the door, Scott was back with Benny and Ong, slaking his thirst with grapefruit juice and stealing some guava and lychees from the platter on the table.

Benny's mind was miles away this morning. The business problems had taken over from the simpler matters of staying alive, and he was remote, detached, and thoughtful. Once the two agents had him safely down to the basement and into the Mercedes, he sat silently working over rows of figures in a notepad, clicking rapidly on a pocket calculator and occasionally muttering something under his breath. He hardly seemed to notice as the limousine drove through the morning crowds in Singapore, accompanied by the ever-present pair of police cars, and he only looked up when they arrived at an expanse of partly-built offices on the northern edge of the city.

Three other limousines were parked neatly abreast of each other. Ong snapped a command to the driver through the radio connection to the front and the Mercedes came to a halt by the other vehicles. The police cars had also stopped and a young lieutenant approached them. Ong wound down the window and spoke shortly. The officer nodded and waved his arms. The other cars were carefully rearranged so that Benny's limousine could move into the middle of the bunch.

Scott looked around. This was not healthy, and he could see the worry on Ong's face reflecting his own. There were lots of buildings around, flat roofs providing excellent bases for a rifleman, and half-built structures that could not have been fully guarded during the night. This location allowed a gunman to take up residence in any of fifty sheltered and hidden spots.

It looked like a killing ground.

"I don't like it," muttered Ong.

"Can't say I'm wildly euphoric myself," Scott responded. "Benny, can this be done without you getting out?"

"Not a chance." Benny was firm, though anxiety showed in his eyes.

Outside, the natives were getting restless. The six businessmen who had turned up were talking in small clumps, faces turned in irritation toward the new arrivals. The police were clearly as unhappy with the killing potential of the site as were the Mongoose agents and Scott could see a little argument breaking out between the lieutenant and one of the business types, a tall, elderly Indian wearing a turban.

"Sorry, mate," said Benny suddenly, leaning forward in his seat and clutching the notepad. "This has to be done."

Giving each other a nervous glance, Ong and Scott got out with him, Ong in front, Scott behind. The police immediately swarmed around them, badly interfering with the process of greetings and handshakes between Benny and the other businessmen. Scott was not unhappy with the melee which formed. Not a gunman living could have picked out Benny, despite his height, from any of the surrounding buildings while people milled around like that.

The group of businessmen shuffled into the walls of the shell of the office building, which took Benny out of danger of a shot from a remote building but opened up the possibilities of a handgun attack from behind any of the piles of bricks or machinery which littered the place.

Heads swinging around all over the place, the agents followed the crowd through the structure. Benny appeared to have forgotten the danger for he was animated, pointing out various features of the building and asking numerous questions. Scott could feel his heart pounding and his pulse thumping in his head. The hunter's sense was working overtime. Something nasty was in the offing. He felt as a swimmer in South Australian waters must feel. The looming, murderous presence of a White Pointer shark could be sensed but not seen.

The group walked up the one stairway which had been built and came up to the roof.

"I'd rather you didn't go out," Scott said to Benny.

The large man shook his head. "So would I, mate," he agreed. "But I have to take one look. We need a water reservoir up here, I have to check it's big enough."

"Christ! Alright, but stay close!"

Benny smiled and nodded.

They walked out in a group on to the horribly exposed expanse of bare concrete. Ong tried to keep everyone close and generally succeeded. But suddenly, Benny let out an exclamation, pointed at something in the far corner and began to walk away from the rest. For just a couple of seconds he was naked to the killer's gaze.

"Benny! For God's sake, get back...." Scott rushed toward him, prepared to tackle him round the knees. A soft breeze seemed to whisper past his cheek just as he got there, he had barely time to touch the big man, shoved him just an inch and a square foot of new concrete wall on Scott's left erupted and became flying white powder. Tiny splinters of concrete stung his cheek and he felt some go into his hair and graze his forehead. Then he heard the shot which had missed his face by a millimetre. *Big calibre rifle,* his mind said calmly to the rest of him. *Probably a 7.62 millimetre. At least a hundred yards away.* Benny was lying flat on his stomach, his hands over his head, saying "omigod, omigod, omigod..." in a low monotone.

The police escort drew their weapons and rushed to the parapet on the side from which the shot had come. A staccato series of orders were being issued into a radio by the police Lieutenant and several men were pointing at the roof of a building in the distance. From behind the protective wall of their bodies Scott dragged Benny into a crouch and hauled him forcibly back into cover.

Benny's face was grey. Now he looked his age, and more. The other businessmen were gabbling hysterically among themselves, looking wildly in all directions. Ong let out a wild yell that silenced everybody.

"Gentlemen!" he called when the noise stopped as if it had hit a wall. "Whoever it was will not try again. He was too close and other police are running in that direction. He needs to get away and that's what he'll be doing. So you are quite safe now."

He was right, thought Scott. In the distance, sirens were weaving an eerie song in the hot morning air as a number of cars converged on the one building which had line of sight on the spot on the roof where they had been standing. *Maybe they'll get the man, and put a lot of concerns out of my mind. Maybe it wasn't Nick. Maybe it was another man called Dieter Konig. Maybe it was somebody totally unknown.* He prayed silently for the last one.

Some order restored, the cavalcade of businessmen and police climbed down to the ground level again. As they got there another police car was scrabbling to a halt in the dust of the unfinished surface. A more senior officer climbed out and as he walked toward them, shook his head in disappointment. Their man had got away.

"In that case, shall we head off to the second site?"

Scott turned at the sound of the Australian tones behind him. Benny had recovered his composure and was grinning at Scott in expectation of his reaction.

"You mean, after all that, you want to keep going?" asked Scott.

The other business men seemed equally astonished. Most were looking pale and shaky, casting longing looks at the safety of their limousines.

"Look mate," said Benny. "The day some shit-head Nazi ratbag with his brains in his bollocks stops Benny Moskowitch from making money is the day I turn Buddhist! Now, this building won't do. I've got to see the other one. Okay?"

Scott turned to Ong standing with the senior officer and raised an eyebrow.

"Actually, it's probably safe enough," smiled Ong. "Our man must have ducked for cover now, he could not possibly make another attempt. He'd need time to get in position. And anyway, how does he know where to go?"

"How did he know where to come for this attempt?" Scott asked, almost without thinking.

Ong stopped and stared at him. "A hell of a good question," he said. "How did he know?"

Scott looked back at him. It was an unpleasant thought.

Despite the events, Benny seemed in high spirits as they left for the drive to the second site, only a couple of miles along the road. As they drove in air-conditioned comfort, Ong made a quiet comment.

"Lousy rifle shot, our man."

"Possibly," replied Scott. "But he only had a day to get a rifle and get prepared. No real time or place to set the sights properly and get used to the gun. And he's not normally a rifleman, anyway."

Ong nodded. "Where do you think he got the weapon?"

It was another good question. Access to firearms in Singapore was effectively impossible.

"No idea at all," replied Scott. "But it means he has a support operation locally. Wonder who?"

"Lots of good questions, you blokes are asking," broke in the sardonic tones of Benny who had been listening intently. "Anyone got any answers?" Nobody in the world could have suspected that two attempts had been made on his life in the last twenty-four hours.

"I've got one," said Scott quietly. The others looked at him. "Somebody in that group of wealthy businessmen leaked the sites," said the Englishman. "Either it's a direct connection or indirect. But it needs checking out."

"I'll get onto it," murmured Ong.

All these new questions joined another couple in Scott's mind and played leap-frog with each other for the rest of the day.

How did Nick know where to come? Only the men in the conference room yesterday knew which sites were being inspected. Where did Nick get the rifle? How was he going to get out of this Singapore island state? Just how extensive was the network for Knights of Aryan Dawn?

He had no answers for any of them.

The second inspection was an anticlimax. Benny bounded out of the car with exclamations of "Now that's more like it!" though the following bunch had to be cajoled from their cars like kittens being coaxed off a tree.

The building was a neat, freshly-finished, three storey structure, with lots of windows, and it was light and airy inside. Benny stood in the middle of the playing-field-sized empty ground floor, spread his arms and rotated happily.

"I'll take it!" he called to the crowd of followers standing close to the walls. "Let's go and have a beer!"

Benny was a happy man.

Ong hurriedly collected everybody, got them into their cars, climbed into the limousine with Benny and Scott and they raced back to the hotel.

"That's it?" Scott asked Benny. "Everything set for a decision?"

"Decision's made!" Benny replied with a wide smile. "I'll be in operation by February."

"So nobody else to see?"

"No! I'll go home tonight, give the news to all those expensive lawyers and accountants and let them get on with it. They'll sign anything that's needed and if they need help, they can ask."

"Simple as that?"

Benny looked at Scott. "Business *is* simple, Scott," he said. "The right decision nearly always stands out like a shag on a rock. Having the guts to make the decision, now that's another matter. All these consulting studies and evaluation committees, they just give an excuse to delay making your mind up and provide somebody else to blame when it gets screwed up."

Scott laughed at his refreshing philosophy. "Okay," he said. "So we get you on a plane tonight and back to Oz. I'm worried our guy will try again."

Benny shrugged. "Can't spend my life hiding from the bastard," he said. "I'll hire a security force. That should keep him out of my hair."

"I hope so," said Scott, with less faith in Benny's judgement than in his courage.

At seven-thirty that evening, the convoy collected for the last time and they took Benny to Changhi Airport. Using the same methods as before, ringed round with bodies they got him inside the Qantas First Class lounge, causing some stirs of interest from the others in there as the uniforms piled in.

Benny recognized some Australian business acquaintances in the lounge and was soon in deep conversation. Ong and Scott sat in a couple of armchairs to one side, carefully watching everybody who came in, but nobody of a passing resemblance to Nick entered.

At nine, the flight to Brisbane was called. They waited until everybody was on board then again walked Benny to the first class section at the front of the Boeing in the middle of a protective ring of bodies. As they reached his seat he stuck his hand out to Scott.

"An interesting experience, young Scott!" he grinned. "Let's not ever do it again!"

Scott laughed and shook his hand. "Take care in that outdoor lunatic asylum called Queensland, won't you?"

"I will. Come and see me if you get down there."

Scott nodded and moved back. Benny turned to Ong.

"Liang Sien, you're one hell of an operator!" he said, beaming widely. "Any time you want to move to Australia, call me. There's a job open whenever you want it. But you'll have to learn to speak like an Aussie. We can't have that bloody Pommie accent in Brisbane!"

"God forbid!" laughed Ong. "Take care, Benny."

They left him to the ministrations of a blond, Adonis-like flight steward and walked out of the aircraft which was immediately closed off in preparation for departure. They walked up to the observation deck to watch the Qantas Jumbo take off, with the mutual feeling that they wanted to see the job completed. Ong also understood that Scott liked to watch aeroplanes any time he could.

As they leaned against the rails with all the other sightseers, a small de Havilland corporate jet taxied past, the sleek lines beautifully set off by the silver and black paint job under the flood lights. "Tumokam," said the single word painted on the tail, above a black square with two red lightning flashes through it. The de Havilland had a Malaysian registration.

"Any idea who Tumokam is?" Scott asked lazily, envying the luxury in which some people travelled.

Ong turned to stare at the craft. "Money," he said shortly. "Private company out of Kota Kinabalu in Sabah. That's East Malaysia, on the island of North Borneo."

"I know it," replied Scott. "Sabah's a pretty conservative Moslem state as I remember. You know the company?"

"Tunku Mohammed bin Kamahl."

"Oh yeah?"

"Tunku's a title. Like a Knighthood in England, bestowed by the king. Mohammed owns millions of acres of cocoa, timber and pepper concessions. He's probably one of the ten richest men in the world."

"Oh." Scott was feeling the heat of the day finally getting to him on top of all the excitement, danger and shock of the awfully near miss with a heavy calibre shell. He found it hard to work up much excitement about Tunku Mohammed bin Kamahl.

"Known to be almost a fanatical Moslem," continued Ong. An edge had crept into his voice and the lines of his body leaning against the rail were no longer relaxed in weariness but taut and angry. Some new thought had reached him and the effect was unpleasant. "Not like most Malays, who are pretty moderate. Rumours tend to float around that he's helped finance some Middle East nasties."

"Not a nice man." Scott began to wake up under the prod of the sharp note in Ong's voice. With a shock of almost lethal intensity, he remembered where he had seen that logo before. Beautifully polished dress shoe pushing back the cuff of a dead man... *"Knights of Aryan Dawn, Mister McIntyre...."* Many of the questions that had been racing through his head like mice chased by angry cats were lying down, answers gripped by tense claws.

180

"A very powerful man," said Ong. "Nobody would search his aircraft when he came in to Singapore or when he left."

They were leaning against the railings, staring at the de Havilland corporate jet with fascination.

"A useful man to know if you wanted to sneak into the city for some purpose of anti-Semitic evildoing, right?"

"Right." Ong's voice had sharpened more as he heard and sensed the explosive tension build in Scott. "Getting heavy guns and bringing them into the city would be easy for such a man too, I suppose."

"Probably. And having an employee treated for gunshot wounds would be a snip, right? No reporting to a hospital or the police. Private doctor would be easy."

"Bloody simple!" The rage in Ong's voice was belied by the casual way he leaned on the railing.

"Just for the hell of it, Liang Sien, why don't we find out just when that aircraft arrived in Singapore?"

"Sure thing, my little *gwai-loh.*"

"And find out which of those rich bastards in the conference room has got ties to Tumokam."

"They'll all have ties to Tumokam."

"Bummer."

In silence for the next ten minutes they watched the de Havilland taxi to the darkness at the end of the runway then thunder toward them, reappearing in the floodlights, lifting off cleanly and folding its wheels away. In his mind, Scott followed through the series of operations and instructions which would be flowing on the flight deck as the graceful little machine climbed into the night sky on its return to Kota Kinabalu.

I wonder if Nick's healthy enough to be having a drink in luxury in the back, Scott thought. *And I wonder if he's worried about the reception he's going to get in Kota Kinabalu for his failure.*

* * *

Another day in Singapore. Nobody to protect, not a lot for Scott to do but wait for Ong Liang Sien to follow through his spider's web of connections and trace whatever facts were available. The flight home left that evening. Scott took a seat across from Ong's desk and accepted a bottle of orange juice.

The Tumokam corporate jet had arrived ten days ago, stayed barely two hours and left, Ong had discovered. Only corporate personnel on board, said the manifest, and there were no records of names of passengers when it left. There was no record of passengers when the plane returned to Changhi on the morning of the attempted hit in the lobby of the Westin Plaza, nor when it left again last night.

Ong's attempts to find the names of the immigration staff who dealt with the arrivals and departures on those days were met by a blank wall. A lot of money had been laid around the place at all levels, it seemed.

"I'll let Jessica tell you," said Ong, and pressed a button on the side of his desk. A moment later, the receptionist walked in. She beamed her sunshine smile at Scott and sat demurely at Ong's right.

"How many of the tycoons at the meeting at the Prime Minister's Lodge are involved with Tumokam?" asked Ong.

"They all are," said Jessica. "I researched every one of them and found many financial ties with Tumokam interests."

"Anything special or out of the ordinary?" asked Scott.

Jessica shrugged daintily.

"Impossible to find out," she replied. "I have rumours, but tracks have been covered pretty well. I have no doubts however, that at least four of the men in that meeting are involved in Tumokam affairs in projects worth billions of dollars."

"So they would follow any orders from Kota Kinabalu, naturally," said Scott.

"Without hesitation," replied Jessica. "All of them could have provided the weapon and medical assistance when your man was hit. My father knows them all well. Not one of them could be trusted to act independently."

"I don't know if anyone can ever touch Tumokam," said Ong, putting his empty bottle of soy milk on the book case behind him. "Too rich, too powerful, too well connected."

"Probably." Scott toyed with his bottle of orange juice, twirled it around on the desk, then he finished it with an angry gulp. "But it gives me the running squitters."

Ong shrugged. "Facts of life, little *gwai-loh*. But if we can wipe out this Nazi connection, we'll have improved the world's pollution level no end."

"I suppose so," muttered Scott, unconvinced. "Have to settle for that."

"You will. Not a bad thing to settle for, when you think about it."

"It's still hard to believe it can be Nick!" Scott squirmed in his chair. "I've known him for eighteen years, now he turns up as the killer I've been hunting for four years. And he killed my parents! It makes no bloody sense at all!"

"There I agree with you. It's too far-fetched. Which only means there must be more to it."

Scott stood up. "To hell with it! I want to go shopping!"

"Spoken like a true *gwai-loh!*"

Jessica giggled and looked like a teenager asked about her boyfriend. "I can give you a couple of stores where you'll get good prices," she said. "Just say Jessica Chiang Hoy sent you."

Armed with her data and name, Scott bought a new camera, a pair of jade earrings for Janette and a couple of Batik shirts. Then he met Ong at the airport for a final beer in the departure lounge, they said their true-blue, British goodbyes with handshakes, a couple of biting insults and not a trace of emotion. Not for anyone to see, anyway.

Chapter 8 – Discoveries

The sight of her as Scott came out of the arrivals gate at Heathrow was like all his Christmases and birthdays come together. They clung to each other, oblivious of the madding crowd milling around them.

"I've started to get very frightened when you go away," she whispered into his neck.

"We always knew it would get complicated," he said with a final hug, then took her hand and began to lead her to the exit.

"I'm not complaining," she said softly. "It's worth every second of it. But I do get frightened."

He looked down at the soft, so-young face with her serious eyes. "Me too. One day, I'll change my operational status and move into something less nervy. But I can't yet."

"I know. We'll survive it, somehow."

"Of course we will. I'm not letting you go now, young woman."

She laughed, and squeezed his hand. "Who's not letting who go?"

"I refuse to answer! Where's your car?"

"There!" she pointed at the car park building across the road. Eventually, they made it out of the airport, onto the M4 and round London to the M1. Scott was happy to sit in the passenger seat and watch her concentration as she drove with the same expression she wore when she was working at her computer terminal.

Just once, she looked sideways at him and smiled. "Good to have you back, McIntyre," she said.

"Stay at my place tonight, young lassie?"

"Try keeping me away!"

"Good!" he smiled and dozed off, despite the ninety miles-an-hour or more that she was maintaining.

He was still groggy from the long flight when they arrived at the office, and he followed Janette almost like a blind man being led. He was halfway to his office when he realized that the day was Saturday. He stopped and said "Er..." which was hardly an accurate interrogation, but when Janette muttered the magic words, "Sir Martin wants to see you," he woke up completely.

Jamieson astonished him by standing up when Scott came in, shaking his hand and echoing Janette's words. "Good to have you back, McIntyre!" he said with a searching look into Scott's face. Scott almost laughed at the coincidence of the echo of Janette's words, but resisted it. The Air Marshal was dressed in perfect RAF off-duty style, a dark blazer with the Squadron crest of his last command, silk cravat, smartly-creased grey slacks.

"Thank you, sir," Scott said firmly.

"Let me pour you some coffee," muttered Jamieson, almost as if struggling to get the words out. Scott was flabbergasted. The Old Man pouring him coffee? What was going on? This was a first to end all firsts.

"Er.. thank you, sir," he managed to respond and watched with fascination as Jamieson poured the steamy liquid into both his own massive RAF mug and a smaller, plain one for Scott. Then he handed the latter one to Scott and returned to his seat. He seemed to be deep in thought.

"Have a doughnut, too," he said as an afterthought. The box was full but after the wonderful food of Singapore, Scott's taste for junk had diminished. He shook his head.

"Ong called me from Singapore and told me the general story and he also sent a complete signal," Jamieson said, putting the

185

blue mug on a coaster and leaning back. "So I'm aware of what happened. You've done a splendid job of identifying al-Yaffi. I believe we can call him Dieter Konig from this point on."

"Or Nick Wallace." The pain was still there when Scott thought of it. An expression of distaste crossed Jamieson's face and he reached forward and took a sip of the coffee.

"Er... yes, as you say. Nick Wallace. I'm truly sorry about that. I know what a good friend of yours he is."

"Was, sir."

"No, Scott. Is. I want you to try and maintain a connection with him, if possible."

"Good grief, sir! How the hell can I do that, now I know what he is?"

"Not easily. But do you think he knows that you have identified him?"

Scott stopped short. Actually, there was no reason for Nick to suspect that at all, he thought. Unless he knew of Scott's trip to Germany and the visit to his parents. Scott could hardly think Nick would have discovered that. Only Jamieson, Allan Hopkins and Scott knew about that trip, except for Janette and Marjorie. Perkins was obviously Nick's link into Mongoose Section and Perkins had been killed well before Scott had planned to return to Germany.

"No, sir, I don't," he said.

"Then try and stay near him," said Jamieson. "We need to know just how far his network extends."

"I'll try, sir. But if I find it's impossible to hide my reaction, it would be safer to avoid him."

"Yes, I agree. Do try, Scott."

Scott nodded, wondering how the hell he was going to be able to do it.

"Sir?"

"Yes, Scott?"

"Do I know the entire story about Dieter Konig?"

Jamieson looked hard at him for a few seconds then picked up the coffee mug and cupped his hands around it as if looking for warmth.

"Explain," he said.

Scott took a few seconds to rearrange his thoughts then released the worries. "I've known Nick Wallace for eighteen years," he said. "If we assume that he *is* Dieter Konig, and all the signs point to that conclusion, then when I met him, he was probably just a recruit into Knights of Aryan Dawn and had learned how to be an Englishman somewhere. But he wasn't al-Yaffi then, and he hadn't started his career of killing people."

"Yes," Jamieson said shortly and continued to watch his agent with care.

"And me, I was just a bright-eyed kid, full of visions of flying fast jets. I'd never heard of you, and anyway, you were still in the RAF commanding a Bomber Group somewhere in Strike Command."

Jamieson nodded. "Mongoose Section hadn't been formed at that time, and wouldn't be for another six years when I retired."

"You sought me out when I left the RAF, recruited me and assigned me to looking for al-Yaffi. The coincidence that he would turn out to be my friend Nick is just too big. What is it that you haven't told me, sir?"

Jamieson sat back, cradled his coffee and looked for a few moments at the photo of himself as a young pilot officer. "I was just as astonished and equally confused when Janette showed me the conclusions about Nick Wallace," he said suddenly, turning back to Scott. "I said the same thing, this was just too great a coincidence. I'd recruited you because you had a personal commitment to getting al-Yaffi but I didn't anticipate this. But if you look at it from another direction it may not be a coincidence at all."

"How so?"

"Scott, you're quite right," said Jamieson, not answering the question. "There's something about all this that you don't know. It's time you learned it."

Scott felt a shock go through him. Jamieson was so serious, so sad, Scott knew the information he was about to hear would be painful. He put his coffee mug on the table and waited. And it was worse than he had expected.

"The bomb in Barcelona," said Jamieson. "Conventional wisdom has always been that it was a mistake, that al-Yaffi was aiming at a trio of French diplomats staying in the hotel during a NATO conference. A rare, but understandable mistake, everybody said."

Cold panic washed like a slimy waterfall over Scott. He couldn't say a word, he just watched Jamieson. The Air Marshal was looking at the blotter on his desk, picking his words with obvious care.

"Scott, it wasn't a mistake," he said. "Al-Yaffi got his intended target. The diplomats were a fog to confuse the issue."

"My parents and sister?" Scott forced the words out through a throat feeling like sandpaper. "How could that be?"

"Not all three of them, no. Just your mother."

"What?"

"Just how much do you know about your mother, Scott?"

Scott was having trouble breathing. Terrible pictures of the scene that had met him in Barcelona, the wrecked building, the bodies on the morgue table, they were fighting for front position in his head with the incomprehensible things Jamieson was saying to him.

"She... she was a teacher, a music teacher, for God's sake, in a girls' school in a small town in Berkshire. What the hell does she..."

Jamieson raised a hand and his power of command worked as it always did. Scott ceased his nearly hysterical outburst and sat back again.

"Tell me what you know about her background." Jamieson had issued an order and Scott obeyed instinctively. His years of military discipline took over, and he calmed down, began to recite what he knew in a controlled voice, not letting himself think about the implications of what was going on.

"She was born in Bristol in 1934, married my father in 1968," said Scott. "I was born two years later. Her parents were both school teachers in Gloucestershire but they died before I was born. She studied music at Birmingham University. I know that she worked in Scotland for a couple of years at a school in Edinburgh then moved to Reading after she met my father at a New Year's Eve party."

Jamieson shook his head. "That's the identity which British Intelligence worked up for her," he said. He paused and looked at Scott as if checking to see if he was ready. "Your mother was born in Warsaw, Poland, in 1930. Her name was Katerina Horowitz. She was Jewish, her parents were killed during the Nazi destruction of the Warsaw ghetto. She was just a thirteen-year-old when she managed to get out from that bloody monstrosity and she joined a Jewish resistance group. She killed her first Nazi when she was fourteen, apparently tripping him up when he walked into an alley to relieve himself, then garrotting him with a piano wire. There were others, later."

Scott stared at him. He could have been drugged, so immobile was he under the heavy clubbing of the words Jamieson was speaking.

"She survived and made it to Palestine in 1945," continued Jamieson. "She fought in the war of 1948 against the Arabs and was recruited by the security forces in 1950. A year later, she went on her own into Syria and discovered a plan for the invasion of Israel by Syrian and Iraqi forces with considerable support from German business and military interests. The Israelis were able to kill most of the Arab leaders of that plot, as well as several of the Germans, all ex-Nazis. It was hushed up for political reasons but in many ways, your mother was considered to have saved Israel. It made her unpopular with the Arabs and with those Nazis who knew about her."

Scott could do nothing but sit motionless. It could have been a story of some unknown person he was hearing, but the tale was so chillingly realistic that he was almost narcotised by it. Jamieson looked at him for a few seconds as if measuring his capacity for any more, then continued.

"Mossad decided that she should get out of Israel and go into hiding to escape the Arabs' efforts which were being launched to kill her. By agreement with the British, she came here and got a new identity. Your father was told the whole story at her insistence before they were married, and he accepted the risks. Everything seemed to be fine, but clearly something went wrong."

Through numbed lips, as if he had just come from the dentist, Scott scraped some words out. An idea had come to him just as Jamieson spoke the final sentence.

"I think somebody was watching her for a long time," he mumbled.

"How do you reckon that, Scott?"

"Maybe meeting Nick at Nottingham was not an accident. Maybe the Knights of Aryan Dawn had given him the assignment of watching my mother through me. Maybe they weren't sure about her and I was a good way of getting near to her and studying her better. Nick visited my home in Reading on a number of occasions. He took lots of photos, especially of my mother."

"Yes. That's what I think happened." Jamieson was looking at him calmly.

"So perhaps that time I met him again by accident in Munich, it wasn't a coincidence either. He'd probably sent all those photographs of my mother to his headquarters, wherever that is, and they'd decided she was who they thought. They decided to take action and I was still the best route to her. I always told Nick where my parents were going...."

Oh God! Now he realized why Nick had always been so interested in his family's doings and why he had taken so many pictures of Scott's mother. Nick had always asked about their holiday plans and Scott could remember telling him that they were going to Barcelona that autumn.

Scott looked up at Jamieson and found the Old Man was studying him with care. The dark eyes were compassionate.

"This is more than I can handle at the moment," said Scott, his jaws and lips still numbed.

"Yes," said Jamieson simply. "But you'll handle it in time."

Scott found that hard to believe just then but inside himself, he knew his boss was correct. Just as Scott had returned to his squadron after burying his parents and Leanne and resumed flying duties with no discernible effect on his skills, he would quickly return to Mongoose readiness.

"Go home, Scott, and get some sleep." The Air Marshal stood up, closing the meeting. "Tomorrow, I want you to track down all of Wallace's movements and see if you can identify any of his contacts."

Scott stood up, stiffly, as if he had been in his chair for hours. "Yes sir, I'll do that."

"Oh, and Scott?"

Scott turned from the door he was about to open and looked back.

"I imagine you'll be working Janette pretty hard when you get back in," said Jamieson. "I've cleared her of all other duties except assisting you. So why don't both of you go home, and choose your own hours from now on?"

Ye gods, the Boss condoning sexual shenanigans in the office! What's the world coming to? Scott managed to smile at the older man and left to give the good news to Janette.

191

A Friendly Killing

Later that afternoon, lying close together in the shadowy dusk of autumnal light sneaking through the occasional gaps in his curtains. In a way which had never happened before, the dams of grief broke open when Scott got home and he had wept for over an hour in Janette's arms before he could regain control. Soon after that, the warmth and softness of her inspired other ideas they explored to the full before finally falling asleep.

"I love you."

"I love you, too. Going away is getting very hard."

"I'm terrified when you do."

"I need to get Dieter Konig before I stop."

"I know."

A long silence.

"Scott?"

"Mmm?"

"Do you think you could do that again?"

"Holy cow, woman! I'm exhausted!"

"I know. But do you?"

"Give me five minutes."

It actually took ten, but he was able.

* * *

They rose early after so much sleep and treated themselves to a leisurely and luxurious breakfast at a restaurant in Acock's Green before going into the office. Scott felt closer to her than ever before and was happy to look at her gentle, lovely face as she studied the menu. Occasionally, she looked up at him and the smile was worth hours of conversation.

They walked out of the restaurant an hour later, hand in hand, thoroughly replete with fried eggs, chips and bacon, lots of coffee, toast and jam. Lunch would be unnecessary, which was just as well because they could be spending a long hard day in front of the computer screen, depending how difficult it was going to be to find the data they were seeking.

They planned the campaign with care, for a huge amount of computer time might be demanded. They sat together by her computer terminal, alone in the room this quiet Sunday morning. Scott carried a second terminal from another desk and placed it alongside hers, so that she could work two together. A couple of other people were in also but they worked in a different section, analysing and filing the signals after they had been decoded. They worked for Janette so it was easy for her to ask them to use another office.

"I've identified the credit cards issued to Nick Wallace," she said, rapidly keying in to the left hand computer terminal line after line of security codes that permitted her to gain access to the computer networks of the financial institutions. The computer screen displayed a short message "Please wait" and she moved the keyboard away. "I also checked out the name of Unsworth that I identified as being the one person who had been both a day-traveller to Geneva and also flew to New York before the Toronto killing."

"Clever lady!" smiled Scott. "What did you find?"

"Diners Club, American Express and a Post Office box in Knightsbridge," she said, with a slightly smug expression. "We'll check out transactions on that card too. It will take a few minutes to log in, so we'll use this one to get into the airline systems." She pulled the keyboard of the second terminal toward her and began to repeat the process of entering security codes. Scott watched with a mixture of love and fascination.

She took his hand for a moment and held it between both of hers. "This is terrible, Scott," she murmured, staring at the left screen which had begun to flash line after line of messages which were inexplicable to him. "I can't imagine how you must feel."

"Nor can I," he said, sadly. "I've had more crazy information that I can properly absorb these last few days. Nick, then my mother... I still can't really believe it."

She gave his hand a final squeeze and let go as the left screen suddenly came alive with a list of action choices. She hit a key and entered the name of Nicholas Francis Wallace followed by a series of numbers.

"This will bring out all Nick's credit card transactions for the last three months," she said. "We can follow a lot of his movements. Then we'll link the data to the airline system and see just what he's been up to."

"Fine," murmured Scott, still rather overawed by the extent of the power she had to pry into people's lives. He had no worries about Janette's ethics, but the thought of all this Peeping Tom capability in the hands of somebody with less personal integrity was definitely scary to him.

She turned to the menu of choices that had appeared on the second screen and again she entered Nick's name and a series of numbers, which Scott now saw were dates specifying the first of June through to yesterday, the last day of August.

She turned to him. "When do you want to get married?" she said with a small smile. He reached for her hands again.

"Last Tuesday!" he said, straight-faced.

"Difficult."

"Not if we hurry."

"Silly man!"

"Yes, madam."

"I suppose we'd better wait until we've cleared up this little matter," she said with a tiny wave of her free hand at the computer screens.

"I think the boss would say the same thing," Scott agreed. "But as soon as possible after that, okay?"

"Okay," she smiled, and turned back to the screens. Nothing had changed on either of them since entering Nick's name and the dates for which transactions were to be selected.

"I think a tea break is in order," she said, rising from her chair in her smooth, graceful motion. "The systems are busy this morning."

"Then to the kitchen, woman!"

She blew him a raspberry. "Your turn to make it!"

He followed her toward the lounge, grumbling audibly about women being out of control ever since some fool gave them the vote. It received an even louder rude noise.

Ten minutes later, they were back at the desk sipping at the fragrant, mint-flavoured tea. A series of lines had appeared at the left hand screen. The other had not changed.

"What I've done," she said, "is to extract all his credit card transactions for the three cards I could find issued to him. Then they were sorted by date so we should see all his expenses in chronological order."

"Great! Should be interesting."

"All right, let's see what we have," she said quietly and pointed at the top of the screen. "July seven, Nick has dinner at a hotel in Berne, Switzerland. He's checked into the same place. He stays there all week, has dinners at various places during the week...."

"Undoubtedly with various stunningly beautiful women," muttered Scott.

"Undoubtedly. Let's not be jealous, shall we?"

"Sorry, miss!"

She grinned at him for a second and returned to the green letters and figures on the black background of the screen.

"Aha!" she said, and looked at the right hand screen which now also displayed lines of data. "That checks with the airline schedules. Look..." She pointed. "Nick flew from London to Berne on the seventh and back again on the twelfth."

"Looks like a legitimate business trip. At least, a trip he could claim to be legitimate business."

She nodded. "Looks like it. And he stayed in England over the weekend. But he flew out on the sixteenth, to Berlin."

"That was the trip he said he did when he made that major sale in Germany."

"Yes, and he checked into a hotel for two nights... dinner again... lunch... looks like he only stayed two nights on the sixteenth and seventeenth... back in again on the twenty-fourth... And there's his return flight to London on the twenty-fifth. That's strange!"

"What was he doing between the seventeenth and the twenty-fourth?"

"Exactly," she said. "There's a complete blank in activities on his credit card and nothing on his travel record."

Scott looked at the notes that he had completed after the first meeting with Allan and Jamieson. "The German military attaché was shot in Milan on the twenty-third," he said. "Nick would need at least a week to prepare such an event, scout out the area, test his guns and all that."

She looked sideways at him. "It could fit, couldn't it? He flies from Berlin to Milan with different identity papers. He does the killing, returns to Berlin, stays another day then flies back to England under his own name."

Scott nodded. "And he's back in time to have dinner with us and tell us about his successful visit to Berlin. Of course he's happy! He probably made three or four hundred thousand tax-free pounds for that killing!"

"My God!" she said sharply. "And he tells us he's likely to get another deal the following week! He must already have been negotiating the hit on Richardson in Toronto!"

"Perhaps he travelled to Milan using the Unsworth name?" suggested Scott. She nodded.

"Let's have a look," she said, and began tapping in extra data. They watched with the excitement of the hunt growing. Suddenly, more lines appeared on the screen.

"Well now, look at that!" she said softly. Scott leaned forward. "This mythical Mister Unsworth flew from Berlin to Milan the day after Nick reached Berlin," she continued, tracing the lines of data on the screen with one finger. "And flew back again to Berlin the day before Nick returned home."

"Let's keep going," he said, waving at the computer screens. She scrolled down to the next batch of information and pointed once more.

"This is where Nick goes off to Berlin again, just as he said he was doing. That's on the thirtieth of July. And here are his credit card details for the hotel and dinner that night. But he's only there for one night. No more transactions from the next day till...." she continued scrolling down the data. "... till Thursday, the eighth of August when he flies back to London from Berlin."

"So there's a gap from the thirty-first till the eighth. Exactly the period covering the Toronto hit?"

"That's it."

"Can we trace the Unsworth transactions?"

"Of course."

Another few minutes passed, and then she pointed. "There it is. The same flight I tracked before. Unsworth flies from London to New York. In fact, here's the flight from Berlin the same morning, connecting with the flight out of Heathrow. And here's his connection to Toronto, in plenty of time to set up the Richardson killing, and the return to New York a couple of hours after he did it."

"Seems to prove it, doesn't it?" Scott felt cold and sad.

"I'm sorry, Scott."

"Well, that's life. It's what we expected. Let's keep going. Any more details for the rest of this month?"

"Looks like it," she said, pointing at the left hand screen. "There's his dinner bill for our second evening out with him in Solihull on the seventeenth that he insisted on paying for. My God, did it cost that much?"

Scott peered at the screen. "It surely did! We had two bottles of the French bubbly, remember!"

"Wow! But Scott! Look! A few days earlier, on the thirteenth, he used his card at a garage in Sutton. And on Thursday the fifteenth, he had either lunch or dinner at a restaurant in Tamworth. Wasn't that the time we thought he was in Karachi when he killed Perkins?"

"Good grief!" Scott stared hard at the screen and studied his notes again. According to the timetable he had worked out, Nick had returned from his Geneva meeting with Perkins on the twelfth. If he was in England between the thirteenth and the seventeenth, he had no time to fly to Karachi and kill Perkins. But somebody most certainly had killed Perkins. Allan Hopkins had found him somewhat dead, as he put it, on the fifteenth.

It emphasized the question he had asked of Ong in Singapore. If Nick hadn't killed Perkins, who the hell had?

"And he's off again," she continued, pointing at the right hand screen. "This time to Stuttgart on the Sunday after our dinner in Solihull. But no hotel, no transactions of any sort. He's got an open return from Stuttgart and he's not used it yet."

"He could have transferred immediately to a flight to somewhere in the Malaysian region using different papers. Wherever he landed, I'd say he was met by the Tumokam private jet. He either went straight to Singapore or somewhere else for the briefing on the attempt on Benny Moskowitch."

"That's the last transaction on any of his credit cards or his airline schedule," she said, sitting back in her chair and turning to him. "And there are no other records for Unsworth. He must have used another name for going to Malaysia or else he flew on a private aircraft."

"That's possible, too."

"I'll print it all out for you," she said, turning back to the keyboards.

"Please, honey, I'll need it for the report to Jamieson. We found all that stuff in very little time."

"He didn't cover his tracks all that well," she replied. "He was getting careless and over-confident."

A few moments of silence passed while they listened to the sighing of the laser printer pushing out the damning evidence against Nick. The sound was the death knell to the friendship that had meant so much to Scott the last seventeen years, almost half his life. It had been meaningless, a play-act designed for Nick to watch Scott's mother and confirm that she was the Polish girl who had destroyed the plans of a bunch of Arab and Nazi maniacs. And with that assurance they had killed her, together with Scott's father and a sixteen-year-old girl who had adored the man who had committed the slaughter.

He realized that Janette was staring at him. The printer had finished its task several minutes ago and Scott was alone in a small hell of his own.

"Scott?" Her voice was hesitant.

He smiled at her. "You realize one thing, don't you?" he said gently.

"What's that?" She looked worried.

"You're the only thing I've got left. I hope you'll stick around."

"I'm not going anywhere," she whispered and came into his arms.

"Yes, you are," he murmured into her right ear. "To my place and straight to bed."

"Good!" she said. "I thought you'd never ask!"

* * *

Monday morning in Birmingham dawned with the first scents of autumn and the tiniest, most delicate feel of the cool to come. September had started beautifully, and everybody in the office had that cheerful expression of being in tune with the elements. Despite the pain and shocks of the last few weeks, even

199

Scott's jaded spirit responded to the glorious weather. The therapies in which he and Janette had indulged to round off a Sunday morning spent in the office also helped.

He spent most of the morning writing up the report without which no activity was complete. The contents of his five or six pages would have made the hair of any normal business reader stand on end, and not even the dry, journalistic tones could hide the impact of the words.

His best friend was an international killer for hire. Nick Wallace was also a weapon used widely by a neo-Nazi group in Germany. For a few seconds Scott wondered if the paranoid minds running the British Intelligence departments would think of suspecting him because of his friendship with Nick then discounted the idea. The friendship was a direct result of Nick's search for Scott's mother. Nick had used him as a conduit to her. Scott was merely the pawn. Jamieson would certainly kill off any silliness in that direction.

The Air Marshal confirmed that himself, early in the afternoon, when he returned from a meeting in London and called Scott as soon as he walked into the office. Scott followed Jamieson's stocky frame that was clad as usual in a superbly cut grey suit, gleaming black shoes and neat grey hat. The doughnut box was sitting by the side of the coffee pot where it had been placed that morning. It was wrapped in a plastic covering to keep the contents fresh and the plastic was still in place. Scott detected a single longing glance at the box from Jamieson as they walked in but Jamieson's discipline held. He hung his hat on the rack and sat at his desk.

"Coffee, Scott?"

"Thank you sir. Can I pour you one?"

"Er.. yes, good idea, why not?"

Kabuki theatre again. Scott acted out his role, Jamieson acted out his, and as always, they ended up sitting across from each other on either side of the massive desk.

"Hell of a story, McIntyre."

"Yes, sir."

"You and Janette did a remarkable job, tracing all those movements of Wallace. Ties him conclusively to the al-Yaffi killings."

Scott said nothing. Jamieson looked at him, the gentleness in his eyes not hidden by the shadows.

"We'll wrap it all up soon, Scott. But you need to try and find his connections. I'm still worried that he may have more conduits into British Intelligence."

"Did Mongoose Two find anything on Perkins, sir?"

Jamieson shook his head. "Looks like simple money problems," he said. "Perkins has absolutely no history to indicate any Nazi leanings. But he was heavily into debt from gambling. Looks like the Knights of Aryan Dawn were able to buy his cooperation. And of course, once he'd helped them to any extent, blackmail would keep him under control."

"How about the Malaysian connection, Tumokam?"

"Obviously the money source. Just how it might tie in with any German business or political bodies may never be found out. We've initiated some inquiries through the German Chancellor but I've little hope of any success there. And the Malaysian Government has already refused any help."

"So what can we do?"

"Just fight our own part of the war, clean up our own house and find any other links that Wallace has. Then we'll pull in Wallace himself. I'll have other people do that, Scott."

"Yes, sir."

"So this is what I want you to do, McIntyre." Scott sat up a little. "Make contact with Wallace as soon as you can," said Jamieson. "Try and show him that you've not yet linked him to this business, that you suspect nothing. He knows who and what you are but if he believes that you are still unaware of his identity, something may slip. If he tells you about any future travels we need to know immediately and place an alert out on anyone who may be his target."

"And if he seems to realize that I do know about him?"

Jamieson's face was grim. "Then you bring him in at once. Or if that's impossible, make sure he doesn't go anywhere."

Scott stood up to leave, returned his coffee mug to the sideboard and walked to the door.

"Mongoose Three?"

"Sir?"

"Stay armed. Stay alert."

"Yes, sir."

Scott thought he saw the old man moving to the doughnut box as he closed the door.

* * *

Kirstie sounded tense when Scott called Nick's office. Making the call had been an exercise in heart-thumping nervousness for him. He had spent an hour working out different things to say to Nick if he got through to him, then finally gave up and decided to play it just as if he knew nothing and was calling to invite Nick out for a drink one evening.

"I'm sorry, Mister McIntyre, Mister Wallace is still in Europe though we expect him back any day."

Kirstie's tension was so strong her voice was a pitch higher than normal.

"Okay, Kirstie, ask him to call me as soon as he gets in, either here or at home. Tell him to call Janette if I can't be reached."

"I'll do that, Mister McIntyre."

Was there a trace of mockery in her voice? wondered Scott. She could not have expected the call and she was obviously well aware of what Nick's real activities were. She had to be, Scott realized. Nick could hardly do what he did, hardly travel under assumed names without her being a part of his support team. *Maybe I was imagining the mockery* thought Scott. *Maybe not.*

* * *

Scott spent the evening alone. He had not had any time to himself since receiving Jamieson's thunderbolts about his family and thus no chance to absorb the shocks. He needed some solitude. Janette had understood his need for isolation and had gone to her own apartment in Edgbaston to get some of her own domestic jobs tackled.

He got home early and made a light snack of cold cuts and fresh country loaf. He had several bottles of beer in the fridge and he decided a night of beer-swilling on his own was justified. He stood in his pleasant but small kitchen while he prepared the food and poured a bottle of Sam Smith's Pale Ale into a heavy glass mug. The first mouthful of cold beer tasted wonderful. He carried the meal back to the lounge room, sat on the Queen Anne settee and let his mind run itself. For the first time ever, he thought about his parents with an outsider's viewpoint.

He had not had any religious upbringing at all. Strange, now that he thought about it. His grandfather from Dundee had been a strict Scottish Presbyterian, that much Scott knew. And yet he had never insisted Scott attend church with him, nor that Scott's father should take him. He must have known about Scott's mother, but Scott knew that the old man had treated her like his own daughter, with much affection between them. She was always welcome at his house, the small cottage he had build in Emmer Green, north of the river, just outside Reading.

Scott had not gone to Sunday School with his friends, and to him, this had always been a source of delight and the envy of the other kids. But he had always thought of himself as simply a Protestant and had declared himself as such on his Royal Air Force application forms. He had attended Church Parades in the RAF, thinking little of it except as a boring way of spending a Sunday morning. Since then, he had gone to church only on special occasions, weddings of friends, a christening or two and midnight mass on Christmas Eve, his special favourite. He had been to a High Mass for the wedding of a Catholic friend, and found it a stirring, impressive event, though no more meaningful as a religious experience than anything else. The lunatic fringe of religion simply made him laugh.

But suddenly, he was Jewish. He knew nothing at all of the religion, having always regarded it as vaguely alien. He had never, to his recollection, been inside a synagogue. But he knew enough to know that the religion was passed down through the mother's line. Katerina Horowitz was a Polish Jew. Instead of being a Scots/English mixture as he had always regarded himself, now he was Scottish/Polish/Jewish. He had known several Israeli pilots during his training days, and was tremendously impressed by the way they always graduated top of the class. What he knew of the Israeli Air Force equally impressed him, as it did every professional military pilot in the world. They were simply the best. But he felt that their superiority was the result of commitment, constant danger and fine tuning, not any outgrowth of religious or philosophical leanings.

And it all meant nothing at all to him. Perhaps his parent's decision to give him no religious background at all was the best preparation of all for facing up to this new fact of life. Scott realized that he appeared to have no religious hangups at all.

Bless you, mum and dad. You did me proud.

His mother must have been one hell of an actress, decided Scott. Never for a second was there any sign that she was anything but an English girl from the south-west of England. Her accent had the slight burr of Gloucestershire, and Scott's musical ear had given him a fine capability to detect accents. Never once had he ever heard anything but Gloucestershire in her voice.

All in all, mother, you were one hell of a woman. As Nick said, you had oomph and pizzazz. I just never realized how much. Dad, you had great taste! I know you'd have both loved Janette, as she would have loved you.

Tears dropped into the Sam Smith ale but he began to get things straight in his head. The grief and shocks of the last few days settled into some private place that need never be disturbed. He was a very lucky man, he realized. He'd had fantastic parents, he would marry a woman of intelligence, grace and beauty, he did a job that mattered.

He drank three more bottles of Pale Ale, finished the fresh bread and cold cuts and went to bed, slightly drunk, but happy.

* * *

Nick called the next day just before lunch. When Scott heard his voice, a thunderous jolt of panic pounded through his body. He fought it hard.

"Hey, Wallace, you old bastard!" he said, as forcibly as he could to hide the nerves. "You've been away a long time!"

"I know. Tough trip, this time."

Nick sounded subdued, a little unhappy. Scott could imagine why. The Singapore event was maybe Nick's first major failure and he had probably taken a lot of heat from Tunku Mohammed bin Kamahl or his staff, never mind the loss of the pay for the botched job. Scott forced his voice to some sort of normalcy.

"Want to go for a beer or two tonight, kid?" he asked.

"Sure, sounds a great idea." Nick's tones were flat. "Need to talk to you. Any suggestions where?"

"What about the Old Mill?"

"Sounds good. Seven?"

"Seven it is. Take care, Nick, see you later."

"Sure, buddy."

Scott replaced the telephone, his hand trembling, stood up and told Marjorie to let Jamieson know about the conversation and meeting. She gave him a long, hard look.

"Backup?" she asked. Scott thought about that and decided against it.

"No," he said. "This will just be a talk between old friends. Not much he can do in a crowded pub and anyway, he still believes I think he's a boring old pill-pusher."

"I'll tell Sir Martin," she said.

"Thanks, Marjorie."

He felt the first sweat of fear in his hands.

He drove carefully down the country lanes on the south-west side of Birmingham to The Old Mill, one of his favourite drinking spots. Following the tree-lined roads, he found it difficult to think about what was about to happen. He and Nick had come to this pub often. It was all external white walls and black trim, oak panelling and dark corners on the inside. The beer was well kept and served at cellar temperatures, cool enough for thirst and just right for bringing out the flavour of the hops.

Nerves were threatening his composure. Luckily, the evening was cool and the sweat on his back, under his arms and on his wrists was reduced by the dusky air. He had on a close-fitting silk shirt under a carefully tailored, dark blue blazer which disguised the shoulder holster of his Browning nine-millimetre. Stay armed, Jamieson had said. You bet I will, Scott had agreed.

He parked the Honda against the tall green hedge at the back of the car park and walked into the pub. It was ten minutes after seven. Inside was warmth and human comfort, soft lights in corners, rosy reflections off polished pewter mugs and the rows of coloured bottles behind the bar. A British pub at its best. Something no other country in the world had ever imitated successfully and the thing he missed most when he was overseas. He was scared.

He hadn't seen Nick's Mercedes when he arrived but he stopped at the doorway and looked carefully at the crowd inside. There was no sign of Nick. He walked to the bar, leaned up to it and placed one foot comfortably on the brass rail. The sounds, smell and feel of a real pub surrounded him like donning a favourite old sweater.

"Evening, Scott! What can I get you?"

Angela was as cheerful as ever. A neat, compact woman in her late forties, wife of the publican, she ran the lounge bar with a friendliness and efficiency that one would expect of a one-time Petty Officer in the Women's Royal Navy.

"A pint of your best bitter would go down a treat, Angela."

"Coming right up!"

She gave him her regular cheerful grin, took a heavy pint pot, placed it under the spout of the tap and pulled on the large brass handles of the pump.

"Your lovely lady coming in tonight, Scott?" She wiped the foam off the top of the beer mug and placed it in front of him.

"Slumming it tonight, love! Bloody Wallace is coming in at any moment!" For a moment, the atmosphere and her familiar presence made him forget that his old friend, Bloody Wallace was an international killer.

"My God! Two sexy bachelors at my bar, unattached! I'll have to watch the place and make sure no women are left unattended!"

He grinned at her and took a long pull at her excellent beer. The strong flavour worked wonders on his nerves and he felt himself begin to settle down. He turned round, leaned back against the bar and tried to behave as if it was any other evening in his favourite pub, with his best friend about to join him for a friendly chat about the world. He looked at some of the patrons, wondering what they think if they knew of the reasons for Scott's presence at the bar.

A huge man in a blue suit which could have been used as a car cover was standing with three other men, all holding pint pots of beer, nodding affably. Two men in farmer's overalls leaned against the bar a few feet away from Scott, jointly reading the Daily Telegraph sports section laid out on the bar. They had the timeless look of men who spent their lives growing things. Their pipes were inclined at equal angles away from each other to allow a clear sight of the newspaper as they bent over it. A young man leaned sideways against a pillar, holding his beer mug protectively against his chest. He wore a red sports shirt over blue jeans. A logo of some sort on the back pocket indicated the jeans were priced above rational levels. His companions were two similarly dressed, smart young men of some affluence, and a petite woman in a short grey dress and hair down to the backs of her thighs. She wore a blue denim cap at the back of her head and managed to look cute despite the get-up.

Good English people, mused Scott, warm and secure in their Englishness. They lived with that calm certainty inbred in all of them that God was an Englishman, that British ways were best and that foreigners had no idea about how to do anything. There'll always be an England and all that. *Nick would like to change that,* he thought, and he turned back to the bar.

A moment later, he saw Angela's face break into the warm smile of welcome and flirtation that only one person other than her husband could cause, and the familiar old voice spoke behind him.

"Already pissed out of your tiny mind, I suppose, McIntyre?"

A tiny cold shiver ran through Scott, then he killed it, smiled and turned around.

"Wallace, you old bastard!" he said. "Just because you can't keep civilized time I have to get the beer poured first! Angela!" Scott waved at her. "Another pint for this pathetic old fool here!"

Just for a second the two men stared at each other. Nick's face was thinner than Scott remembered, his obvious tension reflected Scott's own and there was no warmth in his eyes. He leaned up against the bar alongside Scott and seemed to flinch slightly as his body touched the wooden edge. Scott looked sideways at him. There was an expression of pain in Nick's face.

"You okay, Nick?"

"Hell, yes! Just a bit tired, that's all. Had a bitch of a couple of weeks in Switzerland this time."

And Singapore and Kota Kinabalu, thought Scott. *Was that flinch of pain the effect of a bullet in your right side from a Singapore cop?*

"Well, Nick," he said. "It's time you earned all that fabulous wealth, anyway."

A fresh pot of beer was placed in front of Nick by the well-manicured hands of Angela.

"I suppose so." Nick looked as subdued as he sounded, not quite the gale force of a normal Nick. He picked up the beer with his left hand. "Cheers!" he said, and buried his face in the foam. His right hand stayed gripping the edge of the bar as if for support.

"Good health," muttered Scott, and took another pull at the familiar taste of bitter hops.

"How's Janette?" asked Nick, putting the mug back on the bar and leaning on both elbows. He kept his face looking down, not giving Scott his usual smile.

"In good shape. She sends her love. She's a bit tired too, worked pretty long hours while I was away the last few days." Scott sensed the massive dark void between them. They were playing some awful, essential game and the opening moves had not yet been completed.

"Where were you, this time?" asked Nick. "Another boring economic conference?"

Christ, Nick, you know bloody well where I was. You saw me. I was trying to stop you putting a bullet in the large body of Benny Moskowitch in Singapore. What are you doing, testing me? How the hell do I keep this up?

"No, just some Euro-currency debates in Milan," said Scott. "Nothing as thrilling as your exploits."

This was like some old, stately pavan. They stepped carefully around each other, going through paces, which would ensure nothing touched anything sensitive, avoiding awkwardness. People and conversations flowed around them. Bodies moved up to the bar and left, loaded with glasses or occasional trays. The smell of fresh-cooked meat pies floated gently through the bar and mixed with the odour of hops and liquor.

"Scott, this is getting difficult, this line of work."

I bloody bet it is. And I'm the one making it difficult, you bastard. Are you getting round to telling me something?

"What's the problem, kid? The pharmaceutical market getting tight?" *Or is the Mongoose Section beginning to close in too much for comfort? Has killing been so easy for you the last eight years that some real opposition is hurting you?*

Nick said nothing but picked up his beer mug awkwardly with his left hand, seemed to jerk a little with a flash of pain and took another draught. He looked to be thinking deeply about something.

"Yeah, the market's getting tough. I'm not sure I can keep this up," he muttered, so softly that Scott wasn't sure he had heard him.

Keep what up, Nick? The pretence that you aren't some vicious Nazi thug called Dieter Konig? That you haven't killed at least twenty people in the last eight years? That you didn't slaughter my family that had taken you into our home and given you their love and friendship? Or is it just the pretence that you were my friend for seventeen years that's causing you problems? Come on, you bastard! Let's have this out!

"What, the business pressures?" said Scott. "Hell, Nick, I thought you revelled in it!"

"Yeah, the business pressures," replied Nick. "Sometimes I wonder if it's worth all the tension and the danger to get this sort of result."

Tension and danger, Nick? You're supposed to be a pharmaceuticals marketer. Are you trying to find out if I'm stupid, or what?

"Tension and danger, Nick? What sort of business are you in, old son? Pharmaceuticals, or international espionage?"

Nick looked sideways at him, and the icy stare said it all. Then he dropped the thunderbolt.

"How did you get on with my parents, Scott?" he asked calmly.

Scott stayed hunched over his pot of beer for almost a minute, staring at the small streams of bubbles and breathing in the odour of hops. His brain seemed to stop working for a while. *How the hell did he know?* said his mind, over and over and over again. *How the hell did he know?*

"How the hell did you know?" he asked.

"You were followed all the way from Heathrow to Osnabruck."

"Why didn't you stop me?"

Nick shrugged. "We decided that would cause unnecessary attention. At the time, we still didn't know how much you knew. It seemed reasonable to leave you alone and you'd probably go down a dead end."

"So when did you decide that I hadn't?"

"Tonight," said Nick. "You're too tensed up. You've obviously caught on but I'm buggered if I know how."

"Too complex to explain."

Scott felt as if they were on a small island in the middle of a rushing torrent. The waters of social interaction boiled around them, leaving them isolated, alone, dealing with matters which had no place in the warmth and safety of an English country pub. He wondered what the people around them would think if they knew the subject of conversation of the two men leaning up against the bar in such companionable discussion. He and Nick were carrying on the conversation as if they were in a confessional, and nothing they could say would have any effect afterwards. They were out of time, out of reality, meeting in a world that had never existed before and would cease to be, the moment they broke the fragile bubble surrounding them.

"What the hell happened to Dieter Konig?" asked Scott.

Nick shook his head in confusion. "Dieter Konig!" he muttered, as if savouring an old, once-familiar name of a lover from an earlier lifetime. "I haven't heard that name in twenty years!"

Scott waited and let him indulge the pain and memories.

"I ran away," said Nick, looking into his beer mug. "My parents were old and tired already, by the time I was ten. They pretended that the war had never been, that Germany had not been defeated. They didn't see the American and British aeroplanes flying a hundred feet over their heads, nor the tanks in the countryside. Foreign armies in Germany! We had been betrayed for the second time in thirty years and they didn't care! Well, I did! And I wanted to do something about it!"

Scott's throat was dry, and he drank deeply of his beer.

"I knew that a group of the old men from the war were still meeting from time to time," Nick continued. "Singing the old songs and pretending that the Third Reich would rise again. I found them and they put me in touch with a more realistic organization."

"Knights of Aryan Dawn."

Nick nodded at his beer. "That's right. You learned about them in Chicago, I suppose?"

"Jesus Christ, Nick! You can't really believe all that crap? You want another Hitler, another Holocaust? You want the concentration camps again?"

"Don't be stupid, Scott!" Nick looked rapidly at Scott, then returned his gaze to the bar. "That was all unnecessary! Like all good ideas, the idiot politicians screwed it up! But the idea was right! We *are* racially superior! Not just Germans, that was stupid, but all of us, the white, intelligent races! Look at the way the other mobs screw up everything! Do you want to live in another Zimbabwe or Uganda?" He looked back at Scott.

Scott said nothing, but stared at his old friend. Nick's face was alive, some of the colour was back, his eyes flamed.

"The winners tell the history," Nick continued. "So all you hear about Germany is the Holocaust and Hitler's excesses! But look at the facts, Scott, the *facts!* We lifted ourselves up from the ashes after the first war, and became the greatest power in the world. Then we did it again after the second war. Look at our science, our engineering! We're still the supreme country!"

"And you prove it by killing people like Arnold Richardson and Benny Moskowitch?"

An expression of distaste flickered over Nick's eyes.

"Most of the killings were to make money for the Movement," he replied. "Those crazy Arabs have the money and if they want me to shoot a few Jews, I'm happy to take their cash. People like Moskowitch are a real threat anyway, they can influence public opinion. Richardson, we thought, could eventually become Prime Minister of Britain. We had to get rid of him."

So you don't mind shooting a few Jews, Nick? My mother was a Jew. That makes me one. Will you mind shooting me, old friend? Will that make it a cleaner world for you? Will it touch anything behind those cold eyes when you complete the murder of a family that thought of you as one of their own?

Their small, evil, island universe was suddenly invaded.

"Another pint, boys?"

Angela's wonderfully sane, happy face intruded on them, taking their beer mugs away. Scott had to fight to return to the present time and place.

"Er.. yes... yes, please, Angela."

"Christ! You two look like you're planning the end of the world! Cheer up, for God's sake or I'll have you thrown out of my bar! You're killing the trade!"

"Sorry, love!" said Nick with a grin, and received the smile he could always get from a woman. "We've both had a rough couple of weeks."

"Bloody looks like it! Wait a sec, I'll get your drinks."

The two men studied the act of pulling the two mugs full of draught bitter in silence and waited for her to place the drinks in front of them. When she walked away to the other end of the bar, Scott took a drink, put down the mug and the veil of isolation closed round them again.

"So, how were my parents, Scott?" The pain was in Nick's face as he looked across.

"Old. Very tired. Still grieving for you. They have all your old things in the room upstairs they think of as yours."

"Jesus Christ! You looked through my things?"

"The models of the Mercedes and the Jaguar are still there, still wrapped up."

"Good God! And my books?"

"All there. Complete with the swastikas in the flyleaves and your comments in the margins. That's what told me Dieter Konig was my target. I hadn't related him to you though, at that time."

"When did you do that?"

"On my way to Singapore. It all just clicked, after I put a few things together. I remembered that the killing in Toronto was done with something clever in pharmaceuticals. Remembered how a waitress in Geneva described the man she served while he talked in English to another man she recognized from a photo I showed her. Then I ran a check on your school records and found the forgeries. Found the gaps in your story."

"God almighty! You were busy! We didn't follow you after you reached Hanover again, thought you'd just go back to Birmingham."

"We?"

"The Movement."

214

"And you're supposed to be racially and intellectually superior? What sort of fuck-witted stupidity was that?"

Nick stared at his beer. "You found somebody who remembered me talking with Perkins in Geneva?"

"A pretty little waitress who thought you were her knight in shining armour!"

Nick smiled, his memory back in another time. "Right!" he said. "I remember her! God, she was a sweetheart!"

"Then I saw how you'd always been away when any al-Yaffi event took place," said Scott, bringing him back to the present. "I just tied it all together."

"I see." Nick studied his beer mug intensely. "That was always the risk but nobody checks out things like that."

"We did. I did. Jamieson did. And you'd be surprised what the German security forces have got on you."

That was stretching things a bit, thought Scott, but maybe it would make Nick a little cautious before he killed anyone again. He looked sideways at Nick's drawn, pale face. Just for a second, he felt the warmth and concern he would feel for his best friend if he looked so unwell. He stemmed it. This man had killed his family.

"Where did you grow up then Nick, if not in Newcastle?"

"Southern Ireland. The Movement had its connections there since the war. I spent three years in a little country town making sure I could pass for an Englishman. When I was sixteen, they moved me to Tyneside to get the local accent and polish off the training."

"And did you always want to be a killer?"

"Why not? Cleaning up the world seemed a great idea. I have no trouble with any of my jobs. All the targets were threats to the Movement."

"And what about Wilhelm Scheidinger? What sort of threat was he?" asked Scott. The coldness being shown to him was frightening. It was an insight into Nick that was brand new.

"He was a communist and getting too strong in the new Germany. But that was a lousy balls-up! Perkins was a traitor to us!"

"How so?"

"He was supposed to lead you off in another direction. He'd been our man for five years, feeding you all the crap about Mustapha al-Yaffi with the wrong pictures and descriptions. He was not supposed to direct you at another of our operations!"

"So why did he suddenly give us this break?"

"No idea. Maybe an attack of conscience, or something. But it looks like he deliberately pointed you at that Chicago event to alert you to the influence of the Movement. Then he panicked when Allan Hopkins called him to set up a visit. He wanted to talk to me about getting out of it before anyone found out what he'd been doing. When you said that you'd been in Chicago, I nearly wet my pants!"

"So you killed him?"

"I didn't. Somebody else did."

"Who?"

He looked sideways at Scott for a moment, and the old Nick grin appeared for a second. Scott felt he could have wept.

"Don't be bloody stupid, Scott!"

Scott stood silent for a few moments, still hardly believing the conversation which was taking place. Why was Nick telling him all this? He would know that Scott would take action immediately to have Nick arrested by British Intelligence. Cold ice worked through his veins. Somehow Nick must know that Scott would not be able to tell anyone. Was he to be killed this evening? The weight of the Browning in his shoulder holster was comforting, but not enough to still the fear.

"Why my parents and sister, Nick?"

Nick stared into his beer. "Scott, I never knew that was supposed to happen, believe me!" he said after a few seconds. "I followed orders and made contact with you in Nottingham so that

I could get near enough to your family to check her out. The Movement had somehow been given a pointer that she was someone they'd been hunting for years. But I really felt like your friend and I loved those visits to Reading. I sent the photos of your mother to my people but I didn't know who she was or why I was doing it."

"But you killed them anyway."

"No I didn't. You know me, Scott, you know my methods. I've always worked at close quarters. Bombs are not my style. Somebody else did that one."

Scott was numbed with the pain of peeling away the scars in his mind from the deaths of his family, and the horrors of hearing Nick calmly confirming what he had suspected for the last few weeks. But under the pain was a curious sense of relief. Nick had not been the killer of his family. Somehow, that helped. He stood away from the bar, pulled out his handkerchief and blew his nose, looking behind him at the crowd of cheerful people in the bar and wondering if he could ever again be like them.

"Must have been a hell of a shock when you found out I'd joined the Mongoose Section," said Scott, turning back to the bar and grasping his beer mug.

"I'll say it was!" agreed Nick with a small smile. "I learned it from Perkins, and I nearly had a fit!"

"And you recognized me when you killed Arnold Richardson in Toronto?"

"Of course I did."

"How did you feel about that?"

Nick shrugged. "I had a contract. Nothing I could do about that but I didn't feel happy about it. It was the first time we'd met professionally, so to speak, but I knew it would have to happen some day."

"And the next time in Singapore. Would you have killed me, Nick, if I'd had a gun?"

"Of course! I'm a professional and I had a contract directly from our main financier."

"Tumokam?"

Nick stared. "Christ! You know about Tumokam?"

"Saw the plane leaving in Singapore, recognized the logo, put two and two together."

Nick turned his face back to his beer.

"Why are you telling me all this, Nick?" said Scott, picking up his beer mug draining nearly half the pint of beer in one swallow. He put the mug down and saw the expression of satisfaction on the other man's face. Nick seemed to let out a sigh of relief.

"We won't see each other again, old son," he said with a small smile at Scott. "I just wanted you to know that I was not quite as bad as you thought. The al-Yaffi period is over. I'll be in Germany from now on, organizing the Movement to take over at some time."

"And what happens now? You're going to wrap up the McIntyre family saga by killing me?"

"No. You're still my friend, Scott, always will be."

"So?"

"I'm flying out tonight to rejoin the Movement. Now that we have a single Germany, our work is gathering momentum."

"And why won't I stop you?"

"Because you'll be out cold in about ten minutes. I'll have all the time I need to get out of the country."

"Something in my drink just now?"

"Clever old Scott!"

Scott stood up straight, pulled a ten-pound note from his hip pocket and put it on the bar.

"You're a bastard, Wallace," he said. "I'm going to stop you. If whatever you put in my beer works, then I'll get you later. If I can, I'm going to get you now!"

Nick's face was sad. "You won't make it, Scott."

"I have to try."

"I know. 'Bye, Scott."

Scott ignored him and walked out. If he had ten minutes, he had time to get to the car, use his car phone and call up Jamieson to alert the security forces. Trying to use the gun would be a dreadful mistake. Nick might also have one, or he might have an armed colleague standing nearby, and starting a shoot-out in a crowded pub was not the way to go. He walked into the cool night and the first twinge of the drug made itself felt. He had difficulty getting his bearings to the car, but somehow worked it out and began to walk toward the car park. Within twenty yards the walk had become a stagger. By the time he had reached the car, his vision was blurred and multiplied and nausea was striking his guts.

He had no idea how long he stood leaning up against the door fumbling with his keys. It became one of those nightmares where everything he did made things worse. He finally made out the key with the plastic cap, took an eternity of attempts to put it in the key hole, opened the door and collapsed into the seat. He tugged the car phone out of its clasp, tried to focus on the numbers... *have to put the key in the ignition, Scott.... Oh God, I can't see, where the bloody hell is that ignition?* His hands wouldn't do what he told them... *don't drop the keys, don't drop the bloody keys... switch on, for Christ's sake, switch it on!* Ten thousand years passed while he waited for the phone to light up, and it beeped at him with a hellish, shrieking sound that burned pathways in his brain that would never heal. Outside, the country was twirling insane pirouettes like his head. Jamieson's number was... *oh God, what is his number?...* three... A hundred years passed before the phone beeped after he had pressed the key. Five... more gaps in the cosmic eternity. *Surely I remember that beep being instantaneous when I press the button....* four... Then the great nothingness roared up from the pits of hell and swept him away over the edge of the precipice.

He hadn't had ten minutes, after all. Nick had been lying again.

* * *

His spine was being twisted up around his head and he could hear the creaking. Pain was shooting through his arms and legs and somebody had poured thick glue over his eyes. His arms had been strapped down against his sides and he must have been eating rotting garbage before he went to bed... He stirred, and his knees cracked against something... *where the hell am I?*

He managed to open one eye and a dirty grey light oozed into his head. A massive thick wall of brown dirt stood a hundred feet high in front of him... *hang on!* That was the top of the car's dashboard. He was in the Honda, crunched up in his seat, leaning against his right arm that was jammed up against the door. The taste in his mouth was horrible. A hot cup of mint tea would do the trick...

The door on his right was suddenly opened and he nearly fell out, saved only by an instinctive grab at the steering wheel. He stared up into the grey sky that was almost blotted out by two massive, monstrous shapes. One bent down over him.

"Sleeping off the last night's over-indulgences, are we, sir?" Powerful arms pushed him back into his seat. The monsters refocused in Scott's eyes and became a couple of youthful-looking police officers. Behind them, their white patrol car with its colourful strip down the side was purring gently like a comfortable cat. Scott tried to move his arms and some of the pain eased.

"No," he tried to say, but only a croak came out. He worked at clearing his throat. "Help me out, will you?"

The officer leaned in and grabbed his shoulders. Scott fell against the thick blue-coated arms and let him haul him out. With his legs clear of the steering wheel he was able to push himself out the last few inches and tried to stand up, nearly falling again.

"What the hell!" snapped the second patrolman and seized Scott's arms again with far more force than was suggested for merely helping him to stand. "Pete! He's got a gun!"

Scott was thrown forward against the side of his car and his hands were pulled sharply behind him. Cuffs were snapped on his wrists in an incredibly efficient manner and he was turned round to face the two officers. He nearly vomited from the foul taste in his mouth and the violence of the moves.

The officer named Pete slipped a hand into Scott's shoulder holster and removed the Browning. He showed it to the other who looked at it with interest.

"That's a military-issue Browning," said the second officer and stared at Scott. "Care to explain this weapon, sir?"

"Wallet," muttered Scott. Both his eyes were open now and dawn was getting brighter than his head liked. The headache was acting up like a foundry hammer and he didn't think he had more than a few more seconds before he really threw up.

"What?"

"Get my wallet," repeated Scott.

Pete obliged, removed the wallet from Scott's blazer and held it in front of him.

"And now?" asked Pete. He was being very careful, thought Scott through the haze of illness. But he understood why. The military Browning meant most likely that Scott was either a member of the Irish Republican Army with a stolen weapon, or the gun was legitimately his, making Scott possibly a superior officer to the two patrolmen.

"Check the plastic card with a holographic picture," Scott mumbled through the nausea.

The two patrolmen looked at each other. The second one nodded at Pete who looked through the credit cards, driver's license and automatic bank teller cards till he came to the Mongoose Section identity card. He pulled it out.

"Bloody hell!" he said. "Never seen one of these before!" He passed it to his partner who studied it intently.

"Nor me!" The second officer pulled out the keys and swung Scott round to unlock his hands. Just as he pulled the cuffs, away the nausea took over and Scott doubled up vomiting over the Honda's rear wheel. For a few seconds he gagged while crazy thoughts ambled through his mind.

What the Australians call throwing a Technicolor yawn, he thought as rationality fought to get back in his head. He stood up straight and wiped his mouth with his handkerchief. His insides felt a lot better.

"Thanks," he said. "I wasn't drunk."

"Sure!" said Pete, disbelief showing all over the faces of both officers.

"You can check with Angela if you like. I had less than two pints." Scott was sure they would know Angela and Bob. Everybody in the area knew the owners of the Old Mill Pub.

"So why this...?" Pete indicated the inside of the Honda.

"Drugged," replied Scott.

"Yeah, yeah." Scepticism shouted from both faces.

"Wait," said Scott, and sat back in his car seat. The key was as he had left it last night, still switched to the auxiliary so that the electrical devices would work. He reset the phone which beeped at him and he dialled the private number he had been trying to enter the previous night. He left the phone in its cradle so that the hands-free microphone and loudspeaker would operate, letting the cops listen in on the conversation.

"Jamieson!" snapped the voice from the loudspeaker. Only one ring. The Old Man must have been wide-awake, thought Scott, or had never lost the airman's ability to wake up like a cat, instantly alert.

"Mongoose Three, sir. Wallace caught me last night, drugged me. He's leaving the country for good to return to Germany. We need a check at all airports, coastal departures, maybe get European forces to watch for his arrival. He's had...." Scott checked his watch. It was five-fifteen. "...eight hours start."

"I see." Jamieson paused for a moment. "I'll handle it." The sound of his telephone being snapped down reverberated in Scott's head like a sonic boom. He pressed the "End" button on the car phone and looked at the police officers. They were eyeing him with respect.

"I need to go," he said to them.

"Of course, sir."

"Thanks, officers." Scott closed the door, switched on the engine and somehow steered his way back to the office, thankfully early enough to miss the rush hour. He stopped long enough at a transport restaurant to buy a bottle of orange juice. He drained the lot at the counter, to the amused faces of the long-distance truck drivers doing grievous bodily harm to their mountainous plates of sausage, egg and chips, slathered with tomato ketchup and washed down with huge mugs of strong tea. The juice took the taste of rotting garbage from his mouth, but did nothing at all for the sense of total ineptitude that covered him.

* * *

"You let him walk all over you," Jamieson said. His voice was expressionless, the statement not so much pejorative as merely analytical.

"I turned away for about three or four seconds to blow my nose." Scott wasn't being defensive. Jamieson's style and the training the Mongoose agents had all undergone removed the disparaging element from reviews. Instead, performance was evaluated with a cold, dispassionate analysis of errors from which they could learn for the next time.

"That's all it needed," Jamieson replied. "Never give anyone even a second without being watched."

"Yes, sir. Did anyone get any sign of him?"

Jamieson shook his head. "Not a flicker. He's safely in Germany, well hidden. We've alerted their security forces."

It was eight o'clock in the morning. The scene was as always; steaming coffee pot, ignored box of doughnuts. The taste in Scott's mouth still was enough to kill off any appetite. Kabuki theatre to fill both their coffee mugs. The Lancaster roared its never-ending path through storm clouds that would never die. A steely-eyed, forever-young Vulcan pilot grinned at them from the other wall.

"I suppose that ends the al-Yaffi episode, sir?"

"It does. But you can tell yourself that you helped stop him, McIntyre. Your final identification of him probably saved a number of lives."

"But there are other problems, sir."

"Oh?" Jamieson lifted his blue coffee mug, sipped carefully from it, looking calmly at Scott over the rim.

"Wallace still has a connection somewhere in the department. He knew about my trip to Osnabruck to see his parents, he knew we had linked him to the al-Yaffi persona. His airline schedules and credit card records show he couldn't have gone to Karachi to kill Perkins, but somebody certainly did kill him. I feel there are loose ends all over the place."

Jamieson studied him carefully. "The only people who would know enough to leak information to him are you, me and Mongoose Two."

"Plus Marjorie and Janette," said Scott, finally letting out the small horror which had been sitting in his mind since that morning, as evil tasting as the after effects of the drug.

Jamieson's face was expressionless. "And, as you say, Marjorie and Janette."

"Pretty frightening range of choices, sir."

"Do you have any reason to doubt any one of those five names, McIntyre?"

"No, sir."

"Nor do I. Every one of us, including myself, has gone through security vetting at the most intensive level. Sometimes we are re-checked, again I include myself, without our knowing it, at random intervals."

"Then it's hard to imagine," said Scott, a dull sense of failure rising in him.

"Almost impossible."

"Almost, sir?"

"McIntyre, my father once told me there are only two absolute truths in the universe."

"Yes, sir?"

The Air Marshal leaned back in his seat, both hands cradling his coffee mug. "The first absolute truth," he said, "is that there are no other absolute truths in the universe."

"And the second?"

"The statement that there are only two absolute truths in the universe."

Scott thought about it. Tried out a couple of possible objections and rejected them. He let his mind spin in neutral for a few seconds, remembered a debate at a Sunday afternoon gathering at Jamieson's house in Sutton where Jamieson had proved quite successfully to a group of scientists that the statement 'one plus one equals two' was not an absolute but merely an approximation. He decided that he couldn't match Jamieson in the game of abstruse silliness but he recognized that the Air Marshal had let the conversation deviate into nonsense as a way of easing Scott's mind.

"I see, sir. So what shall we do?"

Jamieson sipped the final drops of coffee and put the mug back on his desk, leaning forward. "Nothing," he said. "I want you to read up on some other cases we may have to deal with soon and otherwise catch up on some training, gunnery practice and a refresher course in unarmed combat."

"What about Wallace's Europharm office here?"

Jamieson looked at his watch. "The police will be raiding it right about now. The woman, what's her name?..."

"Kirstie Schwering, sir."

"Right. Kirstie Schwering will be arrested and her background thoroughly checked. The Swiss authorities have been notified about the organization and we can leave it to them."

Scott stood up and replaced his mug on the table next to the coffee pot and the unopened doughnut box.

"Sir? Is it also an absolute truth that these doughnuts vanish by a miraculous daily process of transubstantiation?"

Jamieson bowed his head over his papers and refused to look at him, but Scott could swear his shoulders were twitching.

"You've got me, McIntyre."

"You mean, you really do eat the damn things, sir?"

"No, McIntyre. I mean that you've just found a third absolute truth."

For the first time in four years, Scott laughed out loud at one of Jamieson's jokes. *Score one to the old bastard.*

Chapter 9 – Australia

Scott had a quiet week. By Mongoose standards, that is. That afternoon, he read through case files of some events which Mongoose One and Two had experienced over the previous twelve months, and he found out that Allan Hopkins had been researching Knights of Aryan Dawn for over a year. Allan seemed to have very few solid facts about them.

On Tuesday, Scott drove down to the Royal Air Force station at Henlow, where, in a small hangar on the edge of the airfield, he re-established painful communications with RAF Regiment Flight Sergeant Eric Mullins. Mullins flung him around on the mats, kicked him brutally in the ribs and placed a death lock on his head, all in the first thirty seconds.

"You're a mite out of shape, Mister McIntyre," he said calmly, letting Scott stand up again. Mullins had not even raised a sweat on his immaculate blue and white shorts and shirt. The flight sergeant stood a full head shorter than did Scott and weighed perhaps thirty pounds less.

Scott staggered to his feet, breathing like an asthmatic horse. He let his shoulders sag and his head drop. "You're right," he gasped. "I'd say I need...." and launched himself at the flight sergeant with a high kick to the head. He did brutal damage to the air where Mullins had been, then the other man's toes caught him in the back of the knees and Scott collapsed again.

"I agree, sir," said Mullins, politely. "You do need exactly that."

227

Scott swung round, flung himself full length, caught Mullins' left foot and twisted himself another full turn. Mullins fell sharply to the mat, wriggled free, leaped fully over Scott and landed with a rib-crunching sprawl on his back.

"Better, Mister McIntyre, better," he said, breathing as easily as if he had never moved. "Long way to go, though."

He stood up to let Scott breathe. Scott had awful problems doing it. He hauled himself to his hands and knees, carefully watched the foot swinging in his direction, then dropped flat, twisted onto his back, seized the approaching foot, flung his legs up over his head and completely reversed his position from lying on his back to his belly again. Mullins went flying off the mat, rolled into a tight ball and ended up hard against the wall bars twenty feet away.

"Well, well, well!" he said. "What a nasty little mongoose we have here, then!" Mullins was grinning from ear to ear, walking back toward Scott with a slight limp. Scott was feeling almost as bad as when the police opened his car door outside the Old Mill Pub. He raised his hands in surrender.

"Peace, Flight! Give me few moments!"

"Certainly, Mister McIntyre. Sure you're all right?"

"I'm quite sure I'm not," Scott replied, bending over and leaning his hands on his thighs.

"Pity," murmured the flight sergeant, kicked away Scott's arms, swept his feet backwards from under him, picked him up round the waist as he fell forward, spun sharply and threw him against the same spot by the wall bars where he himself had come to rest a few seconds earlier. Scott made the worst mistake of all and lost his temper. He stood up, ran at Mullins, feet flew up at his head, flats of hand struck at his neck.

When Scott woke up a few minutes later he was lying on the mat. Mullins was sitting cross-legged a few feet away, looking at him calmly.

"I think you'd better stay on until tomorrow, sir," he said. "We have more work to do."

"I think you're correct, Flight."

"You forgot one of the first lessons we taught you here, Mister McIntyre. You got angry. Never works."

"That may just be Jamieson's fourth absolute truth," Scott muttered to himself.

"Pardon, sir?"

"Nothing, Flight. Now will you please walk well away from me so I can get up and go to the showers?"

Mullins laughed softly, rose quickly to his feet in one smooth movement and walked out of the room. The first rule of his lessons was that while they were both in the gymnasium, anything was fair game. Once the flight-sergeant was out, Scott was safe to get up. He still made certain that he was alone, before he somehow made it to his feet and to the hot showers.

He had lunch in the officers' mess, feeling nostalgic familiarity with the way everything was done. Blue uniforms with the double wings of pilots and the single wings of navigators and technical officers filled the dining hall. There were not many operational aircrew staff here, but Scott heard a lot of conversations of the "..so there I was, upside down, five hundred knots, nothing on the clock but the maker's name and I said to my wingman..." variety with accompanying waving of arms to simulate combat flight. *God, how I miss it!* He thought.

He ate lightly, as much to leave his bruised ribs with as little work to do as possible, as to keep himself still active for the afternoon gunnery practice.

The combat field was of the police training variety. Buildings around a square, windows open, shapes would flash up in front of the combatant, some of the shapes would be designated "friend," others "foe." Scott carried his Browning and stalked around the buildings, nerves tightly wound. Eight times he shot a pair of bullets at a moving shape, six times he held his fire. After the tenth shot, he snapped the magazine out of the pistol and replaced it with a full one, despite the three rounds still left. Running out of ammunition and firing an empty gun was frowned upon as an error that could leave one slightly dead. Scott had learned to keep a running total of remaining bullets in his head. When the whistle sounded, the supervising officer was pleasant about it.

"Nice shooting, sir." He was an elderly warrant officer with a chestful of decorations. "Not a wrong shot, anywhere. Now let's go and do the touchy-feely bit, shall we?"

He took Scott into the building at the entrance to the gunnery range. In a small office, Scott sat at a desk with his eyes covered and proceeded to dismantle, re-assemble and load from a tray of mixed calibre bullets, his Browning, a Beretta nine-millimetre automatic, a Heckler & Koch semi-automatic rifle and an elderly Colt forty-five revolver before the warrant officer would let him go.

He spent a quiet evening in the television lounge of the Officer's Mess, talked briefly to a couple of squadron leaders over dinner, retired early to his room and only woke up when the batman banged on the door at six-thirty bringing his freshly-polished shoes and a mug of tea. Then he repeated most of the activities of the previous day. In the morning, Scott spent a sweat-soaked ninety minutes in which Flight Sergeant Mullins had shown him a series of combat moves and rehearsed him thoroughly before letting Scott try them out. After several minutes of exhausting action, Scott had thrown Mullins to the mat, placed a bruise on his cheekbone and got him in a headlock.

"Passable, Mister McIntyre, passable," said Mullins, croaking slightly from Scott's wrist pressed against his throat.

"Thank God for that!" muttered Scott, released him and began to walk out.

Mullins kicked him behind the knees, brought him crashing to the floor, twisted his arm behind his back and threatened to touch his heels with the back of his head.

"Naughty little mongoose!" Mullins said gently and finally let him go, walking quickly to the showers before Scott got any nasty ideas about killing him.

Scott grinned painfully to himself as he steered the Honda through the evening gloom on the M1 Motorway back to Birmingham. Janette would be horrified by the bruises, the split lip and the creaking bones but she would have an excellent therapy for it, Scott was certain.

He was not mistaken.

* * *

"McIntyre! Get in here, immediately!"

Jamieson's voice sliced through Scott's ear to which he had pressed the telephone when it rang at his desk. He had never heard such urgency before. Normally, Jamieson was calm, steady and rock solid. Scott put the phone back and walked rapidly to his office. There was no point in running and causing a general panic throughout the whole place.

When he got in to the Air Marshal's office, he saw something he had never seen before. Jamieson was at his desk with the red telephone in front of him and the handset clasped close to his face. Only one person he would be talking to, Scott knew, and that was the prime minister.

"It's an immediate need, Prime Minister," Jamieson was saying. "They have requested direct assistance from Mongoose Three."

He looked up at Scott and waved him to the seat across from his desk. Then his eyes focused into the distance as he returned to the conversation with his boss.

"Yes... yes... I agree, Prime Minister, the ramifications could be extreme. The Australian connections with these people could be bigger than we thought.... Yes, Prime Minister... yes... by this afternoon... thank you, Prime Minister."

His side of the conversation reminded Scott of the brilliant television comedy *"Yes, Prime Minister,"* and he struggled to keep a straight face. Jamieson replaced the handset, opened the desk drawer and put the telephone away.

"Benny Moskowitch," Scott said calmly. "Nick's people are trying to recoup the damage done in Singapore."

"Correct," said Jamieson. "He's received death threats and some bullets have gone through his window recently. The Queensland State police are being remarkably incurious about it, which I find interesting."

"So do I," commented Scott. "Could be political pressure there from some fascinating sources. Benny told me a lot of Queenslanders in high places would be great members of the Waffen SS."

"Possibly. So Benny contacted the Federal Authorities and he seems to have some clout there."

"I bet he does," Scott grinned. "And they said...?"

"They said, 'Yes, Benny, no, Benny, three bags bloody full, Benny.' And he asked for you, specifically."

"And I'm on this afternoon's flight, I assume?"

"You'll be met in Sydney by a representative of Federal Security. He'll see you through immigration."

"And will the Australians be with me while we try and help Benny?"

"They will. One of them will, anyway. The State Government has agreed to Federal help. They have no wish for any terrorist unpleasantness, whatever the more extremist loonies in the area might want."

"Oh, yeah?"

"McIntyre, this isn't the Queensland that Moskowitch was talking about. The current mob may still be weird but they're not fascists."

"That's very encouraging, sir."

"Don't be sarcastic, McIntyre."

"No, sir."

"And be careful. The political implications for all of us are very heavy. The Australians don't want to find out they've had a nest of Nazis in the place, least of all in Queensland. And if they do, they don't want it broadcast. The Germans are sensitive about the whole thing. It's a bad one, Scott."

"Any chance of more help? How about Mongoose Two?"

Jamieson looked pensive. "Actually, Mongoose Two has already asked if he could be assigned to this mess as well. If I can free him up quickly I'll send him along."

"Thank you, sir."

"You'd better get going, McIntyre. Shots are already being fired down there."

His face was already turning to the doughnut box as Scott stood up. Scott didn't dare try and wait to see if Jamieson would stand up before he opened the door. The Old Man's sense of humour looked fragile today. Anyway, Scott wanted to grab a few moments with Janette before he caught the shuttle to Heathrow.

* * *

Beaches.

For half an hour or so, it seemed that beaches were the only thing to see. Sydney's air traffic control was directing the Qantas Boeing 747 around the coast line north of Sydney for a lengthy period before the controller allowed it into the pattern for the approach to Kingsford Smith Airport. The complex trail weaving through the Australian skies at an altitude of only five or six thousand feet allowed the passengers to goggle at what seemed to be endless miles of yellow sand alongside clear blue waters. Scott heard some restless murmurs from seats around him. A few people could hardly wait to get to the sand and the topless swimsuits of Australia's surf nymphs, it seemed. Scott thought

233

that they might be upset to discover that in early September, it was still only late winter or early spring, and there might be a dearth of beach nymphets, at least this far south.

The massive barn-door-like flaps reached even further from the trailing edge of the Boeing's wings, engine pitch dropped another few notches and the aircraft straightened on to the approach from the north. To his left, Scott watched the Opera House, the Bridge and the spires of Sydney float by. The City on the Harbour was having another of its endless sunny days. Even at this early hour, several sailing boats were flying multi-coloured spinnakers over the harbour waters.

"Just one goddammed beautiful day after another," somebody had said sardonically to him on his last trip here. And in early September, winter was barely over. Scott had to turn his standard Northern Hemisphere concepts over in his mind to get clear that Spring was about to start and Summer would bring Christmas and the New Year.

Suddenly, red roofs were flashing under the wings, ugly industrial buildings seemingly only a few feet below, the wheels gently touched down and the massive machine was slowing on the runway stretching out into Botany Bay. A few small fishing boats anchored in the Bay's shallow waters sat solidly in the calm. One or two faces turned from contemplation of the surface to watch the Boeing taxi off the runway and begin the return path to the terminal building.

The flight attendant completed her "Welcome to Sydney" speech and Scott pulled his overnight bag from under the seat in front. He sensed the shadow bending over him and sat up.

"Mister McIntyre?" said the flight attendant in the Qantas uniform.

"Yes, Linda!" said Scott. "Good morning!" It was eight o'clock, local time.

"Good morning!" She bent lower to whisper directly into his ear. She smelled of something delicate and flowery and her skin was almost perfect. "You're being met at the doorway by a Mister Cooper. He'll take you off before anyone else leaves."

Her curiosity was obvious, but Scott didn't satisfy it.

"Thanks, Linda," he smiled at her and she stood upright, clearly piqued. He stayed in his seat for the last few minutes of the lumbering journey into the gateway. Crowds of welcoming people lined the observation deck. They must have risen early for this arrival, thought Scott, but most international flights into Australia arrived early in the morning after overnight journeys. By ten-thirty or so, the international terminal would look like a deserted mausoleum.

The engines died with a regretful, fading whine and passengers began to stand up and reach for their bags in the lockers. Scott picked up his small bag and jacket and moved to the spiral staircase down to the main cabin. He got another curious look from Linda and the same from the tall, thin, male flight attendant standing by the door. Muted thumps indicated the connection to the mobile passageway and the door was manhandled open. Several men stood at the entrance, most of them dressed in the airline's uniforms. One, however, wore a more sober dark suit with a light blue shirt and a red tie knotted in a service-style double-Windsor. *Ex-military, I'd bet the mortgage on it,* thought Scott. The man was about Scott's height, lean of build, dark-haired and sported a neatly-trimmed moustache. He looked closely at Scott.

"Scott McIntyre?"

"The very same."

The man grinned widely, displaying good teeth and friendly eyes. "G'day!" he said. "I'm Phil Cooper." The vowels were decidedly Australian, decided Scott. Cooper took Scott's outstretched hand and shook it firmly. "Let's go!" he said. "Customs and immigration have been cleared." With a wave to the two flight attendants still watching them curiously, Scott moved out of the doorway behind the Australian. Instead of continuing the walk into the terminal, Cooper opened the door to the outside, just a few feet away and led him on to the steps.

It was cool in the open. Scott felt chilly in his shirt sleeves and put on his jacket. The sun was bright enough to cause a squint and indicated the day would warm up considerably as time wore on.

"Beaut day!" said Cooper, and began to walk down the stairs to the ground.

"Bloody oath!" replied Scott, and Cooper turned, laughing.

"You've been here before?"

"Two years ago," replied Scott, as they reached the concrete surface. "Nothing too active, just helping one of your people trail a killer."

A large, white Ford Falcon sedan was waiting, the engine running quietly. Phil opened the back door and waved Scott in, following him. As soon as they were seated, the driver spoke briefly into a hand-held microphone and began to move off. The car followed the taxiway toward the end of the building and took a small road along the side of the airfield. Idly, Scott watched a 747 of Royal Thai land on the same runway he had recently used, then a couple of Airbus' took off in quick succession, their roar of engines subdued inside the car.

The drive was very short. Within minutes, they had stopped alongside a neat Gulfstream jet, the same model as the ones the FBI had supplied to fly Wilhelm Scheidinger and Scott's temporary partners, Bill and Allison between Chicago and St. Louis a few weeks ago. It seemed like years had passed since then.

Scott looked at Phil. "Government plane?" he asked. The Gulfstream had no markings beyond the Australian "VH" registration number.

Cooper shook his head. "Benny Moskowitch corporate plane. We're going straight up to Brisbane."

"Strewth!" Scott was finding it easy to slip back into some Australian vernacular. Benny must have had more impact on him in their few days in Singapore than he had realized.

They climbed up the stairway to the front of the Gulfstream and were met by a middle-aged woman dressed in a simple business suit.

"Good morning gentlemen," she smiled. "I am Gretta Hilstein, Mister Moskowitch's personal assistant. If you would take your seats, we will be off immediately." And indeed, the engines were already growling as power was fed to them for the initial start-up.

Inside, the decor was simple but comfortable. At the front of the cabin, three seats on each side facing the middle. At the back, two tables, each with two seats on either side, useful for conferences. In the middle, two pairs of conventional seats facing forward.

With a longing look at the flight deck where the two pilots, one of whom he noticed was a young woman in the co-pilot's seat on the right, were busy going through pre-flight checks, Scott walked behind Gretta and took a seat at one of the tables. Phil sat opposite him, facing the rear, and Gretta walked back to the front and pulled the door closed and locked. Then she took one of the right-hand seats and snapped the buckle of her seat belt.

"Great way to travel!" said Phil, and stretched his arms above his head.

"You bet!" Scott replied. "Benny does himself proud."

"You met him in Singapore, I understand?"

"Just for two days. How much do you know about all this?"

"A bit. Let me introduce myself!" He extracted his wallet and pulled out a card similar to Scott's Mongoose identification card. It had the same style of holograph picture of a Phillip James Cooper, Australian Secret Intelligence Service. ASIS. Scott knew of that organization but this card did not look like the standard ASIS card. He looked at the Australian.

"It's a section much like yours," Phil answered to Scott's silent query. "Few people know about us, we're headed up by a retired General. Similar mission to yours, too."

"Interesting," said Scott and returned the card. As Cooper put the wallet away, Scott saw the handle of the pistol in his shoulder holster.

The Gulfstream had begun moving and taxied straight to the western end of the second runway for a cross-wind take-off. Scott watched the flight deck, but from here could only see a hand on the throttle and an occasional profile as each pilot looked sideways at the other or out at the surrounding scenery to check clearances. They received immediate permission for take-off, judging by the rapid way the aircraft moved onto the runway and began accelerating firmly. Just as they crossed the north-south runway, the nose lifted and they climbed sharply into the flawless pastel sky.

"Tell me about the situation in Brisbane," said Scott.

"Three days ago," Phil started, "a bullet went through the window of Benny's Jaguar about a mile from his house. He drove like hell for home and called the local police. They came and looked, seemed totally uninterested and told Benny it was probably a hunting accident. No worries, mate."

"But Benny was worried, I assume?" smiled Scott.

"Benny was bloody furious! It was the third time in a few weeks that somebody had taken a shot at him and he was ropeable!"

"I can imagine," murmured Scott.

"Not a pretty sight," Phil added. "Trouble was, it got worse. Another bullet went through his lounge window the same afternoon and then one of the barns on his estate was burned down. Swastikas were painted on the side of another barn overnight and he's had a few nasty phone calls threatening a repeat of Auschwitz as a personal family event. He called the cops again but they said it was just kids at play and would he please leave them alone?"

"I suppose they had more important things to do, like collecting their payoffs from the gambling clubs and prostitution parlours?"

"Undoubtedly!" Phil smiled gently. "At that point, he called up Canberra and made use of his extensive Federal Government contacts. I gather he was practically through to the Prime Minister's office before he was satisfied."

"What happened to the private security forces he said he was going to hire?" asked Scott.

Phil grimaced. "They worked for two days then told Benny they had to give up on the job. They left within an hour of telling him. The head of the company refused more information."

"Pressure from high places?"

"You bet."

They paused as Gretta arrived with coffee served in well-shaped, attractive mugs with broad bases for stability. Heavy, chunky pieces of modern art held sugar cubes and cream. She placed the mugs on the table and she moved back to the front of the aircraft out of earshot. *A lady of discretion, our Gretta,* thought Scott.

"Anyway," Phil continued. "It seems some high level communications went on between Canberra and the Queensland State Government in Brisbane. The end result was stalemate. The State government is not happy with the possibility of having a neo-Nazi group in the country but apparently there are some heavy political influences up there that make it difficult for them to interfere." He drank his coffee without adding any cream or sugar and replaced the mug on the table.

"Benny did say that a lot of political heavies in Queensland would be well-regarded members of Hitler's Storm Troopers," said Scott, mixing sugar into his coffee.

Phil nodded. "Some of the bastards would be a bit far right even for Hitler!" he commented with a small smile. "Anyway, that's when Benny called for you to help. Said he trusted you and nobody else. You obviously made quite an impression!"

"The reverse, if anything," said Scott. "But if I'm to help, I need armoury. Can you supply?"

"Do fishes crap in water, mate?" Cooper answered deadpan and stood up to get a bag from a compartment above the other table. He dropped it heavily on the seat next to him and unzipped it.

"Browning nine-millimetre, automatic single-action, shoulder holster, silencer, three boxes of shells, low velocity," he recited like a shopkeeper selling groceries. He handed the packages over to Scott who unwrapped the gun from its protective covering of soft cloth. He checked the movement, ejected the magazine and began filling it. Cooper watched without expression.

"Who told you my preference?" asked Scott.

"No idea, mate. Just came in my packet of orders so I drew the equipment from stores like the boss said."

"I see." Scott stood up, removed his jacket, strapped on the shoulder holster and placed the Browning in the socket, checking the free movement. It got the same professional examination that he had received from Bill and Allison in Chicago, and from Jack Carstairs in Toronto. Up front, Gretta was deliberately not looking in their direction.

Phil returned to the bag. "One Uzi, three magazines, box of shells. There are more refills for everything at Benny's place. There are also some rifles, more handguns. Courtesy of my boss, delivered yesterday in an unmarked car which happens to belong to the army."

"Nice to have pals in high places," said Scott.

"Bloody oath!" Phil answered.

Scott took the Uzi, a beautifully compact weapon. From the flight deck a startled face flashed at them as the co-pilot saw the movement of lethal ironware. Scott watched her profile as she said something to the captain whose face he had not yet seen. He saw the pilot's hand wave her attention back to the instrument panel. She was clearly ordered to forget what she had seen, and her face returned to checking instruments obediently. Scott grinned at the implications that such sights were not entirely unknown in Benny's organization. Maybe running a big industrial empire was not simply cash flows and good business sense.

Scott put the Uzi back in the bag and lifted his coffee mug. "And are you with me in this thing?" he said to Phil.

"All the way, mate! Trouble is, any more of us and we'd have political problems. I reckon the cops in that area are nervy as long-tailed cats in a room full of rocking chairs. And somewhere among them there's somebody who knows what's going on and is very happy about it."

"Any idea who?"

Cooper shook his head. "Not a smell of it. But my boss wants to know who it is as much as you and Benny do. So it's up to us."

"What happens when we get to Brisbane?"

"Benny has a car waiting for us at the airfield. We go straight out to his country place and play it by ear from then."

"Are we likely to get any opposition?"

Phil shrugged. "Who the hell knows? This is Queensland after all."

"Benny said it was the greatest outdoor lunatic asylum in the world."

"Benny understated the case," said Phil with a straight face. "It's also one of those asylums where the inmates run the joint. So watch your rear end!"

"Nice!"

By mutual consent, they stopped talking for a time, and Scott turned his attention to the outside view. They were flying a mile or two off the coast and the endless stretch of coastline seemed mainly comprised of white sand. The water looked beautifully clear. Inland, the country stretched into infinity, light brown under a pastel blue sky. He had always remembered how Australia's colours were different from anywhere else he had ever seen. They were lighter, more delicate, like a nationwide water colour painting by a French Impressionist. Inland, where the desert started in earnest, the harsh reds and browns were again unique to themselves, just as the whole country was.

Scott fell asleep.

Twenty minutes later, he woke up sharply. His pilot's senses had never left him and the tiny change of pitch of the engines had worked like the loudest alarm clock. An equally minute alteration in the angle of the aircraft told of the start of the descent. The table was clear of coffee mugs and accessories, and Phil was dozing in the front seat. A small clatter from the galley told him where Gretta was.

He stayed awake as they dropped down from the thin, cold skies thirty-five thousand feet above the sea, looking at the world's largest outdoor lunatic asylum. It looked much like any sub-tropical land in the southern hemisphere except for those pastel colours. Scott had the disturbing sense that, of all his missions for the Mongoose Section, this was his biggest, his toughest and had the most evil possibilities. The evidence suggested Scott was about to meet the successors of Hitler's Storm Troopers in this dangerous, beautiful and unique land. He wondered how many of them would come out of the encounter alive.

A few minutes later, they landed.

The warmth struck his face as the door to the Gulfstream was opened. With the added temperature was a fragrance that had not been in the air in Sydney. It was redolent of flowers, of different trees and scents Scott had not experienced for some years. He climbed down the stairs breathing in the air with enthusiasm. The gentle warmth felt wonderful. Several hundred miles north of Sydney, and an hour or so later in the morning had given the sun a greater chance to warm up things.

Phil and Gretta followed him down the steps after he had stuck his head in the flight deck and greeted the two pilots. The co-pilot had given him an uncertain look from under her light brown hair tied at the neck with a small ribbon, and the captain had merely smiled without humour or warmth. He had a hard face that reflected a greater age than his mere physiological thirty or so years. Benny employed an interesting mixture of people, Scott decided.

A large Jaguar was parked by the stairway, the engine running. *I could really get to enjoy this life of an industrial leader,* thought Scott. *All private jets, limousines and people bowing and scraping in front of you. And also people shooting at you. But what the hell, I have that anyway, and only on the miserable pay I get from Her Majesty's Government. The deal would be worth it.*

He waited for Gretta to reach the ground and let her lead them to the car. When it was obvious that the car really was for them, he opened the rear door for her and received a friendly smile of thanks as she climbed in.

He took a look around as Phil stood with him. They were about fifty yards from the terminal and Scott could see faces watching with curiosity and perhaps envy. He wondered which was friend and which was enemy. Things were not as clear as they were in standard warfare. No uniforms, no flags, no automatic 'Identify - Friend or Foe' radio frequencies which transmitted the correct signal. Maybe a few tattoos of small red lightning bolts on a black square might be found among the silent watchers. Or maybe not. He looked once more at the line of faces and saw one more at the end. Just on the side of the wall where the window ended, he saw a police uniform. Under the peaked cap, a face stared down at the group by the Jaguar. Might mean anything, he thought. Cops were common enough at airports. Or it might be one of those who displayed no interest in investigating bullet shots aimed at Benny Moskowitch.

He followed Phil into the back of the Jaguar and they moved out of the airport onto the road. The rear compartment had spacious seats and a dark screen hid the driver from their view.

They spoke little as they drove, just a few questions from Scott about their destination.

"It's about sixty kilometres," said Phil.

"You've been here before?" asked Scott.

"Since yesterday. I got there in the morning to check out the armoury and the local ground."

"Anything obvious?"

"It's not good," said Phil with a look of worry. "There's lots of cover for anyone moving in, lots of protection for a sniper."

"And what's the house like?"

"Big, solid, stone. Good protection. Large verandas all round for cooling, two stories and a basement."

"Pretty large target for just us two to protect."

"What do you mean, two?" Gretta chimed in with some indignation. "You think I'm just going to sit there like some Victorian maiden, squeaking with panic?"

Phil and Scott looked at each other briefly.

"Can you use a gun?" asked Phil.

"I can use a gun," she replied calmly.

Scott studied her carefully. She was about five-foot-three, slight of build, probably in her fifties with grey hair neatly styled. She observed his study with a small smile.

"I've been with Benny and his wife for over fifteen years," she said softly. "This is not the first time we've been threatened."

"I see," said Scott, swiftly re-evaluating his impression of her. The steel in the middle-aged woman was showing.

"And there's also Jacob," she said.

"Jacob?" Scott was curious at the small amusement she was displaying.

"Benny's son," she answered. "He's driving."

"And he can use a gun too, I'm certain."

"Rather well," she said with a smug smile.

"Of course." Scott tried to hide his own smile and failed.

The rest of the ride passed in silence. About half an hour after leaving the airport, they drove through a small town claiming to be Ipswich. Scott smiled at the difference between this neat little town with lovely wooden buildings and wrought iron balconies, and the English town of the same name. *About an average temperature variance of fifteen degrees Celsius on any day apart from the physical appearances,* he thought.

They left the two-lane highway heading west, diverging more to the north. Now Scott was seeing countryside, the eternal eucalyptus trees, occasional signs warning of kangaroos or koala bears crossing and they drove along a single lane road for more miles. They passed through tiny villages, a larger one called Marburg and turned north, well into rural Queensland by now. Just after Glenmore Grove they left the sealed road and spent ten minutes on a gravel road before turning into a gateway of what looked like a sizeable working farm. Phil was right, thought Scott. Lots of gum trees and a few walls for any attacker to use as cover. The house was slightly elevated on a grass hillock that would give the defenders some advantage in scanning the country. It was a spacious, lovely structure, built in light grey stone with the wide veranda round all four walls which was a standard feature of Australian country homes. Two huge barns stood about a hundred yards away from the front of the house, one of them a burned out hulk, just two walls standing, and smoke still trickling out into the air. The other had large whitewash patches on the side, presumably where the swastikas had been covered up. Apart from the buildings, emptiness spread for miles of fields and gentle hills. Not another building was in sight.

The Jaguar crunched up the gravel to the wide square area in front of the house and stopped by the front door. Scott opened up his door and climbed out. Gretta did the same on her side, followed by Phil. Scott stretched and looked around. The silence was striking. He heard the curious whiplash call of a bird in the trees. It was a uniquely Australian sound. So was the hysterical yabbering of a Kookaburra, the weird bird call that sounded like raucous, mad laughter. Scott grinned at the noise then watched as the driver's door opened and a giant climbed out.

Jacob Moskowitch looked like his father. He was perhaps an inch taller, a bit wider and sported the same massive nose of personality that Benny had. He offered Scott his hand that swallowed the other man's as he took it.

"G'day!" he said with a wide grin.

"G'day," Scott responded, getting a crick in his neck from looking up at him. "Where the hell are we?"

"About sixty kilometres west and a bit north of Brisbane," said Jacob with a smile. The voice was deep and mellow, like a singer in a relaxed mood. "You passed Glenmore Grove on the way. The nearest town is Corriwongle, about five kilometres to the north of us."

Scott smiled his thanks then thought about their position. "Maybe we should all get inside? You're a big target."

Jacob nodded, looked around with the far-sighted stare of a woodsman or pilot and opened the front door for them. They all filed in and he brought up the rear.

Inside was a huge entrance hall tiled in black and white squares. Lead-lined windows with beautiful coloured inlays provided a contrast with the cool gloom and some classic, vintage wooden cabinets and tables stood round the walls. Scott thought of what a wonderful welcome this entrance would make when coming in from a Queensland summer's day.

And at last, he met Benny again. His huge shape appeared in the hall.

"Scott! Am I glad to see you!" His powerful voice shook the glass front of the china cabinet by the door as he walked up to him. He gave a friendly wave to Phil as he passed.

"Benny," said Scott, with enthusiasm. "I'm really happy to see you! Just wish the circumstances could be different!"

"Bloody oath!" replied Benny, with the Australian term of forceful agreement. His hair looked a little greyer than Scott remembered it from only a few weeks ago and the worry on his face was obvious. "I always knew there a lot of racist ratbags in this place but they've never used guns on me before!"

"It's probably less a personal matter than an attempt to recover from their balls-up in Singapore," said Scott, as Benny led them all down a corridor into a large, airy room taking up one corner of the house. Windows on two walls looked out onto the sprawling vastness of rural Queensland, graceful antique furniture took up a small amount of space leaving a large spread of polished floor. A woman rose from an armchair by one window. She was tall, at least Scott's height, very slender and she moved with a slight limp. Her hair was light brown with no trace of grey that Scott could see, and her complexion looked unlined. Scott would have thought her about thirty-five.

"Hello," she said. "I'm Helen Moskowitch."

"My wife," said Benny with such obvious pride Scott had to smile. He took the proffered hand. It was soft and cool to the touch. If the documents he had read on Benny were correct, Helen was fifty-eight. The documents had made no mention of Jacob. Scott was intrigued by that.

"My pleasure, Mrs. Moskowitch," he said. "I'm so sorry we have to meet in circumstances like these."

"It will help if you'll call me Helen!"

"Thank you!" he smiled. She walked back to her seat and sat down again, with considerable care. Arthritis, Benny had told him in Singapore.

For a moment, the rest of them stood with that slight awkwardness of strangers in a strange house. Jacob had not come into the room with them, and Gretta had stayed for only a moment before vanishing on some errand of her own.

"For Christ's sake, sit down, you blokes!" said Benny and waved them to any of the several chairs around the place.

"Can I suggest something, first?" asked Scott. Benny stopped moving toward a comfortable looking chair by the window and looked at him. "Let's move all seats away from the windows, and draw some curtains. You've already had bullets through the window, I understand."

Benny nodded, and Phil, Benny and Scott spent a few minutes making the room safer. Phil switched on the light.

"Anytime you go to another room, draw the curtains," said Scott.

"All windows have wooden shutters," said Benny. "Why don't we have them all closed?"

"Good idea!" said Scott. "Phil, you and I should go outside and do that. Could we get Jacob to do the upstairs rooms?"

"I'll see to it," Benny said and walked out of the room.

Scott was worried. If somebody was watching the house through a gunsight, anyone closing up the shutters would make a splendid target. He and Phil walked to the front door, opened it and began to walk round the house locking each shutter in turn. Scott had a creepy feeling between his shoulders that cross-hairs of a telescopic sight were focused on him. He had to force himself to appear calm and relaxed and not scream with a burst of fear. Up above, the rattle of windows indicated that Jacob was also locking shutters over the windows. Fifteen minutes later, Scott breathed again as he and Phil returned inside without incident.

The house was gloomy now. Luckily, the air-conditioning was strong enough to keep them comfortable. They gathered again in the lounge. Jacob and Gretta had both joined them, Gretta sitting in a corner behind Benny.

"Council of war, people!" Scott said, trying to make things a little more light-hearted. "Benny, I understand that Phil's people have already suggested you move out and down to Sydney where it would be easier to protect you?"

"They have. I'm staying." Benny was rock firm. "This thing has to be wiped out, not avoided. No bunch of Nazi ratbags is going to make me leave my home."

"And that goes for me." Helen's voice was calm. She seemed quite happy sitting next to Benny and holding one massive hand. Jacob just grinned. He had an air of quiet competence that Scott liked.

"And what was the last exchange you had with the local police?" asked Scott.

Benny sniffed in derision. "They repeated the old crap that it was just a bunch of kids playing around. They were not prepared to give us any attention."

"You think they've been warned off?" asked Scott to Phil.

"Bet your life," replied the Australian agent, briefly.

"We are betting our lives," said Scott. Phil nodded.

"Okay," continued Scott. "Now as I see it, the whole reason for this thing is that they missed Benny in Singapore. Nick will already have been paid for the job, and it's his first failure. So...."

"Nick?" Benny's voice was harsh.

"The killer's name is Nick Wallace. He used to be known as Dieter Konig. Also Mustapha al-Yaffi. He's a leading force in "Knights of Aryan Dawn," a neo-Nazi group."

"You knew this in Singapore!" Benny looked angry.

"No. I *suspected* this in Singapore. The proof came after I got home."

"And he's acting alone?" Jacob looked curious.

Scott turned to him. "I doubt it this time," he said. "He spent several years as Mustapha al-Yaffi convincing everyone that he was a Palestinian terrorist. He did a lot of jobs under that name and he always used to work alone. But that phase of his life has now ended and he's moving back to Germany to step up the work of building the Fourth Reich. He has to end with a clean record to maintain his status and reputation. This time he'll be using help."

"Jesus!" Phil was staring at him. Scott hadn't given him much detail before, unsure if Phil's briefing had included this material. Obviously it had not. "How do you know all this?" Cooper asked.

"He told me before I left," said Scott.

"He told you?" Phil's eyes were wide.

"Wallace was my best friend for eighteen years. As it turns out, he was using the friendship to check out on my mother."

He had their attention the way an attorney has the attention of a rich man's family as he reads the will.

"My mother was named Katerina Horowitz," he continued. "She was Polish...."

"Your mother was Katerina?" Helen's voice was sharp and Benny jerked with shock. Jacob had let out one compulsive gasp then resumed his calm immobility.

"You knew her?" Now they had Scott's attention.

"We knew of her." Benny was looking sad and he had grasped his wife's hand with both of his own.

"How?" Scott felt tears struggling behind his eyes. Benny and Helen simply looked at Jacob. Scott followed their gaze.

"I spent five years with Mossad before returning to Australia," said Jacob. "Katerina Horowitz is a name we all know

250

well. But we didn't know what had happened to her. That was obviously restricted information."

"Now you know. She went to England." Scott had now learned why Jacob Moskowitch did not appear in any files on Benny. Mossad agents kept low profiles.

"Yes. And it had better stay within this room." Jacob looked at his parents, clearly giving them an order.

"The attack on Benny might well have been to some extent because of you, Jacob?" It had just occurred to Scott.

"Possibly." Jacob nodded his head without expression.

"And you will already know something of Mustapha al-Yaffi, and also of Knights of Aryan Dawn?"

He nodded again. "Something."

"Good. It will help." Scott changed the subject. "What weaponry do we have?"

"The two Uzis we brought with us, plus our two handguns. Two more Uzis here, three more handguns, and two Enfield rifles. Lots of ammunition." Phil recited the list as if preparing for a trip to the supermarket.

"Okay," said Scott. "Benny, Jacob, Gretta, you should keep a handgun with you at all times. Carry extra shells with you."

All the faces in the room were serious.

"The rifles are not likely to be much use in this situation," Scott continued. "If there's an attack, it will be at night. And the cover out there is too good. But let's get them ready and maybe keep them by the upstairs windows in case of possibilities."

Jacob stood up. "I'll see to that," he said.

"Good," agreed Scott. "And you, Phil and I will hold onto an Uzi each. Keep the fourth in here."

"And so what do we do now?" Helen seemed calm but the anxiety showed in the strong grip she was keeping on Benny's hands.

"Today, I'm going into town. I want to talk to the local police and get my own idea of just what the situation is."

251

"I'll come with you," Phil said.

Scott shook his head. "They've already seen you. I'm the stranger, and maybe the British security forces card will swing some weight."

"Not likely!" Jacob grinned. "You'll be seen as a Pommie Bastard, which makes you some form of slime low-life around here!"

"That bad, huh?"

"Even worse," laughed Phil.

"Alright," said Scott. "I'll go and play the Pommie Bastard and see what I can see. Everybody else, please stay indoors."

He received a round of nods and some anxious looks but they let him take the Jaguar and drive into the small town.

Corriwongle had a population of about six thousand if the small signpost was anything to go by. Scott drove at thirty miles an hour, the windows closed and the air-conditioning working hard. The temperature for this late winter's day was well up now, warmer than an average summer's day in England. The town was attractive. White wooden buildings, covered sidewalks and beautiful wrought iron railings along the balconies. There were several pubs with a number of vehicles parked outside each of them. The town hall and the police station were next to each other, both by the main crossroad in the middle of the town. There was a large memorial to World War Two in the middle of the junction.

Scott steered his way cautiously round the left side of the memorial and parked by the police station. When he got out the silence hit him again. Just a subdued humming of lots of flies and an occasional drone of a car engine provided a backdrop to the inactivity. He locked the Jaguar, felt the sun strike his head and shoulders and walked into the station.

The door was simply a fly screen and inside, a long counter stretched from wall to wall. A large notice board held pictures of wanted fugitives, warnings about drug use, pictures of a marijuana plant and assorted announcements. A ceiling fan stirred the weary air making some of the papers flutter at regular intervals. A single policeman in shirt sleeves was leaning against the other side of the counter, filling out a form. He was tall and thin and his nose looked capable of cutting through timber.

"G'day," said Scott, walking up to the counter. *Might as well sound like a local for the first few seconds,* he thought. The officer looked briefly at him through narrow-set black eyes.

"G'day," he said, shortly, and resumed his work on the form. He was making heavy weather of the task, taking a painful amount of time and effort with each entry.

"Who's the senior officer here?"

The cop stopped writing and looked up at Scott. The narrow eyes deepened with suspicion and hostility as the English accent became more obvious.

"Who wants to know?"

"Scott McIntyre wants to know."

"And what's a Scott McIntyre?" The insolence was strong in his voice, and the beady eyes were staring hard. Scott took his identification card from his pocket and placed it gently in front of him. The Australian picked it up and examined it carefully, looking several times at Scott's face to compare it with the holograph picture.

"What does British Security want in this place?"

"That's between your senior officer and me."

The Australian stared with anger at the card, at Scott with huge hostility, and seemed to deliberate whether to believe him. Then he took the card with him and walked to a door at the back. He knocked, opened it, and addressed an unseen person in the office.

"You'd better look at this, Sarge. Some Pom from British Security wants to talk to you."

There was silence for a few minutes.

253

"Alright, send him in," said a deep voice. The constable appeared again and returned to the counter. He opened a flap in the surface and swung it up. He didn't speak, but Scott pushed the swing door and walked to the office at the back.

Inside, a large man sat writing at a scruffy desk, loaded with papers. The dirty cream-painted walls had a few photographs hung at unequal heights. Most were of police groups, a couple of them were of the man in front of Scott, standing with other, unknown men in suits. One of them was a huge mass of fat, so rotund he was leaning backward to keep from falling forward under the weight of the enormous belly.

The man at the desk didn't look up as Scott entered. His head was nearly bald, but he had combed as much of the hair on the sides as he could over the top of his scalp. He kept writing, expecting Scott to stand and wait. It was a typical small-minded trick, and Scott refused to be intimidated. He sat down without waiting to be asked and received an angry look. The sergeant had a round face, with several chins. The complexion was poor, and the large, beaky nose had many veins running through the surface of the skin. He put the pen down.

"What's your business here?" he demanded.

"I'd like my card back, first," said Scott, gently. The sergeant picked up the card from his desk, looked at it once more then tossed it casually at Scott.

"Thank you," said Scott. The tricks of insecure men did nothing to him. "I want to talk to you about Benny Moskowitch."

"Why?"

"Because I've come twelve thousand miles to do the job you people have refused to do. I think that's worth talking about."

"It's none of your bloody business!"

"Really? I'm here because your Federal Government asked me to be here. They agreed with your State Government that I needed to be here, because the local police were doing nothing worthwhile. So it *is* my business. I'll ask you directly. Why are you refusing to protect Benny Moskowitch?"

"He doesn't need protecting. Just because a few kids shoot off some rifles, I'm supposed to put a squad of men to look after him? Don't be bloody silly! And I don't jump just because a bunch of socialists in Canberra or Brisbane tells me to."

"And what about the burnt-out barn and the swastikas? Still a bunch of kids in a hunting spree?"

"Probably!" he snapped, not meeting Scott's eye.

"Who gives you your orders, Sergeant?"

"None of your bloody business!"

"I see. And what will it take before you do consider Benny Moskowitch to need protection?"

"A hell of a lot more than he's already had, that's for sure!"

"I see," Scott said again. The situation was clear. He stood up. "I thank you for your cooperation, Sergeant. I'm sure we will meet again."

The sarcasm was lost on the Queenslander. "I doubt it," he grated. "Maybe you should just get back to England where you belong. We can sort out our own problems here, without any help from you."

"I'm sure you can, Sergeant," said Scott with a smile and walked out of his office. The constable at the counter was still working painstakingly at his form, and gave Scott barely a glance as he walked through the swing door and the fly screen to the outdoor heat. Scott moved behind the wall and listened to the conversation inside. The sergeant had obviously come out of his office.

"Christ!" Scott heard him say. "A bloody pommie protecting a bunch of Jew-boys! That's a pretty sight!"

"Bloody oath!" said the constable. Scott got back in the car. The local culture was pretty obvious by now. No wonder they called it the Deep North, thought Scott. Members of the Ku Klux Klan would feel right at home in Corriwongle.

* * *

Back in the Moskowitch home, Scott felt very much at ease. The natural friendliness of all three of them had somehow established a place for Phil and Scott, and Gretta was obviously a close family friend.

It was just after midday when Scott had arrived, and a lunch of cold meats and fruits was laid out in the dining room. More beautiful antique furniture, a long table of such a deep polish it glowed in the cool twilight of the shuttered room.

Scott shook his head at the offer of beer, and stayed with ice-cold lemonade, as did Phil. The two Moskowitch males poured a couple of cans of Fourex down their gullets. Scott doubted that the alcohol would have much impact on their enormous mass.

Scott told them about the meeting in Corriwongle with the police and received calm smiles. "I'd say they've been given orders not to interfere," said Scott.

"Of course," said Jacob. "

"But you don't know for sure?"

He shrugged. "No, I've never really thought about it. Once I'd come home from Israel, I just settled down to running the farm here. I don't bother with politics."

There was a moment of silence round the table.

"So where do we go from here, Scott?" Benny broke the tension.

"We sit put," replied Scott. "Tonight, Phil, Jacob and I will do a scout around the countryside, see if anyone is watching. Jacob, you're up to that?"

"I walked from Damascus to Haifa without being seen, once. I can do it."

"Obviously. Phil?"

"Of course."

"Good. Carry handguns, Uzis and some ammunition, just in case."

Jacob grinned. "I'll take Alice," he said.

"Alice?"

He bent over and pulled a knife from the region of his ankle. It was slim, with a white bone handle. The edge looked luminous and lethal. "This is Alice. Alice, meet Scott and Phil."

Scott stared at the weapon. Jacob held it with a familiarity that suggested he and Alice had spent much time together.

"Good afternoon, Alice," said Scott gravely. "I hope we never meet on a professional basis."

Soon after eight, and darkness was thick on the land. Scott had changed to dark slacks, black long-sleeved polo-necked shirt and had smeared boot polish on his hands and face. All the highlights had been covered. The Browning was slung in its holster on his shoulder, and he had decided to leave the Uzi behind. The three of them stood in the kitchen with the lights off, getting their eyes adjusted. Jacob had pointed out the nearest shrubbery, a bunch of low bushes about fifty yards away, and all of them would aim for that before separating on different patrols of the area.

"Let's hope they don't have night sights," Phil muttered with some nervousness.

"Bloody oath!" murmured Scott and got a smile from both of the others. Jacob softly opened the kitchen door. They slipped through and Scott closed the door again. It would be left unlocked, but the door from the kitchen into the house was securely locked, and the key hidden under a pile of newspapers.

They ran silently for the bushes and the other two simply vanished from Scott's sight. They seemed to know what they were doing, both of them, thought Scott. He moved to his right and aimed for the area that he would patrol.

The first hundred yards was over clear ground, and he simply ran as silently as he could for the distant gum trees. The moon was covered for that time, and when he reached cover, he sat and waited for his breathing to slow to normal before doing anything else. By the time the moon was out again, he was ready to move. He worked his way carefully, moving his feet in the sliding motion which would reduce the risk of stepping on twigs and making a noise. After twenty minutes he stopped, curled up by a tree and simply waited. If others were moving, he would see them first.

But after an hour, he had heard nothing. He carefully stood up, gently moved his arms and legs to get freedom of movement back again, and walked on. He struck an angle of forty-five degrees to his right, keeping a track of his movements relative to the house in his head. The Mongoose training seemed to work, he decided. He was certain that he had made no noise at all, and continued that way for perhaps half a mile before he stopped and camped down again.

He sat and smelled the Queensland country air. He wondered if Nick had taken charge of this operation or had sent others to do it for him. No, he decided, Nick needed to regain the prestige lost in Singapore by doing this job personally. That meant Nick was within a few miles at the most. Maybe within yards. Scott touched the handle of his Browning for comfort. There could be no peaceful parting again if they met. Scott knew he would have to kill or be killed.

How many men did Nick have in support on this operation? Scott wondered. Not many, he decided. He knew that Nick hated working with others, and would probably have taken just three or four with him. Phil Cooper would be an invaluable support in this war, and the unexpected professionalism of Jacob Moskowitch was a blessing. All in all, Scott felt the odds might be with the good guys.

A twig snapped. Somebody had not learned silent movement through forestry. Scott became even more still than he had been the last twenty minutes. Maybe it was Phil or Jacob moving into his patrol area, and attacking each other would be a very bad idea. But then he heard a tiny whisper, and Scott knew it was foe, not friend. He sat rigidly by the base of the tree, bushes around him, lowered his eyes to hide the whites, and was certain he was invisible to anyone passing.

Three men walked by him, no more than three feet away. Scott could smell the tobacco on the clothes of one of them, a bad case of body odour on another. They moved in single file, moving clumsily. When they had passed his position, Scott carefully stood up, let the men get about ten yards in front, then he followed carefully. They retraced the path Scott had followed to get here, obviously moving toward the house.

They stopped suddenly, and Scott froze.

"The bloody lights are all out," grumbled one of the men. Scott realized they were in sight of the house, maybe a hundred yards away across clear ground.

"No, you can see a bit of light," said one of the other men. "Reckon they've drawn the storm shutters."

"Must be that bloody pommie who's moved in with them," said the first one. "Bill said he was MI5, or MI6 or something."

Scott wondered whether Bill was the constable or the sergeant at Corriwongle police station. Neither had bothered to introduce themselves.

"I don't bloody care what he is, no bloody pommie bastard is going to keep those Jew-boys safe." The second voice again.

"Yeah, there's still only three of them in the place. Mind you, I wouldn't want to meet that Benny bloke on my own!"

"Or his son. That bastard's even bigger!" The third man finally spoke.

"Shit, they're only Jews! They'll go down with a couple of slugs in their guts, just like a white man!"

259

Interesting, thought Scott. They didn't know about Phil and they didn't know about Gretta. Scott suspected that for a little middle-aged woman, Gretta might pack a nasty sting with the Beretta nine millimetre she had slung at her waist. The way she had checked it, loaded it, and put it in the holster when Phil gave it to her indicated a level of familiarity with the weapon which the average personal assistant would not display.

And while they knew about Jacob, Scott doubted they would know about his Mossad background. Nick's army could end up getting a very nasty surprise. For the moment, though, Scott had three armed men in front of him, and he was uncertain what to do.

The clank of metal broke the conversation. They were all three carrying rifles, though of what type and size, Scott could not make out. But the snick-snick of a bolt being drawn and snapped back to pull a bullet into the chamber was a distinctive noise, and from the sound of these, Scott doubted that the men were carrying little twenty-two calibre weapons.

"Wait on, I've got to have a pee," said one of the trio.

"Shit, Fred, you should have gone before!"

"It'll only take a minute! We've got all night!" With that, one of the shadows put his rifle down, stood up from the crouched position all three had taken, and walked straight at Scott. The agent moved quickly to one side, held his breath and Fred walked past, his arm almost touching Scott's chest. There was very little light, but enough to move by, and the man walked a few feet further before stopping. Scott heard the tiny zipper noise as he opened his trousers and then the fluttering noise of urine striking foliage. This seemed a good opportunity for action.

His gun butt swung sharply at the man's head and Fred collapsed without a sound. Scott had timed it perfectly. The gunman would be out for a few minutes with a bit of luck. Scott stepped gently back to the other two.

In the dim light, he could see they had adopted a woodsman's stance for shooting. They were sitting down, knees up, and their left arms supported by their knees, holding the rifles. Scott waited.

"Shit, where's the hell's Fred?" complained one of the men.

"Who cares?" said the other and opened fire. A massive jolt shook him. It was certainly no twenty-two rifle he carried.

"Good evening, gentlemen," said Scott into the echoes of the explosion.

"What the fuck..?" shouted the one who had just fired, and swung round behind him. He had barely time to work the bolt and put another bullet in the chamber before Scott's bullet took him squarely in the head. The man dropped with a slight crunching of undergrowth. *My second kill,* thought Scott. He felt nothing.

The other man was totally frozen. He was still sitting in his firing position, motionless.

"Now you won't shoot, will you?" said Scott gently. The other man's head waved from side to side.

"Good. Drop the rifle, but open the bolt first, there's a good boy." The gunman did as he was told, moving slowly as if numbed, or drunk. In the dark and the bushes, he had no idea where Scott's voice was coming from. Scott stayed hidden.

"Now, stand up." The man stood up. The moon was out, and immediately in front of him was clear ground. He was perfectly silhouetted against the grass.

"Walk into the moonlight, my friend, about five paces and stand still," said Scott. The gunman moved like a faulty robot, jerky, uncoordinated as he stepped into the open. In the light, Scott could see his eyes wide open in shock. "And now we will stay here for a while," Scott added.

Still hidden completely from the gunman, Scott moved back to where the first man, Fred, was still lying flat out. He had to search a while, but finally located the huddled shape. He quickly checked for other weapons, but the rifle he had left behind appeared to be the only thing he had brought to the party. Scott located Fred's collar, took a strong grip and simply hauled him to the clear spot where the other man was still standing motionless. It looked like he had no idea that Scott had been away. Scott dumped the unconscious Fred on the edge of the moonlit ground and retreated to the shadows again.

"Okay, pal. Come and pick up your little mate, here," he said. Slowly, the gunman moved to the man on the ground, bent over and took him under his arms, hauling him to where he had stood in the moonlight.

"Now we'll stand still and wait," said Scott. "If you even scratch your bum, you get a bullet in the head, right?"

The man nodded, in that same shocked way he had moved earlier. Scott waited ten minutes by his best guess, then spoke in a normal voice.

"Phil? Jacob? You blokes around?"

"You bet, mate! Been here five minutes!" Scott recognized the voice of Jacob.

"Three for me!" said Cooper.

Scott hadn't heard a sound. "Anyone else around, you reckon?" he asked.

"Not a chance." Jacob's voice, and Scott believed him. Jacob and Phil were professionals.

"Okay," said Scott. "I'm moving out with the third body. He's dead." He groped and found the collar of the dead man, ignored the blood and the gritty substance that was probably his brains, and pulled him out to drop the body by the other two men. The one standing gave a terrified glance at Scott, and then at the body.

Two shapes materialized out of the trees just a few feet from where Scott had been standing. The enormous shape of Jacob would have scared a grizzly bear, thought Scott, and watched with interest at the reaction of the prisoner. No grizzly bear he, and he was so frightened, it was pathetic to watch. Scott walked back into the bushes and came back with the three rifles, laying them on the grass in front of them.

"Any suggestions, Jacob?" he asked.

"The second barn," Jacob said, softly. "We'll chain them up in there so nobody can get them out."

"Sounds good," said Scott.

The unconscious man began to stir. Scott's estimate of time had been way out, the little sleep had lasted nearly fifteen minutes. He waited for Fred to groan and move a bit more, then nodded at Jacob.

"Want him to stand up?"

"What a good idea," Jacob grinned, his teeth white in the moonlight. He reached down, grabbed the collar of Fred and pulled. The man leaped upwards as if bounding off a trampoline. He landed back on his feet with another groan, weakly pulling at the hand on his collar.

"Good evening, little man," said Jacob in a friendly sort of way as the eyes opened and stared at him. "My name is Jacob Moskowitch. And how are you, tonight?"

The little man, who was about six foot and heavily built almost shrieked in terror and tried to move away from the face smiling at him so gently. He might have been shackled in chains, for he moved about an inch.

"I said," repeated Jacob, with some menace. "How are you tonight?"

Fred moaned again, and was violently sick on the grass.

Jacob let him drop. "Obviously he's not very well," he said.

"Can't imagine why," replied Scott.

"Will you two silly buggers stop clowning around?" Phil was nearly choking with laughter, the relief of the end of dangerous action providing the common reaction of near hysteria. "We need to get these specimens put away!"

"This is true," said Jacob, and pointed at the one man still on his feet. "You!" he said. "Pick him up!" He gestured at the body.

263

"And you! Help him!" He gently kicked Fred who was now on his knees, slowly getting up.

The two prisoners somehow managed to get hold of the arms and legs of the body and hauled it, sometimes dragging it on the ground, but generally making their way under Jacob's guidance to the nearby barn. The three agents carried a rifle each. The trip was perhaps a hundred yards, and it took twenty minutes before Jacob pulled open a door and switched on a light. A weak glow shed a dim, shadowy gloom on the scene.

Scott looked at the three men who had arrived with guns. The body had no face at all. Scott's bullet appeared to have caught him just in front of the left ear and removed everything forward of that spot. The last man was red-haired, and Fred, the one Scott had knocked out in the bushes was a young man in his twenties, with a moustache. Jacob looked at him in contempt.

"I thought better of you, Fred. You worked for us for three years! Your family got a Christmas hamper from us each year!"

The young man stared at his feet and said nothing.

"Scott," said Jacob, turning away from Fred. "There's a length of chain with padlocks against that wall over there. Bring it over, will you?"

Scott found the chain and did as he asked, watching as Jacob wound chain carefully over the wrists of both living men, locking them so that escape was possible only to a Houdini. Finally, the chain was locked round a main beam supporting the roof.

"Okay, let's go and get dinner!" said Jacob, cheerfully.

"Hey! What about him?" It was Fred shouting, panic in his eyes.

"Who?" asked Jacob innocently.

"Him!" shouted Fred, trying to point at the body lying about four feet away from him.

"Oh, him!" said Jacob, picking up the rifle he had put on a bale of hay while attending to the chaining of the prisoners. "He's okay, he can't get away!"

And he led the other two out of the barn, switching off the light, ignoring the howl of terror that came from the chained men inside.

Mossad bred them tough, decided Scott.

Scott thought about his reactions as they ate. He had just killed a man for the second time in his life. After the first time in Chicago, he had slept badly, with nightmares, and the awful memories kept returning to his mind in slow motion for weeks afterwards. He kept seeing the waiter's face as the bullet took him in the forehead just above the nose, how his body collapsed to the floor and seemed to shrivel in size as the life left it.

This time, he had none of these reactions. He felt as indifferent as if he had just stamped on a cockroach. The man he had killed represented the people who had slaughtered Scott's mother's family during the war, and then killed her with his father and his sister in a casual blast of an explosive, surely the most cowardly way of murdering anyone. Scott didn't know the dead man's name. He didn't care. Dinner tasted great.

The meal was subdued, however. The bullet shot from the heavy rifle by the man in the bushes had hit the wall and not gone through the window, but Benny and Helen had heard the shot, followed rapidly by the smaller sound of Scott's pistol.

"I killed the one who fired the rifle. The other two are locked up in the barn," said Scott, when asked by a pale-faced Helen. He didn't think the Moskowitch family were people to be sheltered from unpleasant facts.

"Maybe this will convince the police?" suggested Gretta.

"Not a chance!" put in Phil. "They'll be more likely to charge us with murder and hush the whole thing up. This way, we'll leave the next stage to them, and see what happens."

"How frightening it is," said Helen, "that here in Australia, we seem to have a Nazi group big enough to control the local police.

This was always supposed to be the country of refuge for people seeking an escape from this sort of thing."

"Frightening, yes," said Benny. "Surprising? Not when you think about it."

"No?" Phil turned a questioning face at Benny. "I've always thought of my country as one of the most liberal, free places in the world."

"In many ways, it is," agreed Benny. "But remember how we started, as a prison colony ruled by rejects from British society. There was always a military autocracy about the way this place was governed. Remember the leanings toward the Axis powers during the war? Nazi-style philosophies have had good soil in this state for many years."

"And you should look at Australia's history just after the war," added Jacob. "When the country finally agreed to take in European refugees, the official policy was to take only Northern Europeans. The secret forms we've seen since, actually used the word "Aryan" as the preferred type of immigrant, and immigration officers were specifically ordered to exclude Jews and Hispanics."

"It's not the image that most of the world has about Australia," said Scott with a frown. Benny and his son were expressing uncomfortable ideas, and without the light-hearted manner in which he had done it in Singapore in the last discussion.

"No, it's not," agreed Jacob. "But it's the case. Meanwhile, we had better prepare for the next instalment of this saga."

"I suppose so," said Scott. "Phil, shouldn't you be reporting what's happened?"

"But how will he do that?" asked Gretta with a worried look. "You can bet your life our phone is tapped."

"No worries!" Phil was smiling. "I use a computer!"

He stood up from the table and went to his bag still sitting by the wall where he had left it after extracting the Uzis that morning. He took out a case and opened it.

"One NEC laptop!" he announced proudly. "I type my report into this, hook it up to the phone and transmit it directly to Canberra."

"Better do it quickly!" suggested Scott. "Before they cotton on to what you're doing."

Phil nodded, opened up the machine and began tapping a short report into it. Within five minutes he had finished, carried the computer to the telephone on the china cabinet, unplugged the phone and plugged a connection from the computer into the socket. He pressed a few more keys, the computer beeped at them, and Phil examined the screen.

"Okay," he said. "They've got it."

"Good," said Scott, with a small sigh of relief. "At least somebody knows what we're facing here."

Phil was replacing the telephone connections. "Oh-oh!" he said.

"What?" Jacob was the one to ask, alarm in his voice.

"They've caught on. The phone's dead."

"Nice!" commented Scott. "That means we can expect some further action quite soon." Despite the tension, he yawned hugely.

"Bed for you, young Scott," smiled Jacob, who was probably a couple of years younger than Scott. "Phil and I will take watch for the rest of the night. I doubt much more will happen till tomorrow evening, anyway."

"You're probably right," said Scott, feeling the effects of thirty hours of travel and the exploits of the day catch up with him abruptly. Gretta showed him upstairs to a small, comfortable room, and he barely had time to get his clothes off and climb into the single bed, before the blackness took him.

* * *

Scott groped for his wristwatch and discovered it was seven in the morning. He had woken to the screaming hysteria of the Kookaburras that echoed around the house in the dawn chorus that was so common in rural Australia. It sounded like a mob of drunken hooligans laughing at some silly joke. Sleep was impossible with that racket.

Wonderful smells were wafting into his room, fresh coffee, bacon... bacon? In a Jewish household? Well, maybe. He hoped so, he was well into his British breakfast passion. He wasn't disappointed, either. By the time he had found the bathroom, shaved, showered and generally restored himself to life, the entire household was round the table attending to what looked like a Royal Air Force breakfast. Fried bread, bacon, eggs, toast, coffee, it was like coming home.

"Nice to see a good kosher kitchen!" said Scott, walking into the dining room. Helen laughed.

"We all grew up in England, even though Benny and I were born in Poland!" she said, grinning widely. "I've still never found anything to beat bacon and eggs for breakfast! Sit down and stop complaining!"

Scott did as ordered, and gave suitably respectful attention to the banquet laid out before them.

"No further action last night, obviously," he said to Jacob seated next to him. Jacob shook his head.

"They would have waited some hours for the three to get back and report," he said. "Right now, it's probably like a hornet's nest, wherever the headquarters are."

"I'd love to know where that is," said Scott, buttering a fresh slice of toast and covering it with home-made marmalade.

"We will," said Jacob softly. Scott believed him.

* * *

The day passed quietly. Scott spent some hours in an upstairs room searching through the re-opened shutter with high powered binoculars for any signs of movement in the trees and saw nothing. At noon, his only excitement was to see a small group of kangaroos bounce lethargically across one of the fields to the west before vanishing into the haze.

The three of them, Phil, Jacob and Scott assumed a pattern of relieving each other for lookout duties and general patrolling of the house. Occasionally, Scott met with Gretta, Benny and Helen who seemed to be handling things with remarkable calm. He said as much to them at one point, late in the morning as he joined them in the kitchen for more coffee. Gentle smiles appeared on all three faces.

"Scott, we are Jews born in Europe before the war," said Helen. "The face of anti-Semitism is not new to us. We have seen Israel and know what it is like to have people nearby whose only interest is in killing us. Living with this is horrible, but hardly a new experience."

Scott began to understand a little of what had made his mother the woman she had been.

The heat built up into the eighties after the rather cold night. Early in the afternoon, Phil and Scott walked over to the barn and inspected the prisoners, while Jacob caught up on his sleep.

The two living ones were pitiful. They moaned when they saw the two agents, and stood up from their slouch against the pillar. The body of the third lay face down in the hay, and that was a small blessing, because the flies were already thick around the head. Turned the other way, the faceless man would have been a nightmare sight.

"For God's sake, let us out of here!" begged Fred. His face was white and he looked ill. Scott saw a bucket standing by a tap in the wall, and altered course toward it. He filled the bucket and returned to the men.

"Here," he said, and held the bucket to each of their mouths in turn. They gulped greedily, and Scott poured the rest over the head of the dead man in the hay. The clouds of flies erupted like a burst of smoke from a volcano, then settled back as the agents walked out.

Scott still felt nothing for the two men, nor for the man he had killed last night.

The day passed as they thought it would, in silent heat. Nothing moved outside, and only the occasional call of a Kookaburra disturbed the somnolent air that hummed continuously with the hypnotic drone of insects. Jacob, Phil and Scott took turns keeping a lookout from the upper windows, having un-shuttered them during the day for this purpose. They stood well back inside the rooms to peer out, trusting that any sniper in the distance would be unable to see inside the darkened area.

At three-thirty, a different sound intruded, and Scott watched as a small Piper Cherokee approached at about a thousand feet and circled the mansion house in a clockwise direction. Phil and Jacob came into the room from where Scott was watching the aircraft through the binoculars.

"What do you think?" asked Phil.

"They're watching us, okay," answered Scott. He could see the figure in the right hand seat, also armed with binoculars.

"Why not scare the hell out of them?" suggested Jacob, stroking his rifle suggestively. It was one of the ones they had removed from the prisoners, and was a beautifully equipped 7.62 calibre Mauser SP66 with a telescopic sight.

"No!" said Scott sharply. "It could just as well be Phil's people having a look for themselves, maybe scouting out the enemy's troop movements. We can't take the risk."

"I suppose not," he murmured, regretfully.

The Cherokee did one more circuit of the house then turned away to the south and vanished.

At just after four, a howling, shrieking banshee thundered about half a mile to the west and vanished, leaving the echoes of its passing reverberating the china.

"F-111," said Scott.

"Very good!" said Jacob. "They're based at Amberly, the Air Force station about thirty kilometres to the west of here."

Scott remembered now, somebody else had mentioned Amberly to him on his previous trip. Two other Australian Air Force bases in this general part of the world, he had learned, one at Williamtown a little up the coast from Sydney, and one inland, near the mining town of Kathleen in the Northern Territories. Both had been equipped with the FA-18 Hornet interceptor fighters to replace the ageing Mirages and were now facing replacement themselves. Scott had known a few Aussies in flight school. Good chance that some of them were stationed in one or more of these bases. It was useful to remember. He settled back in his chair and tried to relax.

They came in the evening.

As the first shadows of dusk began to creep in, Scott was sitting in the lounge, feeling the nerves of impending action. Phil had closed up the shutters in the upstairs rooms and Jacob had completed a thorough inspection of all their weaponry. Little conversation was taking place.

Scott's senses were operating at peak efficiency, and he sat up straight.

"Listen!" he said. Puzzled faces stared at him. They heard nothing. Scott sat for another two seconds and confirmed the sound in his mind. A very familiar sound. He had spent three years making sounds like that, flying the helicopters of Air Sea Rescue, based at Lossiemouth in northern Scotland. Two

271

aircraft, he decided, the whop-whop-whop of the rotors approaching fast.

"Helicopters!" he snapped. "Two of them coming in together! Get ready! Switch off all lights! Take the Uzis, have plenty of reloads!"

He snatched his sub machine gun, grabbed half a dozen magazines, watched as Phil, Jacob and Gretta did the same. Helen snapped off the light and Jacob ran into the lobby where the only other light was on, switching it off with a sweep of his hand.

The four of them with Uzis raced upstairs and flung open the shutters. Each of them took a different room, with a different outlook. In the east, Scott could see the lights of the helicopters approaching, two of them as he thought, flying at about five hundred feet.

God, he thought with longing. *How I'd love to do what Jacob had wanted to do earlier, and use the high-powered rifle to put a shot into those lumbering machines from here.* But he had the same dilemma as earlier. They could just be friendly forces arriving. But somehow, he was certain they were not and he reached for one of the SP66 rifles they had taken from the prisoners and which was still leaning against the wall by the window. All he had was the contents of the magazine, just three shots. Their prisoners had not been carrying extra ammunition. Their mission must have been one of harassment rather than serious intent to murder. Perhaps.

He moved the safety catch, looked through the telescopic sight and watched the first of the choppers lift its nose to slow down and grope for the ground. It was a Westland Whirlwind, an elderly machine which had been replaced years before Scott converted to rotary wing aircraft. Scott visualized the pilot's actions as the Whirlwind moved... ease back on the cyclic to raise the nose, lower the collective and let the fuel injection computer drop the rotor power to maintain constant revolutions...

Both Whirlwinds landed about a hundred yards away. *Dammit, I should have thought!* swore Scott to himself. These craft were obsolete, no Australian military units would be equipped with them, they had to be the attackers. *Why didn't I realize that earlier, and use the heavy rifle to do some damage before they arrived? Very silly, Scott. Try using that supposedly highly trained military mind, you silly bugger.*

He still had a rifle. So did Jacob and Phil. They had eight 7.62 calibre bullets loaded into perfectly-balanced rifles in the hands of experts. They could do a lot of damage before the enemy knew it. Just as Scott thought that, the other two men moved into the room he was inhabiting, in order to get a clear view of the targets.

The side doors of both helicopters slid open. In the gathering gloom, Scott could just see the figures crouched inside, springing into movement. *My God!* he thought. *Maybe eight or nine men in each, this is going to be bloody!* He sighted on the lead figure, wondered briefly if it could be Nick, got the cross hairs on the man's chest and squeezed the trigger gently.

The flash and explosion in the room were horrific. Scott saw the man go down, jerk slightly and lie still. The other rifles in the room spoke authoritatively and two more men went down. Scott worked the bolt, heard the other two do the same, and sent fire and death into the middle of the men swarming onto the grass. A hail of bullets struck the wall above the window, somebody had got the nerve to let loose with a sub machine gun, but as usual, had fired high. It was the common problem, the defenders were in the upper level of a house which was also on a slight hill. They had the high ground, and shooting uphill almost always caused aiming problems, especially with automatic weapons which tended to fire high.

The time for rifles was over, the attackers were too close. Scott reached for the Uzi and moved out of the room. The action from now would be at ground level. He raced downstairs, calling to Helen and Benny.

"Stay out of the line of windows, stay out..."

His message was suddenly confirmed by the blast of bullets that hailed through the shattered shutter of the window to the entrance hall. Small volcanoes erupted in the plaster walls as bullets hit them above head height. Still shooting high, but that wouldn't last long. Benny and Helen did exactly the right thing and lay down on the floor. Scott saw that both of them had taken the spare handguns and he had no doubts at all that both of them would know how to use them. He waved them into the corners of the lobby. The other two suddenly raced down the stairs as Scott had done a few seconds ago. The upstairs position was of no use now, the attackers were too close, protected by the eaves around the house. There were far more than Scott had thought would appear, Nick was obviously determined to wipe out the disgrace of Singapore, and for the first time, Scott had a horrible worry that he might succeed.

He saw a shadow at the broken remnants of the shutter and without thinking, let off a small burst. The Uzi burped gently and someone screamed outside. Scott heard the thump of a body on the wooden balcony floor. Maybe three or four down of the original attacking force, plus seven or eight of the original group caught by the heavy rifles, there were perhaps fifteen or more left. The chopper pilots would probably stay at their controls, rotors flying for a quick getaway if necessary.

Another window shattered under the hail of bullets, Phil calmly aimed at the gap, waited for a glimpse of a person on the other side and released a two second burst. Thump. Another one down. Scott heard the crash of glass from the lounge room, somebody had smashed their way through, and simultaneously a body simply threw itself through the open space of the lobby window. Scott waited a second, saw Jacob hit his first target, he shrank back in his corner, saw a shadow hurtle in from the lounge, aimed, pressed, burp of Uzi and heard the horrible scream as the bullets cut the man's chest into a bloody mass. Not short of courage, these people, thought Scott, whatever their politics.

It was time to take the offensive. Scott did exactly what the last man had done, simply ran at the window, launched himself head first through the open space at an angle so as not to hit the balcony railing straight on. He hit the floor, rolled, stretched his legs and went over the railing, this time landing in the gravel patch outside the front door. He still had the Uzi in his hands, the Browning was in its holster.

He saw men in a group near the door, tried to shoot and found the Uzi was empty... *Christ! Have I let off a complete magazine already?* He snapped the release catch, dropped the empty magazine, reached in his pocket for a fresh one and slapped it into place. *Damn, the shadows had dissipated, where the hell had they gone?*

He crouched and moved softly round the side of the house. He heard a burst of fire from within, a scream. *Jesus! I hope it's not one of ours.* He saw the four of them talking urgently, and he recognized the slender, lean shape. Nick was here! Scott raised the Uzi, let off a burst in their direction, soft sound like ripping cloth as the weapon released a stream of bullets... they all went down, one single choking sound.. *My God! Have I hit Nick? Have I killed my best friend?*

Bullets suddenly flew past his head... *where the hell did they come from?* He ducked, moved rapidly back to the front of the house, away from the flash of the gun, saw another man running, let off a burst... got the bastard! Down he went, rolling hard against the balcony.

Another burst of firing inside the house, another scream burnt through his head. Scott couldn't see any more people outside the house, they must all have got in by now. That gave Scott a problem. To race inside himself would leave him exposed to fire from his friends, he had to get in at a quiet point of the house. He crept round the walls, looking for a broken window without sounds of action in the room. Finally he found one, it seemed quiet inside, he lifted a leg to climb in, still no sounds, shifted his weight to the inside leg, moved his other leg and crouched down again. He was in the lounge room. He stood up... then a crashing blow on the top of his head sent him spinning against the wall, crazy colours ran wild behind his eyes... *I'm hit! I wonder if I'm dead... wonder what it's like to be dead.. at least I'll have all the answers soon... sorry, Benny and Helen.... sorry, Janette...*

Then the blackness stood up and hit him in the face.

* * *

Blood was dry on his face and had gummed up his left eye. Inside his head felt like a steam hammer was demolishing a brick building, and he was nauseous. His legs were crushed under something heavy, and his arms felt twisted. For a wild moment, he thought he was back in his car, being woken by a pair of Birmingham policemen after succumbing to Nick's knock-out pill. The memories of the gun battle came rushing back into his mind, and Scott returned to the present.

What in God's name had happened? His last memory was of something hitting him with dreadful force on the head and then falling into a bottomless black pit. He opened his right eye, managed to move both arms and tried to see what was crushing his legs so badly. The moonlight was quite strong now, and he could see the chunk of masonry on his legs... moonlight? He clearly remembered climbing in through the window, he should be indoors. But the moon was definitely shining straight down on him... the wall had collapsed. *Good grief, the house is a wreck!* He pushed hard at the masonry on his legs and managed to force it off. He was lying in the middle of more bricks and hunks of stone, under the tilting mass of something he couldn't identify... it was the piano! He recalled seeing the piano in the lounge, an old, pitted upright which Benny told him he had played as a child, brought it with him to Australia, and which Jacob had learned to play before he was six.

He struggled upright and looked around. He was definitely in the lounge, or what was left of it. The southern wall was half shattered, a long jagged edge of stone falling from ceiling to floor. The ceiling above was also badly broken, the eaves of the outside balcony completely demolished, and that was the gap through which the moon was shining so strongly. The Uzi was lying by his side, he still had his Browning in the shoulder holster. Two fresh magazines for the machine gun were sticking into his right thigh as he leaned against the piano for support.

Masses of stone and brick lay on top of the wonderful antique furniture, some of which was broken like a child's toy, arms and legs of Queen Anne and Hepplewhite chairs sticking out in sad disarray. This was bomb damage. From the layout of the damage, it looked like the bomb had exploded by the wall, and Scott's survival was solely because he had been by the piano that had taken most of the blast. The blow on the head was most likely from a flying brick.

He picked his way out through the door to the entrance hall that was lying at an angle on one hinge, and he still had light to see, as the front door was totally gone. Nobody was around. He looked at his watch, peered closely at it and moved it under the light... three in the morning, good grief! He had been unconscious for six or seven hours. He looked around, the corridor to the kitchen looked unmarked, and he limped in that direction. The kitchen was almost complete, just the smashed window to reflect the warfare of the last evening. He made it to the sink, opened the tap and took a deep drink of the pure well water that supplied the house. It tasted like champagne. He washed his face and removed the blood that was gumming up his eye. Finally, he was able to take a proper look around.

And he found tragedy almost immediately. Huddled in the shadows of the lobby, was Gretta. She was lying in the corner where Scott had last seen her shooting at one of the intruders. A single hole where her right eye had been told what had happened. She still had the Uzi on its strap on her shoulder, and the nine millimetre Beretta pistol in her hand. She looked relaxed. Scott kept walking, moved to the front door and found another body lying just outside, face down. He turned it over, feeling a painful jerk in his arms and legs as he bent down and pulled at the weight. It was Phil. A line of blood-ringed bullet holes from left shoulder to his right hip stitched a simple line of death across his blue sweater.

There was nobody else around. Scott walked through the whole house, stepping carefully where the darkness was deepest, but not another human was in the place. No Benny, no Helen, no Jacob. And no other bodies. He could distinctly remember the killings. Scott had no doubt that he had killed at least seven or eight of the attackers, Jacob had shot at least one, Phil had shot one... Several men had died under the hail of Mauser shells as they first jumped out of the invading helicopters... where the hell were they all? The invaders must have taken their dead with them, perhaps to avoid any identification that might be embarrassing. Which caused Scott to think of something. What about the men in the barn?

He shouldered the Uzi on its leather strap and picked his way out of the front door again, walked round the house to check on any bodies and still found none. He struck out for the barn. He reached the door, chanced switching on the light and wished he hadn't. The three men were still there.

Somebody had decided they didn't have the time to free the two living ones from their chains and they had taken a suggestion from the man Scott had killed in the bushes. The two chained men were hanging in their tethers still, but without faces or hands. Heavy bullets had destroyed all chances of identification, the faces were simply bloody masses of flesh and bone, the hands were shattered beyond any chance of finding fingerprints. The sight was worse than anything from any horror movie, and for a moment, Scott could do nothing but stare, numbed. He threw up over the straw.

The attackers had missed him. In the blast, Scott had fallen under a pile of shattered wall, under the piano and not been seen. He wondered if the invaders realized yet that he was missing. When they did, Scott was sure they would return, Nick would see to that. They would most likely assume Scott was dead. The damage was so heavy that the chances of anyone living through the storm they had brought with them so slight, that Nick's army would simply send an expedition when it was light, to ensure Scott was dead and identify the body. That gave Scott an idea.

He worked his way back to the house, closed his mind firmly to the thoughts of the bodies of Phil and Gretta still lying dead, and looked around. He needed a reasonable space for hiding. Eventually, he decided on a closet in the lounge that served as a coat storage. Through the slatted door, he was able to see beyond the demolished wall of the lounge and out into the open at the front of the house. A number of coats still hung there, a pair of huge raincoats which could only belong to Benny and Jacob, and a light cloth woman's coat which might be Gretta's or Helen's. Scott had plenty of space.

He climbed back upstairs to the bedroom where he had managed just one night's sleep, pulled the pillow and a couple of blankets off and took them back down. The night was cold, and the floor was hard. No point in being too stoic about things, he thought. He lined the closet floor with the blankets, put down the pillow and curled up under the top blanket. As an after-thought, he reached up and pulled down the woman's coat, too. He shifted the Uzi and the magazines to one corner, pulled the closet door shut, and lay down. He even slept.

Jamieson's training school would have been proud of me, was his last waking thought.

Chapter 10 - A Friendly Killing

At dawn, they came back. Just a single helicopter this time and the sound of the rotor brought Scott awake with a jolt. Crawling worms of tension paraded in his stomach as he checked the Browning and the Uzi and sat upright. His head was still pounding but he tried to ignore it, and concentrated on the more dangerous thumping of the Whirlwind's rotor blades as the machine approached. He prayed that his theory that Nick would not be expecting resistance from Scott's dead body was correct.

He traced the helicopter's path in his mind, heard with an expert's ear the change of pitch as the machine raised its nose to slow down, the pilot moved the collective lever up to increase the rotor pitch to slow the descent, and the drop in noise as the machine touched down. The rotors kept flying, so Scott knew that the pilot was still with the controls. One never left a Whirlwind with its engine running without somebody holding onto the cyclic lever. The enormous force of the blades could tip the aircraft over if the rotor was in any position but neutral. So maybe only two or three men would be coming.

Scott peered out through the door slats. He was lucky. The Whirlwind was just settling on the grass at the edge of the gravel square in front of the house. The men inside were evidently not worried about safety coming in so close, and clearly didn't expect to find any life in the house. The aircraft was pointing away from the building, slightly to Scott's right, so that the sliding door in the right side of the machine faced the house. He watched, tense.

A single man climbed out of the body of the helicopter. He was dressed in a blue flying suit and wore a bonedome, the protective helmet used by aircrew. It was the standard type with a sun visor pushed up and the cloth covering still in place to keep scratches off the blue plastic. Scott had owned one of those helmets for ten years. A pilot sat in the right hand seat, which, in these machines was the captain's position. He wore a similar bonedome to the man now approaching the house. Scott couldn't see whether there was a co-pilot in the left seat.

The lone man walked casually up to the rubble of the house whistling cheerfully. He jumped perkily onto the balcony with a thump on the wooden floor and bent down over the body of Phil. Scott stifled the spasm of rage that went through him as the man kept whistling while he studied Phil's face. The intruder stood up and moved into the entrance hall, out of Scott's vision. Scott crouched up on one knee and removed the Browning from its holster.

He heard the sounds of furniture being shifted as the whistling man moved around in the entrance hall. The man's steps resounded on the wooden floors as he walked into the kitchen and back into Scott's view again. For a moment, the intruder stood silently, examining the body of Gretta in the entrance hall. His steps receded again as he moved to the dining room.

Scott replaced the Browning and gently eased the closet door open. He had no wish for any movement to be visible to the helicopter pilot in case he happened to be looking in his rear view mirror, nor for any squeak of wood on metal hinges. At the narrowest possible point he crawled on his stomach through the door and into the ruin of the lounge, leaving the Uzi and the magazines behind. They would not be of much use in this situation and he would come back for them. From the lounge he painfully inched along the corridor back to the entrance hall. He moved behind one of the china cabinets and stayed down, listening.

The intruder's footsteps started again. He was moving back toward Scott. The steps got louder and Scott held his breath. He was certain his heart was rocking the place, so violently was it beating. The man reached the hall and stopped. He was still whistling. He seemed to stand in indecision for a few seconds then appeared to move toward the stairs. That was enough for Scott. He stood up, the Browning pointed in the other man's direction. The intruder was looking up the staircase as he walked toward it, and didn't notice Scott's movement behind him.

"Good morning!" Scott said loudly. Even under the flying helmet the other man heard him. He swung round with an expression of absolute dismay on his face. It didn't last long. Scott shot him cleanly in the heart and the man collapsed where he stood. Despite the absence of a silencer, Scott knew the helicopter pilot would have heard nothing at this distance, under the racket from the rotors and the soundproofing of his helmet.

He walked up to the body and steeled himself. He almost laughed at his silliness. *Queasy after killing maybe eight or nine men? Don't be stupid, Scott!* He unzipped the flying suit and manhandled it off the body. The hole over the heart was lightly ringed with blood, though at the back it was a mess. But it would have to do. Underneath, the corpse was wearing a white T-shirt, a black sweater and blue jeans. The blood on the shirt and sweater was heavier. At the back it was a nightmare of gore and burnt cloth. The dead man was not carrying a gun at all. Scott struggled into the flying suit. It was a little short in the legs and arms and uncomfortable in the groin, but he would manage. He took off the man's helmet and the inner helmet with the earphones. These were luckily more Scott's size and he slipped both on his head with a powerful sense of a return of old times.

He lowered the visor as much as he could, covering some of his face without interfering with his vision. He returned the Browning to its holster, walked back to the lounge and retrieved the Uzi and the magazine. He took a deep breath and walked out through the shattered wall.

Feeling trembles in his legs and hurting from the bruises of masonry, he tried to walk as jauntily as had the other man. He saw the pilot look backward at him. Scott waved the Uzi cheerfully and gave a rotating wave of his hand above his head, the helicopter pilot's signal to get going. He reached the rear door, and slid inside. The two pilots, and now Scott could see that there were two, sat in a separate compartment a couple of feet higher than the floor on which he was now standing. There was a space between the two areas of the plane but all Scott could see were two pairs of boots and the hips of the men in the cockpit. That suited him fine. He checked the time on his watch, strapped himself into one of the small seats on the wall opposite the doorway and kept hold of the Uzi. If the pilot had seen him carrying it he would probably have assumed Scott had taken it as a prize from the house.

The roar of the engine swelled and the Whirlwind gently lifted off the grass. In one well-coordinated movement the nose swung to the south, dropped slightly as the pilot pushed forward on the cyclic and the whole aircraft lifted and accelerated. *Nice flying,* thought Scott. *Almost Scott McIntyre standard. I bet he couldn't hover for an hour in a North Sea gale while the crew winched an injured sailor off a tanker, though. I had been one of the best.*

The Whirlwind never rose above five hundred feet. *Not a bad idea,* Scott mused, *if a few F-111 fighter bombers were thundering around on low level practice flights at three or four hundred knots.* He kept track of the course and speed as any professional pilot would, with the automatic calculations in his head. They were flying at regular cruising speed, about a hundred miles an hour, Scott recalled, and heading somewhat east of due south. In the chill morning air, it was a cold ride for Scott but he wanted to keep the door open so he could track the course. Somewhere, these Nazi bastards had a base and he wanted it. He wanted the Moskowitch family even more. Just why they had been kidnapped rather than simply killed in their home was beyond him for the moment but it meant there was a chance that all three of them were still alive. He wondered if Nick's was one of the bodies removed by last night's survivors. He felt strangely unmoved by the thought that he had probably killed Nick in the burst of sub-machine gun fire which appeared to take out four of the invaders.

They flew for thirty-five minutes and didn't detour from the generally southern track. So they were about sixty miles south to south-south-east of the Moskowitch farm, Scott calculated. They had flown over some hilly country in the trip. Scott had seen no buildings in his restricted view though he had twice seen railway lines. He suddenly saw a small white building, what looked like a grass landing strip with a windsock hanging limply from a post at one end, a hangar, and a Piper Cherokee parked at the edge of the strip. The Whirlwind flew round the property in a clockwise direction, presumably scouting out possible dangers or simply letting the people on the ground see who was arriving.

That gave Scott the chance to see what there was to see. In addition to the small white building and the hangar there was a larger house about a hundred yards away from the strip. A typical farming home it would seem, nothing to cause interest or suspicion in anyone.

The Whirlwind stopped circling the property and came in for a gentle landing a short distance from the hangar. Inside the hangar, Scott could see the second Whirlwind. Sensible, he thought. A Cherokee parked on the grass would be standard for many Australian properties that could extend for hundreds of square miles. But two Westland Whirlwinds? That could be excessive and might rouse comment. Better to hide luxuries like these. Smaller helicopters were popular for cattle roundups but the Whirlwind was a military machine, good for carrying heavier loads but not very fuel-efficient, expensive to run and maintain. These people had resources, Scott decided. Probably Tumokam in Malaysia, to whom a few million dollars was merely loose change.

The Whirlwind stopped on the grass and the rotors began to wind down, the engine dying with a descending moan from the turbine. The pilots would be leaving in another couple of minutes when the rotor had stopped completely. Scott knew he had to make rapid decisions. He leaned outside the door and looked at the house. Nobody was in view, and while a few windows looked in this direction, things seemed quiet. He had to take a chance. He pulled the Browning out of its holster and he went back to his seat and turned slightly to the right with the handgun gripped firmly and hidden by his right thigh. He kept the helmet on.

The engine stopped and the rotor blades came to a halt. In the silence, Scott heard laughter through his helmet from one of the pilots as both of them unstrapped from their seats a couple of feet above and behind Scott, and climbed out of their windows and down the sides of the helicopter. The captain stood waiting by his side until the co-pilot had walked round the bulbous nose and joined him. Both appeared at the doorway, their helmets swinging from their hands. They looked young, cheerful and suntanned, the perfect image of youthful Australians.

"Hey, Charlie, shift your bum!" one of them called. He had a trim yellow beard and moustache that matched his sun-bleached blond hair. "We've got things to do! Nick needs some help!"

Does he now? Scott thought. So he didn't kill him last night. He couldn't make out what he thought about that.

"Can you come and give me a hand with this thing?" he muttered, keeping his face down and pretending to struggle with the seat belt. The second man laughed uproariously.

"Bloody hell, Charlie!" he said through the laughter. He looked in his mid-twenties and was darker than his friend. His hair was also cut short in almost a military pattern. "No wonder you wear thongs! Never could tie your bloody shoelaces!" Both of them climbed into the compartment, chuckling. Scott straightened, lifted the Browning and shot them both through the head before they knew what had happened.

Their bodies crumpled onto the aircraft floor. Scott watched them fall with a detached thought that in the last twelve hours he had killed maybe ten men, maybe more, all of them Nazis. The idea seemed innocent, devoid of meaning, of no importance. He decided he didn't like the implications of that lack of feeling at all.

He checked his weapons and found he had only three shells left in the magazine of the Browning. He reloaded from the handful he had kept in his pocket. With the Uzi he ejected the magazine and replaced it with a fresh one. He had one more magazine and he moved that to one of the usefully long, slim pockets of the flying suit, then slung the gun on its leather strap over his shoulder.

The sounds of the outdoors crept in through the open doorway. Crickets chirped and a dog barked in the distance. Scott could just hear the sound of a car engine. The smell of grass, fresh air, cow manure and other rural scents all mingled with the cordite in the helicopter and the pervasive odour of oil and gasoline which always hung around powered aircraft.

It was just after eight in the morning and the sun's glow had not yet taken the night's chill away. The flying suit and helmet were still worth keeping on for warmth as well as disguise. In the bright morning sunlight he had a good excuse to remove the visor cover and pull the blue plastic down over his eyes. He pushed the two bodies into the far corner of the helicopter compartment, stepped out, and slid the door shut. He looked around and saw no movement anywhere. He started to walk toward the hangar to minimize the time he was outside.

When he got there, he wondered how those pilots had been so cheerful. They had lost a number of comrades last night and those comrades were now lying in the hangar, stacked like firewood. Scott counted them carefully. He counted sixteen bodies, all dressed in dark clothing. The top one had a deep gash in his throat. He had clearly been introduced to Jacob's Alice who had left a deep impression. Scott moved to the pile and pulled out a wrist from one of the men. Black square, twin red lightning flashes. Knights of Aryan Dawn. Any possible lasting feelings of pity he might have had for these dead men vanished like campfire smoke in a wind. They, or men like them had killed his family, his mother's family and many millions of other poor innocents. And they wanted to be able to do it again. He dropped the wrist and moved out of the hangar.

He walked up to the house. It was a single storey, ranch style place, with two wings growing from a central square. It was much more modern than Benny's place and without the cooling verandas round the sides. Scott steered for the back of the house, his skin crawling with expectations of a sudden shot or merely a shout which indicated somebody had spotted an intruder. But nothing disturbed the silence. A large black Mercedes was parked near the door. Scott touched the hood cover. It was still warm.

The back door was unlocked. He opened it gently, fear scrambling his guts as he did so, but he found nothing on the other side. He was in a kitchen, a huge kitchen. Massive slabs of working tables covered three walls. A table in the centre was like a small aircraft carrier, a refrigerator big enough for a whole cow filled one wall and a monster of a stove with six gas rings filled another. On his left, the fourth wall was a sliding screen, probably opening into a dining room. At the end of that wall was another door. It was a working farm's kitchen. Scott removed his flying helmet and inner helmet, and placed them on a work table.

Now came the difficult bit. He had to explore the house. He still couldn't understand why the place was so isolated. Where the hell was everyone? Even with the bodies in the hangar there must be at least another nine or ten of last night's invaders left. And where was Nick? The helicopter pilot had said he needed help. What sort of help?

Scott flicked the switch on the left side of the grip of the Uzi to single shot firing to conserve ammunition and again swung the weapon over his left shoulder, gripping the stock with his left hand.   Jamieson's school had made sure Scott could shoot successfully with either hand, but he preferred his right for pistol work, and this way, the Browning would be easily available in its shoulder holster. He slowly opened the door out of the kitchen and peered through. It was a large, spacious dining room, with a massive white pine table and ten wooden chairs around it. At the far end, a hallway led into a corridor. Scott could hear voices speaking softly somewhere along that corridor.

Feeling naked in the vast area of the dining room and the massive windows, he walked over the shining wooden floor to the hallway. The voices grew louder, the murmurs echoing in the cool corridor with the same polished wooden floors as the dining room. There were two voices though Scott could not make out the words. Once he was through the hallway, the voices could now be heard to be coming from an open door on the left. One of the voices was Nick's. He sounded tired, perhaps ill, his voice struggling to reach the air in the room. The other voice was Australian, high pitched and unpleasant. It was the voice of a petulant child, angry at being deprived of something. Scott leaned against the wall by the open door and tuned in to the conversation.

"I don't understand why you brought them here!" the Australian whined. "Why not just kill them where they were?"

"I told you," Nick said with a gasp. "We can negotiate for them." He paused and took a ragged breath. "The family's worth a billion dollars. It's worth going for."

"You've got enough cash!" the irritating Australian voice snarled. "That fucking Arab of yours owns half the bloody world! Why not just let him pay up?"

"He's not an Arab. He's a Malay. And I want to get independent of him, anyway. We've got a lot to do."

"I'd still rather kill the Jews," grumbled the Australian, as if having his fun spoiled by an unreasonable parent. "Once we get back in, there'll be plenty of money."

"Maybe." Nick sounded contemptuous of the other speaker. "But you're not back in yet, and it's going to take a hell of a lot of capital to do it." He paused for a few seconds, and Scott could hear a bubbling back in his throat as he took several heavy breaths. "And that's just the State. You want to get Federal power, and that takes a lot more. You've hardly got public backing, have you?"

"Public?" The man almost spat out the word. "Who the fuck cares about the public? Once I'm Premier, we'll get the boundaries reset, and that will take care of that. I've got the plan set up to arrest most of those bloody socialists in Brisbane already, and once we've done that, those fools in Canberra don't have the balls to do anything about it."

Jesus Christ! Scott could hardly believe what he was hearing. Whoever the man in the room with Nick was, he was planning a take-over of the State government. Scott had to assume it would be a military coup rather than a democratic process, but he had no idea how it would be done. Whoever this man was, thought Scott, he seemed prepared to go to any lengths to gain power.

"That's all probably true," said Nick. "But you still need a lot of weapons for your people here. You'll need poison gas to tackle the aboriginal question. And you need aircraft. We'll get the money for the Jews first, then maybe we'll kill them."

Any feeling Scott may still have had for Nick vanished at that moment. This was the real Nazi showing his face. 'The aboriginal question?' *Dear God, is this the local version of The Final Solution which had heralded the gas chambers of Dachau and Auschwitz?* It sounded like it to Scott. And the way Nick talked about 'the Jews,' it sounded as if he was discussing clearing out a cockroach nest. Where the hell were Benny and his family?

The roar of a powerful engine burst into the quiet. Scott slipped back to the kitchen and looked out, just in time to see a semi-trailer arriving with a Caterpillar bulldozer mounted on the trailer section. Two more cars followed the monster and they vanished from his sight in the direction of the hangar. He moved back to the room.

"...the bulldozer we've hired to bury the bodies." Scott just heard Nick's voice as he reached the doorway again.

"It's about bloody time. They'll start to stink the place out in another half hour or so," responded the unpleasant voice of the unknown man.

"That's all you can think about them, is it?" Nick's voice was scornful, but Scott could also hear the increasing weariness in him. Nick seemed to be fading. "They were my friends and my colleagues in the Movement," he gasped. "I'd known some of them for years. And they died fighting for you, remember!"

"They were just soldiers! Soldiers fight. They die. That's their job."

"Parker, you're a bastard."

"Maybe," sneered the other man. "But this bastard will be in charge of the place soon, and then nobody's going to touch me."

"Really?" Nick sounded scathing again. "Just how well are the plans developed since last we met?"

"We've got over four hundred cops in the State as members now. That's an increase of two hundred since we last reported. I've got twelve men in the Party personally loyal to me now. I've got an army of six hundred in and around Brisbane armed with rifles and lots of ammunition, and their section leaders have all got their plans for when The Day comes."

The Day, thought Scott, remembering the reading he had done in recent weeks. In the thirties in Europe, the Nazis had called it *'Der Tag.'* The same thing. The whining voice was still talking.

"The plans include taking over the local radio stations, the TV stations and the newspapers," said Parker. "People are assigned to specific sites, just waiting to get the signal. We'll be ready."

"Maybe." Nick sounded less than certain.

In the distance, Scott heard the roar of the bulldozer starting up. The burial party was at work. He had seen perhaps eight men arrive with the trailer and he hoped all of them would be fully employed on that distasteful task.

"Anyway," said the voice of Parker. "We need to get you to a doctor. You've been hurt pretty badly. We've called our man in Brisbane, he should be here soon."

"I hope so." Nick's voice was barely a whisper, now. His breathing was getting ragged. Scott knew he had to do something fairly drastic and soon. He also needed to know who this man Parker was. He stepped inside the door, the Browning in his hand, the Uzi still hanging from his left shoulder.

Nick was lying on top of a heavy blanket covering a couch. His right arm was bandaged tightly to his chest and blood covered most of the cloth and his shirt. There was blood on his left leg above the knee. His face was deadly white and his eyes seemed to be ringed with black. Exhaustion showed in every inch of him. His cheeks looked sunken, almost a death's head.

The other man was sitting in an armchair across from him. He was enormous, but not in the same way Benny and Jacob were big. This one was simply fat. The face was almost like a football. Chins rippled down to a tight collar like the profile of the Michelin Man. His girth was so huge he couldn't sit straight in the armchair, but reclined, his posterior perched dangerously on the front edge of the chair. The ears were like those of an elephant, fleshy, standing almost horizontally out from his head, and his face was a childlike pink, scrubbed to perfection. The eyes were something else. They were pale, cold, hard like gemstones. The expression of astonishment and dismay on that pink face was almost funny. Scott doubted if humour had any part in this man's life.

Scott stared at the elephantine man for a moment. He recalled having seen him in the photograph on the walls of the police sergeant's office in Corriwongle. He returned his gaze to Nick. The wounded man on the couch was actually smiling.

"Hello, Scott," said Nick. "I was wondering if you'd drop by."

"You look in bad shape, Nick."

"Your doing, kid!" Nick's smile was disrupted by a small cough and a trace of blood shone on his lips.

"I'm sorry." For a moment, Scott truly was. *I'm going to miss you, Nick old friend, whatever it is you've been.*

"You've done me a lot of damage, Scott," Nick croaked. "Here and in Singapore."

"I know. I hope I've done enough to stop this lunacy."

"Not a chance, kid," said Nick, shaking his head gently. "It's too big for the Mongoose Section, even with you in it."

"Maybe. We'll give it a bash, anyway."

"Dieter, who the hell is this man?" The fat man was outraged but looked frightened as well.

Dieter? That was the first time Scott had ever heard Nick called by that name, and it felt alien. Dieter was nobody he knew

293

outside of an old photograph of a lonely kid. Scott looked at the mass of blubber on the armchair and said nothing.

"He's called Scott McIntyre," said Nick. "He's an agent of British Security." Nick seemed to be enjoying himself imparting this bombshell. Clearly, he had neither affection nor admiration for the other man.

"British...?" The fat man stared at Scott, his mouth open. "What the bloody hell is British Security doing meddling in this?"

"Hurting us, that's a fact. Isn't it, Scott?" Nick's voice was getting fainter. He was breathing in small gasps.

"I hope so," Scott replied, looking at him and feeling his own pain. "That doctor had better get here quickly, Nick."

"Not much chance of any success, old pal. Your aim was pretty good." Nick coughed painfully, and wiped blood from his chin.

"I see." Scott could feel sadness welling up. "Who's the fat dogturd in the chair, Nick?"

"His name's William Parker," replied Nick, the faintest trace of his old grin showing briefly. "He thinks he's going to be the Fuehrer of the Queensland First Reich."

Scott stared at the fat man. "And is he?" he asked, addressing the question to both of them.

"Could be." Nick seemed uninterested.

"Where's Benny Moskowitch, Nick?"

"They're all safe."

"Where?"

"Safe."

Scott turned to the fat man. "You want to tell me, dogturd?"

"How dare you!" snapped the elephantine man, his chins wobbling. "I'll have your balls for that!"

"Unlikely. Where are your three hostages?"

"Get fucked!"

The bullet from the Uzi hit Parker in his left shoulder that looked like a side of beef. The impact sounded like a bat hitting a ball and it was followed by a scream of pain. Parker flung his right hand across the vast spread of his chest and tried to grasp his left shoulder but the distance was too great. He collapsed back in his seat, moaning, dribble starting to drool from his fleshy, pink-lipped mouth.

"Where are they?" Scott repeated.

"In the basement." It was Nick who spoke. "No point in cutting him apart, Scott. He doesn't know."

"Pity," said Scott. "I'd have enjoyed the target practise."

"Yes," Nick murmured. "You've changed, Scott. I may have underestimated you."

"It's been done before."

"I'd agree." Nick's voice was a gasp of pain.

"It's time to go, Nick. I'll get you to a hospital."

"No chance, kid. There's no time. It's three or four hour's drive to the city."

"I wasn't planning on driving."

"Then how?... Oh I see, the helicopter. I'd forgotten."

Scott began to walk to toward Nick and looked over at Parker. The fat man was staring at Scott with pained eyes, still moaning and drooling over his series of chins. A less likely successor to Adolf Hitler it would be hard to imagine, thought Scott. He gestured with his gun at the wounded man.

"On your feet, fatso!"

"He'll never make it, either. Scott, I want to tell you something." Nick was gasping louder now. Scott knew that there was no time left to save his old friend.

"What is it, Nick?"

To Scott's right, the fat man was gurgling. Scott stared at him. Parker was gazing with wide eyes at the doorway. There was a look on his face, maybe it was astonishment. Under all that fat, nothing could be certain. Nick was stirring on the couch and his left arm was moving.

A monstrous explosion thundered from the doorway. Nick's face simply vanished in a blur of flesh and blood and his body dropped back onto the couch. The fat man screamed again. Scott was paralysed with shock. Parker struggled to get up, clutching at Scott's arm. Scott staggered as another booming shot came from the doorway, and the enormous weight of the man nearly pulled Scott off his feet as Parker slammed back against the armchair. The pink face stared up at Scott in astonishment, then the light faded from the pale eyes.

Scott turned slowly, unwilling to face what he must see at the doorway.

"Greetings, old son!" said a familiar voice. "Thought I might drop by and enjoy the festivities!"

"Hello, Mongoose Two," said Scott. "I was wondering when you'd show up."

* * *

The stairs down to the basement were steep. Scott led the way, Allan Hopkins following up a yard behind. Both of them had their guns drawn, but so far nobody else had come near the house. A padlocked door at the foot of the stairs stopped further progress. Scott rapped on it.

"Benny?" he called. "You guys in there?"

"Scott! Oh thank God!" It was Jacob's voice.

"All of you okay?"

"We're all here, Scott. Can you open the door?"

"Stand by! And stand away from the door!"

Scott waited for a moment while he heard the sounds of movement inside, then aimed the pistol at the lock. The boom of the explosion almost shattered his head and he had to use another shot to break the padlock. Ears ringing, he pushed the door open.

"Let's go!" he snapped. "Up the stairs! Helen, Benny, you okay?"

"We're fine. You're an amazing man, Scott!" Benny's voice was less powerful than it had been but he was still a giant with a giant's strength. Helen just smiled wearily. She looked in much worse shape.

"Jacob, can you carry your mother?" asked Scott

Jacob didn't answer but simply advanced on his mother who looked like a small girl beside him, and picked her up.

Scott ran ahead and up the stairs. "Allan!" he called down. "Get everyone up the stairs, to the front door. I'm going for the chopper. Bring them out when I touch down outside!"

A wide grin of delight lit up Allan's face and he began mounting the stairs followed by Jacob and his load, and lastly by Benny. Scott ran back to the kitchen, collected the flying helmet, donned the inner one and walked to the door. As soon as he was outside he put the bonedome on his head and lowered the sun visor, removing the cloth cover and slipping it into a pocket. The sun was well up now and the heat was following it. He glanced at his watch.

Ye Gods! he thought. It was just after nine! He had been here merely an hour! He could hardly believe so much had happened in that time. He began to walk firmly to the hangar where the Cherokee and the Whirlwind were both parked. A group of men were standing beside the hangar, watching the Caterpillar gouge a deep pit in the dark earth. The task looked pretty well complete for the purpose.

As Scott passed the hangar and approached the chopper, a shout from the crowd reached through his helmet. He turned to see one of the men waving at him. It seemed to be a summons of some sort. All the other faces had turned in Scott's direction. He shook his head, pointed at the helicopter and kept on walking. They must have got the message that he was on important business because the faces turned back to the pit.

One man, however, did not, but walked inside the hangar and reappeared pulling a small trolley, heading for the Whirlwind.

Scott realised with a wave of relief that the man was pulling out the starting booster for the helicopter. He had forgotten that the elderly Whirlwind had no self-starter and a small sweat broke out on his back as he thought about how close he had come to disaster. Nick's men were well disciplined and trained, he decided and nobody was questioning why the helicopter was about to leave. He pulled down the sun visor over his face, walked round to the right hand side of the machine and began to climb up the steps. As he reached the window of the pilot's seat the noise of the Caterpillar stopped. He turned and looked. The machine had backed away from the site of the pit and the men were filing into the hangar.

Scott climbed into the seat, un-slung the Uzi from his left shoulder and set it down on the co-pilot's seat. It had been some years but the friendly confines of the Whirlwind cockpit welcomed him just as the cockpits of the Wessex and Sea King always had. He looked over the instrument panel and everything looked much as he remembered. In front of the nose, the trolley had been connected up and the operator was giving him a thumbs up. Scott responded and began the series of steps to start up the motor, switched on the electrical supply and the fuel pump, pressed the starter and held it down. The huge rotor arm drooping directly in front of him twitched, the engine groaned and the arm began to move slowly. He increased the fuel flow, the rotor arm picked up speed, the other one came in sight, picked up more speed and finally, the rotor swung completely round and kept going. He sat back, strapped himself in and waited for speed to pick up under the persuasion of over a thousand horses packed into the aptly-named tiny Gnome engine in the nose. He saw a set of throat microphones lying by the left hand seat and decided that it would be a good idea. He groped behind his head, found the radio lead to his inner helmet and reached for the socket that was exactly where he had always remembered it being. He snapped the throat mike round his neck and felt completely at home.

He was happier than he had been in years. He was flying again! He watched the revolutions counter slowly climb up to the required mark, watched the oil pressures and checked the fuel levels. From his reading, he recalled that the Whirlwind had a range of about three hundred miles. The return trip from here to Benny's house, which the Whirlwind had already completed that morning, was about a hundred and twenty miles. The fuel gauge indicated that the tanks were a little over half full. He had plenty for the journey he planned.

He looked to his right. The booster trolley was being hauled back to the hangar and the other men were returning from the hangar, each of them carrying a burden. There were sixteen bodies to be buried. The men walked up to the pit and slung the loads in without ceremony. Scott turned back to the instrument panel. All the gauges were where they should be. He maintained the gentle grip on the cyclic lever in front of him which he had taken as soon as the rotor had started moving. His left hand took hold of the collective lever down by his left thigh. He placed both feet on the rudder pedals.

He eased up the collective lever with the tiniest pressure and felt the chopper start to lift up on its suspension. *I haven't lost my touch,* he thought with pleasure. He eased up a little more. He saw the faces by the hangar watching him. *Mustn't let my rustiness show....* Every atom of his body was concentrated on keeping the cyclic lever in dead centre and letting the chopper rise to two metres above the ground. He saw the grass blowing outwards in a wave from under the nose. *Hold it still.... still.... perfectly still....* He placed a feather-light pressure on the right rudder and the big machine slowly rotated on its axis until the house came into view in his windshield. His movements of hands and feet were so tiny that they couldn't be measured. They were almost totally within his head, not really physical. He eased the cyclic forward the tiniest fraction of a millimetre, countered the loss of lift with an equally minute adjustment on the collective. The bird moved at about ten kilometres an hour toward the house, sitting on an invisible railway line a metre above the ground.

Allan and the Moskowitch family appeared at the front door. Scott nudged the helicopter another few metres toward them. He pressed gently on the left rudder pedal and the Whirlwind rotated to face the north-west and leave the door on the right hand side facing the passengers. With a touch that could hardly be felt in his fingers, he pushed down the collective lever on his left, adjusted the pitch of the rotors with just the tiniest movement backward of the cyclic. The wheels touched. It was a matter of pride not to let the suspension settle completely, to keep the bird half flying, half sitting.

Allan and the others walked out, trying to move rapidly but limited a little by the load of Helen. They crouched against the gale force of the rotors, instinctively lowering their heads from the blades twirling a metre or so above them. The side door slid open, Scott felt the extra weight pull the bird down and corrected the movement. *Christ, Scott! You're good!* He looked down to his right. They were all in. Scott raised the collective lever a fraction more and began to lift up. At a height of three metres he rotated the aircraft round to the north. With more definitive movements, he pulled up on the collective and pushed forward with the cyclic. The fuel feed computer instructed the injectors to pour power into the tiny turbine engine in the nose and the Whirlwind began to soar away, climbing fast.

Over his right shoulder, Scott saw sudden, frantic movement erupting by the hangar. Men were running and picking up objects from the ground. "Shit!" said Scott loudly. "They've got their guns." *Maybe I'll be lucky*, he prayed.

SLAM!

Scott screamed with the sudden, awful pain in his right foot, jerked in his seat and went dizzy for a dreadful moment. The helicopter slung itself upward and round to the west like a stallion rearing from the whip. *God knows what it was like in the back*, thought Scott with a tiny part of his mind. He hoped they had strapped in. Allan should have seen to that, he decided. He would have flown in these things often enough as a naval officer. Scott groaned, gritted his teeth and looked down in horror at blood all over his foot. The whole shape seemed to have changed. *Oh God! How it hurt!* The pain rose in waves from his foot up his whole leg and seemed to wash over him. He fought to keep consciousness and slowly took control of himself despite the trembles that shook him.

"What the hell was all that about?"

The voice shouted into Scott's ears. *Of course!* thought Scott, Allan had also found throat mikes and helmets in the rear and had plugged himself in.

"Got hit in the right foot," Scott gasped, struggling for control. "Hope nobody was shaken loose by all that farting about?"

"No, I'd got us all strapped in. Are you okay?"

"Think so," said Scott, forcing the words through teeth clenched with strain. A wave of nausea nearly made a liar of him. "Looks like the foot is a bit buggered though." *Good stuff, Scott! Play the wounded British hero! Stiff upper lip, old chap, and all that!*

"I'll say!" said Allan. "I can see it from here. You need attention!"

Scott peered down behind his seat. Allan's anxious gaze was fixed on him.

"I'll get it pretty soon," said Scott, bringing his voice more under control again. "Should be about half an hour with luck."

"Where to?"

"Amberly. Bomber station a hundred kilometres north."

"Good. What shall we do about the extra baggage we've brought along?"

Scott struggled to think... extra baggage? Then it clicked. The bodies of the two pilots were still in the compartment. A nice welcome for the Moskowitch family. Scott knew he was sick of the killing. The training people at Central Flying School had been right, he decided, he wasn't cut out for fighters or bombers. Coastal surveillance, air sea rescue, that was his bag. *No more of this killing, please no more...*

He gritted his teeth, tried to program the pain out of his mind and concentrated on the compass. He'd flown here in a general south-south-east direction he had estimated. A reciprocal of three-forty, that should do it. He wished he had the directional indicator code for Amberly then he could tune in and let the direction show on the dial. Or even just the radio frequency. *Ah well, we'll just have to play it by ear.*

"Allan," he called out. "Is everyone okay in the back?"

"We're fine. Just get us to Amberly."

"Keep talking to me, old son. I need something to keep me conscious." The pain in his foot had settled to a grinding agony that threatened nausea and dizziness again.

"Understood," said Allan and paused for a second. "What happened at the house?"

"Bombed. Should be repairable. But tell them Gretta and Phil Cooper were both killed."

"Stand by."

Scott heard him pass on the news to the other three but couldn't hear the responses.

"Allan?"

"Yes, Scott?"

"How did you get here?" The pain was eating up into Scott's knee, and all he could see of his foot was a mass of blood covering the ripped shoe.

"Jamieson caught me in Tel Aviv," Allan replied. "Told me to get straight here. I got a commercial jet to Brisbane. I already had Benny's address so I rented a car and drove there."

"And then what?" Scott was listening to the words in his earphones as if they were a prayer for his well being. They were the only lifeline for him and he clung on tight. The pastel greens and browns of the Australian countryside swum indistinctly outside the cockpit windshield.

"Got there about three this morning," Allan replied. "Saw the damage. Saw the bodies, didn't know who they were. I called the contact in Canberra. Eventually found someone who thought the base might be in that place we just left. Managed to find my way there."

"Good timing."

"I'll say! Wallace was just pulling a gun out while you were bent over that fat slob. I think the other guy had a gun, too."

"Didn't see that one." Scott tried to recollect the scene. He had seen Nick's left hand moving, and as he walked out Allan had pulled a Beretta from under Nick's blood-soaked blanket. He could recall nothing about Parker beyond the mass of blubber.

"I did." Allan's voice was sharp. "I couldn't take the chance."

"Thanks, mate."

"All part of the service."

Scott resumed concentration on the compass. He must have been unconscious when Allan got to the Moskowitch house that morning, he decided. Maybe Allan hadn't driven all that close but parked some way away and checked out the situation on foot. That would have been sensible. *God! my leg hurts.* The throbbing was like a bass drum emitting pain and it was affecting his vision. With the damage done to his head and body last night, this morning's activities had pushed him to the limit.

"No such thing as a limit, McIntyre!"

The familiar words of RAF Regiment Squadron Leader Witherspoon, in charge of Survival Camp training in northern

Scotland rang in Scott's ears. Witherspoon's voice seemed very real just now. A small man, his peacock chest stuck out as he stood rigidly in front of the line of young recruits as they slumped, weary and miserable. Witherspoon had walked with them overnight as they tramped over thirty miles of wilderness without food or sleep. Scott was ready to drop. Witherspoon looked as fresh as a child skipping to school on a spring morning.

"Think you're tired, eh, men?" Scott's group of three all nodded. They were ready for breakfast and their tents as they hobbled back into camp. "Well, stiff shit, lads!" Witherspoon crowed. "We're going out again at once. See that mountain? We're going to the top of it!"

He was right. Scott could have sworn there was no way he would make it up three thousand feet of craggy moorland but somehow, they all did. Witherspoon was standing at the top as Scott crawled the last few yards. He looked like a man on a Sunday constitutional stroll.

"Come on then, McIntyre," he snapped at him in his high-pitched voice which echoed in the airmen's nightmares for weeks after getting home. "Don't roll around like a prostitute on her day off! Move it, man!"

They climbed two more mountains that day before they returned to the base camp again. They had not slept for thirty-nine hours or eaten for the same period. By the time Scott was back at flying school ten days later, he still felt he had limits but they were a long way higher than before.

He shook himself. Almost, he was seeing the little bantam of a man standing in front of him... JESUS! He was down to three hundred feet and swinging off course, thirty degrees too far to the west. He raised the collective, pushed on the right rudder bar to turn back to the north, and screamed as the pain in his foot nearly exploded his head.

"Scott!" shouted Allan's voice in the earphones. "For Christ's sake! What was that?"

"Sorry, pal. Nearly asleep up here and I hurt my foot."

"Be careful! We need you!"

"Sure," said Scott, more to himself than to anyone else.

He brought the helicopter back up to a thousand feet and began to swing his head around. Could be fast jets flying low in the area. He looked at his watch. Just fifteen minutes had elapsed since leaving the scene of all that death. Maybe twenty more to go. The air speed indicator read a hundred knots, more or less cruising speed, but top speed was only a fraction higher.

The countryside was fairly hilly and he had to concentrate on keeping a safe altitude above some of the higher patches. Not much of the country was developed. Most of it seemed to be rough scrub with open areas of bushes. He saw no other buildings. At one point, a flash of colour shook his nerves. It was almost like an explosion off to his right and for a hallucinatory second, he thought it was artillery. But it was simply a cloud of galahs, pink and grey parrots. Several thousand birds in the cloud vanished behind him.

"Scott?" The voice in his earphones broke the slightly hypnotic effect of the pink cloud.

"Yes, Allan?"

"Company."

"Where?"

"Five clicks astern." Allan's voice was terse and calm, the manner of a military officer meeting a situation for which he had been trained.

"The other chopper?" Scott tried to keep his voice the same way.

"Yes," said Allan. "I just opened up the sliding door and had a look."

"Suppose we should have expected that. Just about the time needed to haul the thing out of the hangar and get it going. Any guns back there?"

"Just my Browning," Allan replied. "Ten shots left."

"Shit!" mumbled Scott. "What about the bodies?"

"Stand by."

Scott released the collective lever, shifted in his seat and reached out his own Browning. He wriggled his hand into his pocket, found the last half dozen shells for the gun and slipped them into the breast pocket of his flying suit. He still had the Uzi sitting on the co-pilot's seat with one more full magazine in the lower pocket of his flying suit.

"Scott," came Allan's voice in his ears. "One more nine millimetre, six shots, that's it."

"Okay," said Scott, adjusting the throat mike. "Here, take my pistol and some extra bullets. There's nine left in the magazine. And I've got an Uzi with two full magazines."

"You are a gentleman and a scholar, sir!"

"Use them wisely." Scott reached the weapons down through the gap behind his seat and felt Allan's hand take them. He lowered the nose of the Whirlwind and hauled up the left hand lever a little more, sensing the tiny extra flow of power that the computer fed to the turbine to compensate for the increased drag of the rotor. The airspeed rose to the maximum of a hundred and six knots. He had plenty of fuel. They might just get away with it, he thought.

"*Aircraft at one thousand feet, on course three four zero, approaching Amberly restricted area. Identify yourself.*"

Good God! Scott almost jumped with shock. Amberly must have been transmitting on a series of wavelengths until they got him. He pressed the microphone button on the cyclic lever between his knees.

"Amberly. Squadron Leader Scott McIntyre, Royal Air Force, flying Whirlwind, no registration. Government business. Mayday, Mayday, Mayday."

"Whirlwind, switch to one two one, decimal five and respond."

The emergency frequency all over the world. No Mayday call could be ignored. The air traffic man at the other end was cool, professional. Scott tried to be the same, having already stretched the truth a little with his identification. He leaned forward and switched the radio as required.

"Amberly, Whirlwind," he said as he sat back.

"State the emergency, Whirlwind." The man at Amberly was calm and unflustered. The familiar military tones were a miraculous salve to Scott.

"Government security, Amberly," Scott replied, feeling encouraged and revived by the help which was now available. "Injured pilot. I have bogy approaching from my six o'clock, five clicks. Require assistance."

A small silence rang in his earphones. He must have astonished even the cool professional, Scott decided with a twinge of amusement.

"Whirlwind, Amberly. Give another reference, Squadron Leader McIntyre."

What? What the hell did that mean? Scott was momentarily confused. The Amberly controller had used Scott's name, which was not standard procedure. A hint? Had the station been briefed about possible trouble in the area? Maybe Phil's message through the computer to Canberra had stirred up something and they needed a confirmation from Scott. He had no doubt what the extra reference would be.

"Amberly, reference is Air Marshal Jamieson."

"Thank you, Whirlwind. Steer three two five, descend to five hundred. Come straight in, land at dispersals."

"Roger, Amberly."

Well now! thought Scott, *that seemed to have been the right trigger.* He swung the nose a few more degrees to the left as instructed, and kept going. His leg was almost without feeling by now, which was probably cause for worry. But he was even more concerned about the second helicopter chasing them. They would have switched to the emergency frequency to hear the conversation and would know Scott's plans exactly. Letting Scott's team get away would not be healthy for the Knights of Aryan Dawn. They would have to do something drastic. Scott had about ten minutes to reach the airfield.

"Scott, they're pulling up on our left!" Allan's tone was sharp, but still controlled.

Of course, thought Scott, *they need to have us on their right side so that the open door way could be used for firing at us.* He swung the Whirlwind sharply left, pulled the collective up a notch higher to feed power to the rotor, pushed the nose down into a slight dive and accelerated as fast as he could, trying to cut off the enemy line of fire. It looked like he would not avoid gunfire.

Nor did he. He craned his neck forward and to the left to try and see the other craft, kicked on left rudder and swung the cyclic a little right so that the helicopter was actually flying partially sideways, giving the others the minimum profile as a target. Scott was just in time to see a man leaning from the open door of the other Whirlwind, pointing a weapon. He heard a thump in his earphones and felt the small shock somewhere above and behind him. He pulled back on the cyclic, causing the excess power to be translated into lift and the craft soared a thousand feet as the other chopper passed under his nose. He was about to drop down and tuck in behind in good fighter-pilot style when a new voice resounded in his ears.

"McIntyre Whirlwind, steer immediate two seven zero and drop."

Old instincts swung into action. When somebody says "immediate" in a flying situation, they mean *immediate.* Scott

308

kicked left rudder and lowered the collective, feeling more and more at home in the craft with every passing second. *Maybe I couldn't yet handle a North Sea storm, but by God, McIntyre, you know how to fly these things!*

As he dropped sharply toward the ground he saw the thin line of smoke and barely had time to identify the FA-18 Hornet streaking in from his left. It hurtled past, no more than a hundred meters in front of him, and he saw the tiny puffs erupting from the pointed, aggressive nose. Cannons! Twenty millimetre shells, a hundred a second of them, said some tiny mote of memory in his head. The Whirlwind shook like a frightened dog in the storm of the Hornet's passage, and even through his helmet and the racket of the massive rotors flying above his head, Scott heard the muted thunder of the more than thirty thousand pounds of thrust from the fighter's twin engines.

"Holy shit!" Allan's voice shrieked in Scott's ears.

"What happened?"

"They just exploded!" Allan's voice was high-pitched in excitement.

"Hornets will do that to you," replied Scott, trying to sound cool about the whole thing. His pulse was thundering almost as loud as the engine.

"It sure as hell did it to them! Where in God's name did that baby come from?"

"Not Amberly, that's the F-111 bomber base," said Scott, feeling weaker by the second. "Maybe they called in a strike from Williamtown, a bit north of Sydney. Must have been on patrol nearby already, judging by the time it took to reach us."

"Lucky for us!"

"Agreed," said Scott with feeling. "Though I think they might have been waiting for us. Everyone okay in the back?"

"No problems."

Scott was feeling faint. His leg was completely numb, and his vision was getting blurred.

"Whirlwind, steer three five five. Two kilometres to dispersals. You may climb to get visual contact."

"Roger."

He fed power to the engine to climb so that he could see the airfield directly. At fifteen hundred feet he eased off the power again. He had what he wanted. He could see the enormous spread of the military airfield, lines of F-111 fighter-bombers parked near the hangars. He steered for them, thinking that the crisis was over, beginning to relax slightly.

Too late, he was reminded forcefully of Murphy's Law. Anything that can go wrong will do so. What went wrong was the fuel flow to the engine that cut out as if the engine had been magically removed. The thump Scott had felt must have been a bullet hitting the fuel line or damaging a vital link to the transmission shaft that later broke apart.

Old reactions took over as if he had never left active service. The experience of the last half-hour of flying the helicopter had restored much of the training that took over in his head without any decision of his own.

His hand flashed to the auto-rotation switch. He snapped the rotor free of the connection to the engine, dropped the collective lever to the bottom so that the rotor blades had a minimum angle of attack against the air, and he dipped the aircraft's nose. The rotor was now freewheeling, providing enough lift to allow him to glide the helicopter for a limited distance. He kept his eyes on the airfield and felt sure he could make it. *Thank God I had climbed for height a few seconds ago while I still had power!*

"Scott, what's gone wrong?" came the bellow in his earphones. The abrupt silence must have scared the occupants of the rear cabin out of their minds.

"Quiet, Allan! I'm busy!" Scott snapped, and watched the airfield. The Whirlwind hissed over the perimeter fence at no more than three hundred feet and Scott kept the nose of the helicopter pointed down. The airspeed kept the rotor flying and sustained lift. They reached concrete, and Scott eased back on the cyclic lever to raise the nose and slow the Whirlwind. When he was only three or four feet above the concrete he hauled up the collective lever. The rotor blade angle turned upward, giving maximum lift and maximum drag against the air. The helicopter slowed and sank gently to the ground. The suspension absorbed any bump that might have been.

"Perfect auto-rotation emergency landing, Squadron Leader McIntyre," Scott mumbled to himself and felt the pain of his leg again as his concentration on the landing faded.

He saw the flashing lights of a vehicle approaching and focused his mind on switching off the fuel pumps and electrical devices, letting the rotors slow and finally stop. When he raised his head from the instruments, a man was leaning in through the window by his right shoulder.

"Good morning!" said Scott. "My leg hurts."

He blacked out.

* * *

"We saved the foot but it's badly damaged." The doctor was a short, stocky woman with grey hair and a bad complexion. Her bright blue eyes sparkled with life and energy and a smile always seemed to be hovering at the corner of her mouth. Her white coat hung open over a dark green dress as she sat in the small chair at the foot of the bed. She handed Scott a tiny cup of water and two blue tablets.

"So I can tell. How badly damaged?" The pain had not stopped since Scott had woken up in this small room yesterday. A series of pills had given some relief but not much. But the assurance that he still had the foot was a great boost. He'd had dreadful nightmares about the possibility of losing it. He downed the tablets in one swallow.

"Two bullets hit you," she said. "One shattered the ankle and we've had to fuse that so you have no movement in it. It will be rigid for life but you can walk on it."

"And the other?"

"Did a lot of damage." No messing around with this woman, thought Scott. She was giving him a military person's answer. "You've lost the two toes on the right and a number of bones were broken. We've done as much as possible but it's still misshapen. You lost too much bone and flesh for a complete repair."

"But I'll be able to walk on it?"

"In time," she replied. "You'll need a crutch for some months probably, then a stick. You may be able to manage without anything eventually."

"But I shouldn't plan on trying out for the Scottish soccer team?"

Her lips twitched. "Probably not."

"Never liked soccer, anyway."

"Just as well."

"How long before I get out of here?"

"Couple of weeks. Then you can fly home."

"Thanks, doc."

"No problem." She stood up and walked out of the room.

Scott retreated into the friendly, pain-free darkness.

* * *

He woke up to pain. It was almost as bad as the first few moments after the bullets had hit him in the helicopter, and he couldn't stop the tears springing up in his eyes. He gasped for a few seconds, tried to tell himself to be a man, to grin and bear it. *No limits, McIntyre, remember that, you have no limits, that's what Witherspoon told you. Oh God! it hurts.*

He lost out to the pain and reached for the switch hanging by his right shoulder. A nurse appeared within a few seconds, already armed with a tiny plastic bowl and a cup of water. Scott swallowed two more blue capsules and gripped his mind tightly to avoid screaming.

"Hold on," she said, gently. "It will go away." She was young, Chinese and very pretty. For a moment, Scott was back in the Singapore Airlines jet, getting a large cocktail from Kim Ling Soo. Then the cutting saw stopped slicing into his foot and the whole leg seemed to go numb. He let out a long sigh.

"That was a bad one," he whispered.

"It will get easier in a few days," she smiled. "Trust me! It means it's healing." Her voice was very gentle and sweet. It reminded him of Janette. She busied herself straightening out the bed and removing some paper debris from the cabinet. He watched her, having little else to do, and decided that she was even prettier than Ling Soo.

"Well, you old bastard! As always, in bed, and a gorgeous woman looking after you!"

The voice felt like it could shatter the walls but that was probably the result of Scott's fevered mind. Allan Hopkins's brilliant green eyes almost lit up the room as he walked in. The nurse smiled at him and walked out. Allan took the chair last occupied by the doctor and pulled it up to Scott's right hand side.

"G'day!" said Scott and smiled at him.

"You've been here too long, McIntyre! You're becoming an Aussie!"

"Could do a lot worse," said Scott.

"Just remember old chap, you're British! And we need you back home."

"I need me back home, too. There's a good woman waiting for me in Birmingham."

"She sends her love."

"You talked to her?"

"Yesterday. Called in to report the result of your operation. She's badly upset but relieved you're at least still alive. It was a narrow call, old son."

"I'll say!" said Scott. "That shambles at Benny's house was like the Battle of Waterloo!"

"You survived it," said Allan, looking carefully at him.

"I know. But Gretta and Phil didn't."

"Yes," Hopkins nodded. "Gretta's being buried today. Phil's body was flown to his parents' home in Melbourne."

"Jesus, Allan! What a bloody disaster!"

"Fortunes of war, old pal! Your job was to save Benny and his family and you did that." Allan sat up straight in the chair and crossed his left foot over his right knee. "Jamieson said well done. He was uncontrollable with the excitement."

Even in the sadness and discomfort of lying in bed for so long, Scott had to laugh. Allan had always had the capability to say things in a deadpan way that just broke Scott apart.

"So, what's happened with the Queensland First Reich?"

"The Queensland...? Oh, I see," said Allan. "Our Knights of Aryan Dawn and the local supporters. Quite a lot. That tub of lard yacking to Nick Wallace was William Parker. He'd been some backbench politician in the previous government, one of those thrown out in a landslide some years ago. Corrupt as hell, facing charges on a number of dirty little episodes. We got into his office and looked at his files and found several more conspirators. The Federal Government is working on just how to prosecute them."

"Great!" said Scott. At least something was happening. "What about the police connections?"

Allan shook his head. "Not so easy. No documentation we could find. Nothing to prove any real dark and dirty stuff with anyone."

"The men at that house?" asked Scott.

"Nobody there when we moved in," said Allan with a shake of his head. "We're starting to dig up the bodies by the hangar, may get some identification there and from the two bodies we left in the helicopter."

Scott felt depressed. "So after all that we may prosecute a few politicians in Brisbane? There's a whole bloody Nazi organization here. What are we going to do about that?"

"I'd say you've already done a hell of a lot!" said Allan and touched his colleague's shoulder. "Remember, the local leader's been eliminated, Wallace as the international co-ordinator is gone and the Federal Police are on to the whole thing."

Scott thought about it. Allan was probably right, he decided. He saw images of Nick's face blowing up in front of him as Allan's shot hit him dead centre. Tears were very close.

"I suppose so," said Scott. "I hate the idea of all those loonie police still roaming around, though."

"Forget it," said Allan with a small smile. "They were loonie before, they'll be loonie for ever. This is Queensland."

"Of course, I'd forgotten that!" Scott managed a grin at him. "When are you going home?"

"Tonight. I'm driving to the airport in a couple of hours and getting the Singapore plane. I'll connect to the London flight from there. Jamieson says he needs me back in the office to introduce Mongoose Four and show him the works."

"Great! The doc says I can be out of here in maybe two weeks. I'll fly home then."

"Don't," said Allan firmly. "Benny wants you to stay with them a few days. Jamieson approved of the idea. Says you're on sick leave, anyway."

"Oh." Scott found he liked the idea. Even though it meant longer without Janette, the idea of seeing Benny and his family without the imminent danger of bullets and bloody action was very attractive.

"What about the local police guys in Corriwongle?" asked Scott. "They may get a bit cranky about having us all around there. Especially as I killed a lot of their people."

"Forget it!" said Allan with a wide grin. "The Premier put such a firecracker up that sergeant's bum as he will never forget. You'll get royal treatment if you go near the town."

Scott still didn't feel too secure about the idea but decided he wanted to stay at Benny's house, anyway.

Allan stood up. "Time to go and get that plane. Take care old son, see you back in Birmingham."

Scott reached out his hand. "Okay, you old bastard! Have a good flight. Tell them I'll be back in three weeks."

"Will do. Cheers!" And Allan walked out.

* * *

For two weeks Scott lazed around, bored out of his head. He read everything he could find in the hospital library, which was not a lot. When Benny, Helen and Jacob came to visit it was like a party. They looked wonderful, thought Scott, though the shadows on Helen's face reflected the horrors of the last few weeks. Benny had lost weight. Jacob was exactly as he had been before.

They didn't talk much once Helen had told him about Gretta's funeral, a simple affair at a cemetery in Brisbane.

"Didn't want her lying in Corriwongle," said Helen. "Not after the way the police had behaved. She was our friend for many years." Despite Helen's soft voice, her emotion was strong.

"How's the damage to the house?" asked Scott. They seized on the change of topic with relief.

"Looks worse than it is!" said Benny with a smile. "No structural damage beyond the actual missing wall. It will be rebuilt by the time you get there. The veranda's already been done, the lounge wall was nearly finished by this morning. We're making up a room for you on the ground floor, so hurry up and come home!"

Home! thought Scott. It sounded lovely. He hadn't had a real home to match the security and friendliness of the

316

Moskowitch place since leaving his parents' house in Reading. Not even the comfort of his Birmingham apartment had provided such a feeling.

"Couple of days," he said. "Sure you can cope with me?"

"Try it and see!" said Jacob. "I'll come and get you in the Jaguar when you're ready."

Two days later, Scott tried it and it was wonderful. He spent five days sleeping as late as possible, which was not all that late because the Kookaburras started their lunatic chorus at dawn. He arrived with a wheel chair, tried the crutches on the second day, and managed reasonably well. He spent a lot of time sitting on the veranda, drinking a wonderful range of wines and an occasional beer. Sometimes, they talked, other times he sat alone and just looked at the huge country.

Benny was away for a couple of those days, overseeing his multi-million dollar empire. The work on his new plant in Singapore was progressing well, he told Scott, and business was good.

Scott's favourite time was the early evening. It became almost a ritual that the four of them would sit with their drinks outside on the western side of the house and watch the day turn the wonderful, rich, deep purple of a Queensland rural sunset. They never talked during this process, just watched the colours change, and finally moved quietly back to the dining room for dinner. Scott recovered from the wounds, let his soul heal from the psychic damage, thought a lot about Nick, about Janette and about what he would do when he got home. He thought about how Allan had appeared so suddenly and saved his life. The pain in his foot gradually declined as the nurse had said it would.

But the pain of all the killing would never go away, he knew.

Eventually, the time came to leave. Jacob drove him to the airport where the Gulfstream had been placed at his disposal.

Scott struggled painfully up the stairs, having difficulties with the crutches but finally making it. He leaned into the flight deck and greeted the two pilots who looked with interest at him. The co-pilot still had her hair tied behind her neck and she seemed relieved that Scott was carrying no weapons that she could see.

He took one of the front seats and laid the crutches on the floor, relaxing with a sigh after the struggle up the stairs.

"Would you like a drink, sir?"

He looked up to see another woman, perhaps in her twenties, as neat and trim as any professional flight attendant.

"Er... yes, please!" He had almost expected Gretta and the new face had thrown him for a second. "A bloody mary, please."

She retreated to the galley and Scott watched the crew go through the pre-flight checks. He looked around the empty cabin and wondered if he would ever again have a complete corporate jet placed at his sole service. He decided to enjoy the flight like no other, took the massive drink from the young woman, strapped himself in and relaxed. For the next hour or so, he lived like a business tycoon and loved it.

Chapter 11 - Home for the Fall

Early October, the days were beautiful, the evenings were cool, and the nights were distinctly chilly. A perfect arrangement, as far as Scott and Janette were concerned. After four weeks apart, they had a lot of catching up to do, and her apartment in Edgbaston was rarely occupied. Despite the care they had to exercise with Scott's foot, they managed to conduct some successful recovery and the healing of both his psyche and his foot continued well. But something fidgeted in his mind like a caged bird sensing the presence of the cat.

Sometimes, they talked about the events in Australia, sitting cuddled up on the Queen Anne couch, and Scott relived the moment when Nick was killed. He still wept occasionally but that reaction subsided quickly. He remembered Nick's comments about 'the aboriginal question' and about killing the Jews, and the sadness was replaced by contempt.

Other times, they talked about the future. Jamieson had said nothing so far, because Scott was still supposed to be on sick leave, but they knew his career as a Mongoose was finished. Scott didn't mind at all.

"Are you sure, honey?" Janette was curled up against his chest as he half reclined on the couch, his right foot resting on a cushioned stool. Her perfume was working distracting effects on him.

"I'm really sure," he said. "I know I've enjoyed a lot of it, but being frightened for half my life was not the way I wanted to keep going. The al-Yaffi case is closed. That's what I joined Mongoose section to achieve. And after Australia, I'm sick of the killing."

She stroked his arm. "That really got to you, didn't it?"

"And how! I killed at least twelve men. Twelve! I know they were all Nazis, and I know that people like that killed my parents and sister, but..." It was difficult to go on.

"They were trying to kill you, Scott."

"I know. And they were planning to kill a hell of a lot more too, including the entire Aboriginal population. But I keep remembering the two guys we chained up in the barn. They were just people, working men with families. One of them used to work for Benny. They were real, living people. I've no idea who the others were, but I assume they'd be much the same. I don't want to do it again."

"You won't have to, Scott."

"No. I'll be talking to Jamieson when he gets back this week. We'll see what he has to say. Maybe I can find a job in some other area. Or go into civilian life."

"Whatever you want to do, love."

"Actually, I do know what I want to do."

"Oh? What? Oh! I see! What, here and now?"

"Why not?"

"Why not, indeed?"

The perfume finally had its desired effect.

* * *

It was like coming home. The Lancaster flew its eternal path through the storm, the young man in his flying gear leaned against the nose wheel of the Vulcan, and the coffee pot exuded aromatic steam. The doughnut box had not been opened, as Scott had followed Jamieson in as he arrived.

Jamieson hung up the Burberry's raincoat on the coat rack and waved Scott to his usual seat. Scott was still on crutches, but he had got the knack of sitting down easily, and automatically leaning them against the wall. Jamieson moved to his desk, took his usual glance at the Lancaster and sat down. He was wearing his regular, perfectly-cut, three-piece suit, gold cuff links and Air Force Squadron tie.

"How are you feeling, Scott?" The Air Marshal's eyes studied Scott carefully.

"Perfectly okay, sir. The foot has stopped hurting mostly. Can't walk on it yet, but another month should see to that."

"Can I get you a coffee?"

"Er.. yes! Thank you, sir!"

Scott watched him rise and go to the pot. Jamieson poured the coffee into his own RAF mug and then into one of the guest mugs. Without asking, he poured a teaspoon of sugar into Scott's coffee mug and passed it to him, placing his own mug on his desk at the same time.

"Doughnut?"

"Yes please, sir."

"Excuse fingers."

"No problem, sir."

Jamieson lifted a cream-filled monstrosity from the box, placed it on a paper napkin and passed it to Scott. Again, Scott nodded his thanks and took a bite of the sugar and calorie filled delight. Then he stopped eating and watched in disbelief.

Jamieson took another doughnut from the box, placed it on a napkin and carried it back to his desk, sat down and put the napkin on the desk.

Scott swallowed the mouthful he had taken and washed it down with the coffee, still looking carefully at Jamieson. Was he really going to do this? he asked himself in astonishment.

"Problem, McIntyre?"

"Er.. no, sir."

He did it. Jamieson lifted the doughnut and took a bite, chewed with obvious relish and swallowed it. He stared at Scott, deadpan. But his moustache had a distinct twitch to it.

"Good doughnuts, these," he said.

"I'm glad you finally found that out, sir. That was your first ever, of course."

"Of course, McIntyre." He took another bite, and wiped a trace of cream from his chin. Scott was having trouble keeping a straight face and Jamieson could see it.

"As you said," mumbled Jamieson. "The daily miracle of transubstantiation kept taking these things away. Thought it was time to try one. Never again, of course. Terribly bad for my waistline."

"Of course, sir. I do hope you enjoy that one to the maximum."

"I assure you, McIntyre, I am."

For another three or four minutes, the room was silent as they drank their coffee and finished the doughnuts. Scott felt that this had almost been worth the events of the last month. Then he realized what the implications might be. Jamieson was bringing to an end a game that had been played for some years. It could only mean one thing.

"Obviously, that foot ends your active Mongoose career, Scott." Jamieson wiped his fingers and sat back in his seat.

"I realize that, sir," said Scott. "I'm very sorry."

"So am I. You've been my best man."

"Thank you sir, but I screwed up a number of times."

"Goes with the territory. You should see some of the disasters the others have committed. War never goes according to plans."

"I see. So what happens to me, sir?"

"What would you like to do?"

"I've been struggling with that for a while. And I still don't know."

"Going to marry my Head of Analysis and Coding?"

"Yes, sir."

"Good. She's worth it. Will she keep on working here?"

"That's up to her. I think she wants to. At least until she has a sprog or two."

"Do you want to retire? You can get a reasonable disability pay."

"I know, sir. But that means going into some civilian job. And I'm not sure I could handle it."

"Nor am I. Scott, I have a suggestion for you."

"Yes, sir?"

"You made a lot of friends these last few weeks. The Americans wrote a glowing report on you, which is most unusual. They normally find it difficult to believe anyone could be as good as they are."

"They were pretty damn good themselves."

"Of course. And the Canadians have said you can come and help any time."

"Carstairs is a good man. Despite a dreadful taste in jackets."

"That's what he said about you. A good man, that is. And the Prime Minister has had a formal letter of thanks from his opposite number in Australia for the work you did."

"I'm overwhelmed."

"No need to be. You did well."

"And what is all this leading to, sir?"

"I've suggested that we might pool our resources between those bodies and a couple of others, including the European forces. We need somebody who can coordinate the whole thing, set up the structures, and all the other stuff."

"And have they agreed?" Scott felt a wave of excitement.

"They have. They've agreed you'd be the best man for the job, too."

"Wow! I mean, how extraordinary, sir."

"Precisely. You'll take it, of course?"

"Of course."

"Splendid! Have another doughnut?"

"Thank you sir, I will."

Jamieson let him get it on his own, seeming to recognize that Scott needed to be self-sufficient, even if it did hurt like hell. Asking Jamieson if he wanted another doughnut was obviously not an option, Scott knew, if Jamieson's comment earlier about it being his first and last was to be believed. Scott didn't believe it, but he still played the game. He refilled his coffee mug, somehow making it back to his seat without spilling a drop.

"Can we wrap up some details about the Australian event, sir?" he said as he settled back.

"We need to," said Jamieson. "I've read your report, and some things aren't clear."

"Just two areas that are unclear. First, the assistance I got from the Royal Australian Air Force at Amberly. How did they know what was going on?"

"We had a considerable backup operation going on there," Jamieson replied, looking smug. "One of my old friends is top man with the Australian Air Force. I called him as you were leaving and briefed him on the situation. Once they saw the helicopters involved, they kept a squadron of Hornets in the air nearby. Amberly was on readiness the whole time. And as soon as Cooper's report was received in Canberra, ASIS flew a couple of men up to Queensland to keep an eye on the Moskowitch house from a safe distance. Couldn't be too obvious about it, the State government people were still very disbelieving about the whole thing."

"But they saw what happened?"

"They saw the helicopters arrive and heard the gunfire. They had a look around after the choppers had gone, but didn't see you."

"Did they see anyone else arrive?" Scott was feeling tension rise within him, but was uncertain of the cause.

"No," replied Jamieson. "They said the night was completely quiet after the choppers left. Where were you?"

"I was submerged under bits of house."

"So it seems. Anyway, they also saw the chopper come back the next morning and then leave. They had no idea it was you getting into it, though they heard the gunshot and later found the body. They called Amberly about the whole thing, thinking they might need help getting to you, but the Amberly people lost track of the chopper."

"It was flying at about three or four hundred feet in hilly country. They'd have needed aerial spotting."

"That was the problem. The Hornets weren't near enough for visual contact either. So Amberly was on a high degree of alertness waiting for a call. I knew you'd do something about that."

"But you knew where Wallace's base was, didn't you, sir?"

"No we didn't, until you found it. We've assumed since, that the local people picked Benny as a target for the Singapore event because he was such a rich, high-profile, Jewish business man in the area. Probably thought it would be a great boost to local membership if they killed him."

"But surely the ASIS people in Canberra knew where the base was?"

Jamieson looked hard at him. "No, they didn't, McIntyre. You found it for them."

"But..." Scott stopped, confused. Something was terribly wrong here.

"But what, McIntyre?"

"I'm not sure, sir. Something's not adding up, but I can't see what it is."

"Work on it. Let me know if you come up with anything."

"I will, sir. Did anything else come out of the searches of bodies and aircraft, and things?"

"A number of interesting items. The farm was owned by that Parker bastard under a series of interlocked company names. We traced the Whirlwinds too, after getting a look at the engine numbers, including the one shot down by the Aussies. Both machines were bought from the RAF six years ago by an international consortium. One of them used to be in the air-sea rescue squadron you flew with. Ostensibly, they were bought for working in the oil territories in Brunei."

"No doubt Tumokam was behind it?"

"Of course. Somehow they got the choppers to Australia as part of the financial help to Parker's Queensland Nazi group. We're tracing some more financial dealings too, and the Australian government will be placing a very heavy protest with the Malaysians before too long."

"Won't do any good," said Scott.

"Maybe not. But it will keep that bastard's fingers out of Australia, at least."

"What about Parker's people?"

"All indicted on various charges of corruption, or mere criminal activities. No real proof of the connection with Wallace's Nazi gang, but the Australians are making sure they stay in prison for some years."

"Well, that's something, anyway."

"It's a hell of a lot, McIntyre."

"Thank you, sir."

"Okay. I want you to take another two weeks leave. You're on full pay. Maybe go off and get married, or something. Then come back here, and we'll organize your new position."

"Seems a reasonable plan. Thank you sir." Scott stood up, grabbed his crutches and moved to the door.

"Oh, and Scott?"

He turned, awkwardly. "Yes, sir?"

"Not a word about the doughnuts!"

"What doughnuts, sir?"

"Thank you, Scott."

He hobbled into Janette's office to see her working side by side with one of her analysts. She was a young girl fresh out of college, whose father had been one of Jamieson's friends at

Cranwell and throughout his air force career, according to Janette. She looked earnest, intelligent and not unlike the way Janette herself had looked when Scott had first met her. More like a pretty secretary than an honours graduate in mathematics and computer science. Scott mentally shook himself for thinking like a sexist dinosaur.

Janette saw him watching her, and smiled. "Karen, take a break, will you?" she said. "I need to talk to Scott for a few minutes."

The girl stood up, gave Scott a shy smile, and walked out to the lounge.

"What did the old boy say?" Janette was obviously a little nervous about the meeting with Jamieson. Scott smiled reassuringly.

"I have a nice new job. We're doing a joint venture with the Americans, Canadians, the Aussies and some of the Europeans. I get to be liaison officer."

"But that's wonderful!" Her eyes glowed and she touched his arm.

"I think so, too," replied Scott, stroking her hand with the tips of his fingers. "Some travel, but not the way it's been before. No guns."

"Thank God!"

"He told me to take another two weeks and do something silly, then come back and start."

"Did he mention anything specific that you were to do?"

"It was really very silly."

"McIntyre, I'm going to stamp on your foot!"

"He sort of thought that we might consider the possibility of getting married in that time."

"Oh." Scott could just see the tiniest hint of a smile on the corner of her mouth.

"I told him I'd talk it over with you," he said.

"Really?" She flicked a look up at him, then concentrated on straightening his tie, which had no need of attention.

"Well, you are sort of involved in the decision, you know," he said.

"I am?"

"Colley, I'm going to strangle you!"

Finally she laughed, her eyes sparkling. "When would you suggest, Mr. McIntyre?"

"What, strangling you?"

"Idiot!"

"Oh! The other one! How about next week?"

"Sounds good." The expression on her face was calm and happy.

"Talk to you tonight?"

"Whenever you're ready to leave."

"I need to talk to Allan and meet the new guy. Let's go at about four."

"Let's!"

With another glowing smile from her, Scott set off to make his way to his office. It had been a while since he had been in that room. But as he moved along, banging his crutches against the walls on occasion, something began to run around in his head and took his full attention. Small pieces of a jigsaw puzzle fell into place and he nearly unbalanced as his head swam. He felt a wave of nausea as he reached the door to his office.

Allan Hopkins was at his desk, talking to a tall and good-looking young man in a black blazer with a military crest on the pocket. The stranger had borrowed Scott's chair to sit opposite Allan. As Scott walked in, the young man bounded to his feet.

"Hey, young McIntyre!" said Allan, obviously in a great mood. "Meet Mongoose Four! This is Michael Johnston, Mike meet Scott McIntyre!"

They shook hands. The newest Mongoose looked clear-eyed and confident, and his handshake was firm. Scott liked him.

"Royal Artillery?" said Scott, looking at the breast pocket badge. "Welcome to Mongoose Section. Makes a change from all these naval fools that have plagued us over the years!"

Johnston laughed. "Thank you, sir! Allan tells me it's the flying fools that cause the problems!"

"Christ, drop the sir bit! I know I'm crippled, but don't remind me. And tell Allan that it was a flying fool that saved his skin in Australia!"

"I'll do that, next time I see him!"

There was a loud laugh from Allan. "Oh ye gods, another raving lunatic! I was hoping for a change!"

Scott sat on his desk and waved the latest Mongoose back to his chair.

"So what's the news, Scott?" Allan looked concerned.

"New job, couple of weeks leave first. I'll tell you all about it later on. I need a quiet evening at home tonight, first, though."

"I hope I can persuade you to change that, Scott. We've got a couple of details the Old Man asked me to sort out with you, and this new Mongoose of ours is taking up the rest of the day."

"You're sure it can't wait?"

"You know the Old Man." Allan smiled gently. "He said as soon as possible."

"Then it had better be tonight." Scott tried to keep his voice calm.

"Sure! Why not make it about eight?" Allan beamed cheerfully.

"Eight's fine. Mike, I need my chair back. I've got a report to write."

Mike Johnston stood up. "No problem. Allan's about to take me on the guided tour."

They both strolled out, looking incredibly healthy, fit and handsome young men with jobs of national importance. Jamieson would have to look to some means of protecting his female staff from the impact of both of them walking in on them, thought Scott. He took out a notepad and began writing.

At four, Janette popped her head into his office and waved. She looked wonderful, thought Scott. He reached for the crutches and got to his feet. They walked out through the front to the elevators, with Janette holding his left hand as it gripped the cross bar of the crutch. It seemed to help.

As they drove through Birmingham's rush hour traffic, he told her about his evening's schedule. "I need to talk with Allan for a few minutes about the Australian event," he said. "I have to get some final details from him."

"Can't you do it tomorrow?" She was obviously disappointed. "I thought we had plans to make tonight?"

"We do, dearest lady. I'll go straight after dinner, should be back by nine. Jamieson's orders."

That was enough. The boss' name always gave priority to anything. She finished the drive home, though her disappointment still showed in her face. When they were inside and both had changed into more casual clothes, she touched Scott on his arm and looked closely at him.

"Something's worrying you, Scott."

He tried to hide it. "No love," he said. "Just the foot hurting again. And I'm still a little down about having to retire from active service, even if it does make things easier for us."

"Sure?"

"Certain!" He put his arms around her and held her close, then they nearly unbalanced as he stood on one foot and they broke apart, laughing again. But her smile faded quickly, and he took his seat, aware of what he was causing her distress.

She walked into the kitchen and he listened to her bang some pans around for a few minutes.

At seven-thirty, Scott went back to his bedroom to change to go out. He dressed as he had when going to meet Nick at the Old Mill pub, light blazer over close-fitting shirt. He bent over Janette where he had left her sitting on the couch, touched her cheek and kissed the top of her head.

"Okay, love, we need to be going. Chauffeur duties for you again."

She reached up, touched his face and smiled. There was no sign of her earlier unhappiness. "I'm ready," she said. "Keys in hand, shoes on, your dutiful servant, sir!"

She stood up to join him and they went out.

Allan's apartment was fairly close to Janette's home in Edgbaston, not far from the cricket ground. Twenty minutes after leaving, she stopped outside the four-storey block that housed his spacious three bedroom place.

Scott went through the complex and strained routine of getting himself and his crutches out of the car, stood up and closed the door behind him. Janette had also got out and stood on the opposite side of the car, looking anxiously at him.

"I have to do this, honey," said Scott. "I should be down in about twenty minutes. Keep the heater going."

She understood the rules and resumed her seat, leaving the engine running. Scott turned and made his way up to the front door. He rang Allan's apartment and heard his familiar voice answering through the intercom.

"It's Scott. Let me in, it's bloody cold out here!"

The buzzer sounded and the door jumped open. Scott entered, found the elevator and took it to the top floor. He had been here just once before, about a year ago. Allan was standing by his open door when Scott reached his floor, and the welcoming smile was broad.

"G'day, you Australian reprobate!" Allan said, cheerfully. "Welcome to my humble slum!"

His humble slum was spacious and attractive. Deep blue carpeting was soft underfoot. Dove-grey walls held a Picasso print of "Weeping Woman" on one side, a pair of beautiful Japanese oil paintings on the other. A track lamp on the ceiling was pointed directly at the oils, and the deep purple and gold patterns were almost the focal point of the room. The curtains were open, letting the street lights from the road outside pour an amber glow into the room. A gas fire was lit and two armchairs were positioned for a comfortable conversational place by the warmth. A circular coffee table with a blue slate surface stood between the armchairs.

"Take a seat," Allan said, pointing at the left hand armchair by the fireplace. "Let me take the hardware." He held the crutches while Scott lowered his weight into the comfortable chair, and he leaned them against the wall to the right of his own seat. Allan moved to the kitchen. "What'll you have?" He opened the cabinet to display a large, colourful selection of bottles.

"Got a whiskey?" asked Scott.

"Blended, single malt or double malt?"

"Single."

"Glenfiddich or Laphroaig?"

"Hopkins, you sound like a waitress in a pub."

"The down-side of affluence, my crippled friend! I say again, Glenfiddich or Laphroaig?"

"Yes, please."

"Bloody idiot!" he laughed.

"Laphroaig, then."

"I'll join you."

Hopkins moved back to the coffee table and placed a pair of coasters on the slate surface. He returned to the kitchen, took the bottle of Laphroaig and poured two portions into glasses. A gentle whiff of the peaty smell reached Scott across the blue carpet. Allan walked back to the coffee table and placed the two crystal tumblers on the coasters. He sat down in the other armchair, his back to the window, the amber street lamps framing his head like a halo.

"Cheers!" he said.

Scott waved his glass generally in his direction. "Good health," he muttered, and took a sip of the scotch. The smoky, burnt peat taste worked its way down his throat. "How does our new Mongoose look?"

"Great!" said Allan, enthusiastically. "Hell of a good record in unarmed combat, weaponry and all that good stuff. Got a Master's Degree in computer science as well."

"God, the intellectoids are invading!" Scott took another small sip of one of Scotland's greatest exports. It had been his father's favourite.

"Relax!" said Allan. "You're out of that area, anyway. You can spend the rest of your working days simply directing us muscle-bound men of violence around the place."

"Maybe."

Hopkins appeared to be sensing Scott's mood and the beginnings of relaxation in him ceased. He put down his crystal glass on the coaster. "What's wrong, Scott?"

"Oh, nothing, really. Couple of questions to ask about the Aussie event. Fill in the gaps, sort of."

"Then why are you carrying a gun?" Hopkins sat back in his seat, elbows on the arm rests.

Scott froze. "I'm not certain all of Wallace's people have been cleaned out," he replied. "I'm not mobile, and I have Janette to worry about."

"I see," said Hopkins. His eyes looked hard, and his face was taut. "You said you had questions."

Scott's nerves wound up a notch. There was a coldness in Allan Hopkins he had never seen before.

"I do," Scott said. "What time did you say you got to Benny's place that night?"

"About three, three-thirty, maybe," replied Allan. "Couldn't see a damn thing but I walked around quite a bit and had a look in through the windows." He leaned forward and took his scotch, cradling it in both hands and looking into the delicately coloured liquid.

"You had a flashlight?"

"Sure," said Allan. "Still couldn't make anything out." He wasn't looking at Scott at all.

"You didn't go inside?" asked Scott.

"No. The front door was off its hinges, but I decided to get to a phone instead and ask the ASIS people in Canberra where the farm was."

"So what time did you leave the house?"

"Christ, I don't know! Maybe four in the morning." He took a drink and looked hard at Scott. His eyes were bright. "What the hell is it, Scott? You don't need all this for your report, surely?"

"Bear with me, Allan. How long did it take you to drive to the farm?"

"About two hours. Country roads, some unsealed. Not a fast ride."

"Not for a hundred kilometres, no. Trouble is, there's no direct route. You'd have had to go back into Ipswich and out again, a total drive of a hundred and eighty kilometres. At night, unfamiliar roads. Then, as you say, a lot of unsealed highway the last thirty kilometres. Two hours isn't practical."

Allan went immobile in his seat. His brilliant green eyes stared at Scott, obvious even with the amber glow behind his head. "Scott, what the hell is all this?"

"Allan, there were two ASIS men watching Benny's house the whole time. They saw the attack, they saw the choppers leave, they saw one come back next morning and leave with me aboard, though they didn't know it was me at first. But the one thing they did not see was you arrive to have a look around and then drive off."

For a second or two, shock radiated in Allan's face. The presence of observers was nothing he could have forecast, thought Scott. Hopkins replaced his glass on the coaster and leaned forward toward Scott.

"Bloody hell, Scott! A couple of Australians? They were probably pissed out of their tiny minds and sleeping in the car!"

"I don't think so. And you said you looked in through the windows and that the door was off its hinges?"

"Yes! What of it?"

"You didn't notice that one complete wall had been demolished? You could have seen quite a lot of the interior without peering in through windows."

Hopkins said nothing, but simply stared across the table without expression.

"And anyway, there's another problem," said Scott.

"Oh? What?" The contempt and anger in Hopkins' voice now, were powerful, biting. Allan Hopkins was anything but Scott's friend at the moment.

"The problem is that nobody knew where their farm was. Nobody. Not Jamieson, not ASIS. Nobody. So you couldn't have called Canberra because they certainly didn't have any idea. So you must have known yourself. You never went to Benny's place. You drove straight to the farm. Which means you're part of it, Allan."

"Crap!"

"Sorry, Allan. The only explanation. And I think you killed Perkins in Karachi."

"What the hell are you talking about? It was obviously Wallace who followed him back from Geneva and shot him!"

"Not a chance. We found credit card transactions by Nick in England for the days when he was supposed to be doing the shooting. No way he could have shot Perkins. I think you did it."

Hopkins stared at him, motionless. "This is why you're carrying a gun," he said. "You think I'm the double-agent?"

"You told Jamieson that you had done a computer search for Perkins' name on flights coming into Karachi," continued Scott, ignoring Allan's words.

"So?" Hopkins' voice was glacial.

"You said you didn't find one. But when we sat with Janette looking for Perkins' travel movements, we found him on the flight from Switzerland. So either you didn't look properly, which is not like you, or you didn't look at all."

Allan looked into some unknown distance for a few moments. "Why would I do a thing like that?" he finally asked.

"You were killing off a traitor. You and Nick had realized that Perkins was trying to warn us. He'd been supposed to misdirect us away from Nick's Milan killing, which he did, but only by pointing me at another killing in Chicago by one of your people. Nick said that's what warned him that Perkins had turned."

Hopkins was watching him, immobile as a lizard on a rock.

"Then we got the lead to the Toronto event," Scott continued. "That came from Perkins too, by way of Mossad and the Egyptians. That was a direct pointer to Nick this time, and you realized Perkins had to be silenced."

There was still no movement from Hopkins. He could have been frozen.

"And talking of Nick," said Scott. "He told me that I'd been followed all the way to Osnabruck when I traced his parents. He knew something that only Jamieson, Marjorie and Janette knew apart from you."

"So why couldn't it have been one of those who told him you were going to Germany?"

"It could. The idea haunted me for a long time. But all the others knew that I was going to go to Geneva after I'd spoken to the Konigs. You didn't know that because you'd already left Jamieson's office when he ordered me to do it, and Nick only knew I was going to try and find his parents. So you had to be the one who told him my plans, otherwise he'd have known about Geneva."

Hopkins still said nothing, but stared hard at Scott as if trying to force Scott to retract his words.

"I thought back to the moment when you shot Nick," said Scott into the silence. "He was just about to tell me something about Mongoose Section. He was dying, he knew it, and I think he wanted to do one last thing for me. You shot him to stop him telling me about you."

Allan said nothing.

"And you shot Parker to keep your cover intact," Scott continued. "What was going on, Allan? Had you written off the Australian project and decided just to maintain secrecy?"

Their eyes locked. For half a minute they sat like that. Allan reached forward, took his scotch glass from the table and drank deeply. He sighed heavily as if in defeat.

"That's about it, Scott. I had never agreed with the project in the first place. I always thought it was lunacy. The Australians don't have the discipline for the Movement. That maniac, Parker, was totally off the wall. You'd just about killed the plans, so this was the best way to wrap it up."

"So how long have you been part of Knights of Aryan Dawn, Allan?"

"Since naval college. I could see the current European organization was leading to another bloody disaster in time. There was nobody strong enough to run things properly."

"And you wanted to take us back to the thirties, is that it? Jesus Christ, your grandfather died in the North Sea fighting the German Navy and you want to bring it all back?"

"That's not it at all!" Allan was irritated. "I don't want a Hitler or an SS and the concentration camps! I just want a strong leader and these people had the right idea. This plan for European unity won't work! It won't stop the Japanese, and the

337

Americans don't understand the implications! We need a properly united Europe and Germany's the most logical country to make it happen!"

"Not Britain?"

"No, no way!" Contempt ran over Hopkins' face. "We'll have a socialist government again in a few years and we'll be back in the old stupid ways. It has to be Germany! When I was at naval college, I met people from the Movement in Germany and they showed me what the plans were. They made sense, that's all!"

"And so you joined Mongoose Section, and went around killing people, while actively preventing other assassinations. Pretty logical!"

"More than you think!" For a second, a smile warmed Allan's face. "We needed money and there were lots of people prepared to have targets hit. It was good business for us! I'd use my job to get rid of other assassins and leave the market clear for Mustapha al-Yaffi."

"Nick did a pretty good job," said Scott. "He must have valued your support."

"Nick?" Allan laughed outright. "You really got suckered in, didn't you?"

Scott raised his eyebrows at him, trying to ignore the sudden wave of panic he felt in his chest. What was Allan leading up to?

"You think Nick Wallace was the leader of this thing?" Hopkins said with contempt. "The evil and mysterious Mustapha al-Yaffi?"

"Of course," Scott replied. "That's where all the evidence pointed."

"Wallace was a useful killer," snorted Hopkins. "But that's all he was. I was the one who planned his events. He went where he was ordered. He was just one of several."

"You planned his events?" Scott was feeling scared now. Where else had he gone wrong? "And did you plan all the other events for the Knights of Aryan Dawn?"

"That's what a leader does," replied Allan in contempt.

"Including the Barcelona bombing?"

"Including that. We'd wasted years looking for that woman. She'd cost the Movement a great deal."

"That woman was my mother." Scott was having trouble breathing. "And you killed my father and a sixteen-year-old girl who was my sister."

Hopkins shrugged. "Jews," he said. "Just Jews."

"Like me."

"That's right. Just like you." Hopkins crossed his legs and his lips curled as if a bad smell had reached him. All pretence of being a friend and colleague had wafted away before the winds of his hatred.

"Did you do that job yourself, Allan?" Scott waited in dreadful tension for his answer.

"No," said Hopkins. "You've already taken care of the man behind that one."

"The man in Chicago?"

"Helmuth Weber was his name."

Scott felt a massive load fall away from him. At least he had avenged his own demons. He prayed Hopkins was telling him the truth.

"And did you do any of the killings?" he asked.

"Of course. Had to keep my hand in."

"There never was a Mustapha al-Yaffi, was there?" The truth hit Scott like a sunbeam out of a storm-laden sky.

"That's right," said Allan with a small smile, and looked back at him. "You silly buggers swallowed everything we fed you. Wallace did a few killings, I did others, my people did the rest. The whole thing was a story from the start. It kept you all running around like headless chickens."

"And some of the killings, especially the ones you were actually sent out to do, they just got rid of the competition?"

"Correct!" Hopkins grinned over his scotch glass. "Standard business strategy!"

"Business has just come to an end, old pal. Time for you to wind down the company and liquidate."

"Bullshit!" snapped Hopkins. "Just what do you think you can achieve?"

"We can wrap you up nice and tight, for a start."

"Only for a time! As soon as my people find out, which will only be a matter of days, we'll take action that will cut you apart!"

"Really? Such as?"

"They'll do something heavy, I assure you. We may get some British Jihadists to do it for us. They never need an excuse. Or we may get Tumokam to finance something. Or we may do it ourselves. But something will hit you hard! And we'll keep hitting until I'm released!"

"That's what Jamieson said you'd do," said Scott, softly.

"You've told Jamieson?"

"Of course."

"And what did he say?"

"He said to put you out of business." Scott had no difficulty with the lie.

Hopkins' contempt was blistering. "He doesn't have the guts! He's an old British aristocrat and British aristocrats don't play that sort of game. It's not cricket, you know!"

Scott drew his Browning from his shoulder holster and pointed it at his colleague. "But Jamieson's not an aristocrat," he said. "He's the son of a Yorkshire coal miner. That's why he asked me to do it."

Hopkins stared at him, ignoring the gun, looking as if he was seeing Scott for the first time. For another half minute the silence boomed in the pleasant apartment. Allan leaned back in his armchair. "Are you seriously telling me," he said. "That you've come here to kill me?"

340

"My orders," agreed Scott. "Also my choice and my preference. You've caused too much grief, Allan. And after all, isn't that why you invited me here, to kill me?"

Hopkins stared at Scott. He looked briefly at the gun in his hand and placed his hands behind his head.

"It was," he admitted. "I was going to leave for Germany immediately."

"Just like Nick. Seems I've got to you just in time."

"I have to admit," Hopkins said, "I seem to have underestimated you as well as the Old Man."

"Jamieson, certainly," agreed Scott. "Me, I've just changed a lot the last few weeks."

"No, you've just reached your potential," said Hopkins. "Which means things look a little bleak for me, right now."

"I suppose so," Scott responded. He felt weary, sad, almost defeated. Allan had been his friend for four years, entertained him with his wit and sardonic humour. The only closer friend had been Nick and Nick had betrayed him. It was happening again.

Hopkins looked at the scotch glass in his hand and took a sip. He seemed amazingly calm for the circumstances but he was made of steel, that much Scott knew. The small movement made Scott twitch nervously but he kept his gun pointing at Allan. His foot was beginning to hurt like hell.

"Scott, are you really sure you want to do this?" Allan frowned at him in puzzlement. It was hard for Scott to believe that Hopkins was really aware that Scott was about to kill him. Scott was still not certain that he could. He breathed deeply and tried to forget what he had believed Allan had been the last four years, and to focus on what he had actually been. He was not just one of the killers of Scott's family, but the man who had ordered a bomb placed to kill them and had then treated Scott as a friend.

341

"I'll offer the Nuremberg defence that your old Nazi gods offered fifty years ago," replied Scott. "I'm just following orders. Except that I really do want to follow this one. Just like they did."

Silence echoed round the room. Hopkins looked around, as if studying the place for the first time. "Seems a bit extreme to me," he murmured, almost to himself. He took another drink of scotch and seemed to consider before speaking. He looked at Scott.

"We've had a lot of fun in our time, why spoil it now? You're not going to achieve anything by it, after all."

"Believe me, it has to be done." Scott's heart was pounding so heavily he was sure Hopkins could hear it and know his panic. His hands were clammy and he was afraid he would lose the grip on his gun. He squeezed a little harder, and felt the sweat in his palm.

More silence. Hopkins studied his glass and Scott looked at his face. Some of the colour had gone but that might have been the effect of the amber lights outside. Hopkins looked up, glanced around the room and looked longingly at the door, as if seeking escape.

"It's funny," said Hopkins. "We live for years knowing that each day might bring our own death. I never thought it would come in such a damned civilized manner."

Scott said nothing.

"Do you think about dying, Scott?" asked Allan. He almost appeared to be begging for a friendly word.

"A lot, recently," said Scott. "Especially during the event in Australia. It was very close."

"I've killed a lot of men," murmured Hopkins. "And not all of them were for the Movement, whatever you might think, Scott. Many of them were genuine enemies of my country. I suppose I'm wondering if I'll be meeting them again, soon."

Scott was feeling waves of appalling emotion. Despite the dreadful reality of what had to be done, he was hearing his old friend and colleague talking now, much as they had talked in previous, more friendly meetings.

Hopkins looked directly at Scott. "I know you have to kill me, Scott," he said. "It's the position into which we've been placed by our own choices. I still regard you as my friend."

"I'm a Jew, remember," said Scott. "Just a Jew. How could you regard me as a friend?" The pain inside was grating, as if something was scraping against his heart.

"Odd, that," nodded Hopkins. "I've always known what you were, even before you did. And I'll make no excuses for what I believe about your race. But you're still my friend."

"Not in my view," replied Scott.

"So you'd better get on with it, then," said Hopkins. His voice was calm.

"Have you said everything you want to?" asked Scott. The pain was burning him.

"I don't think you can do it." Hopkins' voice had lost some of its elegance and smoothness. A hint of tension had finally appeared. But he was correct. Scott was not sure himself that he could do it, either. *Kill him? My one remaining friend? Dear God, I effectively killed my very best friend only a month ago. He would have died from my bullet within minutes if Allan had not silenced him so suddenly. Can I really do this?*

"You don't know me as well as you think," answered Scott, remembering how Nick had admitted the same thing to him only a few weeks before. *I didn't know myself as well as I thought, either. I killed a number of men in Australia in that dreadful twenty-four hour period in Queensland, but that had been in the heat of battle. Being shot at makes a great stifler of conscience.*

Allan looked more confident. Maybe he had seen the doubts in Scott and seen the sweaty hand trying to grip the pistol. He started a movement of his hand toward the cushion of his armchair. He glared at Scott defiantly, perhaps trying to keep Scott's eyes away from his moving hand.

"Okay, if you insist! Then do it!" The challenge was thrown like a gauntlet onto the floor between them.

Scott froze for a second at the insanity of the words hurled at him. In that tiny moment, Allan moved. He turned to his right and seized one of Scott's crutches from against the wall. Scott tried to fire, but his training failed him. He had not healed enough from the recent events and he was a lifetime too slow. The crutch swung viciously and struck Scott's hand with a crack. The Browning dropped from his crushed fingers. As it fell, Scott saw Allan's face, wild with rage, his bright hazel eyes flashing with fury and exhilaration. The crutch went flying, continuing the arc of the sweep which had disarmed Scott and Allan's hand dropped to his thigh, dug inside the cushion of the armchair and reappeared with a small hand gun. It pointed at Scott's eyes.

For one dreadful instant, Scott stared at the gun and felt his soul break into pieces at the awareness of his immediate death.

"I've failed," were the only words he could bring to his mind.

The boom of a gunshot seemed to explode his head and Scott knew what it was like to die. He felt his ears collapse within him as a furious, murderous bee thundered into his head and the universe became sparks within jet blackness. He saw Allan's face dissolve and become a riotous mix of colours and blood as his head slammed back against the armchair, blood splattered in a fine mist against the glass of the window, distorting the beam of the amber street lamp. Allan's back arched for a second, threatening to spill his chair backward then his body slumped. A final small tremor shook his left leg and he went still. Silence fell in the room and Scott discovered that he wasn't dead. The pain in his head dissolved and he felt sweat pouring down his back and his legs.

"Sorry, Scott," said Air Marshal Sir Martin Beresford Jamieson. "We were almost too late." Beside him, Janette had a pistol pointed firmly at Hopkins' body. Her face was calm. Scott blacked out for a few moments.

"Janette called me as soon as you came in," said Jamieson. "I have a key to all your homes and I came here. I managed to open the door without either of you hearing me. Thank God I wasn't any later."

Scott was still sitting in the chair in which he had almost died. He felt unable to speak, so dry was his throat and so serious the trembles in his body. "Janette?" he croaked.

She smiled gently. "It just smelled wrong," she said. "It wasn't essential that you visit Allan this evening. I thought back on the things you had told me about how he arrived at just the right moment, and..."

"Came to the same conclusions I had," Scott finished for her. She nodded. Scott stared at her pistol, a Beretta automatic. She looked down at it, as if having forgotten she was holding it. But the muzzle remained pointing at the body in the armchair.

"You don't know everything about me, Scott," she said softly.

"I wouldn't let my daughter work for me without being capable of looking after herself," said Jamieson.

Scott looked at him for a second, then shook his head. "No, I suppose not," he replied, too shattered to comprehend fully. He stood up with pain and difficulty, and limped to where his gun had fallen. Painfully, he bent over and picked up the Browning. He moved over to Hopkins' chair, keeping his gun pointed at the shattered, bloody head. Hopkins was certainly dead. Scott looked down at the body's right hand that was just holding the handle of a small twenty-two calibre pistol. He pushed it until it dropped it on the carpet, well away from Allan's seat. He limped back to his chair and leaned against the back of it. Jamieson watched him without expression.

"It's done, Scott," the Air Marshal said. Janette finally tucked her Beretta into her bag. Scott realized the explosion of the gun had actually been the bullet passing within inches of his ear.

"Yes, sir," Scott finally was able to say. "Not bad for an old bloke."

"Thank you, Scott," said Jamieson. "A hell of a way to wrap this thing up."

Scott didn't reply. He looked at the scene in the room. The tears flowed freely down his face. Then he pulled his gun out again. He stood upright and turned to Jamieson.

"Not entirely wrapped up," he said.

Jamieson looked back and saw Scott's gun pointed firmly at him. His expression didn't change. There was only a small gasp of indrawn breath from Janette. Crushing the pain into some quiet place in his chest, Scott tried to ignore her.

"You have a problem with something, McIntyre?" The Air Marshal's voice was calm.

"Yes, I do. I have a problem with the death of my family."

"I thought you had come to terms with that, Scott."

"Oh, I have, sir. But what I haven't come to terms with, is something Nick told me the time we talked in the pub."

"Which was?" Jamieson seemed calm, his eyes fixed firmly on Scott's, not on the gun pointed firmly at his heart.

"Nick said that Aryan Dawn got a mysterious lead to my mother being the woman they had been hunting for years. Who the hell could have given it to them?"

Jamieson was silent, but his eyes widened a little.

Scott worked hard to keep talking. "It occurred to me that letting that little detail slip would be a good way of getting a trace on Aryan Dawn's organization in England and the connections to Europe. All you had to do was watch and see who came to check her out."

"You think I did that, Scott?"

"Not you, personally. You were still in the RAF when that happened. But someone did, and probably a someone you know."

"I was still in the air force, yes," agreed Jamieson. "But I was already preparing a move to counter-terrorism. I knew everything that was going on."

Scott felt the pain try and leave the small prison in his chest, and firmly suppressed it again. "So you knew about throwing my mother to the wolves?"

Jamieson nodded. "And endorsed the idea," he said calmly. "But we got caught. We never suspected that charming young Englishman Nick Wallace was a Nazi agent. And the *modus operandi* in Barcelona, that was so far off standard that we got confused."

"So my parents and my sister died because you were too dumb to catch on?" Scott felt a tide of hatred burn through him.

"Yes, Scott," replied Jamieson. "We made a bad mistake, and three people died."

"That's it?" Scott was dumbfounded. "My family died, and that's all it means to you?"

"No, not all," said Jamieson. "There has not been one day since, when I have not loathed myself and everything I stand for. Most days, I have seriously considered resigning from the service. Many days, I have looked at my gun and thought about resigning from life."

The answer was so unexpected, that Scott swayed against the seat back. Deathly weariness threatened him and his knees trembled. The Browning in his hand seemed to weigh a hundred pounds.

"You've heard all the clichés about war, Scott," Jamieson continued. "You were fed enough of them at training school. About the necessity of sending men under your command into action that will probably kill them. Clichés, but true. And the war against terrorism is even worse. We saw the growing power of Aryan Dawn and the links to al-Yaffi. We had to draw them out."

"And kill my family in the process."

"It was your mother's suggestion, Scott."

Scott gasped as if hit in the guts.

"As I said, the method threw us," continued Jamieson. "We simply never anticipated a bomb. We had twelve armed men around the hotel, looking for an assassin. Three of those men died in the blast, as well."

Scott folded into the chair as his legs failed him. He slipped the gun back in his shoulder holster, too weary to think.

"You're going to face the same problems in your new job," said Jamieson. "You're going to make decisions that will kill men in your care."

"Then I can't do it," mumbled Scott.

"Perhaps. But I think you can. Any commander who doesn't hurt when it happens is not a true leader. You have to keep the objectives in focus."

"The world stinks."

"It would stink a lot worse, McIntyre, if we let it. Remember what someone once said. 'All it needs for evil to triumph is for good men to do nothing.' It's true."

"And what we do, is that just a different sort of evil?"

Jamieson smiled, a sad, tired smile. "Want to kill me, McIntyre? Will that repay you for the death of your family which I helped bring about?"

Scott closed his eyes. For a moment, he remembered his gentle mother, her smile when she talked about the girls at school. Leanne laughed at him through a thickening mist of years. His father looked at him with that worried, affectionate expression he had worn during his wife's absence. Then he saw the bodies piled up in a barn in Queensland.

"No, sir," he said.

Once more he hauled himself to his feet and went to the telephone on the bookshelf. He dialled the number he had once hoped would never be necessary for him to remember, but somehow had always stuck in his mind. Jamieson watched without expression.

Only one ring sounded. "Operations," said a calm voice in Scott's ear. "Identification?"

"Mongoose Three."

"Code verification?"

"Blackstone five three niner."

"Verified," said the calm voice. "Requirement?"

"Clean-up crew," said Scott.

"Location?"

He gave Allan's address. There was just the tiniest break in the even tone of the other man's voice. He would know the address.

"Ten minutes," said the voice and the phone was replaced. Scott remained standing, his weight on his crutches.

"I'll go now," said Jamieson. "You have everything under control, I believe. You and my daughter have a difficult discussion to get through."

Scott looked at Janette. She was standing motionless, looking down at the carpet.

Scott nodded at the Air Marshal. "I'll talk to you when I get back," he said. Jamieson gave a small wave of his hand in acknowledgement and walked out of the door.

The silence rang like a bell for a few seconds.

"His daughter?" Scott broke the emptiness.

Janette finally stirred from her frozen position, moved to Scott's side and touched his shoulder. "He's never let anyone else know."

"Colley? Your mother's maiden name?"

"Yes. My idea."

"Does this change things for us?"

Her hand moved to his cheek. "Not for me. It's up to you. Can you handle it?"

Her warmth and gentleness seemed to soak through him. He moved his hand from the crutch handle and placed it on her waist and managed to kiss her cheek. For a few moments, they stayed like that, despite the baleful presence of the corpse in the other chair.

The buzzer sounded exactly eleven minutes after Scott had phoned earlier. Scott hopped to the door and pressed the button to open the entrance downstairs. He waited, heard the elevator ascending and opened the door.

Two men came in. Just like in Chicago, when FBI Special Agent Bill Webster had called for someone to take away the body of the unknown German gunman, these two were dressed in working overalls. They had the name "Bryant Cleaning Services" across their backs. One of the men pulled a cart with a heavy device on it, tubes wrapped round a large barrel, the other pushed a large laundry basket on wheels.

They walked past Scott with just the briefest nod, ignoring Janette entirely. They looked at the body on the chair and at the blood on the window. There was more blood and material on the armchair.

"You'd better go, sir," said one. "We have a fair bit to do. We'll lock up."

That was standard operating procedure. Scott nodded, and clumped his way out.

Without speaking, he and Janette climbed into the car. She put the key in and started the engine, then looked at him.

"Are you sure?" she asked. Her voice was a whisper. She reached over and took Scott's hand in hers. He gripped it firmly for a moment, ignoring the pain of his bruised fingers, then released it and put his arm round her shoulders. For several minutes they clung to each other and she wept into his shoulder.

"Scott, I was terrified," she whispered, tears distorting her voice. "When I finally realised what the situation was, and that

Allan..." A storm of weeping made her whole body shake. He held her tight until she calmed down.

"Let's go home," he murmured into her hair.

She sat back in her seat, put the car in gear and moved away. They were silent as she drove.

"Janette?" he said, about five minutes from home.

"Yes, love?"

"Do we still have a date for next week?"

She shot a quick smile across to him. "Yes, love."

"And I suppose the Old Man's giving you away?"

"Yes, love. He won't miss it."

"Will it be okay if I stand there with a cane? I can get rid of the crutches by then."

She smiled again. "Yes, love."

"Good. Let's get home and start planning a few things."

"Yes, love."

Scott laughed. "I do love obedient women!"

"Tough!" she said, the smile still warm on her face.

The rest of the drive home was fine.